The Best of Times

A Novel of Love and War

The Best of Times
A Novel of Love and War

Terence T. Finn

Ivy House
Publishing Group
www.ivyhousebooks.com

PUBLISHED BY IVY HOUSE PUBLISHING GROUP
5122 Bur Oak Circle, Raleigh, NC 27612
United States of America
919-782-0281
www.ivyhousebooks.com

ISBN: 1-57197-410-5
Library of Congress Control Number: 2003114471

Printed in the United States of America

In memory of
Louis B. Kohn II
Helen Griffin Purcell
and
John F. Finn, Jr.

ONE

That the Foreign Secretary was to be among her dinner guests did not trouble Helen Trent, nor did the fact that a high-ranking American was to accompany Sir Anthony. She was, after all, the wife of a senior British diplomat, accustomed to entertaining, comfortable with protocol. Sir Robert Trent was Deputy Permanent Secretary for Colonial Affairs. He had been a classmate of Anthony Eden at Oxford where they had shared an interest in Oriental languages. His appointment as DPS was the result of their longstanding friendship, though Sir Robert was quite talented and doing his job rather well.

Helen was a nearly perfect wife for Robert. Well educated, of good family—her grandfather had been an admiral in the Royal Navy and her father a respected physician—Helen could hold a conversation with anyone. She could speak with wit and insight on most matters—a necessity for the diplomatic service—all the time appearing to be genuinely interested in what the other person had to say. That at times she found the conversation tedious simply highlighted her skill. Helen had discovered a key to success in conversation—

simply ask the other person what he or she thought. Men loved the question, for they loved to talk and hear themselves talk. Women, who were rarely asked their opinion, welcomed Helen's questions. They responded eagerly, often with wisdom. Frequently, Helen would muse at how easily this technique worked. She thought it unfortunate that men did not more often listen to women.

Helen was an attractive woman. Men found themselves drawn to her, although she did not return their attention. Helen thought she looked quite good, particularly for a woman of forty-three. Her weight was down, her hips remained slim, and her legs still drew admiring glances. She alone thought her mouth too large. Men seemed fascinated by her breasts, which she considered, like her mouth, too expansive. Her skin was decidedly white and soft, but with little color. Before her death in 1933, Helen's mother would comment that her daughter was a pale little princess that neither sunshine nor make-up would change. Helen liked the white tones of her skin. They stood in contrast to her hair—deep black, rich and full, too long perhaps for someone her age, but when piled upon her head, it looked stunning. Helen thought her hair to be her best feature and was secretly proud it contained not a touch of grey. When dressing, Helen would look at herself in the mirror and note approvingly. She had retained the good looks of her youth. Indeed, she had added to them.

Men noticed Helen Trent, but her interest in them had waned. Upon Peter's death, she had assumed that romance no longer was to play a part in her life. Peter had been her first great love. She thereafter believed he would be the last. Helen thought that life provided but a single opportunity for such an experience. Early on, she had realized hers. She had then placed in cold storage any hope of finding another man to cherish.

With Peter, the romance had been joyous beyond words, a relationship marked by sexual intimacy, laughter, and respect. Helen was no prude. Indeed, with Peter she had had a merry time. But he was gone and the men she now met were either self-absorbed like her husband or interested only in a bedtime tumble.

Helen had always wanted more. She admired men of substance, respecting the energy and talent that accompanied success. She noticed men of means, for Helen Trent enjoyed the comforts of life and had little desire to do without them. She appreciated men whose sense of humor matched her own. In recent years, several gentlemen had pursued Helen, even after her marriage to Robert. To them all, she was indifferent. Helen remained faithful to Peter's memory and to the man whose name she bore.

A *nearly* perfect wife, Helen was all that Sir Robert Trent wanted. A hostess of great charm and skill, a proper partner for success in the Colonial Office, Helen was a pleasant companion, someone who made life for this British civil servant easier than it might have been otherwise. Helen fit into his life like a puzzle piece. She added polish and respectability, and made few demands upon him, except regarding the care of her daughter. Sir Robert thought her to be an excellent wife. That he no longer slept with Helen troubled him not at all. That she was not a truly contented woman he did not notice.

"My dear, you will be ready soon, I trust. Our guests will be arriving shortly." Helen was sitting at the dressing table and Robert had come into her bedroom.

"I'll be ready in a moment or two." It would be more than that, but there was little sense in telling Robert. He'd hover about, somehow thinking his presence would speed up the process. It was a habit of Robert's she disliked, but one she had been unable to break.

"Anthony may be a tad late, but he assured me yesterday that he would be coming. Said he'd never dream of missing one of your dinner parties. Called them marvelous. But the others will be on time, including the American."

"And who exactly is this American?"

"His name is Warren Smith. He is what the Americans call an Assistant Secretary of State. He's their man for Africa and runs the entire show. The Secretary and his deputy, Mr. Welles, care little about Africa. So Mr. Smith is the man to see."

Helen thought it quite reasonable that the American Secretary of State, counterpart to Anthony Eden, paid little attention to Africa, given that in 1943 America was waging war around the world. She ran a comb through her hair, noting its luster, and turned to Robert. "Well, I shall be sitting next to him and will keep him entertained."

"I have no doubt of it."

"Do you know how late Sir Anthony will be? It might be awkward if he's not arrived by nine o'clock."

"Not to worry my dear. Anthony is usually quite punctual. Hates being late. I'm sure he'll not keep us waiting. He's looking forward to the evening, a bit of a break from the Foreign Office, and from Winston." Sir Robert smiled and looked at Helen. "You're looking lovely tonight, my dear." He wandered out of her room, leaving her to finish getting ready.

Helen looked at her hair. She knew other women thought it too long, but she liked the way it looked. She took out her lipstick and added a touch of color to her lips. Helen used little make-up and was proud of the fact. Peter used to call her his natural beauty. She liked that and smiled sweetly at the thought.

Standing up, Helen eyed herself in the mirror. Her dress, a dark burgundy, was smartly styled. She had worn it before, and would have preferred something new, but wartime shortages had made fine clothes difficult to obtain. With a high neck and long sleeves, the dress, which she adorned with a grey Italian silk scarf at her shoulders, created the effect she had sought. Simple, yet elegant. Decidedly feminine, but not too much so. She examined herself in the mirror, turning to see if her slip was showing. It was not. Another look in the mirror. Helen would laugh when vanity was equated to women, but she admitted there was some truth to it. One last check in the mirror. Now it was time to give a dinner party.

Four days earlier, Helen was in the pantry, about to make some tea, but addressing François Sabotier, a chef from the Collingwood, Sir Robert's club, who would prepare the meal. "And what exactly is a DuBarry salad?"

"Madame, it would be perfect for your party. It is a salad with small pieces of cauliflower, gently steamed with lettuce and garnished with radishes and sprigs of watercress, dressed with a vinaigrette and added lemon."

Helen had used the Collingwood before, with great success, but François Sabotier was new. The regular chef had taken ill, and the club had sent over Monsieur Sabotier, whose credentials were said to be impeccable. Helen certainly hoped so. Dinner with the Foreign Secretary needed to be flawless. François seemed nonchalant, indifferent, somewhat condescending. She thus concluded he was genuinely French.

"I'd like to serve rack of lamb."

"Ah Madame, rack of lamb would be most nice."

Helen was not sure he meant it. "What do you recommend we serve with the lamb?"

"Madame, we might serve, let me see, yes we might serve peas à la bonne femme. That would be peas, browned onions, and diced bacon. Very nice, yes. And we begin with a celery consommé."

Helen wondered where she would obtain all this food. Wartime Britain endured severe food shortages, made worse by rationing. No one starved, but many people went without. Eggs, meat, and fruit were always in short supply. Oddly, restaurants prospered and seemed to suffer less than individuals. Unlike some of her friends, Helen would not utilize the black market to secure additional foodstuffs, though she could certainly afford to do so. "I shall have some difficulty in getting this food."

"Not to worry, Madame. The Collingwood has available what we will need."

"Well, that's a relief." Helen was relieved, for unless one dined out, food was something about which one had to worry. Like many in England, Helen looked forward to the day when the shoppes of London and throughout the kingdom had shelves full of food. To her, and to many in 1943, victory against the Germans meant not only an end to the fighting, but also an end to rationing and to the shortages of food. "Shall we have roasted potatoes as well." This was not a question.

"Of course, Madame." But François' face said no. Then he remembered how the English loved their potatoes. At least this time they would not be boiled. "And what would Madame care to serve for dessert?"

"I was thinking we would have trifle." She knew it was not elegant, but she liked trifle and wished to serve something English.

"Ah, trifle. How English! And so very nice." There was that word again. Helen would learn over time that when François described something as nice, he meant ordinary. "But instead, Madame, let me suggest we serve a crème brûlée. It is most elegant." François emphasized the third syllable. "And I make, if I may say so, a superior crème brûlée."

Crème brûlée. Full of cream and butter and sugar. Helen liked it, but she'd rather have trifle, yet she wanted to keep Monsieur Sabotier happy. Successful dinner parties required contented chefs.

"Yes, a créme brûlèe would be splendid."

François beamed. "Very good, Madame. For you I make the best créme brûlée there is." The French, he believed with some truth, had invented gastronomy and French cooking, as French wine, was considered unequalled. Even German generals wanted French cooks. Vive la France.

Helen was pleased. The menu was fine. The food apparently was available. And Monsieur Sabotier was happy. He had won the "Battle of Desserts," but Helen was more than pleased. The smile she wore came from knowing, as few in England did, that crème brûlée, despite its French name, originated in Cambridge where it had been known as "burnt cream." God Save the King.

"Monsieur Sabotier, may I offer you some tea?"

Fifteen minutes before the party was to begin, all seemed in order. Monsieur Sabotier was in the kitchen moving quickly but calmly, clearly in control. Helen had brought out the silver and fine china the day before, and had set the table in the morning. Dinner for fourteen. It called for a great deal of work. Helen knew what to do, and did so expertly, but much had to be accomplished. Thank God for the Collingwood. They had sent over Hoskins who had worked for the Trents before and knew the routine. And Monsieur Sabotier seemed to be doing well, judging by what she witnessed.

"Monsieur Sabotier, the guests will be here soon."

"Yes Madame, I am ready. We shall serve the first course promptly at half past eight."

Helen prayed that Sir Anthony would be there by then, envisioning François insisting on beginning the meal regardless of whether the principal guest had arrived. Helen smiled, knowing Robert's reaction should that occur. Unlike François, her husband thought that guests outranked food at dinner parties. Helen agreed, though there were times when the latter seemed more interesting. Tonight, though, this would not be the case.

In addition to Sir Anthony, his wife Beatrice, and the American, guests would include the Ashcrofts, John Pennington, and his wife Harriet. Jane Ashcroft was Helen's best friend. Her husband Herbert was a surgeon and medical director of St. George's Hospital. Pennington, a businessman who had given lavishly to the Conservative Party, was a quiet, yet pleasant fellow whose reserved manner concealed a sharp mind and large fortune. Harriet was quite different. She was outgoing and funny, full of energy, and liable to dress outrageously. She adored John Pennington, and not for his money. He, in turn, was smitten. Helen envied their happiness.

Jane Ashcroft and Helen had gone to Roedean School outside of Brighton together, remaining close ever since. They had met Harriet at a Christmas reception and the three had become best of friends. They confided in each other, shopped the same stores, and more than once traveled the continent together. Fortunately for all, the husbands got on well.

Both Herbert Ashcroft and John Pennington knew Eden. They did not know Wilfred Grimes, an RAF Group Captain assigned to the Colonial Office whom Sir Robert invited to the dinner party.

With Mark Stewart, a colleague of Eden, and his wife coming, they would be short two women. Helen thought it important that men not outnumber the women. Too many men and the party turned into a business meeting, or worse, a political rally. Helen wanted neither, at least not tonight, so she had invited Clara Harris. Mrs. Harris was a neighbor. She was a widow of an army colonel lost at Dunkirk. Now, without much money and alone in the world, she faced an uncertain future. Yet she was a woman of dignity and strength, and Helen enjoyed her company.

Sir Robert was not pleased with the invitation to Mrs. Harris. He thought they should invite someone with influence, so he chose the remaining guest. She was Lady Roberts, a woman well known in Conservative Party circles. Her maiden name has been Edna Jones, and Helen thought her insincere, far too ambitious, and slightly vulgar. Her marriage to Lord Roberts had surprised many, not least of whom was Lord Roberts who enjoyed having a young attractive consort who occasionally provided him memorable physical pleasures. As Lady Roberts, Edna enjoyed her husband's money and the many doors now open to her. Tonight, Helen observed, she was about to have dinner with the Foreign Secretary of Great Britain.

Clara Harris and Lady Roberts. One the choice of Helen Trent, the other of Sir Robert. Each spoke volumes about their sponsor. Helen was satisfied with the arrangement, though not pleased. Life, she knew, was a series of compromises—some big, some small. This was one of the small ones. At least Clara would be there and Helen hoped that her neighbor would enjoy the evening.

There was a knock on the door and, as Hoskins was in the kitchen assisting François and Sir Robert was upstairs still dressing, Helen went to answer it.

"Good evening, I'm Warren Smith and I'm afraid I'm a bit early. This is 28 Temple Court, the home of Sir Robert Trent?"

"Yes it is." Helen was smiling. "Do come in. Let me have your mackintosh. I'm Helen Trent and we're delighted you're able to join us tonight." Hoskins arrived and took the raincoat from Helen. He then discreetly disappeared.

"I do apologize for being early, but it seemed silly to wait outside, especially given the rain."

"Quite so. It's so nice to meet you, and we do want you to stay dry."

Smith smiled in return. It was a warm smile and gave character to his otherwise undistinguished face. He was a short man with grey thinning hair. He wore a navy blue suit with a striped red tie, and had a folded white handkerchief in the left breast pocket of his suit. This made him look like a successful New York banker, which he was. Like many senior officials in the American government, Smith was someone who had signed on for the duration of the war, giving up a lucrative position. He was a dollar-a-year man, a friend of Sumner Welles who had arranged his appointment as Assistant Secretary of State.

"That's hard to do in England."

Helen was still smiling, half because it was her job as hostess and half because this American seemed to be a decent fellow. "That's why England is so green and the flowers so rich in color. Don't you have rain in America?"

"Yes, though not as much as here. Actually it rains only on Tuesdays and Thursdays."

"How boring. Must be why you have deserts in the West." Helen knew her geography. It had been her favorite subject at Roedean, and her library was filled with maps and books about maps. Her hostess duties called. "May I get you a drink?"

"Yes, thank you."

"Whiskey, gin, or perhaps some sherry?"

Smith loved a glass of whiskey, but had yet to see an ice cube in England, so he took the safest route."

"Sherry would hit the spot."

"Here 'tis. Do sit down, and make yourself comfortable. Sir Robert will be down shortly." Helen poured herself a glass of sherry and led Warren Smith to the blue sofa in front of the fireplace. The Assistant Secretary sat down and took in the room. It was a large space, predominately informally decorated with blues and off-whites. The blue was soft and went well with the mostly beige rugs. Smith thought the room to be comfortable, almost cozy, not stiff and busy as he expected English upper class homes to be. There were a number of brass lamps producing a warm light that was blocked to the outside by the ubiquitous and ugly blackout curtains. Because German raiders still flew at night, London remained dark, and air raid wardens descended on any homes that showed light to the outside. Warren Smith wondered whether his wife would approve of the decor and decided she would. To the side of the fireplace, there was a small oak table on which a number of framed pictures stood. Most prominent was a picture of an older gentleman in uniform and one of a young girl in school dress. He wondered who they were and sipped his sherry.

"How long will you be in England, Mr. Smith?"

"Please, call me Warren. About two weeks. I'm here to discuss what to do with North Africa with our British friends." The Allies had vanquished Rommel's Africa Corps four months previously, and the entire coast from Casablanca to Alexandria lay in British and American hands.

"Sounds terribly important. What else do you think should be done?"

Warren Smith recognized the hook and decided to accept the bait. He had always found talking an issue through to be helpful.

"Well, my government's position is that no decisions need to be made now. Military governors can run the show in the near term. The sherry is lovely." He took another sip. "Sometimes people make decisions before they have to."

"And do you share your government's views?"

The American looked across at Helen Trent, holding his hands tightly together, a habit he employed when contemplating a decision. He liked this woman. She had a sense of humor and seemed intelligent. She also was pretty in a very British sort of way. He concluded he could trust her.

"Actually, I do. It's the long term I'm worried about."

"How so?"

"Well, you Brits want to restore the previous colonial governments, which means reinstating the French and possibly the Italians."

"Is that a problem?"

"In the long run, it might be. The Algerians and Moroccans and Tunisians seem to think that the coastline belongs to them."

"Surely you don't believe these Africans are ready or capable of governing themselves." Helen staunchly supported the British Empire. Not without reason, she believed it had brought much good to the world.

"Not yet, but they will be. Our countries, yours and mine, are fighting for survival. We're defending freedom and liberty. I'm not sure we could, or should, keep these principles to ourselves."

"It is difficult for me to conceive of Africa without the presence of France and Britain. I can't imagine the colonies governing themselves."

The conversation was beginning to resemble a meeting at the State Department. Smith decided that the Trent's living room was not the place to pursue the matter, though he would have liked to hear more of what Sir Robert's wife had to say. It was time to deflect the conversation with some humor. "Besides, one hundred and sixty years ago, your king and his ministers were saying the same thing about us."

"Point taken. But think how much better off you might have been had George the Third defeated George the Washington."

"But then, Mrs. Trent, I would not have the great pleasure of being here tonight."

"That would be a pity. Here, let me have your glass and I'll get you more sherry."

"That's a pretty young girl in the picture there."

"Thank you. That's my daughter, Claire. She's down at school."

"How old?"

"Fourteen. She's a dear. We see her next at Christmas time."

"I bet you can't wait."

"How true. You must have children of your own."

Smith thought of his girls. Grown and now leading their own lives. "Two girls actually. Both married. I get to play with grandchildren. One of life's great pleasures."

"I'm sure it is, though I shall have to wait awhile." Mention of Claire made Helen momentarily forget her guest. Dear Claire. Sweet and bright and ready to blossom. Peter would be so proud. Christmas could not come too soon.

The dinner party was proceeding well. The guests all had arrived on time except for the Foreign Secretary who, fortunately, had come ten minutes before Hoskins was to serve François' food. Eden was then forty-one. He was tall, elegant, and articulate. As Foreign Secretary under Winston Churchill, Eden was both powerful—for Britain was a primary player in the world then at war—and weak, for Churchill chose to make many decisions himself. Committed to the Empire, believing fiercely in the moral and intellectual preeminence of Britain, Sir Anthony thought the sun would never set on English territory. Despite Churchill's shadow, Eden was a most successful diplomat. In 1943, his influence was great and his prestige enormous. His failure as Prime Minister was years ahead. For now, he was someone to be reckoned with, a major actor on the world's stage.

Lady Roberts thus was pleased to be seated next to him. Sir Anthony was less pleased, though he admired her good looks and knew her husband to be extremely wealthy. Another benefactor for the Conservative Party perhaps? The Tories would face a difficult election at the end of the war. England was worn out. Her finances were imperiled, her economy near ruin, and her people tired, but determined to build a new and different postwar Britain. Eden perceived electoral danger, and knew a wealthy supporter would be most helpful.

"Lady Roberts, you're looking lovely this evening."

"Thank you, Sir Anthony." She did not blush.

Helen touched her hair, admitting to herself that Lady Roberts looked quite good, although she thought her guest wore a far too revealing dress.

"I'm sure all the men have noticed, and approve," Sir Anthony complimented.

Sir Robert hoped Wilfred Grimes took notice. He looked at the Group Captain who was conversing with Herbert Ashcroft. A nice young man. On assignment to the Colonial Office. Sir Robert hoped to get to know him better.

"You are simply too kind, Sir Anthony."

Eden gave her a look of interest and approval, one he had given to numerous diplomats across numerous conference tables.

Lady Roberts thought she had permission to proceed, and wished to push on to a new subject. "Sir Anthony, when will we see Parliament dissolved and a new election?"

"Ah my dear, that's a question for Winston. I am but the poor Foreign Secretary."

"But I wish to help. Besides, elections are such good fun, and we must keep those awful Socialists from power." To Edna Jones, socialists were but two steps above the Nazis.

Eden shared the last sentiment. Clement Atlee as Prime Minister. What an ungodly thought. Such a little man for such a big office. Perhaps he should pay greater attention to this woman, if her husband were as rich as Bobby Trent had indicated. Atlee at Downing Street. The idea was intolerable, though Eden realized it was not far-fetched.

"My dear, the war at last is going well. Winston is hopeful and I am as well. I suspect we'll see an election in '45 or '46. And I should much like to have your assistance."

"And you shall have it, at election time and before. I do so want to be involved."

Eden's mind had wandered back to Clement Atlee. "There is much to be done, and we conservatives must not be overconfident."

"Surely we will win." Edna had turned to Eden and put her hand upon his shoulder. She knew most men found her attractive. "And I am going to help you in every way possible."

Helen presumed she meant in ways beyond financial. The remark certainly had been suggestive. Edna Jones was not above using feminine attributes to realize her ambitions. She had told Jane Ashcroft she had seduced one Tory official to become a member of the Conservative Party Advisory Committee on the Arts. Helen was neither surprised nor, as she had admitted to herself, shocked. But she was disapproving. Helen realized again she was not fond of Edna, Lady Roberts. Why, the woman had practically propositioned the Foreign Secretary!

Helen was about to say something when the thought occurred to her that perhaps Lady Roberts had meant no such thing. Helen's pale face turned slightly red. Edna used sex to have her way, but she employed money as well. All Edna had said was she wished to aid Eden and the Conservatives in the next election, and everyone at the dinner party interpreted the remark to relate to money. Helen felt embarrassed, and looked about to see if her guests noticed her discomfort. Maybe it was she who was thinking about sex. Without realizing she did so, she ran her hand through her hair, and remained quiet. But she still did not care for Edna Jones.

Anthony Eden was neither fazed by Lady Robert's remark, nor by her hand, which he deftly removed. "You are too kind, Lady Roberts. I should like your assistance, and would welcome it. Eden turned towards Mark Stewart. "When the time comes, do speak with young Stewart here."

"I shall do just that." Edna Jones turned her eyes upon the Foreign Secretary's youthful assistant. Elizabeth Stewart gave her handsome husband a swift kick under the table.

Shortly before dessert was served, Helen struck up a conversation with Group Captain Grimes. "How are you getting on at the Colonial Office? It must be quite different from the RAF."

"Yes, it is, but I rather fancy the change." Grimes, who never was without a cigarette, inhaled in a somewhat theatrical fashion, yet politely blew the smoke away from the dinner table. "Along with being a bit like a private club, the Air Force can be too regimented for me. Being away from it for a while may actually be a relief, if I may say so."

Helen thought the Group Captain's last remark a bit odd, but remained silent. The officer continued to speak.

"But let me change the subject. I must say that your beautiful home speaks volumes about its mistress' excellent taste and her eye for color and decor."

"How kind of you to say so."

"I simply adore the way you've done the living room. Despite my uniform, I'm not overly fond of blue. But in your lovely home, it looks just marvelous." Grimes took another puff on the cigarette. "Light blues and soft whites, elegant fabrics, a splendid mix of old and new. It all works so terribly well together."

The conversation went on in this vein for several minutes, terminating only upon arrival of the crème brûlée. Helen found Grimes an engaging individual. He was witty, observant, and obviously at ease in the presence of females. She thought he seemed out of place in the Royal Air Force.

As dessert was served, Warren Smith was conversing with Clara Harris. She was a dignified woman, small in size and austere in appearance, but surprisingly gentle in character. Smith understood why Helen Trent cared for her. Despite her loss, Clara Harris spoke of the war without bitterness.

"My father died at Ypres and now dear William is gone. These Germans have brought such pain and suffering to the world," she said in sorrow rather than anger. "There must be something about the Germans that lead them to such evil." It was a question as much as a comment.

"I'm not sure, Mrs. Harris. Economic conditions and inflation made their money worthless, and the German military tradition all seem to have driven them mad. Twice I might add."

"I do hope it ends soon. So many have been killed. So many have been hurt." Clara Harris, upon whom much pain had been inflicted, felt the pain of others.

"I don't know when it will all end," responded Warren Smith. "But, as Sir Anthony has said, the war at last seems to be going our way."

Clara Harris seemed relieved, which Helen Trent noticed. Helen also wanted the war to end, but she wished for victory as well. "I do hope Sir Anthony is correct. The killing is awful, but Germany must be defeated."

"You're right of course, dear, but all this bloodshed is dreadful," responded Clara.

"Clearly, the bloodshed is terrible," said Helen, "but England and America must triumph if decency and democracy are to prevail. Warren, what do you think?"

"I agree with you both." Though new to the role, Smith was a diplomat. And he really did agree with them both. The killing was dreadful, yet victory had to be achieved. Decency and democracy had to prevail. Smith turned toward the older woman. "Mrs. Harris, it is important for the future that Germany be defeated. Japan too. But we need to defeat them, not destroy them."

"So that it doesn't happen all over again."

"Exactly, exactly. We've taken our lumps so far, but for now, the tide seems to be turning."

The tide was turning. North Africa belonged to the Allies who, in July, had invaded Sicily. The island fell in thirty-eight days, at the cost of eighteen thousand casualties. In September, the Allies turned their attention, and guns, to Italy proper. British troops crossed the Straits of Messina. American soldiers landed at Salerno. Continental Europe, at last, had been invaded.

But the war was far from over, and the outcome was by no means certain. The campaign in Italy would falter, plagued by bad weather and bad generals. Normandy had yet to be invaded. Indeed, D-Day was nine months away. The strategic air war against Germany was entailing heavy losses, especially among the Americans, who insisted on bombing in daylight. In the Atlantic, U-boats remained a menace. And Russian troops who, in January, had halted the German invasion at Stalingrad, still faced well-equipped, battle-tested Panzer divisions intent on winning. In September 1943, victory for the Allies lay in the future. And the killing, so repugnant to Clara Harris, was to continue, with the end to bloodshed still not in sight.

"The sooner the killing stops, the better off the world will be." Clara Harris was looking at them both. "I am no pacifist, and I know it's important that we win. William always said that if England were to fight, England must fight to win. But destruction has become the norm. Too many people have lost their lives."

"Too many to be sure," Warren Smith spoke. "But at last we seem to be making some real progress."

"Quite so, old boy, quite so." Sir Robert had joined the conversation. "Monty beat the Germans in Africa and in Sicily, and now he will defeat them in Italy. Side by side, with you Yanks, of course."

Warren Smith had to hide a smile. Sir Robert had remembered an American was his guest. But Helen's husband had more to say.

"We have them on the run. We've hit them in the soft underbelly of Europe. And they've run out of steam in Russia. We should strike next in Central Europe—Greece or the Balkans."

Smith sensed trouble. Striking north from the Mediterranean was Winston Churchill's preferred strategy. "Hit the Hun in the belly," he'd say, "where he's soft." But the Americans, particularly George Marshall, the Army's Chief of Staff, wanted a cross-channel invasion, striking first into France and then into Germany itself. FDR had promised Stalin a second front to relieve pressure on the Soviet Union. But in 1942, the Allies were too weak. Invading North Africa had been the best they could accomplish. Yet the campaign in Africa was a sideshow. The major battles were taking place in Russia. General Marshall, with President Roosevelt supporting him fully, insisted the next step was in Northwestern France. Meet the Germans head on. Make the Nazis fight two separate wars, one to their east, one to their west.

"Well, I hope the fighting in Italy goes well. I'm told the terrain favors the defenders." Smith decided not to debate grand strategy, having reminded himself he was only an Assistant Secretary of State. Besides, he was attending a dinner party.

"It is going well, and no doubt will continue to do so." Sir Robert was not giving up. He wished to impress upon the Yanks the wisdom of Churchill's strategy. As many in England did, he felt the Americans did not do strategy well. "We'll be in Rome in a month. Then across the Adriatic into the heart of Europe."

Smith noticed Eden was listening. Helen was also.

Bankers are cautious. So are diplomats. Warren Smith was both and he decided not to accept Sir Robert's challenge. Perhaps a comment to Helen on the dessert. The crème brûlée was superb. No, that would not do. Too transparent. "Well Sir Robert, I trust General Eisenhower and your General Montgomery will come up with what's best." It was weak and he knew it.

It didn't work. Sir Robert pursued the issue. Helen wondered if her husband was trying to impress Anthony Eden. "My dear fellow, the Navy controls the Med and we'll soon have all of Italy. Hitler's southern flank is vulnerable. Monty can strike north and pierce the Third Reich."

Sir Robert made it sound simple. The American knew it was not. The Foreign Secretary then entered the discussion.

"You see, my good man, if we now strike into Central Europe, we keep the pressure on Hitler and secure a more advantageous postwar position."

Smith knew that was at the heart of British strategy. They wanted to keep Russian troops from occupying the middle of Europe. Not unreasonable, but Ike and General Marshall knew the Allies had to first defeat the Germans. That required an invasion into France—confront Hitler's armies in the west and defeat them. Liberate France, Belgium, Holland, Denmark, and Norway. Politically compelling and militarily sound. Warren Smith would not be at the meeting where Churchill, and Eden too, would have to accept the American position. But that was months away. Now he needed to respond to Britain's Foreign Secretary and to his Colonial Office host.

Sir Robert spoke first. "Quite so, quite so. We push into Germany from the South. Monty can do it. You Yanks need to join the party."

How best to answer what clearly was a challenge? Smith wanted to be forceful, but not impolite.

"Well, my friends, the truth is we're not ready to challenge Hitler directly, neither in Central Europe nor in France. "We need time. Time to build up our strength. Time to assemble a war machine the likes of which the world has never seen, for that's what it will take. The Germans are strong. They are far from finished and we are not yet strong enough."

He looked at Helen and then to her husband. "Sir Robert, consider the geography. To the south of Germany and Central Europe lay the Alps. Hannibal crossed them, but I'm not sure Monty can." Sir Robert's blood rushed to his face, which looked like it might burst. The Englishman was about to speak, but Smith preempted him, and turned to Eden.

"Before we plan the postwar world, we need to win the war. That means defeating the German armies. Back in the States, we have an expression—first things first."

"My dear fellow," Eden said, "invading France will be very costly, in American and British blood."

"War is a bloody business," said the American.

Helen looked at the Foreign Secretary. He had taken no offense.

"You see, Mr. Smith, I'm concerned about the future in Central Europe. Our friend Mr. Stalin is not someone to be trusted."

"Sir Anthony, I'm concerned about Mr. Hitler. His armies are the roadblock to peace. Defeat them and the war is over."

"And what then?" Eden now spoke forcefully. "Europe will be divided, with the Soviets controlling vast amounts of territory."

Warren Smith did not trust the Russians, but he knew that FDR did, or at least wanted to give Stalin the benefit of the doubt. "Stalin is an ally. Not a gentleman perhaps, but an ally. The best way to help him and to defeat the Germans is to invade from the west. The war is not a political exercise. It's a crusade. Against a dark and evil madness that has infected half the world."

Inwardly, Eden sighed. Americans were so naive. This war, like all wars, was indeed a game of politics. It was more terrible than most, with extremely high stakes, but a game, nonetheless.

Warren Smith knew he should stop. He had made his points. No need to go further. Eden was looking at him. The Englishman appeared calm with a look on his face that conveyed interest and understanding. Smith bet he gave that look to everyone. He knew the Brits thought Americans to be naive. Woodrow Wilson's legacy. *Perhaps we are. But without trust and ideals, we'd be just like the Europeans.*

"Mr. Smith, I suspect I shall have this conversation again."

"Sir Anthony, I'm certain the President and General Marshall look forward to it."

The rain had continued during the evening. It was a light rain, more pronounced than a drizzle, which itself was normal for this time of year. Combined with the chill, for the temperature had dropped, the rain signaled a change in season. The wonderfully warm greens of England were giving way to cold grays and dark blues. Gardens once full of flowers would soon be bare. The river Thames would see fewer and fewer pleasure craft. Heavy clothes, which so often identified an Englishman, would be taken from chests and drawers. Harsh weather, not yet arrived, was on the horizon. The constant was rain. As always, England would see much rain.

The foyer at 28 Temple Court was filled with umbrellas. It was late, a little after 11 P.M. and the guests were beginning to depart.

"My dear, everything was splendid. You did your usual smashing job." Jane Ashcroft was putting on her coat, looking at Helen through the reflection in the hall mirrors. "Herbert and I enjoyed ourselves immensely."

"I'm so glad. I thought it went rather well."

"Perfect, just perfect." Harriet was speaking. Hoskins was holding her coat, but she was not quite ready to leave. "Helen, dear, you do these things the way they should be done. And you look marvelous. I love the burgundy on you."

"Helen, the crème brûlée was marvelous."

"Stop it, you two. It was a very pleasant evening, at which thankfully nothing went wrong."

Harriet and Jane looked at each other. They knew their friend did not take to compliments easily, especially about dinner parties. Helen thought they were simply part of the job every diplomat's wife had. And anyone with a modicum of social graces could give one. That it took genuine talent to host successful dinner parties Helen did not believe. Harriet and Jane knew better. Their parties, pleasant affairs competently organized, lacked the sparkle and perfection Helen sought and achieved when guests came to dinner.

"I should say everything went off in royal fashion. And Jane's correct; dessert was marvelous. Where did you ever find that chef? Everything was so good."

"Harriet, the chef is new. He's from the Collingwood. If one's to have a good dinner party, one must have a fine chef. It's really quite simple." Helen thought it to be rather obvious.

"Well," said Jane, "I shall talk to the Collingwood staff the next time I give a party. Good night, dear."

"Good night. Harriet has said we must have lunch soon, and I agree. I'm free next week. Thursday or Friday would be best, though."

"That's fine with me. I'll confirm with Harriet, and ring you up."

Harriet was putting on her coat. It was a brilliant red, trimmed in black with oversized gold buttons. Helen thought it too flamboyant, but admitted it looked good on Harriet. "Helen, I do love that dress of yours. Typically elegant."

"Just a little frock." Helen laughed, remembering that it had been an expensive little frock. Helen had paid twenty pounds for this dress, but it fit well and looked terrific. "Actually, it's one of my favorites. I like the look and the color."

"Good-bye dear. Lunch soon. I shall look forward to it." And Harriet was gone, on the arm of Sir John.

Helen thought they made an odd pair. But she knew them to be totally dedicated to each other. It was all too sweet. They were truly in love. Helen wondered, and envied, what they would do upon arriving home.

"I want to thank you for a lovely evening." Warren Smith had come up behind Helen.

"You're most welcome. We're delighted you were able to join us. I hope my husband and Sir Anthony didn't make you uncomfortable. The conversation was becoming quite intense."

"Not at all. It's my job. Defending my government's position comes with the territory. However, I do have a favor to ask of you."

"Of course."

"Well, it's still raining outside and I was wondering if I might borrow an umbrella. Seems I left mine at the hotel. I'm going to walk Mrs. Harris home, and I'd like to keep her, and myself, dry."

"Certainly." She was already in the foyer reaching for one. "Here in England, houses come equipped with umbrellas, by proclamation of the Crown."

"I have no doubt of that. Thank you again."

"Helen dear, thank you so for having me." Clara Harris was now speaking. "I had a most pleasant time. Dinner was lovely. Everything was exquisite, as always. And now this American gentleman is going to escort me home."

Helen took both of Clara's hands and squeezed them gently. "Clara dear, do take care of yourself. I'll come by next week and check on you."

"Not necessary. But do come by for tea."

"Lovely idea. I'll do just that. Bye now. Stay dry."

Helen Trent watched Clara Harris and Warren Smith leave together. She felt a twinge of envy. Clara had had a good marriage and the American seemed to have one also. Two children. That counts for something, although she knew that no one outside a marriage ever knew whether a husband and wife were truly happy. It could be sheer ecstasy or prolonged antagonism. Or, as she knew so well, marriage could simply be cordial coexistence.

"My dear, that was a lovely party." Now that the guests had departed, Sir Robert had changed into a smoking jacket. He was standing in the doorway of Helen's bedroom, feeling content and pleased with himself. He had hosted a successful dinner party for his friend, the Foreign Secretary. The dinner itself had been excellent and Hoskins had served with his customary efficiency. He had met his Colonial Office obligations by inviting the American who seemed to have enjoyed himself. His wife had been charming and looked most presentable. His friend, Lady Roberts, had met the Foreign Secretary, a longstanding goal of hers, and now was indebted to him. And young Wilfred Grimes had seen a level of society ordinarily denied to him and might now be more amenable. When the world worked to his liking, as it had this evening, Sir Robert Trent was convinced he enjoyed good fortune and proper recognition, both necessary for a move beyond the Colonial Office. Sir Robert wished to be an ambassador. Ottawa would be nice. Perhaps Stockholm. Maybe even Rome. To become one, he knew he must have a wife such as Helen. Thus, he intended to keep her happy and, if not happy, at least content. He would make her life comfortable and interesting. More importantly, he would provide for her daughter, whom he knew she adored. And Helen, in turn, would play the role designed for her.

"Yes, it seemed to go quite well."

"I think Tony had a pleasant time."

Helen was combing her hair. She knew her husband liked briefly to review how things had gone. He did so after every affair. The habit was endearing, and Helen wondered whether Robert alone did this or whether men in general sought the views of their wives about social events they had attended together. "He seemed to. I wish I had had more time to speak with Beatrice. She seemed tired. The poor dear must be under great stress."

"No doubt. I noticed that your friend Jane Ashcroft was talking with her. And Harriet Pennington. So Beatrice had plenty of company. I must say, though, the American was a bit odd. But, most of them are."

"Oh, I thought he was most pleasant." She was sitting at her dressing table, taking her earrings off.

"All this nonsense about invading France. Winston's right. We need to punch Hitler in the belly, from Italy. I do wonder about the Yanks."

Helen could see that her husband was about to get all worked up on the question of strategy. Time to change the subject. "Lady Roberts seemed to enjoy herself. She looked quite lovely."

"Indeed. Splendid, I thought, quite splendid." Helen wondered whether he meant how Edna looked or how successful her introduction to Eden had been.

"I'm so glad Clara Harris was able to come. She's such a dear. I think she had rather a good time."

"I'm sure she did. I must say, Helen, I do not understand why you insisted she be invited."

"Please, not again. Suffice it to say she's my friend and our neighbor."

"True enough. I rather enjoyed dinner. It was quite tasty. Hoskins told me the chef was very much in charge. A bit difficult is what I think he meant. But the results were excellent. Tony told me it was the best meal he had had in some time."

Helen thought the Foreign Secretary of His Majesty's Government deserved fine meals. "Well the chef is new, from your club, and very French."

"The French do have a way with food. They certainly cook better than they fight."

Helen was conscious of how expensive a fine dinner party was. Cocktails, wine, food, service—it all added up. At times, she felt guilty that she and Robert enjoyed a comfortable life when so many in England faced shortages in food and clothing. But if the war were to make life in London totally bleak, without any elegance and enjoyment, then that, she believed, would be a small victory for the enemy, which Helen Trent did not want them to achieve. "Here now, be good enough to unzip my dress." Helen had gotten up and turned her back to Sir Robert.

He pulled the zipper down, but without emotion, as though he were opening a closet door. Helen remembered when Peter would take her dress off. Not always at her request. Her dress would fall to the floor and he'd run his hands down from her bare shoulders to her waist. Then he'd turn her around, kiss her gently and tell her to remove her dress completely, which she would always do. Peter would kiss her again and again, telling her how beautiful she was. God it felt good and the excitement would run through her body and her heart. Best not to think of such things.

She put such thoughts aside, at the same time marveling at her ability to do so. She then finished undressing. A kiss for Claire, whose picture rested on the night table, and then Helen Trent climbed into bed and turned off the light.

TWO

The grey stones of Wycombe Abbey no longer echoed with the laughter of young girls. Northwest of London, the Abbey had been a school for privileged youngsters who embraced their studies while sighing, giggling, and scheming, as female adolescents do, all the time dressed in the school uniform of a green plaid skirt and a simple white blouse. And because the Abbey, like most buildings in Britain, lacked central heating, the girls invariably wore heavy blue sweaters, which had the yellow crest of the school sewn onto the front.

The girls were now absent, though uniforms were still evident. The school had been forced to relocate by the Air Ministry. The Air Ministry sought additional facilities for the Royal Air Force, which in turn gave the Abbey to the Americans who needed a headquarters for the fleet of bombers that had arrived in England in the spring of 1942. No yellow crest was evident on these uniforms. They were brown, and many had silver wings above the left front pocket. Sewn into the left arm of the jacket, up by the shoulder, was a patch that would become one of the most honored in American military history. The patch was a circle of blue, with a white and red star set within a yellow winged number eight.

Wycombe Abbey had become the headquarters of VIII Bomber Command. The bomber fleet now approached 300 aircraft, squadrons of B-17s and B-24s that from their bases in East Anglia could reach into Germany, delivering destruction and death from the air. The Eighth Air Force, to be known to history as the Mighty Eight, was the instrument by which the Americans hoped to validate their theory of daylight precision bombing. Their goal was to destroy Germany by air power alone, thus voiding any need for an invasion of France that all acknowledged would be bloody and difficult. Air Force strategists wanted to prove the invincibility of well armed, long-range aircraft striking the enemy in broad daylight. Daylight enabled American bombardiers to pinpoint key military and indus- trial targets. Collateral damage would break the morale of the German people. The Americans hoped to destroy the Germans' abil- ity to wage war, and also their will.

Not everyone agreed. The British thought the doctrine to be suicidal. Early in the war, the RAF had sent bombers out in daylight with disastrous results. RAF Bomber Command was now a night force. Its Lancasters, Halifaxes, and Sterlings sought out German cities by night, employing area bombing rather than precision strikes. Losses remained heavy and the target was frequently missed, but Bomber Command would persevere, occasionally suggesting to the Americans that the Eighth Air Force adopt its own commitment to the night sky.

American army generals thought that their counterparts in the Air Force were simply wrong. Marshall, Eisenhower, Patton, and the others all believed, correctly it turned out, that in the end, American soldiers would have to invade France and defeat the Germans on the ground. Air power, these officers argued, should be a tactical force assisting the G.I. Joining these generals in opposition to daylight pre- cision bombing were the admirals. Whether in the Royal Navy or America's, sea officers viewed the conflicts against Japan and German as essentially maritime warfare. They believed resources spent on long-range bombers should be devoted to surface ships and submarines.

Despite the skeptics, proponents of air power remained determined. The United States was fielding twelve combat air forces in what Hap Arnold, chief of American's air force, called a global war. Not all were strategic in character. But in September 1943, the case for daylight strategic bombing rested upon the wings of the organization now headquartered at Wycombe Abbey. And no one was more determined that the Eighth Air Force would succeed than its commander, Lieutenant General Ira C. Eaker.

"Damn it, Dick, I don't want excuses. I want answers." Eaker, who rarely swore, was speaking to Brigadier General Richard Harrison, his Director for Fighter Operations at Wycombe Abbey.

"I know that, General. I just think the problem is that our fighters don't stay close enough to the bombers." Harrison was uncomfortable. The Eighth Air Force was losing bombers faster than they could be replaced. And every bomber shot down meant the loss of ten trained crewmembers. The bomber boys blamed their fighter escorts. The escorts thought they could be more effective hunting German fighters wherever they were than by staying tied to the B-17s and B-24s whose slower speeds made escort work all the more difficult. "We need to keep the escorts close in, where the bombers can see them and make sure they don't go running around the clouds in pursuit of the Germans. Let the Jerry fighters come to us."

"I'm not sure that's the problem. We don't have enough bomb groups, and we're losing our best, most experienced crews. I want to raid Germany and I don't have sufficient strength to hit the Krauts where it hurts."

Harrison looked at Eaker. He thought striking at Germany now was premature. Surely Schweinfurt had proven that. "But raids in France are safer, and we can do real damage to Jerry's transportation and supply system."

"True, but the Eighth is a strategic air force." He emphasized the adjective. "Hell, we can blow up every railroad yard in France, but that's not going to put the fear of God into Germany. And if we don't strike at Germany proper, we make the case for the ground hogs that air power is a tactical tool." Eaker looked straight into the eyes of his subordinate. "And General, you can be absolutely certain I'm not going to do that."

Eaker had been one of the founders of the modern American air force. During the 1930s, when the United States focused on things other than its military, Eaker, with Hap Arnold, Carl Spaatz, and others, had kept the faith. With little money, no public support, and admirals challenging their every proposal, Eaker and his air-minded colleagues had laid the foundation for a modern air force, one competitive with the RAF and Luftwaffe. In 1939, when the war began, the Army Air Corps was small and outclassed. Six years later, the air force built by these pioneers ruled the skies above Europe and Japan.

Harrison knew Eaker was upset. Though a fine pilot himself, he was miscast in the job he held. Director of Fighter Operations was a key position in the Eighth Air Force and Richard Harrison was simply not up to it. He belonged elsewhere. "General Eaker, I'm going to call my group commanders together and issue new orders about escorting procedures. We'll keep those fighter boys glued to the bombers."

"Do that if you think it will work." Eaker believed in letting subordinates run their own affairs. Unlike many in high command, Ira Eaker knew the importance of delegating authority. His job, he believed, was to think ahead and orchestrate the pieces. The man at the top had to navigate into the future. The results of Eaker's approach were often beneficial. The flaw lay in not always finding the right man for the job. "I want my bombers protected."

"They will be, General, and then we'll get on with the job of striking at the heart of Germany."

"That's what I want to hear." Eaker paused, and took out his pipe. "And have happen."

Ira Eaker knew fighter escort was not a simple affair. Two types of aircraft were available for the tasks: the P-47 and the P-38. The former did not have the range needed while the latter, which did, performed poorly in cold weather. Moreover, rendezvous between fighter and bomber were difficult to accomplish, often because of bad weather. And Eighth Air Force fighter groups were too few in number to keep the Luftwaffe from beating up the bombers. Eaker was not certain Harrison understood the complexities involved, but the man had a fine record, seemed eager to please, and was well regarded back in Washington.

"I want results, Dick," said Eaker, implying that the lack thereof would bring about changes in command.

Harrison heard the words, but not the message. He felt secure and was comfortable at Wycombe Abbey. Director of Fighter Operations was a job he liked. Being DFO was a solid career step. With luck, he thought he'd soon win that second star. Major General Richard Harrison. That sounded good. His wife back in the States would like that. She had come to enjoy the perks associated with a husband of high rank. Though he disavowed them publicly, Richard Harrison enjoyed the perks as well.

Before replying, Harrison looked around him at Eaker's office. For such an important post, it was a modest space. There were two flags behind a standard issue Army desk flanking a credenza. Standing upon the credenza was a row of bulky black binder notebooks, kept current by Eaker's staff. The notebooks tracked progress of the Eighth Air Force buildup. Each notebook covered a different component. Subjects included aircraft repair and replenishment, crew training, navigation, airfield construction, logistics, combat operations, intelligence, health and morale, weapons development, et cetera. It was these pieces that Eaker orchestrated.

On top of the desk was a carved wooden sign stating simply "Commander Eighth Air Force," which was placed to the left of a small brass lamp. Near the lamp were four wooden box trays marked "In," "Out," "Urgent," and "Signature." They were the flight path for paper that confronted Ira Eaker each day. Lieutenants, majors, even colonels dealt with throttles and triggers. Commanding Generals dealt with paper. True, Eaker had flown on the first B-17 raid the Eighth had conducted on August 17, 1942, but he had to seek permission to do so, and he went along as a passenger, not a pilot. It was his only mission. For Ira Eaker, issues arose, were framed, discussed, and decided by paper. Of course, there were meetings. The U.S. Army, of which the air force was a part, could not function without them.

Harrison thought Eaker had too many meetings. Better simply to make the decision yourself and have the necessary orders issued. But Eaker wanted to hear what others had to say, particularly subordinates. He liked to question them and test their thinking. It was a technique he had acquired from his friend in Washington, Hap Arnold, who now commanded the entire air force and who, in August, had let him fly on that first mission.

Near the desk was an old wing chair, the kind one might find in a comfortable New England home, which is where Eaker had found it. The chair belonged to Eaker's sister who had given it to him for Christmas in 1938. She had said that the chair, covered in a brown, gold, and blue pattern, went so well with his uniform that they, he and the chair, belonged together. Eaker had accepted the present readily. It had since become part of his official baggage and accompanied him wherever he went. The general used the chair a lot. He would review lengthy documents there, rather than at his desk, and he could often be found there at night, after dinner. It was a place where he did much of his thinking. It was also where he could devour a favorite book, something not connected to the war. Such reading was how Ira Eaker relaxed. The Army's Chief of Staff, George Marshall, went horseback riding. General Eaker read. At the moment, he was reading Rafael Sabatini's *Scaramouche*. On the small table next to the chair, aside a pipe rack, was his next book: Robert Louis Stevenson's *Master of Ballantrae*.

The chair faced a fireplace. Eaker's staff kept the fire going all day as the General liked to stoke, tinkering with the fire as he did his pipes. The fireplace provided charm to the room, which perhaps, given the room's purpose, it did not need. But it also provided warmth, which the Americans believed the entire Abbey required. Colonel Baldwin, Eaker's chief meteorological officer, liked to update his boss on the weather practically hourly so as to stand by the fire and get warm.

Atop the fireplace was a beautifully crafted wooden mantle, above which hung a large portrait of Miss Eleanor Steeples, headmistress of the school during the 1920s. In the portrait, Miss Steeples wore neither a smile nor fancy dress. She seemed austere and unfriendly. Actually, this was not the case. Miss Steeples had been extremely outgoing and fun loving. Surprisingly, she liked the portrait. It conveyed the image expected in a school known for strict rules and propriety. To her, the painting portrayed what parents of the rich wanted to see in the headmistress of a school for young ladies.

In the portrait, Miss Steeples is wearing a dark blazer and green plaid skirt. The picture was dark and rather dreary save the yellow crest embroidered upon her jacket. General Eaker's officers had wanted to remove the portrait upon taking possession of the building, but Eaker said no. He wanted the picture there to remind him and his staff that they were guests of the British and but temporary occupants of Wycombe Abbey.

Below the portrait, a small photograph in a simple wooden frame stood on the mantle. The picture was of six men, all in aviator flight gear. The men were the crew of an Air Corps Fokker monoplane who, in 1929, had set a world endurance flying record. In the picture, Captain Ira Eaker was the aviator second to the left. Fourth from the left was Major Carl Spaatz who, as Lieutenant General Carl Spaatz, turned over command of the Eighth Air Force to Eaker on December 1, 1942 departing for the Mediterranean where he commanded Eisenhower's air force in North Africa. Eleanor Steeples was not the only individual whose picture hung on the walls of Ira Eaker's office. Near the window, four photographs were on the wall to the left of the fireplace. Of the same size and in identical frames, they were all formal portraits. The first was of Franklin D. Roosevelt, the President of the United States, who, as Commander-in-in Chief, led all of America's armed forces. Next to FDR's picture was that of General Arnold. Third in line was a photograph of Winston

Churchill. Eaker had discussed air strategy with the Prime Minister at Casablanca earlier in January. The final picture was that of King George VI. The monarch had visited Eighth Air Force facilities and General Eaker considered him a regular guy if indeed a king could be described in such informal terms.

At Casablanca, Churchill and FDR met to plan Allied strategy. Among the subjects discussed was daylight precision bombing. The Prime Minister had wanted the Americans to switch to night attacks, as the RAF had done. General Eaker was tasked to dissuade him. He did so, and brilliantly. Eaker, who had attended law school while in the Air Corps, prepared a one page brief, discarding a much lengthier paper his own staff had prepared. The General had learned that sometimes less is better. More importantly, he included in the brief a phrase that caught Churchill's attention. Eaker said the Allies would hit the Germans "round the clock." The British by night; the Americans by day. The phrase resonated with Churchill. The upshot was that the Prime Minister withdrew his objection to American strategy. Eaker had secured a future for daylight raids. His air force was to find it a costly enterprise.

"I want results too, Sir, and I'm going to get them." Brigadier General Harrison said and walked over to the window. He had not understood the meaning of Eaker's comment. Harrison thought his job safe and that he only needed to build up the fighter force. He should have known, but did not, that no job was ever truly secure. Harrison knew that Eaker wanted the bombers protected. The simple way to do that was to keep the fighters close in. He would issue the necessary orders and the bomber boys would be satisfied. Harrison understood that the bomber boys ran the Eighth Air Force. Keep them happy and all would be well. "The fighters want to go find the Luftwaffe fighters, which leaves the bombers exposed. I'll make sure they don't."

Ironically, Herman Goring employed the same tactic in the latter days of the Battle of Britain. Facing mounting Luftwaffe losses over England and responding to complaints by his bomber crews that German fighters were off chasing Spitfires instead of flying close escort, the Field Marshall ordered his fighters to weave about the bombers, staying within sight of the slower craft.

The tactic did not work in 1940. And it was not going to work in the winter of 1943-44. For while close escort did keep enemy fighters from wreaking havoc, it did not result in many of the enemy being shot down. Therefore, they could return again and again to harass and deflect the bomber formation. Early on, when U.S. fighter strength was limited, the practice of close escort made sense. But as the fighter force grew in number, as it did that fall and winter, the tactic became outdated. The tactic that would win the air battle would be to free the fighters and have them seek out the enemy— let them destroy the Luftwaffe interceptors wherever they were.

General Harrison wanted to play it safe. He was a conventional man who was comfortable with conventional tactics. He not only kept the American fighters confined to the air space near the bombers, but he also kept them above 18,000 feet. P-47s, which were doing most of the escort work, were kept from pursuing German fighters down to the deck. Bomber crews wanted to be able to see their escort, which they could not do if the P-47 went after the attacking German. When pressed, the enemy could dive away, safe in the knowledge that the American pilots would not follow. Harrison, and others too—General Gilbert for example—argued that at lower altitudes, fighters were vulnerable to ground fire as German antiaircraft guns were more accurate. They pointed out that the Eighth could ill afford to lose fighter aircraft. That was true, but tied to the bombers, American fighters were not going to destroy the Luftwaffe. They could do so only with the freedom to go after the Germans regardless of where they were. Once shot down, Fw-190s and Me-109s were not available to strike at B-17s and B-24s the next day. General Harrison, who should have known this, did not. He was committed to close escort. And he intended to issue the necessary orders, the ones he had promised earlier, as soon as his meeting with General Eaker was over.

"General Eaker, I do have some good news." Harrison had moved from the window and was standing beside a large globe that sat upon an antique wooden frame across from Eaker's wing chair.

"I can always use some of that."

"The buildup of fighters is going well. Two new groups, the 15th and the 89th, have arrived in Liverpool and move to their bases early next week."

Fighter aircraft were shipped to England via boat. Upon arrival, the aircraft were reassembled and checked out, thereupon assigned to groups whose personnel had arrived also by ship. Bombers, with their longer range, were flown directly to England. The route, some 2,119 miles, went from Gander in Newfoundland to Prestwick in Scotland. Later on, fighters also were ferried across the Atlantic, employing external fuel tanks to extend their range. These fighters flew formation on a single bomber, which carried out the extensive navigation required.

"How long before they become operational?" Eaker questioned.

"About four weeks. Maybe five if the weather doesn't cooperate," Harrison replied.

"Dick, that's an awfully long time. Can't we get them ready sooner?"

"I wish we could, General, but the truth is, these guys need some real life training. When they arrive in England, our fighter groups simply are not ready for combat."

"Yes, I know. That damned training establishment. You'd think with all the time and money they have, they would do a better job."

"I agree, General, but we've got to work with what we have."

In this instance, Harrison was correct. In 1943, fighter groups arriving in England were not sufficiently trained. Despite extensive instruction, American pilots were not prepared for the rigors of combat flying in Europe. Bomber pilots needed to improve their formation flying. Fighter pilots had to learn new tactics. All of them needed experience in radio procedures and local navigation. And, most of all, they needed to practice flying in bad weather. Having been taught to fly in the clear skies of the Southwest, American pilots were ill equipped to handle the rain and clouds that filled the skies over England and the Continent. The two new groups would need much time and hard work to get ready.

The American fighter arm was organized around groups. Comprising three squadrons of twenty-five aircraft each, the group was the principal tactical unit. Although squadrons retained individual identities, the aircraft went into battle as a group, with squadrons positioned at different locations relative to the bombers.

"We're going to need them. Fifty more fighters. That's good, Dick, but we need many more. I've got 300 bombers with more on the way, but our fighter strength is not where it needs to be."

"I know that, General, and we're working hard to build up the force. I feel we're making genuine progress."

"We are making progress, Dick, and we've come a long way."

The Eighth Air Force had come a long way. A year before, as Eaker was beginning the buildup of the Eighth, General Arnold had issued a most unwelcome order. To support Eisenhower in North Africa, Arnold ordered aircraft of the Eighth dispatched to the Mediterranean. Groups arriving in England expecting English weather and General Eaker were diverted to General Spaatz and the desert. Thus, raids by the Eighth Air Force in 1942 were modest affairs. Attacks that winter employed about one hundred aircraft. The first raid upon Germany occurred in January 1943 when ninety-one B-17s were sent to Wilhelmshaven. At one point in 1942, Ira Eaker had only one fighter group in his command. But by September of the following year, the drawdown had stopped. Eaker was beginning to build momentum. He was assembling the strike force envisioned when he had first landed in England nineteen months earlier.

"The new groups, they're all P-47s?"

"Yes, Sir."

"Well, it's a good airplane. Rugged, reliable. With plenty of fire-power."

"Yes, Sir, it is a good airplane. Dives better than anything in Europe." General Harrison did not like the P-47. He had flown one on a few test hops in August and thought the airplane too big and too heavy.

Harrison also had flown the P-38, which he thought to be a better aircraft. However, his favorite fighter was the P-39. Built by the Bell Aircraft Company, this plane was unusual in that the engine was positioned aft of the cockpit with the propeller driven by an extended shaft. Rejected by the British, the P-39, nicknamed the Airacobra, was not a success, despite a nose cannon that was lethal in the ground attack role. Yet the plane had found favor with the Soviets. Their air force used the cannon to destroy scores of German tanks. Early on, the Eighth Air Force had numerous P-39s. These were sent to North Africa, where the need for aircraft was urgent. Most of the P-39s were gone by early 1943. Harrison was sorry to see them depart. General Eaker was not. He wanted a fighter that could safeguard his bombers.

"I just wish it had longer legs." Eaker was lamenting the P-47's range.

"I have some good news on that score as well, Sir."

Eaker's face displayed surprise. There had been little good news of late. The inability of the P-47, his principal fighter, to accompany the bombers the full distance to their targets was cause for concern, not only at Wycombe Abbey, but also in Washington. Both statistics and common sense indicated that Eighth Air Force B-17s and B-24s suffered fewer losses when shielded by fighters. But the P-47s could not stay with the bombers for very long. Though its range was greater than that of the RAF's Spitfire, the P-47 usually turned around near Aachen, along the German-Belgium border. Luftwaffe pilots would await their departure before bouncing the now unescorted bomber force.

General Eaker had stopped fiddling with his pipe, so anxious was he to hear what the Director of Fighter Operations had to say. Harrison liked giving his superiors good news. He believed that good news was likely to rebound to the messenger's credit, so he had looked forward to speaking about fuel tanks.

"The 108-gallon tanks are about to arrive."

"From our British friends?"

"Yes, Sir. They'll enable the P-47s to have a range of about 325 miles."

"Excellent." Eaker was truly pleased. "What a mess this whole business has been."

"My own view, General, is that it took the Brits far too long to manufacture the tanks."

"Don't be too harsh, Dick, we've not done a good job with that ourselves." Eaker, who liked the British and got along with them exceptionally well, knew why American-made tanks had not been available—because Air Force strategists had seen no need for such devices. Single engine fighters were not expected to conduct long-range escort. Hence, external fuel tanks to extend their range were unnecessary. Armadas of four-engine bombers, capable of defending themselves, would be conducting daylight precision bombing. With reason, the B-17 was nicknamed the Flying Fortress. Like the B-24, it bristled with machine guns. These would deal with enemy fighters foolish enough to contest the target sky.

"I'm told that American-made fuel tanks, good ones, will be on the docks shortly. I've arranged for transportation once they're unloaded from the ships," said Harrison.

The first American-made tanks had not worked well. They were ferry tanks used to fly the P-47s across the Atlantic. Bulky and made of an especially stiff paper, they degraded aircraft performance and could not be used above 22,000 feet. Therefore, Eighth Air Force engineers designed a steel tank of their own, which the British agreed to manufacture. Shortages of steel in England forced the manufacturer to extend delivery dates. The Americans, by now desperate to extend the P-47's range, thus purchased a British-made paper tank that worked reasonably well. General Eaker knew that external fuel tanks for fighters had not been the Eighth Air Force's finest hour. The request to the British for assistance had irritated many of his officers who thought British engineering to be second rate. Eaker knew better. He pointed out that the Brits had far greater wartime experience than them and that the Eighth Air Force had much to learn. Eaker was a quiet, extremely capable, and tactful man. He disliked the arrogance he saw in many Americans and consistently preached the need for modesty and cooperation. His best speech had been one of the shortest ever given by an American general. At a community gathering in High Wycombe, near the Abbey, Eaker had addressed a large group that included many Englishmen who expected a long-winded and typically brash American speech. Eaker had recently arrived in England and said simply, "We won't do much talking until we've done more fighting. We hope that when we leave, you'll be glad we came."

"I'd like a full briefing on the fuel tanks, Dick. I want to hear what the British have done and have not done. And tell me what our own boys have accomplished. Spell it all out and, most importantly, tell me with specifics what the impact is on P-47 range and tactics."

"Yes, Sir. I'll put that story together for you." As he spoke, Harrison was seeing himself giving orders to Colonel Arnie to prepare the briefing. He would then retreat to his office and review the material by himself, emerging only to have specific questions answered. Harrison used his staff extensively, but rarely sought their advice.

Talk with Miss Hayes and have her find time on my schedule for the briefing. I think Thursday is good. I'm having lunch with Air Marshal Harris, so maybe we can do it right after."

"That sounds good to me. I'll check with her."

"Come to think of it, why don't you join us at lunch?"

"I'd like to General Eaker, but let me decline. I've got some meetings scheduled I'd prefer not to miss. If that's all right with you, Sir."

"Yes, that's fine. Just check with Miss Hayes."

"I will do that, Sir."

General Eaker met often with Air Marshal Arthur Harris. Harris was the commander of the RAF's Bomber Command. A leading proponent in Britain of strategic bombing, Harris had reinvigorated the Command, which had done little to harass or harm Germany early in the war. In May 1942, Harris had assembled one thousand planes to hit Cologne. Some were training planes and some were wrecks patched together, but the night raid had been successful. It helped restore Bomber Command's credibility and further convinced the RAF that bombing Germany at night was the best way to win the war. Not surprisingly, General Eaker and Harris got along extremely well. They shared a belief in the primacy of air power. Moreover, they simply liked each other, discovering in passing that they had the same birth date. Harris had been particularly helpful to Eaker in setting up the Eighth Air Force, providing substantial assistance, which the American both needed and appreciated. About a month after Eaker arrived in England, the Air Marshal had given him the large globe that now sat in the office at Wycombe Abbey. In return, General Eaker had given Harris a finely detailed model of a B-17.

General Harrison was slowly spinning the globe as he excused himself from the luncheon with Harris. He didn't like the British. He thought them arrogant and condescending. *At war for over three years, the British have few victories to show for their efforts.*

On one hand, Richard Harrison agreed with the British. Like their Fighter Command, the DFO favored fighter sweeps over the Continent. When P-47s were not escorting bombers, the General sent them out, hoping to entice the Luftwaffe into combat. This was an aggressive strategy, appealing to many in the Eighth Air Force. But the strategy failed to achieve its goal. Recognizing that P-47s by themselves posed little threat, the German fighters stayed on the ground. They were interested in bigger fish, namely B-17s and the other heavy American bomber, the B-24.

"Excuse me, Sir, but I thought you'd like to have the latest forecast." Colonel Roger Baldwin had slipped into the room. After speaking to Eaker, he nodded a respectful acknowledgement to Harrison.

"Come in, Roger."

"Thank you, Sir."

Baldwin was thin, slightly bald, and wore glasses. His uniform jacket bore few decorations and on Baldwin, the jacket somehow looked more like a comfortable tweed coat worn by a college professor. That was not an inappropriate description since the colonel had taught physics and meteorology at MIT prior to enlisting in the Army Air Corps. A graduate of Dartmouth College, Roger Baldwin was friendly and informal, a man who seemed out of place in a military organization. But Baldwin was a patriot. He was proud of the Eighth Air Force, pleased to be part of it, and worked very hard at his job. Ira Eaker knew him to be expert at understanding weather and fought to retain Baldwin when he had been earmarked to accompany Spaatz to North Africa.

"General, I think tomorrow may offer us some decent weather. The initial signs are good. The front is moving off and Iceland reports clearing."

Harrison stopped spinning the globe and eyed Baldwin, who was standing in front of the fireplace. "What about France and close-in Germany?"

"I can't say for sure. Conditions suggest they'll be clear."

"Clear for how long?" inquired Eaker.

"Long enough for a mission, General. But keep in mind that these are early estimates. I'll know more in a few hours."

"Roger, what we need is reliable information about target areas."

"I know that, General. I'm afraid weather forecasting is still as much art as science, although I do have an idea how we might improve things."

"I'm listening."

"Well, what we need are measurements at the target site and along the way. So why don't we send out aircraft to get the data?"

"Because we don't have aircraft that can do the job," answered Harrison, just as Baldwin had expected. "P-47s don't have the range or equipment bay. And B-17s, which do, cannot survive in groups of two or three, much less alone."

"Correct. But the British have a plane that can. Why not borrow a few Mosquitoes from the RAF?" Baldwin had done his homework. The Mosquito was an extremely fast, twin-engine plane made of wood. Employed by the British in a variety of tasks, the plane used its speed and high altitude to stay clear of German fighters. Although it was a small craft with only a pilot and navigator as crew, the Mosquito had great range. It could fly from Britain to Berlin and back.

"Can a Mosquito carry enough weather instruments?"

"Yes, Sir, it can."

Eaker peered at his weatherman, whom he liked. "How do you know?"

"I went over to the RAF station at Hadley and looked at them last week with some engineering folks. It's a very nice aeroplane." Baldwin pronounced all three syllables.

Eaker's eyes disclosed his amusement. Baldwin was widely known at Wyecombe Abbey for having little interest in aircraft. His passion was weather, not aviation. "I don't suppose you flew in one?"

"Oh no, Sir, I don't like to fly. But I did examine the Mosquito's bomb bay and we could fit our instruments into it. And the pilots told me they could fly over Jerry flak and outrun Jerry fighters."

"Yes, I'm sure they did. Well, it's an interesting idea. I'll talk to Air Marshal Harris about it and see what he thinks."

"Excuse me, General, but the group commanders are ready for you when you're ready." This time, the interruption came from Major Harris Hull, an aide to Eaker who had been one of the original six officers to accompany the General to England in February 1942.

"Thank you, Harris."

"Well, gentlemen, it seems I'm needed elsewhere. You're welcome to join us." Eaker was inviting all three men to the meeting. Being staff officers, they were not always included when line officers, in this case, commanders of the Eighth's bomber squadrons, met to discuss operational matters.

The distinction between line and staff was clear and sharp in the Eighth Air Force. Between the two types, a rivalry existed. Staff officers felt their colleagues on the line did not appreciate the larger picture nor understand the complexities of a large organization such as the one headquartered at Wycombe Abbey. Line officers complained that staff officers lost sight of essentials and had forgotten, if indeed they had ever known, how difficult it was to fly a B-17 to Germany and back. The rivalry led to good-natured ribbing. Roger Baldwin was often the target. Pilots were amused by his unwarlike demeanor and by his disinterest in airplanes.

Richard Harrison basically disliked most line officers, for he believed they undervalued staff work and thought their pilot wings ensured insights somehow denied earthbound individuals. The irony was that Harrison himself was a pilot with the same arrogance and simplicity he so disliked in line officers.

General Eaker worked hard, with success, to harmonize the two sets of officers. He knew both were essential, and he encouraged each to attend the other's meetings. His hope was that they both would better understand the difficulties each faced and would recognize the expertise the other brought to the table.

Eaker had convened a meeting of his bomber group commanders to review tactics and discuss what might be done to reduce losses. July and August had been difficult months for the Eighth Air Force. At the end of July, Eaker had mounted a series of raids into Norway and Germany. Fifteen B-17 groups hit targets in Bergen, Kiel, Hamburg, Hanover, Kassel, and Oschersleben. For six days, Eaker sent out up to three hundred aircraft. Considerable damage was done even though bad weather hindered operations. Losses were high. Over one hundred B-17s went down. Aware that the Americans now constituted a threat from the West, the Luftwaffe had reorganized air defenses. Fighters were redeployed from Italy and Russia to confront the Eighth. Whenever Ira Eaker sent forth his armadas, Me-109s and Fw-190s rose to defend Germany.

The ensuing air battles were fierce—none more so than Schweinfurt. On August 17, 1943, the anniversary of the first B-17 raid, General Eaker dispatched 376 bombers to Schweinfurt where the manufacture of ball bearings was concentrated and to Regensburg where Messerschmitt had an important factory. P-47s escorted the attack force part of the way and then turned homeward as fuel ran low. The Germans were waiting for the Fortresses. The results were disastrous. Sixty bombers were shot down. Fire and smoke from the crash sites marked the route to the two targets. Additional aircraft were so damaged upon return as to be written off. Eaker believed the Eighth had won a costly battle. The media portrayed an aerial victory. They were both wrong. The battle was a defeat for the Americans. Damage to the targets was substantial, but hastened dispersal of German industry, which made its destruction more difficult. Moreover, though bombs blew out walls, set fires, and disrupted production, they did not destroy heavy machine tools. And the claims of enemy fighters destroyed put forth by Eaker's aircrew were grossly inflated. Air gunners believed they were driving the Luftwaffe from the skies; bombardiers believed they were blasting German industry. Neither was the case. In July and August, the Eighth Air Force had struck hard at Germany, with courage and sacrifice, but Germany was a hard nut to crack. And the Eighth had come off decidedly second best.

"Dick, I'd like to see you after this meeting." Eaker was speaking to General Harrison.

"Yes, Sir. Anything I can prepare for?"

"No, just come by the office and have Miss Hayes buzz me. Besides, I want you to hear what the group commanders have to say. After all, you are my Director of Fighter Operations."

Eaker left the room. The others followed, with Harris Hull stepping aside first for Eaker and then for Baldwin. The weatherman spoke as he left Eaker's office. "Yes, these fellows love to see me. I sometimes think they believe I actually make the weather, rather than attempt to predict it."

Bad weather constantly interfered with operations of the Eighth Air Force. Because of poor visibility, aircraft were grounded, recalled, and diverted to the secondary targets, which themselves were often obscured. Rain, frost, and ice all made flying difficult. For one-fourth of its stay in England, the Eighth stood down due to inclement conditions.

Eaker realized he could do little about the weather, but he was determined to change whatever needed to be changed in order to improve the fortunes of his force. Navigation, fighter escort, gunnery, formation flying, and the like were thus all on the meeting agenda.

The bomber commanders were in attendance. These men, who led the B-17 and B-24 groups, were responsible for the success of daylight precision bombing. They believed they were hitting Germany hard—and they were. But combat makes men realists and these gentlemen knew all was not well. They did not read press releases. They read casualty reports, and had seen Fortresses fall in flames.

Eaker respected these men. Many he had hand picked. Eaker dealt with them openly, and encouraged full debate. Unlike many of high rank, Eaker kept discussion focused. He steered debate towards first understanding the problem and then considering solutions. The General had little tolerance for tangents and none for speechmaking. He would bore in on the preferred solution so that upon conclusion of the meeting, there was no confusion as to what had been decided.

The meeting had lasted most of the morning. Eaker had started the discussion and then mostly listened as the group commanders marched through the agenda. Toward the end of the meeting, Eaker had stepped out briefly to speak with General Harrison. He returned accompanied by the three staff officers.

"Ten-shun!"

The men stood up as their commanding general entered. The room was large and contained six elegant Gothic shaped windows whose lead frames held old, uneven glass. The room had been the visitor's lounge at the Abbey school. Its comfortable furniture had been removed, as had twin cabinets used to display the school's fine china. In the middle of the room stood eight ordinary wooden tables. These were arranged in a square with plain chairs placed to the outside. The group commanders occupied these chairs, save one. Staff officers sat in identical chairs along the walls. To the left on a small table was an overhead projector directed at a portable projection screen. Nearby, sitting on the floor, was a Bell and Howell film projector. Target maps of Europe adorned two walls and a single American flag stood behind the empty chair.

"Thank you. Please be seated." General Eaker slid into his chair and immediately began to relight his pipe. Quickly glancing at those sitting with him, he saw faces that showed fatigue and the strain of combat—but no fear. He felt proud to command such men.

"Colonel Ellis, please continue."

"I was just finishing up, Sir, saying that our escorts too often leave the formation and go diving after Jerry. I know they want to get the bastards and that a 109 shot down today won't be around tomorrow. But squadrons are left unprotected and we get beat up pretty bad when there are no P-47s around."

"I know. General Harrison and I were just discussing that."

Ellis continued, "When the fighters make the rendezvous and stay within sight, we do pretty well against Jerry. But left to ourselves we're damn vulnerable."

Eaker said nothing, but his expression signaled agreement.

"What we need, General, are more P-47s around more often." Ellis knew he was speaking for everyone around the table. "With fighter escort, we can hold our own."

"What we need, Sir, are longer range fighters that can go with us all the way," said Donald Archer, whose group had suffered high losses on the Schweinfurt raid.

"Well, they may be coming. In the meantime, we're adding drop tanks to the P-47 and are working a number of fixes to the P-38."

Richard Harrison then spoke, "I'll be meeting shortly with fighter group commanders to emphasize the importance of staying with the bombers. And I'll be issuing new orders to that effect. I'm also going to remind them that they're forbidden to go below eighteen thousand and that anybody who does it may get court-martialed."

The last two words put a chill in the room. Silence followed. Eaker thought clear orders would be sufficient and was surprised Harrison had mentioned court-martials. He knew though, that at least half the bomber group commanders would support such drastic action.

Ellis and Archer had nothing else to say even before Harrison's remark, so the meeting appeared to be over. General Eaker was cleaning out his pipe as he looked around the room. He asked if anyone had something else they wished to bring up, implying that otherwise it was time to depart. They did not.

"We're finished here, but please remain seated. There's something else I wish to say to you all." The general had moved from the table and now stood in front of one of the Gothic windows. He paused, in reflection, and then addressed the men in the room.

"I want to tell you I'm extremely proud of you. You've taken the battle to the skies over Germany and are hitting the Nazis hard. We've suffered losses. Brave men, many of them our friends, are gone and will not coming back. And I suspect the sacrifice will continue because we are going to continue to strike targets in Germany. We will hit them during the day and the RAF will blast them at night. Around the clock, we will strike again, and again, and again. No place in Germany will be safe. No enemy will escape the wrath of the United States Eighth Air Force.

"Our force is growing. Last spring, we could put up just one hundred planes. Now we can assemble three times that. Next year, we'll put up five hundred, and even more later on. We are becoming democracy's longest sword, the most powerful aerial army the world has ever seen. And it is you, the men in this room, who will bring this about.

"You are all brave men. True warriors. America is proud of you. Hitler fears you. And I am honored to be your commander."

No one spoke. The silence in the room echoed respect and camaraderie. Eaker's words had come from the heart. That was clear. His eloquence surprised the assembled officers who rarely heard their commanding general speak with passion. Baldwin, Hull, and a few others knew how Eaker felt, but they too had been moved.

"Ten-shun." Donald Archer boomed the command, and the spell was broken. The men stood to attention and Ira Eaker, with pipe in hand, walked out of the room.

"Democracy's longest sword. Not bad, not bad at all," mused Harris Hull.

"And the damndest thing is that it's true," added Roger Baldwin.

The next day, Richard Harrison stood outside General Eaker's office.

"I'll tell General Eaker you're here."

"Thank you, Miss Hayes."

Moments later, General Harrison heard Eaker say, "Send him in." Miss Hayes reappeared at Eaker's door, beckoning Harrison through.

"You wanted to see me, Sir?"

"Yes, Dick. Come in. This will have to be brief. I'm on my way to meet the leading citizens of Cambridge." Eaker, who was packing his briefcase with papers his secretary had just given him, did not invite Harrison to sit down.

"I wanted to ask you about the fighter groups. Actually, their leaders. I've read the reports and have met them all, but I wanted to hear how you feel about them."

Harrison, who was good with data, but uncomfortable with intuition, at first fumbled with the answer. "I feel fine about them, General." That sounded stupid and Harrison knew it, but he recovered.

"Basically I think the groups are well led. Morale is good and the groups put up a full complement of aircraft. Of course, with the new groups, we'll have to wait and see."

"True enough. Who's the best?"

"I'd say Colonel Hubert Zemke of the 56th."

"Any aces?

"A few—Charles London, Gene Roberts, and some others. I'm trying to downplay the ace thing. This is a team effort and puffing up a few pilots isn't healthy. I'm trying to have the press focus on the group, not on individuals."

"Quite so." Eaker did not sound completely convinced. "Any problems?"

"Not many, but I might have a problem with one of the group leaders. Actually, he was the deputy group leader. The group is the 19th. Its commanding officer, Colonel Carl Phillips, went down on a training flight near the Pas de Calais."

"I remember. A real shame."

"His deputy is the new C.O., but I'm not sure he's up to it." In fact, Harrison disliked the man intensely and wanted to sack him.

"Keep me advised."

"Yes, Sir."

"What's the man's name?"

"Forester. Lieutenant Colonel Thomas Forester."

THREE

After the first World War, in which German Zepplins bombed the city, foreshadowing future terror from the skies, London was a city of enormous energy. Lacking perhaps the romance of Paris, it had nonetheless great museums, great architecture, and great wealth. Larger than New York, London stood alone in finance, insurance, and trade. Although located in the south, London was the center of England, the seat of government—and with a port central to economic well-being, the city thrived. So did the arts. London nurtured music, dance, and the theater. During the 1930s, the city was cosmopolitan and full of confidence, despite war clouds to the East.

By 1943, in the fourth year of the war, London had changed. The city was dark. Streetlights and neon signs were turned off. Blackout curtains blocked light from homes throughout London and its suburbs. The city was dark so that German bombers, flying at night to avoid the RAF, might not easily find their target. Although the Luftwaffe struck London, the bombing in 1943 was much less severe than the Blitz, the intensive aerial campaign against the city three years earlier. But the bombs did cause damage. They brought death and destruction to London—and fear. People were afraid for their lives and for the lives of their friends. The bombs also brought a lack of sleep to people in the city. Few could sleep through air raids. The result was a populace profoundly tired, with spirits further aggravated by food shortages and limited supplies of clothes and drink. Rationing was extensive. Most Londoners faced hardship in their daily routines. Cinemas and museums flourished as people sought relief from the war and its impact upon the city. Fine arts, however, did not do as well. Writers and other artists contributed their talents to the war effort, abandoning stage and studio. The Opera House at Covent Garden was closed—the only opera house in Europe to remain dark for the entire war. In September 1943, the city was showing signs of physical and emotional stress. Much in London was drab and worn. With victory still distant, the city soldiered on. The rains that struck Big Ben that September and the cold winds that swept across the Thames signaled a hard winter.

To the east of Big Ben, off the Old Brompton Road near the Victoria and Albert Museum, lay Earl's Court, the section of London where Helen Trent and her husband lived. Earl's Court was a desirable location, though not as fashionable as Chelsea. That men of substance lived in Earl's Court pleased Sir Robert. He enjoyed having men he wished to know as neighbors.

The house at 28 Temple Court was substantial—not grand, but certainly not modest. Georgian in design, the house had been renovated in 1927 by its then owner, a bank executive whose finances collapsed three years later. Sir Robert, at the time a promising but still mid-level civil servant, was able to purchase the property at a bargain price with funds given him by an elderly aunt. The house had large rooms on the first floor. This made it suitable for entertaining, which Sir Robert enjoyed, for he saw social occasions as opportunities to advance his career. In this he was correct. The dinners and receptions put on by his wife in fact had contributed to his professional success. Helen liked entertaining as well. She found pleasure in meeting men and women of accomplishment and style. The price of this entertaining was the occasionally tedious individ-

ual—men who defined pomposity and women who lacked any trace
of style. Helen had come across more of the former than the latter.
She disliked such men, but felt only pity for the women. They were
sad creatures. She believed that women, in what clearly was a man's
world, needed everything they could muster in order to survive.

Except for a library, the second floor consisted mostly of bedrooms. These were small, but had surprisingly ample closet space. The
largest bedroom belonged to Claire. Now that she was away at
school, the room remained tidy. Helen had the two bedrooms at the
South end of the house. These were separated by a large bathroom,
which featured an immense porcelain tub sitting delicately on four
cast iron legs. Helen loved to take long baths in the late afternoon.
She would fill the tub with hot water, then soak and let the suds
gather about her body. Her mind would wander and she would relax
totally. A quick scrub would follow. Afterward, she would rinse off
using a flexible shower hose from which water flowed gently.
Stepping out from her bath, she would smother herself in thick cotton towels. All this took place in front of a large mirror. Helen
thought the entire process to be self-indulgent, if not slightly
wicked. She thus enjoyed it immensely.

The smaller of Helen's two rooms was her bedroom. The other
she used for dressing and as a study. She had decorated this room in
soft peach and ivory. Upon her dressing table she kept the picture of
Peter taken when they had visited Florence. The photograph captured Peter's special expression, the one he had when telling her how
much he loved her. "I will love you till the end of time," he would
say, and he made her believe it to be true. Helen treasured the picture. She could still hear his voice speaking those words. The room
overlooked a small garden at the rear of the house. Helen spent
comfortable hours in the room. She would attend to her correspondence, read, and listen to music on the BBC. And she would gaze
down upon the garden, marveling at the array of colors nature could
produce.

Sir Robert had the two bedrooms at the north end of the house.
He also used one as a dressing room and study. His view encom-

passed not the garden, but the garage. The garage housed a 1937 SS Jaguar saloon motor car. With petrol and tires unobtainable, the automobile was never used. Yet Sir Robert kept it in working condition. However, he had little need of the car as the Colonial Office provided him with both automobile and chauffeur.

"I must say, Helen, I do not think you've thought this through." Sir Robert was in the kitchen, finishing breakfast, and about to depart for the office.

"Actually, I have."

"Well, it doesn't appear so."

"I don't understand why you find my doing something for the war effort to be so objectionable."

"Because, my dear, whatever you were to do would hardly make the war end sooner."

"That's a rotten thing to say." Helen was upset. "What if everyone thought like that?"

"Everyone is not the wife of a senior official in His Majesty's Government. It's perfectly fine for the lower classes to have their women work in factories, but hardly appropriate for you."

"Robert, I'm not going to work in a factory."

"Well, what are you planning to do?"

"I don't know. I just think it's time for me to contribute, to help out."

"You already are contributing."

"I am?"

"Yes, my dear, by being my wife. By being the companion to the Deputy Permanent Secretary for Colonial Affairs who needs a charming, competent wife at his side. There are social obligations to fulfill, obligations which have political overtones and which, as you know so well, are part and parcel of my position."

"But Robert, don't you see, that means I'm but an adjunct to you."

"So?"

"So that's not enough!"

"Helen, let me remind you that you're my wife. You carry my name. Your place is by my side."

"Not now, Robert. England is my country, too. And it's time for me, as me, not as your wife, to be by England's side."

"God, you sound like Mrs. Miniver." Sir Robert was referring to actress Greer Garson's award-winning portrayal of a brave English housewife at the time of Dunkirk.

"And what's wrong with that?"

"Nothing I suppose. But why now? All of a sudden you have a patriotic urge?"

"I can't answer that. I don't really know. It's something I've been thinking about for some time. All I know is that I must again do something to help." In 1940, Helen had served part-time as a driver for the Ministry of Health. The job had been part-time because Claire was then at home and needed care. When her daughter went off to Roedean, Helen had worked full-time, again for the Health Ministry. This arrangement did not last long, for Helen had been injured when a lorry crashed into the motorcar she was driving.

"Robert, all across England women have left their homes and gone to work in real jobs. Many are in the Service. Jane Ashcroft's sister drives lorries for the RAF. Clara Harris's niece works at Vickers building airplanes."

The war had brought a change to British life. Women had left their homes and gone off to war, in support of their country's crusade against the Nazis. Women served in all of the forces. They handled communications, worked in intelligence, provided transportation, and did countless other tasks, thus freeing men for combat. British women also worked in factories. In the States, such females were called Rosie the Riveter. In England, they had no such fancy moniker. But they worked as hard, and turned out warships, fighter aircraft, and other instruments of war. Their impact on production was significant. So too, in a more subtle way, was their impact on British society. Women became freer, no longer completely dependent on men. Class consciousness remained, but this too became less rigid.

Such change was not always welcomed nor accepted. Men such as Robert Trent objected to women achieving any measure of independence. Of course, not all women wished to leave the home. But many did and the war provided an opportunity to do so. By war's end, over five million women had joined the work force, and thousands more served in the military. Now fully recovered, Helen Trent was once again anxious to do her part.

"That's all very noble of them, but your place is by my side."

"I'll be there, Robert." She paused. "When I need to be. I'm not leaving you, nor am I asking your permission. I'm simply going to find something worthwhile to do." *Why,* she asked herself, *is this man being so self-centered. Is he insecure or simply blind to my needs.* The thought crossed her mind that it was both. "The dinner parties will continue."

"They must. I expect you to act like my wife."

Helen pondered the last remark. *Act like my wife. God knows I've tried to do just that.* A wife sleeps with her husband. A husband makes love to his wife. Robert showed no interest in such things and actually had feigned illness when Helen, in a most revealing silk nightgown, had attempted to seduce him. Helen remembered that she had little difficulty in convincing Peter to make love. Once they even had one another in the garden. At 28 Temple Court, however, the garden was only used to grow flowers.

"I will act as I see fit." After a pause, she added, "That includes my job as hostess of this house." Though the conversation was becoming acrimonious, Helen was not seeking to battle with her husband. "Robert, I neither wish to fight you, nor to engage in threats. And I certainly won't do anything to harm your career. But I need to step out from your shadow and I'm determined to do something, although I don't know what, to help win the war. Others have and I must too. Will it make it difference? I think it will. I'm certainly going to try."

"My dear, you're acting foolish." Sir Robert regretted the remark as soon as he said it.

"I am not and I resent your saying so," she retorted quickly.

"I meant no offense. I just think there are numerous ways for you to occupy yourself here at home. And be truthful here, many of the things women are doing to win the war are either silly or unbecoming."

"There's nothing silly about working in a factory or serving in the navy, or the army, or whatever."

"Perhaps not for some, but for a woman of your . . ."

"You're speaking nonsense, Robert." Helen cut in, having heard before what her husband was about to say. "My position, as you call it, requires me to do something. I must say my staying at home can hardly be supportive of your career. I would have thought you'd want me out and about, visible for all of Westminster and Whitehall to see."

"My dear, I want you to act sensibly and to remember your station."

"I always do Robert, on both accounts."

"Well, now I must be off to work. The colonies need governing." Sir Robert had changed the subject. He did so whenever conversation with Helen became tense. The Deputy Permanent Secretary for Colonial Affairs preferred harmony to conflict, especially at home. He had married Helen to enhance his career and to secure a level of comfort. When either of these appeared threatened, Sir Robert became unsettled. He now knew Helen was determined to find something to do for the war effort. That was tolerable, he concluded, as long as she respected the unspoken boundaries of their marriage. By her remarks, she appeared to do so. Sir Robert believed she was foolish. She would enlist in some noble cause, surrounded by a group of ladies who would bustle about and probably get in the way. The activity would not likely contribute to the real winning of the war. Spitfires and pounds sterling did that. It was all for appearances. Britain united—one king ruling one people. He thought it mostly rubbish. Sir Robert considered himself wise and perceptive. People were not equal. Not in talent, not in wealth, and certainly not in manners. And they never would be. Only the Americans believed in equality, which illustrated how little they knew and how naive they were. As for women, they had their place. They were companions to men, and mothers. Their role in society was simple and well defined. They had no place in business or government. They belonged at home where their contributions were genuine. Yet he knew appearances mattered, and there was something to what Helen had said about visibility. Men in high places would see the wife of Sir Robert Trent contributing to the war. That might indeed be beneficial. So Sir Robert relented, silently. Wisely, he did not voice approval. That would reignite disagreement. He simply acquiesced. And, in changing the subject, both he and Helen understood that she had won.

"Have a pleasant day," said Helen.

"Thank you, my dear. I shall be dining at my club tonight. Don't forget we have dinner plans for tomorrow with Donald Iverson and his wife." Iverson was a close friend of Sir Robert and, like Anthony Eden, a classmate at Cambridge.

"Yes, I have it on my calendar."

"Good. Good-bye." And with those two words, Sir Robert Trent was gone.

Helen went back into the kitchen and had a second cup of tea. As always, she used the tea service her mother had given her the year before her death. The service was chintzware. This English pottery, ablaze with color and flowered patterns, had been manufactured in England for over 250 years. Helen's mother had purchased the set in 1922. Although the service was now a collectible, Helen used the china nearly every day. There was a pot, six cups and saucers, and a creamer. Claire had broken the sugar bowl. At first, Helen had not liked the service, but now, with her mother gone, she cherished it. The chintzware was a link to someone she had dearly loved. It recalled sweet memories of her mother and of her own childhood.

The kitchen clock said 9:25 A.M. and Helen knew that today's activities were about to intrude upon morning tea. It would be a full day. She had an 11 A.M. meeting at the Brooklands Library and then lunch with Jane and Harriet. She then planned to shop for something fun to send Claire, returning home in the late afternoon for her bath and a quiet evening at home. She was looking forward to the meeting, which she expected to be an interview, and to seeing her two friends. Helen did not mind that Sir Robert was to dine at his club. She enjoyed her own company and liked having the house to herself. But first, Helen needed to tidy up the kitchen. She did so efficiently and went upstairs to dress. At one time, a maid would have been present to prepare breakfast and keep the house clean. However, once Claire went off to school, Helen thought the maid to be unnecessary and dismissed her, despite Sir Robert's objections. Helen had done so gently and thought the young woman would be upset. Not so. The maid seemed pleased and Helen learned later that she was working in a munitions plant outside Birmingham.

St. James Square was in the heart of London. Situated between Piccadilly and Pall Mall, just off Regent Street, the Square was the location of the Library. At 11 A.M., Helen Trent was to meet Miss Hilda Farrell, an assistant librarian in charge of volunteer services.

From Earl's Court, the library was too great a distance to walk. Helen decided to take the bus. Driving was out of the question, and Helen disliked the underground, which she found too confining. Besides, she rather liked the bus. She would sit on the upper deck and watch the people on the streets. A game she played with herself was to imagine the purpose of the people she saw walking along the street. But the reason had to be incongruous with their clothing. A soldier might be out on a mission to find milk for a kitten. A woman in fine clothes might be seeking employment as a cook. A nanny with a baby carriage might be a fashion model about to be photographed. The game was silly of course, but that was part of the fun. Helen and Jane Ashcroft had played the game while at Roedean. Helen later taught and played the game with Claire. The goal was to find great contrast between what people wore and what they were doing. Helen was amused that she still played the game, even when riding alone.

A Number 74 bus took Helen Trent down Cromwell Road past the Victoria and Albert Museum to Knightsbridge. There she transferred to a Number 14 bus, which traveled along Piccadilly. Traffic was not heavy this morning; it rarely was now that fuel was scarce and no private motorcars were being manufactured. Helen soon found herself near her destination, stepping off early so as to have a short walk. "A walk is a good thing," she often said to Claire. Helen enjoyed walking and, weather permitting, took a walk each day. Along the bus ride this morning, she had seen an immaculately dressed army officer whom she imagined was about to play rugby. She had also seen a heavyset woman loaded down with packages. The woman appeared to be in a hurry. Helen decided she had entered a foot race.

—⁂—

Hilda Farrell was not having a good day. She had slept poorly the night before and because of train delays, had been late for work. Her newspaper, the *Daily Mirror,* had gotten wet, making it awkward to read. And her appointment book was completely full, portending a difficult day. Moreover, the Brixton Labour Party meeting she had attended over the weekend was still troubling her. She considered the meeting to have been a farce. Miss Farrell thought the Party was getting soft, in part the result of the wartime coalition with the Conservatives. *Damn Tories—so self-righteous, rich, and full of themselves,* she thought. They owned the banks and the means of production. Their goal, she believed, was to hold down the working class and continue a life of privilege. That would not continue. Hilda saw change in the wind. She was convinced that once this bloody war was over, socialism would triumph. Then, the fools in the Party would be dispensed with, their places taken by those truly committed to a new Britain. Hilda Farrell was a true believer whose passion was politics. She found little time for the arts or love. She hated the Tories, disliked Americans, and worshipped Ernest Bevan.

All this meant she had little regard for women of wealth who wished to volunteer at the library. Yet her job was to interview anyone who indicated a desire to help. A few volunteers were men too old for the military and unable to perform the rigorous duties of air raid warden. Mostly she met with women. Because working class women were at jobs, Miss Farrell interviewed women who were either very rich or simply well off. That she seemed ill suited for this particular job did not trouble her, for she did not notice. Nor did the Brooklands Library. Armies are not the only institutions to place square pegs in round holes. Wealth, she considered, was first manifested in clothes and speech. Hilda Farrell resented such wealth, largely because she knew so many without. She herself had few clothes. To her they were a functional necessity, not instruments of beauty. Hilda believed the imbalance of wealth in Britain was obscene. She had dedicated her life to redressing such disparities.

Hilda Farrell's anger at Britain's rigid class structure was not unreasonable. In 1943, the country was extremely class conscious, despite the war's leveling effect. Like that of the United States, Britain's democracy was a torch of freedom, but not of equality. Speech, dress, and occupation all identified an individual as belonging to a certain class. What surprised Americans was how accepting of class distinctions the British were. Upward mobility was not a national characteristic. Men such as Sir Robert Trent epitomized the privileged class and many shared his disdain for those less well off. Some people in Britain believed education and charitable works would, over time, enlarge the middle class and alleviate the misery of the poor. Jane Ashcroft's husband, Herbert, held to this view. Both he and Jane set aside time to provide assistance at St. George's Hospital to those in need. Other people, whose number was greater than the Conservatives realized, shared Hilda Farrell's determination to shake the foundations of British society. Hilda envisioned a Britain where the state ran companies with an eye not just to profits, but to the welfare of employees as well. Health care would be available to all, at reasonable cost. Education would be free. Her Britain would eradicate class and become a truly progressive society, a beacon for Europe and the world.

But in Hilda Farrell, there was arrogance equal to that of Sir Robert. Less visible than his, it came from a belief that both the forces of history and tenets of justice were on her side and alone. Evil

nested in the hearts of her opponents. The Tories were not just electoral opponents, they were wicked. If Hilda Farrell was dedicated,
she was also intolerant. If she saw the wrong in Britain, she was blind
to its good. If she hated the rich, she sanctified the poor. Unfortunately, she nurtured the very consciousness of class she found so
objectionable in others.

At precisely 10:58 A.M., Helen Trent knocked politely on the
door of Hilda Farrell's office.

"Yes?"

"Excuse me. I'm Helen Trent and I'm here for my appointment."

"You'll have to wait."

"Of course. I'll be here in the sitting room." Helen sat down in
a space too small to qualify as a sitting room. The room itself was
sparsely decorated. There were three chairs and a small table that
held a large lamp. The colors were beige and dark brown except for
the rug, which was off white and jade. The rug was a bit too large
for the space, but seemed to be of a better quality than the other fur-
nishings. Helen concluded that the rug had been a donation to the
library. On the wall, next to a formal portrait of the King, hung pictures of two older, but distinguished looking gentlemen. Who they
were was not at all obvious. Perhaps they had been heads of
Brooklands. On the opposite wall hung a brightly colored poster
depicting a triumphant farmer and factory worker. Text on the
poster appeared to be Russian. Helen doubted George VI enjoyed
looking each day at Bolsheviks who tended to hold monarchies in
low esteem.

For what seemed to be a long time, Helen was considering what
gift to purchase for Claire when the door to Hilda Farrell's office
opened.

"Please fill out this form." Hilda handed Helen a single page and
disappeared back into her office.

Fortunately, Helen always carried a pen with her, which she now
took from her pocketbook. Unwrapping the pen from within an old
handkerchief Helen used to prevent damage should the ink leak, she
glanced at the form using the pen as a marker. Grandly titled *The*

Brooklands Library Volunteer Assistant's Personal and Related Data Form,
the form requested basic information: name, address, date of birth,
height, weight, education, and occupation. The form also requested
related experience. Helen wrote down the first two items listed. As
always, she printed neatly rather than writing in script, the legacy of
Miss Packenham's class at Roedean. Then Helen wrote May 11,
1900; 5 feet, 7 inches; 9 stone; Roedean School and two years at
London University. No degree. Helen had been on track for a First
in Geography when her world changed. She met Peter and suddenly
the university seemed not terribly important. Her father was upset
at her leaving school. "You'll regret this, my child," he told her. And
he was correct. She did come to regret not having a degree. But that
was much later. Peter was irresistible, and she had gladly gone to him
when he begged her to join him in France. They married soon after,
to the relief of her father and mother. God, what delicious memories they were. However, they were memories, and she knew she
now had to focus on the library form. Occupation. What should she
put down? Helen sensed that Miss Farrell would be unimpressed
with the term housewife, so she carefully printed the words "civil
servant wife," realizing that this too would not likely impress the
young woman. At least the words were true. She was the wife of a
civil servant. And Sir Robert Trent at times made her feel as though
she held down a job. Next was experience. Here Helen felt she had
much to offer the library. She could write, she enjoyed books and
their authors, she was well traveled, and she was skilled at dealing
with people. Helen wondered whether Miss Farrell would agree that
these attributes were useful. Perhaps. Perhaps not. Helen decided she
would speak on the subject of experience rather than write something that might appear conceited. She left the space blank and
carefully rewrapped the fountain pen in its handkerchief. After placing it back in her pocketbook, she returned to thinking about
Claire's gift.

"You may come in now." Hilda Farrell was standing at her door
addressing Helen. Next to Helen was a woman of Hilda's age who
had come into the sitting room while Helen was filling out the

library form. Hilda's face brightened when she saw her friend. "Hello, Bridget. Do sit. I won't be but a minute."

Helen entered Hilda Farrell's office. For a moment, she stood behind a chair until Hilda beckoned her to sit.

"Mrs. Trent, is it? I gather you wish to work at Brooklands."

"Yes, I'd like to help in some volunteer capacity."

"I see. Why the library? A woman of your position might be more suited to something more exotic than a library. Perhaps the Red Cross or the Entertainments Service." The latter was the Entertainments National Service Association. Headquartered on Drury Lane, ENSA organized entertainments for Britain's military forces wherever they served.

"Well Miss Farrell, I'm terribly fond of books and believe in libraries. I thought you might be shorthanded what with the Services calling up so many of our men."

"Quite so. Actually, we are understaffed, although our collection is intact." That was correct, but six months later when the Luftwaffe returned to London, the library was badly damaged. "What do you think you might do?" As she asked the question, she was filing away Helen Trent's completed form.

"I'm not sure. I could catalogue or do research. I know something about maps and might assist in the library's cartography division." Helen considered adding how keen she was to help, but thought better of it. This young woman seemed likely not to be impressed by enthusiasm. Sitting across a desk from Hilda Farrell, Helen Trent noticed that the librarian was neither a woman of style, nor one who seemed the least bit interested in her appearance. No doubt, Miss Farrell performed her duties exceptionally well. That she dressed so plainly did not matter. Helen knew this intellectually, and believed it to be so. But deep inside, where emotion at times over-rules reason, she thought it unfortunate that Miss Farrell dressed as she did.

As the interview progressed, Helen sensed antagonism on the part of Hilda Farrell who had yet to respond to the suggestions made as to what she might do. "How interesting. Tell me, Mrs. Trent, why would a lady such as yourself wish to work with ordinary folk? We're not very fancy here at Brooklands."

What a strange question. Helen believed she had, with every good intention, come to volunteer at an institution essential to the city of London. "Miss Farrell, as I mentioned before, I'm here because I'd like to help."

"Yes I'm sure you would." Hilda had a touch of sarcasm in her voice.

Helen took offense at the woman's tone. She had little patience with discourtesy. Smiling, she replied calmly, "Libraries, Miss Farrell are for everyone. At least they were when I was your age."

"Do you collect books, Mrs. Trent?"

"I do, and read them as well."

"So you have a library, all of your own?" The emphasis was on the last two words.

"As I suspect you do as well, Miss Farrell. Don't we all who love books?"

Helen now realized that for Hilda Farrell, the interview had been but a morning chore, now mostly completed. She imagined Hilda checking off the name H. Trent on a list of things to do. *How many other people had been treated so brusquely?* she wondered. Helen understood that there was little chance of obtaining a volunteer position at the library. Most likely, the chances had been nil from the very start. But she had made the effort in good faith, and she knew there was little more that she could do. The world is full of unpleasant people and Helen Trent had had the misfortune to meet one at the Brooklands Library. She was disappointed, but not discouraged. She already had decided to accelerate her quest for worthwhile work. But first, it was time to terminate this conversation. Helen rose from the chair. Presenting her best diplomatic smile and extending her hand, she said, "Miss Farrell, I've taken up much too much of your time. Thank you for seeing me. I should like to help out here at the library. If that's possible, do ring me."

Hilda was caught off guard. Usually, she ended the interview. She took Helen's hand and was gently pulled up from her desk and then towards the door. "I shall do that, Mrs. Trent," she stammered. She was not telling the truth and knew that the woman across from her knew it. "Thank you for coming in."

"Good-bye, Miss Farrell. Do have a pleasant day." Helen then departed, walking through the small sitting room. As she did so, she heard Hilda Farrell address her friend.

"Bridget, do come in. I have just the job for you."

Once outside, Helen decided not to worry about what had just transpired. Obviously, the interview had not gone well and there would be no volunteer work at the Brooklands Library. Standing alone in St. James Square, Helen realized that she could either stew about the situation or dismiss it from her mind. She chose the latter. But, before doing so, she decided she must learn from the experience. In this, Helen merely was following the advice she so often had given Claire: "We must learn from all that happens to us, particularly when it's unpleasant." She could hear herself speaking to her daughter. Now she smiled within as she imagined Claire replaying the words back to her. The difficulty was that Helen Trent was uncertain as to what the lesson was. She had prepared for the meeting. She had arrived on time. She had dressed appropriately. She had tried not to appear too keen. Helen was at a loss to understand what she might have done differently to secure a more favorable outcome. Then the thought struck home, and she was amused by its simplicity—nothing she could have done would have altered the outcome. The problem, if that was the correct word, lay not with her. The problem belonged to Hilda Farrell. Miss Farrell, Helen reasoned, was an unhappy creature, a young woman with a chip on her shoulder. *Poor thing. Life is inevitably unfair and its benefits are not equally shared. No doubt, she wishes to change the world. Well good luck to her. The world could use a remake. Just don't replace one set of injustices with another, nor hurt people in the process.*

As Helen Trent left St. James Square walking north to the restaurant where she was to lunch with Jane and Harriet, she wished Hilda Farrell well. Helen carried no grudges and shortly would forget the entire episode. Before doing so, however, she had one final thought about the young librarian. And that was that before Miss Farrell began to change the world, she would do well to learn good manners. To Helen Trent, rudeness was inexcusable.

—⚭—

"Men are strange birds." Jane Ashcroft was speaking to Harriet Pennington as they sat in a restaurant awaiting their friend. The eatery was called Fogarty's, and it was a favorite of Helen's. Situated off Oxford Street in what once had been a dress shop catering to women of high fashion, the restaurant specialized in French cuisine, despite its name. The two women had arrived early, thus obtaining a choice table by the window where they could watch Londoners come and go. They observed mostly men. Men in uniform. Tradesmen. Men wearing bowlers and carrying umbrellas. Old men and young men, though more of the former than the latter since many of Britain's young men were abroad. Perhaps this parade of men outside Fogarty's explained why Jane had changed their earlier topic of conversation and was now focusing upon the male species. "I sometimes wonder what they really need and how they think."

"The answer is a great deal and quite differently from us."

"Harriet, I love Herbert. He really is a dear man, but he doesn't listen. He hears what I've said and then proceeds to solve what he thinks my problem is. It's all well intentioned, but it's not what I need or want."

"John's the same. Men tend to focus upon solutions, which is hardly the point."

"Sometimes I wish only to converse with him, to share my feelings and tap into his."

"Jane, Herbert's a man of medicine, in charge of a large hospital. His job is to make people well, to cure what's wrong with them. That's what doctors do. He thinks he's supposed to do the same at home."

"You're right, of course. He works terribly hard at St. George's and he cares so much. But when he's home, I want to be close to him, talk through what's on my mind and find out what's on his."

"Ladies, may I bring you some tea?" The waiter had appeared and given a menu to both Harriet and Jane. "Two of you today? We have a lovely pea soup and we're featuring sole à la niçoise. That's grilled, seasoned with tarragon, mixed with anchovy paste, and finished with capers and olives."

"Actually, we're expecting a third person, but tea would be lovely." Jane ran her eyes quickly down the menu, as did Harriet.

"Pea soup sounds splendid, but we'll wait for our friend. I'll have tea as well."

"Very good. I'll bring the tea." After leaving a third menu on the table, the waiter departed.

Harriet continued, "I'd prefer a nice gin, but John says I mustn't, so tea it will be."

Jane did not want to talk about food and drink. She wanted to talk about men. "I wonder if all men are the same. I mean, do they all think life is simply a journey? The purpose of which is to fix whatever's wrong with the world? Herbert is a dear man, kind and loving and really a good sport, but to him, everything is a situation he should rectify. He listens, then makes a diagnosis, and offers up a solution—even when I don't want a solution. I just want to sit and talk, to hear him speak and to engage his feelings. I get so frustrated. I just need a little understanding. Sometimes I just want to shake him hard."

"But you don't."

"Of course not. I just sit there and watch this brilliant man whom I love go on to the next problem and its solution. Is John like that?" Jane already knew the answer for she and Harriet, and Helen, had had this conversation before.

Harriet Pennington was deeply in love with her husband, and felt a duty to protect him. Extremely wealthy, John Pennington was a man who at times kept to himself. "John is the dearest man in all the world, and like your Herbert, hard working. Unlike some in this country, he *earned* his fortune." Harriet emphasized the verb, and went on.

"Somehow, and I do not know why, John and I speak the same language. We're really quite different. He's quiet, I'm not. I drink, he doesn't. He attended the university. I attended the school of hard knocks. But the two of us communicate. John says we're on the same wavelength, whatever that means. It's perfectly marvelous."

"Helen and I have always said the two of you are a perfect match."

"It's true. But I've come to realize that often John needs to be alone, off in his own world. And when he's there, I stand aside. At first, when we were just married, I didn't. But now I do. I've come to realize that at times, John requires only his own company. He's off by himself. It's a world I do not enter. I think when he's there, he's calculating what needs to be done. And resting. Somehow, all at the same time."

"Don't the two of you talk?"

"Yes, when he's ready. We do share our feelings and we communicate with words, and by touch, and with our eyes. But only when he's back here. I'm excluded from that other world. It's simply the way it is. But he always returns. It's like a short trip to another world. He's there, and then he's back."

"How odd."

"Not really, Jane. I believe it's the way men are. They're problem solvers like your Herbert. And travelers, like my John." Harriet Pennington may not have had much of a formal education, but she was full of insight. "I don't like it when he's off in that world, but I've come to accept it. Part of nature's plan. You see, John always comes back and when he does, he comes back to me. He squeezes my hand and tells me I'm his true love. It's a signal we have."

"That's very sweet."

"Yes it is. John is a very sweet man. That's why I love him so."

"You're very lucky."

"I know I am. John and I do well together." Harriet's eyes twinkled. "And not just with words."

Jane giggled like a schoolgirl. "Harriet Pennington, do I assume you're referring to sex?"

Harriet answered in a mockingly meek voice. "Yes Mother Superior, I am. Please forgive me, but my husband is a fine lover. He satisfies me and I take good care of him. And Herbert?"

"No complaints. Dr. Herbert Armstrong Ashcroft, the somewhat stuffy Medical Director of St. George's Hospital, has been known to do some very unstuffy things in bed, and," she paused, "on the stairs. He has but one habit I cannot seem to break."

"And that is?"

"Well, after we make love and we're lying quietly in each other's arms, it is a perfect time to share our most intimate thoughts, which we begin to do, and then it happens."

"What happens?"

"He falls asleep. Sometimes right in the middle of a sentence."

"My dear Jane, of course he does. John does too. All men do." Harriet was smiling. "Poor things, they seem not to have much stamina."

Jane was the most serious of the three women. She suddenly became reflective. "Harriet, we are truly fortunate. There are two fine men out there and they belong to us."

"Lover, friend, and husband all in one. I do count my blessings."

"And then there's Sir Robert Trent."

"His Majesty's Future Ambassador." Sir Robert would have been surprised to learn that Helen's two best friends were aware of his ambition. And he would be quite annoyed by their disapproval. "Should that happen, I trust the Foreign Office would send him off to one of those little countries in South America that no one knows about."

"Now be nice." Jane was also a gentle person.

"Why? The man is simply dreadful."

"Be nice because the man, dreadful or not, is married to Helen."

"A fact that never ceases to bewilder. Why in heaven's name did Helen marry such a person?"

"First of all, he's not all bad. Robert is certainly very smart and good at what he does. He is perfectly pleasant, if a bit pompous, but then who in government isn't?"

"He's a bore."

"No, he's not. He can be rather engaging and he takes perfectly fine care of Helen and Claire, too."

"True enough. But she never should have married him. Marriage is an affair of the heart. It's not a contractual agreement to simply coexist."

"Sometimes it has to be."

"Nonsense."

"Harriet dear. When Peter died, Helen was left quite alone. Her mother was ill and there was Claire to care for. This was before you and John met her at Christmas. Herbert kindly lent her funds to get by, but she was determined to make it on her own. Unfortunately, she had difficulty in finding work. She had no degree and, after much looking about, found work in a dress shop somewhere near here. The salary was modest, just enough to keep her and Claire afloat."

"I hadn't realized her situation was so dire."

"Yes. Helen went through hard times. She became particularly worried as Claire got older. Without additional funds, the child's future was not bright. This time she refused Herbert's offer to help, insisting she would find a way to manage."

"Enter Sir Robert?"

"Quite. At first he was rather charming. Even warm. He took a liking to Claire and was most attentive to Helen. It seemed a perfect match. No, not perfect, but very solid. A good second marriage. Helen seemed happy, and the four of us had some jolly good times together."

"I remember. That's when John and I first met you. It was Christmas 1938 at the Ashley-Martin's reception. If I recall correctly, Helen seemed happy."

"Yes, I think she was. Contented. That's a more suitable word. Helen was contented."

"What happened?"

Well, you saw what occurred, as I did. Robert changed. He withdrew. At times he would disappear. He kept long hours at the

Colonial Office and spent more time at his club. Oh, the externals were there. He and Helen entertained. They traveled. Helen did all that was expected of her, and more."

"Ah yes, Helen Trent, the perfect wife."

"On the surface, certainly so. But inside, she was not the same person. She is still fun to be with, still a fine and strong woman, but, mark my words, something is missing."

"I see that, too. I sense all is not well with our friend Helen Trent."

"I'm afraid so." Jane Ashcroft's face was showing the concern she felt.

"Did I hear my name mentioned? Are you two telling tales out of school?" Helen had arrived and sat herself down at the table. Before doing so, a wistful look crept over her face as she sat down. Neither Jane nor Harriet noticed. "I should never let the two of you get together without me."

"We were not talking about you," said Harriet with a straight face.

"Absolutely not." Jane stated solemnly. Then they both burst out laughing.

"You two are awful."

"Not so. We were having a serious conversation," Jane was grinning, "about men."

"And we decided, Jane and I did, that while they seem to lack stamina, they make the world slightly more interesting than it otherwise might be."

Helen turned to each of her friends. "Of that, I'm not sure. Do remember this war was started by men that seem to have a proclivity for killing each other." Helen believed this to be so, as do many women. But she sensed the remark had been far too serious in the context of her friends' conversation. She told herself to lighten up. "Men are interesting, at least some of them, but they do tend to be awfully needy."

"That may be, but Harriet and I find having men in our lives makes life rather colorful, especially at bedtime."

Jane's remark resulted in an awkward few seconds of silence as all three women realized one of them slept alone. Jane wished she had said something else. Harriet, too, was embarrassed, but recovered quickly. "Well colorful or not, we seem to be stuck with them."

"We do indeed," responded Helen.

"But we must always remember what the Church of England had us all say on that fateful day." Jane and Helen looked at each other wondering what their unpredictable friend was about to say. They were not disappointed. "For better or for worse," Harriet paused, "but not for lunch. So we will dine without the company of men as God intended ladies in the afternoon to do."

"Madame, may I bring you some tea?" This was not the waiter of earlier, but an older gentlemen who was speaking to Helen.

"Yes, Henry. That would be marvelous. You're looking well."

"Thank you, dear lady. An ache or two here and there, but not as many as before. It's good to see you looking well, Helen."

"Thank you, Henry. Do take care."

"Helen. You know this man? I'd have thought he's not your type."

"Hush, Harriet. That's Henry Fogarty. He owns this establishment and I've known him for years. He's a wonderful and kind man. Now, and I'm changing the subject, what are we going to eat?"

As always, Helen found dining with Jane and Harriet enjoyable. The food was excellent; Henry was a better chef than shopkeeper. The setting was pleasant and the company most agreeable. Helen told Harriet and Jane about her meeting at the library. They were sympathetic and appalled at Hilda Farrell's rudeness. Then the conversation turned to more pleasant subjects. The three friends talked about their children and their own lives. They talked about old times together and they planned new adventures. They reviewed current fashions and current films, and inquired of mutual acquaintances. They even discussed the war, wondering what life in England would be like once the shooting stopped.

Helen cared for these women and knew they returned her affection. She also knew that they perceived all was not well with her.

Helen Trent's life had a hole in it. She herself knew something was missing. Helen wanted a man in her life—someone to protect her, someone to confide in, and someone to be cherished by. For several years, Helen had projected an image of indifference to men. Acquaintances thought she simply had no interest in the opposite sex. At times, she believed this facade, or tried to. But when she was honest with herself, and Helen could be brutally honest, she knew the truth. She needed a man to love. Robert Trent was not that man. She knew that. Odd how he had changed once they had settled in. How strange that the spark had died almost before it had ignited. She had chosen poorly, but Claire was provided for and her life was not altogether unpleasant. Helen and Sir Robert had made an agreement, unspoken, but nonetheless real. And a bargain was a bargain. For all his faults, Robert was living up to his end. Helen Trent expected to honor hers.

Upon conclusion of lunch, the three friends went separate ways, agreeing to meet again in a fortnight. Harriet was off to visit an aunt who was elderly and unwell. Jane was going to St. George's Hospital where she did volunteer work twice a week. Helen headed for Harrods. Her daughter loved surprises, so Helen intended to purchase a soft warm scarf and mail the surprise down to Roedean. Helen smiled at the thought that schoolgirls were like their mothers, they could never have enough clothes.

Harrods was at Knightsbridge, on the Cromwell Road not too far from where Helen lived. Before heading there, she decided to walk along Regent Street, the site of fine shops large and small. The street was not crowded. Buses were most prevalent. Most were red, a few muddy brown, and fewer still were green and yellow. All were the trademark double-deckers. Taxis were available, although only about half of London's prewar fleet of eight thousand were running. Motorcars were noticeably absent. Like the Trent's SS Jaguar, private automobiles were in garages and rarely driven. Of the cars that did traverse the streets of London, most were official transport, conveying high-ranking men to their meetings. Of these, more than a few were American, identified by the white star and military serial numbers painted on their sides.

To Helen, the sidewalks seemed more crowded than the street. Most Londoners were still at work, yet Regent Street had numerous pedestrians. People were out in large number, walking with what seemed a sense of purpose. Many were women. Some wore the uniform of the Women's Auxiliary Air Force or its counterpart in the army or navy. These women reminded Helen Trent of her desire to find worthwhile work. Something she had said to Sir Robert this morning came to mind. "England is my country, too." Well, it was true and although her country was tired and showing signs of wear, Helen was intent upon contributing to England's victory. But first she needed to find something for Claire. Along Regent Street, her eye caught the window of a small store she had not noticed before. The window contained hats. The store appeared to be a millinery, although the window displayed other items. All were lovely. There were scarves, pins, and several cashmere scarves. Helen was looking at the hats, one of which she thought gorgeous, when she saw a scarf that would be perfect for Claire. Then she heard a voice behind her that she recognized, but could not place.

"Hello, Mrs. Trent. This is a lovely store, isn't it?" The voice belonged to Warren Smith.

"Why, Mr. Smith. What a surprise. What brings you here?"

"Warren, please." He was again asking Helen to address him by his given name. "I've just done some shopping for my wife. It's a very nice store."

"Yes, it seems to be. I'm looking for something to send my daughter."

"Well, let's go in. Here, I'll come with you."

The two entered the shop, which was stocked with an assortment of goods, similar to those in the window. As they browsed, Helen learned that Warren Smith was shortly to return to the United States. His official business had ended two days earlier. He had stayed on, at his own expense, to visit the city and bring gifts back to those at home. They chatted for some time as Helen considered what she might purchase. Their conversation was easy and both appeared to enjoy the chance meeting. Helen learned again that the American was happily married, devoted to both his wife and family. She told him he was fortunate and Smith readily agreed. Warren Smith learned that this woman, whom he found charming and bright, was seeking useful work to assist the war effort. That gave him an idea.

"Helen, I think there's something that might be perfect for you. And real, that is, genuinely useful."

"What would that be?"

"I've heard at the Embassy that the Army, that is our army, actually the Army Air Corps, is putting together a group of Englishmen, ladies too, to advise us on how to accommodate the large number of American airmen now arriving in Britain. Many of these fellows will be in London on duty or on leave. The city will be teeming with Americans, mostly youngsters, and the generals want some advice on what we might do to ensure that London and these kids do well together."

"Sounds like a splendid idea. You Yanks are going to find England, and London too, far different than what's at home."

"Indeed we are."

"What might I do?"

"Dear Mrs. Trent. You would be perfect to serve on the Committee."

"As a member?"

"Absolutely. You know London, are terrific with people, and have the common sense we're looking for. You'd be perfect. And it would be perfect for you."

"Well, I should like to help, and it does sound splendid. Perhaps I should assist in some informal manner."

"Nonsense. You should be on the Committee, and I'm going to see that you are. You have no choice in the matter." Warren Smith looked at this Englishwoman he admired and pointed a finger at her. "Uncle Sam wants you."

Helen's face expressed acceptance. "I suspect Mr. Roosevelt would be disappointed if I declined."

"Very much so," Warren Smith replied. "As would His Majesty the King."

"Well, then I accept."

"Let's see," Warren Smith was now thinking hard. "Yes, I want you to contact Colonel James Dixon at the American Embassy. He's the Deputy Air Attaché, and chairman of our planning group that is putting the committee together."

"Colonel James Dixon." Helen repeated the name so as to remember it.

"Jimmy Dixon is a friend of mine and I'm going to tell him that we've found an important member of the advisory committee."

"That's very kind of you."

"My pleasure. It's no trouble at all and you're perfect for the job. But promise me one thing."

"What's that?"

"That within three days, you'll go to the Embassy and meet with Jimmy. He'll be expecting you."

"I promise."

"Fine. That's settled. Welcome to the war. Now let's pick something out for your daughter."

Helen and her American friend spent another half hour looking for Claire's gift. Finally, Helen decided upon the cashmere scarf she had seen in the window. Warren Smith insisted upon paying for the gift, to which Helen objected. But he did so anyway, saying he wished to thank Helen once again for the lovely evening last week. Helen finally relented when she realized he would not be deterred. Plus, she did not wish to make a scene in public. As they left the store, Helen said again what she had spoken inside. "You really should not have done that."

"We'll just have to differ on that, Mrs. Trent. I would have liked to have met your daughter."

"Yes that would have been nice."

"I must now say good-bye, Helen. I have very much enjoyed meeting you and would have liked to spend more time here. Alas, duty calls, as does my home."

"Good-bye Warren Smith." Helen reached out and gave him a gentle kiss on the cheek. "Take good care and come back and see us."

With that, they departed, never to see one another again. Their lives had crossed and would continue on in different directions. Helen made sure she had the box containing the scarf and walked slowly down Regent Street towards Piccadilly. From there, she would take the bus to near Earl's Court. As she walked, she looked forward to being home. By the time she arrived, it would be time for her bath.

FOUR

From the cockpit of his P-47, Tom Forester scanned the skies, searching for enemy aircraft. He did so continuously, turning his head from left to right, then right to left, and checking behind his aircraft as well. Forester knew that the pilot who first saw the enemy gained a tactical advantage. No German fighters were in sight. At 21,000 feet above France, the sky was suddenly empty.

Minutes before, as the 19th Fighter Group had rendezvoused with Eighth Air Force bombers that were returning from a strike at chemical plants near Soissons, northwest of Paris, aircraft were everywhere. The Luftwaffe had come up to fight. Twenty Me-109s, their yellow noses clearly visible against the grey clouds, had attacked the B-17s head on. Fortunately, Forester's group had been well positioned. The P-47s, placed above and to the sides of the bombers, had intercepted the Germans before their cannon fire had ripped into the B-17s. Tom led the top squadron into battle with a simple "Let's go get 'em" as his planes engaged the enemy. In no time, the sky was crowded with warplanes. Me-109s and P-47s turned, dove, and climbed, seeking to destroy the other. No ballet—the resulting combat was an airborne rugby match.

Forester had assembled his group over England and directed its flight southeast across the Channel to France. Once over occupied territory he had spread out the formation leading the P-47s to the assigned rendezvous. Still under his control, the fighters had stationed themselves around the returning bombers. Altitude was then 28,000 feet. Forester's task was to escort the B-17s back across France, and he had put his aircraft where they could best do their job.

Forester's group consisted of forty-eight aircraft in three squadrons, each with sixteen P-47s. Four aircraft had had to abort, returning to Bromley Park prematurely. Two of these experienced radio problems. The other two had had rough-running engines. Tom later learned that one of these P-47s did not make it home. Its pilot was never heard from again. That left forty-four aircraft to safeguard the B-17s. A sufficient number, although Forester knew that numbers alone would not carry the day.

The Luftwaffe pilots were good. Well trained and experienced, they flew with skill and courage. Their Me-109s and Fw-190s were fine aircraft, fast and maneuverable. In the hands of aggressive pilots, and Tom knew the Germans to be very aggressive, the Focke-Wulfs and Messerschmitts were dangerous opponents. Scores of Spitfire pilots, many of them *hors de combat,* would attest to that.

Forester's pilots were learning fast, but their inexperience showed. Upon arrival in England, their group commander, at Tom's urging, had put them through rigorous training. Weather permitting, they flew every day. General Harrison thought their fuel consumption too high, and had said so. But Forester persisted, convincing Carl Phillips that it was wiser to make their pilots safe than to keep the General content. The fighter pilots of the 19th Group learned new radio procedures and improved their gunnery. They practiced formation flying. They became much better at navigation and they developed tactics for escort and air combat. Forester worked them hard, aware that the Luftwaffe would show no mercy in the coming battles.

Even so, the results had been disheartening. The 19th Fighter Group had lost as many aircraft as it had shot down. Yet this record was better than several other groups in their initial encounter with the Germans. Moreover, as both Phillips and Forester had pointed out to Colonel Arnie, Harrison's right hand man, the bombers escorted by the 19th had come through with minimum losses. Clearly, Forester's insistence on training had paid off. But still, there were empty bunks and damaged aircraft at Bromley Park, which, with the few kills recorded, reflected the mixed results being achieved.

In September 1943, American fighter pilots in Ira Eaker's Eighth Air Force were inexperienced, a condition only time and leadership, would overcome. Yet the pilots of the 19th Fighter Group remained undaunted. Eager to confront their adversary, they readily took to the sky hunting for Germans. They believed their cause to be just. Their P-47s, if lacking in range, were rugged, high performance planes with considerable firepower. And in Tom Forester, they had a group commander who knew what he was doing and in whom they had absolute faith.

Once the battle had been joined, Forester no longer was able to control forty-four aircraft. He had led the top squadron into the fray. Additional Me-109s had appeared, no doubt vectored to the scene by German air controllers. These aircraft also attacked the B-17s, but from the rear. But they too were intercepted by P-47s as the group's other two squadrons engaged the enemy. As the battled raged, as planes circled, dove, and climbed back to reengage, the squadrons dispersed and the air mass surrounding the bombers became a series of individual combats. P-47s stalked Messerschmitts, Me-109s fired at P-47s. Through it all, the B-17s flew on, at 220 miles per hour, shooting at any aircraft close enough to threaten, regardless of whether the plane bore a white star or black cross. B-17 gunners were a nervous lot and the barrels of their .50 calibre machine guns grew hot as they blasted away at any fighter within range.

In leading that first attack, Forester had singled out an Me-109 whose guns were sparkling, creating a bright red line of fire leading directly to one of the B-17s. The pilot of the Me-109 saw the descending P-47s and turned away, rolling left and diving to gain speed. The bottom of the German fighter was painted blue to blend in with the sky when viewed from below. Forester, with the advantage of height, easily followed the maneuver because as the aircraft rolled on its back, the blue contrasted with the green and brown of the earth below. His P-47 flew past the damaged Fortress, which, despite the attack, maintained formation. With its throttle pushed forward for maximum power, Forester's plane roared down after the Messerschmitt.

Aware of the danger posed by the pursuing P-47, the German turned again, increasing the angle of his dive. Seeking protection in a blanket of clouds below, the German was confident he could outrace the American. He couldn't. The P-47 was a big ship, the largest, heaviest, single engine fighter in World War II. Thus it was fast in a dive, very fast. As Forester's air speed indicator passed 400 mph, he saw that he had gained on the enemy and would soon be close enough to fire.

He then checked his rear, and smiled at what he saw. Astern was his wingman, Lieutenant Robert Ennis, in position to fend off any attack.

"Trumpet, this is Red Two. You're clear." Trumpet was Forester's radio call sign. Group commanders in Eighth Air Force Fighter Command warranted their own identification. Red Two was Ennis.

"Roger, Red Two."

Ennis did not answer. He wanted to speak, but did not. The lieutenant knew that Forester insisted on radio discipline. Communication between aircraft was to be kept to a minimum. The reason was simple. When one pilot spoke, another could not. The channel essentially was blocked when a pilot employed his radio microphone, so an urgent warning or critical command from another flyer could not be transmitted. In combat with the Luftwaffe, that could be fatal. So, again and again, Tom had taught his pilots to be brief and to communicate only when it was essential to do so. "No chatter, gentlemen, no chatter. Speak only when you must and then keep it short" were words each pilot in the group felt he had heard a hundred times. Now Ennis was practicing what Forester had preached.

The lieutenant also wanted to shout words of encouragement as the P-47 he was guarding closed in for the kill. This was Robert Ennis's first encounter with the enemy and he was plenty excited. So, as a cheerleader might at the big game, he yelled, "Go get 'em, Colonel," at the top of his lungs, but prudently kept his transmitter turned off.

Forester was excited too. His heart was beating fast and, while his palms were not sweaty, the adrenaline was flowing. Forester was inwardly conversing with himself as he did whenever something important was happening or was about to happen. The conversation was calm, somewhat clinical as if two friends were engaged in discussion after class. Tom the instructor was telling Tom the student, *Fly the plane. Stay focused. Check your rear. Aim steady. Get in close.*

At four hundred yards, he opened fire. The P-47 carried eight powerful machine guns, four in each wing. When Forester pressed the trigger, they exploded in anger, throwing a barrage of bullets at the fleeing Me-109. No hits were registered. Forester realized he had fired too soon. The German turned again, still seeking the protection of the cloud below. Altitude was now 16,000 feet. Forester recalled General Harrison's rule about no air combat below eighteen thousand. He considered it stupid.

The P-47 turned with the Me-109. Forester fired again, a three-second burst, and saw his aim was wide. But he was closing in. No aircraft in any air force could outrun a P-47 when both planes were heading straight down. A touch of left rudder and another short burst. Again there was smoke from the wings of the American plane. This time lines of fire converged at the right side of the German craft. Small pieces flew off, but there was no explosion. *Steady now. Stay with him. Check your rear. Fire!*

It was the cloud that saved the German. Though damaged, the Me-109 found a safe haven in the thick watery mist that covered portions of France this particular day. The pilot of the Me-109 had learned a lesson. Do not attempt to out dive the American P-47. The tactic had worked against the RAF. Its Spitfires, one of the most graceful planes ever built, could easily be outrun. But holes in the fuselage of Messerschmitt suggested the tactic would not work against those big fighters the Americans employed to escort their B-17s and B-24s.

Forester also learned a lesson. It was a lesson he learned each time he engaged the enemy. Don't fire too soon. Get in close. Closer still. Then open up. Tom Forester was not a crack shot. To hit an aircraft ahead that was moving along three axes was not easy, despite the simple geometry outlined in gunnery practice. The 19th Fighter Group's commander could score strikes only when on top of the target. In this, he was not unusual. Most Eighth Air Force fighter pilots were poor marksmen, as were their British and German counterparts. A few Americans were skilled at aerial gunnery, but most, like Tom Forester, were not.

The 19th Fighter Group had one such expert, Leroy Richards. Lieutenant Richards was a natural. He flew like Lindberg and shot like Davy Crockett. Nicknamed "the Kid" because of his youth and boyish character, Richards hailed from the mountains of Kentucky. Major Harry Collins, the 19th's Intelligence Officer, said that the Kid was born not with a silver spoon in his mouth, but with a rifle in his hand. The Kid invariably responded to Collins with a "Gosh Harry, I just do a lot of hunting, which ain't all that hard." Richards thought everyone could shoot as well as he, which they could not. This sweet, good-natured youngster from Beverly, Kentucky was a dangerous foe when in the cockpit of his P-47. Already he had shot down three Me-109s. If he could keep himself alive, Richards had a proclivity for getting separated from his squadron, the Kid would likely become a top-scoring ace of the Eighth Air Force.

Forester was aware he was no Kentucky sharpshooter, and he made no attempt to suggest otherwise. He told himself and his pilots that lessons he preached applied to himself as well as to others. Tom Forester was an honest man. Honest with his flyers. Honest with himself. This was one reason why the men of the 19th Fighter Group respected their commander. Another was that Forester did what he asked others to do. Forester, the average shot, flew his P-47 in close to the enemy. Then he got in closer. Often the results were satisfactory. At this very time, a badly shaken Me-109 pilot was nursing a damaged aircraft home to base.

"Red Two. This is Trumpet. Let's go back upstairs."

"Trumpet. Red Two. I'm right with you."

The two aircraft employed the momentum of their dive to hasten their climb back to the bomber formation. P-47s were notoriously bad at gaining altitude. In Europe and wherever the P-47 flew in combat, a common tactic was to use the great speed achieved in a dive to propel the bulky craft skyward. The higher the altitude, the better the P-47 performed. So pilots would dive, and then zoom upward, seeking to place their planes up top whenever possible.

Forester and his wingman soon rejoined the B-17s, which were by now some seventy miles from the coast. What they saw pleased them both.

Much of the bomber fleet was still intact, although the battle was still in progress. A few gaps existed among the B-17s squadrons and one bomber was in trouble. Its left wing was on fire. One landing gear had dropped down, and the aircraft was swinging out of the formation rising to the left. Suddenly, it began to fall in what clearly was a final dive. Tom saw dots emerge from the stricken plane, crewmen taking to parachutes. One. Two. Three. Four. A B-17 carried a crew of ten. Where were the others? *Come on you guys, get out.* Forester was pleading for the remaining crew to leave the falling craft. Five. Six. Then it happened. The B-17 exploded, creating a massive fireball of red and black. Pieces of metal, and men, rained through the smoke. In seconds, the large aircraft had totally disappeared.

Forester looked and saw six parachutes, counting them twice to be sure of the number. Upon landing at Bromley Park, he would need to tell Harry Collins what he had seen and he wanted to be certain of the count. Six men were floating in the sky—tiny figures swinging back and forth. Soon to be prisoners of war, their tour of duty prematurely ended. Forester wondered whether the pilot of the B-17 was among the six. *Oh God no!* One of the chutes was smoking. Then, like a match, it flared as the canopy caught fire. With nothing to hold the air, the man rocketed downward in a terrifying, solitary last flight. Forester turned away. He felt sick at the thought of what that person had felt when he saw his chute catch fire.

Tom Forester had never used a parachute. The truth was that he feared doing so. Jumping out of an airplane, in Forester's mind, was an unnatural act and he got queasy just thinking about it. Forester had mentioned this fear to Harry Collins, but not to any of his pilots. Collins, a big man with a sharp mind, had laughed and told his commander to relax.

"Hell, Colonel, you'd be nuts not to be afraid. Jumping out of an airplane is not something God intended us to do. I doubt whether any of our intrepid airmen want to jump. Except of course for Perkins, and we all know he is certifiably crazy."

Lieutenant Oscar Perkins was a pilot who drove and drank like a mad man. Forever accepting a challenge, regardless how dangerous, Perkins was considered by all to be out of control. No one expected him to live much longer.

Collins's remark made Forester feel better, at least temporarily. Of course, the group commander wore a chute each time he flew. Specifically, Forester, as many P-47 pilots did, strapped on a U.S. Army Air Force S-2 parachute that served also as a seat cushion. As a cushion, he found it comfortable. As a tool of escape, he had serious doubts. Tom Forester was not afraid to fly and he showed courage in confronting the Luftwaffe. But the group commander of the 19th Fighter Group remained thoroughly uneasy at the thought of departing his P-47 by parachute.

Forester had been back with the bombers for less than a minute when two Me-109s, coming out of the sun, attacked.

"Trumpet, break left" shouted Ennis into his radio. The lieutenant had not identified himself, wishing to convey the message as quickly as possible, and assuming Forester would recognize his voice.

Upon hearing the warning, Forester immediately pushed his control stick forward and to the left. This raised the aircraft's left aileron and lowered the right one. It also positioned downward the elevators attached to the horizontal stabilizers at the rear of the P-47. The effect was instantaneous. The big fighter rolled to the left and headed towards the ground. Simultaneously, with his left hand, Forester advanced the throttle. Nose down and turning, the P-47 accelerated rapidly. Employing the rudder as well, whose controls were foot pedals at the front of the cockpit, Forester kept the aircraft in a diving turn, hoping to thwart the aim of the two Messerschmits.

"They're still on you, Trumpet." called Ennis.

"Roger, Red Two." Forester could see for himself that the Me-109s were still in pursuit for over his right wing tracers of cannon fire appeared. In pursuit of the American were F-model Messerschmitt's. The Me-109Fs carried a single 20 mm cannon in the nose of the aircraft that fired through the propeller hub. Supplementing the cannon were two machine guns, one mounted in each wing. Strangely, it had less firepower than the Me-109E, which it replaced.

This modest armament and the greater speed of the P-47 when diving would enable Forester to escape. His airplane hurdled downward and began to outdistance the Germans. As he drew ahead, the tracer fire stopped. When he reached 15,000 feet, he reasoned the enemy would be gone. A look back revealed this to be the case. The P-47 carried a rear view mirror centered at the forward end of its framed canopy. Forester had exchanged the standard mirror for a circular RAF mirror, which he and other American pilots found more useful. Several glances into the mirror confirmed that his tail was clear of Me-109s.

"Red Two. This is Trumpet. Where are you?" No answer. "Red Two, this is Trumpet. Where are you?" Ennis did not respond.

Time to regain altitude again. Forester pulled back on the control stick and the P-47 headed upward. The group commander was worried about his wingman. Ennis was a good flyer and a likeable young man. Though new to his squadron and to combat operations, Ennis had seemed alert and dependable. His quickness in calling out the two Messerschmitts had been commendable. Forester made a mental note to compliment Ennis when next he saw him—if he saw him again. The possibility that the Me-109s had downed the newcomer was not farfetched.

"Trumpet here. Do you read me Red Two? Come in Red Two. I'm northwest of Amiens, climbing to twenty-one."

There was no response. Ennis was either shot down, damaged and heading home, or flying nearby, but with a dead radio. Radios in the P-47 had been causing difficulty. Indeed, the first combat mission of P-47s on March 10, 1943 had been a failure due to malfunctioning radios. The basic problem had been solved, but difficulties kept cropping up. Forester hoped Ennis was okay. He wanted all 19th Fighter Group pilots to be safe, but he particularly wanted his wingman to stay out of trouble. This was not solely out of concern for Ennis.

Wingmen were integral to fighter operations everywhere. The basic fighting unit in the sky was two aircraft, a leader, and his wingman. The leader hunted for the enemy. The wingman kept guard and protected his leader from attack.

This two aircraft formation was called an element. Two elements and four aircraft formed a flight, which in both the RAF and U.S. Army Air Force comprised the smallest unit sent into battle. In 1943, squadrons usually consisted of three flights, each identified in radio communications by color. The Americans used red, white, and blue. Later, when additional aircraft became available, a fourth flight was added to squadron strength, with the colors green or yellow chosen as the new flight's radio call sign.

The four aircraft flight flew in what was termed the "Finger Four" formation. In this formation, the lead aircraft was out in front. His wingman flew to the left about 100 feet back, and stepped down slightly for maneuverability. The second element leader was approximately 150 feet to the right of the flight leader while his wingman was positioned a further 100 feet to the right. The formation of the flight reflected the relative position of the four fingers of the right hand when holding the thumb underneath. The middle finger would be Red 1, the index finger Red 2. The pinky would be Red 4 while the ring finger would be Red 3.

Each fighter squadron had its own radio call sign, which almost always was a two-syllable word. The 19th Fighter Group consisted of the 340th, 341st, and 87th Fighter Squadrons. Their radio call signs were Snowflake, Boston, and Cowboy, respectively. Thus, any aircraft of the group could be contacted by radio using a verbal code. The two-syllable word specified the squadron. The color meant the flight. And the number identified the position of a particular aircraft within the flight. For example, "Cowboy Blue Four" was the wingman of the second element in Blue flight of the 87th Fighter Squadron.

This day, Forester was flying with the 340th squadron, leading Red flight. The 19th's group commander would fly with one squadron for two weeks or so, and then move to a new squadron. This enabled him to learn how well the pilots of a particular squadron flew. It also let him instill his tactical ideas into the group at various places and gave the pilots of the 19th the opportunity to fly with and learn from their commander. Wherever he flew, Forester was "Trumpet." The call sign immediately identified the voice on the radio as the group commander. Pilots, already alert when in the air, perked up when they heard the words, "This is Trumpet."

Forester had chosen the radio call sign shortly after the 19th Fighter Group had arrived in England. Harry Collins had come into the Operations Room early one morning, when the weather precluded flying, and told his commander that he and the three squadrons each needed new call signs.

Forester responded, "Tell the squadron commanders to pick their own signs. Two-syllables only. I'll go along with what they want, assuming it's reasonable."

"What's reasonable?" queried Collins.

"Nothing profane or silly. Shitface or Bonehead will not do. Tell 'em to use their heads."

"Yes, Sir. What about you?"

"What about me?"

"The group leader needs a call sign as well, Colonel. As a group commander, you're entitled to your own call sign. Actually, you have to have one. There's no choice. It will identify you or whoever's in charge that day."

At that moment, Major Wilbur Williams, the group's adjutant, entered the room. He said good morning to Collins and to Forester, and went over to a small table by the coffee and donuts on which sat a record player. Williams selected a seventy-eight disc and soon the sound of Harry James was floating through the room. Williams loved the big band sound and had brought his own collection of records to England. Forester knew nothing about music, but enjoyed listening to it immensely. When Harry James hit some high notes on his trumpet, Forester just smiled, and turned to his Intelligence Officer.

"There it is, Harry."

"Sir?"

"The call sign. Listen."

Harry Collins was a smart fellow. Quick and thoughtful, he had been a small town businessman before volunteering for the Air Corps. He had wanted to fly, but had been too old and had poor eyesight. So, sensibly, the Army had made him an Intelligence Officer. He was good at the job, and was much appreciated by Forester. Collins liked Forester. He found the group commander to be thoughtful and extremely well organized. He knew that the pilots of the 19th Fighter Group respected their leader who, by all accounts, lacked neither skill nor courage in combat. In time, Collins also had come to realize that Forester had a sense of humor and liked to play word games.

Collins understood they were now playing a game. Forester was challenging his Intelligence Officer to guess what the call sign would be. There had been a clue. Collins knew he must think fast. Something had triggered Forester's mind to come up with the call sign. But what was it? Bingo. The music. Wilbur Williams and his record collection. Forester was humming the tune. The call sign must be "Bandman." Harry James led the big band. Bandman worked because it signified someone in charge, orchestrating a diverse group of talents. As a group commander, Forester had to do the same thing.

"I've got it, Colonel."

"And it is?"

"Bandman."

"That's good, Harry, real good. But it's Trumpet. Listen." The sound of Harry James's horn was smooth, clear, and penetrating. The song was "It's Been a Long, Long Time." Tom Forester gave his Intelligence Officer a friendly smile and pretended to play the trumpet.

At 21,000 feet, Forester leveled off. There was still no sign of Ennis. As he searched the sky looking for his wingman, the red fuel warning light on the instrument panel of his aircraft still had not gone on. The P-47 had two internal, self-sealing fuel tanks located in the forward part of the fuselage. Together they held 305 gallons of aviation fuel. The flight manual called for the auxiliary tank to be used first. The pilot would then switch to the main tank. When the light went on, the main tank had 40 gallons remaining. This provided about twenty minutes of flight time.

Forester turned his aircraft to the northeast. The P-47's engine was running smoothly and a quick glance at his instruments indicated all was well. However, clouds were beginning to build up. What had started out as a clear day was turning sour. Ahead, the south of England was covered with clouds, and the front was heading east. Once again, aircraft of the 19th Fighter Group would have to let down in the clouds.

Tom avoided flying in a straight line for more than fifteen seconds. The enemy loved to attack out of the sun and a plane cruising along in a straight line was an easy target. So Forester turned his P-47 and kept a sharp lookout. Without a wingman, he was vulnerable. Therefore, he constantly checked the sky about him.

Below lay France. From 21,000 feet, it looked peaceful. Farmland and a few roads. The colors were varying shades of green and brown. Some crops appeared yellow and the roads were dark black, like shoelaces laid across a quilt. No towns were in sight, though Dunkirk was dead ahead, some 40 miles distant.

Suddenly, Tom was thinking of his father who loved France and had fought there in the Great War. Dad was a banker in New York City. Successful, he and his wife Marjorie lived on the north shore of Long Island. Their house, in which Tom and his older brother, William, grew up, overlooked the Sound. The family belonged to the Port Washington Yacht Club where John Forester kept a 35-foot sloop, which Marjorie had christened *Reward*. The sloop spent little time at sea. Not that Dad didn't like to sail. He loved nothing better than to take *Reward* out in a stiff breeze with his family aboard. Tom and Will would crew while Marjorie enjoyed simply watching her three men in action. But John Forester spent much of his time at the bank. Unlike some in his profession, he had survived the Depression. Yet he would never forget the havoc it wreaked nor would he, from 1929 on, ever take wealth for granted. So Tom's dad worked long hours and took care to invest his money prudently. One result was that he was extremely well off. Another was that he saw little of his family.

John Forester was extremely proud of his younger son. He was pleased that, upon graduation from Dartmouth, Tom had planned to pursue graduate studies in Modern European History. He was less pleased when Tom had put on hold plans for a Ph.D. "There's a war coming, Dad, and this country had better get ready to fight." At first, John Forester had disagreed. Like many Americans, he believed Europe's problems need not become problems of the United States. He told his son, "Let them stew in their own mess. One American Expeditionary Force is enough." But in time, he came to share Tom's view that Adolf Hitler was truly evil and a threat to all that was good in the world.

Marjorie had cried upon learning that Tom had enlisted in the army. She had feared for her husband when he had fought in the trenches, and now she was afraid again. John Forester approved of his son's decision. He also was supportive of Tom's desire to fly. In June 1940, he and Marjorie took the train to Texas where they attended Tom's graduation from flight school at Randolph Field. "I'm proud of you, son," the older Forester had said when the ceremony was over. "Those wings of yours set you apart. Wear them safely, and with honor." He then hugged his son who welcomed the embrace. Marjorie Forester stayed quiet. While Tom and John Forester talked about what it meant to be an officer and pilot in the United States Army Air Force, she said nothing. Her hand simply took a handkerchief to her face and wiped away the tears.

Forester's P-47 was approaching the French coast. Time to put aside thoughts of his father and tend to the business at hand. There was still no aircraft in sight. Clouds covered most of England, but above France, they had cleared away. The sun was bright and the air cold at this altitude. Despite no wingman, Forester felt good. At this moment, he imagined that he owned the sky. Flying a high performance airplane gave one an enormous sense of agility and power. The twenty-six-year-old commander wanted to enjoy the freedom flight provided. This feel of flying was special. It gave Forester a sensation he had difficulty describing, but one he liked immensely. Once he had tried to explain the feeling to Will, but the attempt was not a success, so Tom kept to himself the joy of riding among the clouds. It was a true pleasure, one he felt each time he took to the air.

Forester continued to scan the skies. Turning his head from side to side, checking the rear through the mirror. He knew now was not the time to contemplate the joys of flying. Below, French airfields were presently occupied by the Luftwaffe. Once home to the Armee de l'Air, their hangars now housed Focke-Wulfs and Messerschmitts. Forester stayed alert.

Three thousand feet above him, two aircraft had spotted his lone P-47. With guns armed and gunsights on, they headed downward. Tom saw them, but did not dive away.

"This is Trumpet. To the two P-47s diving just south of Dunkirk, identify yourselves."

"Hello, Trumpet. This is Snowflake Red 3 and 4. Are you okay?" The two aircraft approaching Forester's belonged to the 340th Fighter Squadron. They were part of the flight Forester had been leading. "At first we thought you were a German."

"Trumpet to Snowflake Red 3 and 4. "I'm fine. Form up on me. How's your fuel?"

The pilots of the two aircraft obeyed their commander. Upon reaching 21,000 feet, they tucked in astern of Forester. "Fuel is a tad low, Trumpet. Light blinked on a few minutes ago." That was Snowflake Red 3.

"Roger. Keep your eyes peeled. Where's the squadron?

"Don't know, Trumpet. We followed you down and broke up a Jerry attack. Other Germans hit the bombers from the rear and it became a free for all."

No longer did Forester feel vulnerable by flying alone. The arrival of the two P-47s lessened the likelihood of any unpleasant surprise by German fighters. Six eyes, Tom reasoned, were better than two.

One of the two P-47s was flown by a particularly aggressive pilot. Snowflake Red 3 was Captain Vincent Granelli, from Providence, Rhode Island. Forester knew him to be a good pilot, someone completely unafraid to tangle with the Luftwaffe. What Forester did not know was that Captain Granelli was one of those individuals for whom violence is normal behavior. Eager to have physically fit men in uniform, particularly those with an aptitude for flying, the army overlooked his dubious background. Despite a disdain for rules and a certain contempt for authority, Granelli did well in the army, opting for the Air Corps where he had shown considerable proficiency in flying. His tendency toward violence was known to his squadron mates, but his combat record, numerous engagements with the Germans and an Me-109 to his credit, made commanders overlook any shortcomings.

At Group Headquarters, Harry Collins knew that Captain Granelli would sooner or later make trouble for the 19th Fighter Group. He had not said anything to Forester, but had spoken with Wilbur Williams. The Group Adjutant had replied that Granelli was indeed a bad apple. "One of these days that guy will screw up bad," Williams said.

The three aircraft were now approaching Dunkirk. The sky remained clear and Forester could see much of the town ahead. Dunkirk sat on the coastline and, prewar, had been both a busy seaport and popular resort. To the southwest and northeast of Dunkirk, the coast of France was a great line of demarcation. On one side lay the grey chopping water of the Channel across from which was England, weary but nonetheless determined after four years of war. On the other side stood the green and brown fields of a once proud country now occupied by German troops. To Forester and other Allied airmen, the former signaled safety and a warm bed. The latter meant loss of freedom and a cold bunk in a Prisoner of War camp.

The beaches at Dunkirk had been the site of an English defeat turned into an English victory. Early in the war, a British army had crossed the Channel to bolster French forces facing Hitler's panzer divisions. In May 1940, the Germans attacked. Bypassing the Maginot Line, they moved swiftly into Holland and Belgium. In ten days, the Wehrmacht gained more territory than the Kaiser's army had in four years. The French Army, dispirited and poorly led, collapsed. The British Expeditionary Force did not collapse, but outgunned and outmaneuvered, it failed to stop the German Blitzkrieg. By May 30, surviving Allied troops had withdrawn to a pocket around Dunkirk. Then, Hitler told his victorious army to pause, in order to regroup for anticipated battles in the south. This gave the Royal Navy time to arrange the safe removal of over 330,000 troops. A British army had been defeated in battle, but not destroyed. In England, this "Deliverance at Dunkirk" had been celebrated. Britain could replace the equipment left behind on the beaches, but not the men. They had been saved and would fight another day.

As the three aircraft flew over the French city, Forester decided upon a course of action. He had time to engage the enemy again, though not for an extended period. They could mix it up over the Channel, but not pursue the Luftwaffe deep into France. Getting back to Bromley Park was paramount. A P-47 ditched in the sea or crashing short of the field was an aircraft lost and a pilot endangered. Tom had twenty-two missions under his belt and had often come home with but a few gallons left in the tank. Time and time again, he would tell his pilots to concentrate on fuel management. Now, over Dunkirk, he told himself to do the same thing. "Snowflake Red 3 and 4, this is Trumpet. Stay with me. We're not going home just yet." Tom banked his plane to the right, as did the other two pilots who by radio acknowledged their commander's instruction. The small formation flew northeast, parallel to the coastline. At 21,000 feet, the three airmen could see well into Belgium, with Ostend in the distance.

Forester figured their new course would lead them to the Luftwaffe. Often the Germans would put up fighters along the coast after the main American strike force had turned home. They hoped to catch stragglers or damaged aircraft attempting to reach England. The commander of the 19th Fighter Group hoped to do some catching of his own. He calculated that the coast of Belgium adjacent to France was a likely spot to intercept the Luftwaffe.

Ahead to the right of the P-47s, about 10 miles inland, were two aircraft. One was streaming a long wispy trail of blue-black smoke.

"Trumpet, this is Red 3." Granelli had dropped his squadron's call sign. With just three aircraft in the formation, he felt no need for the lengthier identification. "Off to our right, about 4,000 feet below us."

"I see them, Snowflake Red 3." Tom had the two aircraft in sight.

"Let's go down and get 'em, Trumpet." Granelli was eager to score. He thought the two planes were sitting ducks and he was anxious to open fire. The Captain smelled blood. "Let's go get the bastards."

"Hold your position, Red 3" Forester had no difficulty in letting someone else have an easy shot. And he wanted all his pilots to have the experience of shooting guns in anger. But he had seen something Captain Granelli had not. Why would two aircraft, one obviously in trouble, be flying west in a straight line? Forester wanted to verify what he suspected. "Let's get a little closer."

Within twenty seconds, Forester spoke again. "This is Trumpet. They're Spitfires. Repeat Spitfires."

The two aircraft were indeed RAF Spitfires. Already a legend, the Spitfire was Britain's premier fighter aircraft. Nimble and a joy to fly, yet deadly in combat, the Spitfire was hindered by its limited range. At its best in a defensive position, as in 1940 when the plane rose to defend England, the Spitfire in 1943 was tasked to fly fighter sweeps over occupied territories. These sweeps were intended to draw the Luftwaffe into battle. They did so rarely, for the Germans would engage Allied fighters only when the bombers were present. Spitfires, with their short legs, were ill suited for escort work. So the RAF assigned them to fighter sweeps or to bomber support when the big planes were either starting out or returning home.

The two Spitfires the three Americans had stumbled upon belonged to an RAF squadron based at Chase Hill, an airfield northeast of London. The squadron had put up sixteen Spitfires that morning in a sweep to Belgium. This time, the tactic had worked. The Spitfires had clashed with fourteen Me-109s in a fierce battle. Three Germans went down, as did three British planes. Several aircraft were damaged, including the Spitfire now trailing smoke. This smoke was likely to attract unwelcome attention. The Spitfires' squadron commander was in the other plane attempting to shepherd the damaged craft home to Chase Hill.

"Heads up Snowflake Red 3 and 4. We have company." Coming down the coast, vectored by German ground controllers, was a gaggle of Messerschmitts. Spread out in two lines abreast, the Me-109s were hoping to surprise Allied aircraft whose crews might be less vigilant now that their home airfields were close by. Painted dark grey, almost black, the Messerschmitts Forester had seen had bright

red propeller hubs. These stood in contrast to the otherwise menacing appearance.

"Bandits at twelve o'clock high." Forester was now telling his
two compatriots where the Me-109s were. Hour marks on an imaginary watch face indicated direction. Six o'clock meant dead astern.
Three o'clock meant ninety degrees to the right of the direction
being flown. The Messerschmitts were directly in front of the P-47s.
"I count at least fourteen."

"Oh Jesus." That was Snowflake Red 4.

"This is Trumpet to Snowflake, Boston, and Cowboy aircraft. If
you're near Dunkirk, come join a party. We're at angels twenty-one
and could use some help."

"Trumpet, this is Snowflake Red 3. The Spitfires are turning
away."

"Roger Snowflake Red 3. I see them. Let's cross over the Spits
and break into the Jerries."

The two British planes were now in considerable danger. Upon
seeing the Germans, they had banked to the left and were building
up speed as they sought to flee. One of the Spitfires continued to
spew smoke. The other kept station and was ready to defend his
cohort. He had not yet seen Forester and the other two P-47s.

The three American aircraft now turned, over flying the British,
heading directly towards the Messerschmitts. "Snowflakes, this is
Trumpet. Line up to my side. We'll hit them three abreast, on my
call."

"Oh Jesus." Again, this was Snowflake Red 4 who had left his
radio on. But he brought his aircraft along side of Forester, as did
Granelli.

Intently, Forester kept track of the Germans. He had to gauge
exactly when to begin the attack. Outnumbered, Forester knew his
three aircraft flight might well not survive. For a moment, a brief
moment, he was afraid. His knees felt limp and he became conscious
of height. Forester recognized the symptoms. Occasionally, fear was
a co-pilot of the 19th Fighter Group's commander. When it
appeared, he acknowledged its presence, but told himself that fear

would have to wait for a more convenient appointment. He was too busy to be frightened. There were airplanes to lead and other airplanes to fight. *Fear would have to take its turn, which is later, back at Bromley Park.* Once on the ground Forester would confront this inevitable feeling and let it shake him down. But in the air, it had to be put aside, which is what Forester now did.

"This is Trumpet. Stay steady." Eager to do battle, Tom became confident. He even felt the odds had become about even, which they had not. "On my call, gentlemen . . . now!"

At the instant of Forester's command, the three P-47s jerked upward to meet head on the first line of German aircraft. Twenty-four machine guns were blazing as the three aircraft flew through the enemy formation, disrupting the Germans who were about to attack. In truth, the Me-109 pilots had been surprised by the audacity of the Americans. They had expected the P-47s, given the odds, to turn away.

After passing through the Luftwaffe line, Forester looped his aircraft and headed back. Snowflake Red 3 and 4 did the same. "This is Trumpet. Let's go get 'em."

Forester led the three P-47s down into a steep dive. Several of the Me-109s were within striking distance of the Spitfires. Forester focused on the lead Messerschmitt. This time he got in close before firing. At 200 yards, he pressed the trigger and held it down for four seconds. In those four seconds, the guns threw out 960 rounds of heavy fire. The results were devastating. Almost all of the bullets ripped through the canopy of the Me-109. Before shards of glass could shred the German pilot, his head exploded as Forester's fire ripped into his face and skull. The German was never aware of what happened. He died instantly. His body slumped forward onto the Me-109's control stick. This caused the plane to nose down. Trailing no smoke and looking remarkably undamaged, the Messerschmitt and its mangled pilot flew straight down. This last flight took fifty seconds whereupon the plane impacted violently with the ground There, in addition to creating a large crater, the Messerschmitt killed several prized cows belonging to a dairy farmer who was unaware of the airborne drama unfolding above his land.

Forester paid scant attention to his victim once he saw his bullets strike home. Though his gun cameras recorded the episode, his focus was elsewhere. A second Messerschmitt was attacking the damaged Spitfire.

The little British plane was less sturdy than the P-47. Almost fragile, it could not absorb much punishment. Tom glanced at the Spitfire. At once, he realized its precarious position. Forester pulled his P-47s control stick to the right, at the same time kicking the rudder pedals. The big plane shifted direction. *Stay calm. Keep your speed up. Check your tail. Fire!*

Once again, Forester's aim was true. The second Messerschmitt, dark grey and black like the others, flew for nine more seconds. Then, with engine and fuel tanks riddled with the fire of Forester's guns, it exploded. The entire aircraft and its pilot simply disappeared in a bright orange fireball, which then fanned out sixty yards. Accompanying the fireball was a tremendous noise, which Forester only vaguely heard. He flew through the exploding flame, instinctively closing his eyes as the P-47 passed through what once had been a man and his machine. In two seconds Tom's plane was through and beyond the now fading fireball. Two seconds more with the throttle pushed forward to Military Power and the P-47 gained even greater speed. Forester knew the fight was far from over. He pulled the stick back and the aircraft headed up to where the Germans were still trying to shoot down the Spitfires.

The very number of Messerschmitts made the German task more difficult. They simply got in each other's way. The Luftwaffe pilots needed to be cautious when firing, for fear of hitting one of their own. The three Americans had no such inhibitions. If it flew, it was probably German. So the P-47s fired short bursts whenever an aircraft was in range. Tom piloted his plane with wild abandon. His goal now was simply to force the Messerschmitts to break off their attacks. He fired often and succeeded in diverting at least ten Me-109s from their goal. Forester saw little of Granelli and nothing of Snowflake Red 4. Hopefully, they were safe. In a battle such as this, there was little he could do to help.

In fact, Granelli had done well, with but one exception. He had damaged several Messerschmitts and twice had saved a Spitfire from certain destruction. Unfortunately, he also had once fired inadvertently at a P-47, briefly hitting the left wing of the plane. The P-47 was Forester's. Only when Sergeant McGowan, Forester's crew chief, examined the damage did this become known. Granelli thought he would be in serious trouble. Not so. Forester dismissed the incident with, "Things like that sometimes happen." He knew how easily harm could come from friendly fire. However, Tom did request that Captain Granelli reread the aircraft recognition manuals published by the Eighth Air Force.

Snowflake Red 4 didn't do as well as Granelli. He flew hard and had fired often, but his aim was off and no German fighter felt the sting of his guns. Yet Snowflake Red 4 had managed to avoid getting shot down. He and his plane had survived, In this battle, which became part of 19th Fighter Group lore, that alone was an accomplishment.

Forester leveled off and spotted yet another Me-109. This time, the enemy was flying parallel to Forester's P-47, at the same altitude. The two aircraft turned toward each other. With a closing speed of over 700 mph, they raced forward. Forester could see the red nose of the Messerschmitt. It looked like a red ball with which one might play stickball. Suddenly, it erupted with bursts of fire and accompanying smoke. The German pilot had triggered the Me-109s cannon located upon the aircraft's Daimler-Benz engine. Forester judged that his adversary had fired too soon. He estimated the two aircraft to be 600 yards apart. *Stay calm. Get in close.* Seconds later, Forester pressed his own trigger and empty gun cartridges immediately spewed forth beneath the wings of his P-47.

The 19th Fighter Group's commander did not actually see his fire strike the Me-109. But again, his aircraft's gun cameras recorded the action, filming pieces flying off the German plane. The P-47 and Me-109 passed within six feet of one another. As they crossed,

Forester caught a glimpse of the dark grey and black Messerschmitt. It looked rather foreboding and Forester, for an instant, was reminded of the evil the plane represented.

Ten seconds later, Forester's P-47 was enveloped in clouds. He turned to the left, hoping to break free and rejoining the battle. The clouds had moved in from the west and it was nearly a minute before his P-47 emerged into open sky. No Germans were in sight. What before had been awash with aircraft was now empty, except for two aircraft off to the right, about 3,000 feet below. They were P-47s, which Forester identified as Granelli and Snowflake Red 4. Both appeared undamaged. But where were the Messerschmitts? Had they given up? Did they run out of ammunition? Actually, the Me-109s were short of fuel prior to the engagement. After a few minutes of battling the P-47s, they reluctantly had had to return to base. Their commander, an experienced Oberstleutnant, was extremely agitated. Not only had he lost three pilots and their planes, but his group had also failed to down the Spitfires.

"Trumpet. This is Snowflake Red 3. Red 4 and I are about 4,000 feet below you."

"This is Trumpet. I see you both. Hold position. I'm coming down. Form on my wing."

"Roger, Trumpet."

Forester brought his plane down and the two P-47s flew into position. The three aircraft were now well out over the water, where the English Channel and North Sea merge. Northwest lay East Anglia, home to Bromley Park and the other airfields of the Eighth Air Force.

Forester checked his fuel. Now it was time to get back.

"This is Trumpet. We're going home. But keep your eyes open. Our German friends may still be about."

"I think not, Colonel. I saw them break off and head east." This was Granelli. In the excitement, he had discarded radio call signs.

"Trumpet. This is Snowflake Red 4. Sir, the Captain's right. The Messerschmitts broke off the combat."

"Roger Red 4. Red 4, are you okay?"

"Yes, Sir, I'm fine, but I don't have much fuel."

"Snowflake Red 3, what's your condition?"

"Trumpet. Red 3 here. I'm alive and well, but ditto on the fuel."

"This is Trumpet. Reduce your fuel mixture and ease back your revs. Follow me down, we'll descend gradually."

A few seconds later, Snowflake Red 4 was on the radio. "Trumpet, this is Snowflake Red 4. Two aircraft at three o'clock low. I think they're Spitfires."

They were Spitfires. In fact, they were the two aircraft the three P-47s had just rescued off Dunkirk. Now at 6,000 feet, the Spitfires were struggling to reach the shores of England. Just inland near Deal, the RAF had established emergency airfields for aircraft not capable of reaching their home base. The Spitfires were heading to these fields. Their course would take them across Forester's flight path, but below the P-47s.

"This is Trumpet, Snowflake Red 3 and 4. Stay in position. I'm going down." As the two Spitfires passed underneath, Forester rolled his plane to the right. Completing the roll, he swooped down to the left, holding the throttle in check so as not to build up speed nor to use more fuel than was necessary. The P-47 came down and approached the Spitfires. Fortunately, the RAF pilots, recognizing the shape of the big American fighter, took no defensive action. They continued to fly towards the shore. Both were now trailing smoke, but were seemingly under control.

Forester flew along side the lead Spitfire. The British plane was small in comparison to the P-47. It was painted grey and dark green, with its national insignia a red circle surrounded by a thin white line inside a blue circle that was outlined in yellow. The canopy of the Spitfire was pulled back. The pilot, who commanded the squadron based at Chase Hill, seemed unperturbed, hardly aware of the blue smoke emerging from his plane's Merlin engine.

As Forester pulled even with the British craft, its pilot turned to the American and with his left hand gave Tom a thumbs up. Forester interpreted this to mean all was well. He was half correct. The RAF officer was conveying his thanks as well. Forester responded by sliding his canopy back and then doing something he later thought was overdramatic. He looked directly at the Spitfire pilot, no more than 50 feet across, and brought his right hand up to his forehead in a quick salute, which the other pilot returned. The gesture was simple, yet telling. It conveyed respect and camaraderie. It also, Tom realized, was something he would have done were they all starring in a Spencer Tracy movie.

The three aircraft were now passing over the white cliffs leaving the Channel behind. Once over land, Forester moved his P-47 away from the Spitfires, which were dropping their wheels in preparation for landing. Looking once more at the RAF pilot who had returned the salute, Tom gently rocked the wings of the P-47 and climbed out to the right. As the two little fighters touched down upon the emergency field, Forester was flying north, shortly to rejoin Granelli and Snowflake Red 4.

These two pilots were expecting their group commander. They were not expecting to sight another P-47. As Forester caught up with them, he spoke to them both.

"This is Trumpet, Snowflake Red 3 and 4. There's a P-47 coming into our right. Check four o'clock."

"I see it, Sir," responded Snowflake Red 4.

"Roger, Trumpet. I wonder who it is?" asked Granelli.

"We'll see. He's apparently joining our flight."

The new P-47 did as Forester predicted. Coming in from the east, the big plane moved in. There were several holes in the plane's fuselage and a patch of rudder was missing. But the P-47 appeared stable with the pilot fully in control. All of which made Tom appreciate again the ruggedness of the P-47. He quickly reflected that while the fighter could not climb worth a damn, it certainly could absorb hits from the Luftwaffe. The new arrival now was 100 feet away. Its pilot had pulled back the canopy and was waving. He also rocked his wings as he eased his plane down and to the left of Forester's. It was Ennis.

"This is Trumpet. Hello Snowflake Red 2. Are you okay?"

There was no response. So Forester tried again. "Snowflake Red 2, this is Trumpet. Can you hear me Red 2?"

The answer was obviously no because Forester heard no response. Tom assumed Ennis's radio was dead. He had seen the damage to the newcomer's plane. The hits to the fuselage were just aft of the cockpit where the P-47's radio was located. Apparently, voice communication would not be possible. This seemed not to faze Snowflake Red 2. He had pulled up even with Forester and was waving again. Somewhat self-consciously, Tom waved back. Group commanders were supposed to be aloof and unemotional. But Forester was glad to see his wingman safe. And he smiled to himself as he waved again.

Forester also was glad that Ennis's P-47 had not been lost. While Tom valued pilots more than planes, he knew that in September 1943, fighter aircraft were in short supply. He thus wanted to bring home the same number of P-47s with which he had started. Pride was involved as well. Forester wanted the 19th Fighter Group to excel. The group was important to operations of the Eighth Air Force. Moreover, it was his group. He was its commander and its record was his record. And he wished his name to be associated solely with success.

Ahead were the clouds that now rose several thousand feet. Bromley Park was fifty miles to the north. There was no way to avoid the front.

"This is Trumpet. Tighten up Snowflakes. We're about to go into the soup."

Ten seconds later, the now complete flight—Snowflake Red 2 off to Forester's left with Red 3 and 4 staggered down to the right— disappeared from view. Flying in close formation, but with visibility severely restricted, each pilot could see only the plane next to his own. The four planes continued their descent. Each pilot was hoping that the clouds that enveloped their flight and covered much of England north of the Thames did not extend all the way to the ground.

FIVE

The office belonging to Colonel James Dixon was small, but tastefully decorated. Located in a house on Grosvenor Square across from the American Embassy, the office was on the second floor in what had been a child's bedroom. The house itself now belonged to the Americans. Their government had purchased the building to increase the space available for Embassy offices. Additional space was needed to accommodate the growing American presence in England. London was already full of U.S. uniforms. The Yanks were not only forging an air force to bomb Germany but they also were starting the buildup for the army's invasion of France, now but nine months away.

Dixon's office measured 12 feet by 12 feet. The walls were painted soft yellow, the ceiling an off white. Fluted crown molding covered the juncture of wall and ceiling. Bookshelves were built into one wall while two large windows provided ample light. On the floor was an expensive rug. Along with an antique table, which the Deputy Air Attaché used as a desk, and two chairs, the rug gave the room elegance unusual for a governmental office. Dixon had had such an appearance in mind when he had bought the rug from an Indian merchant in Paddington. The Colonel might be an Army Air Force desk jockey, but Jimmy Dixon did not wish to live like one. The office looked, and felt, like a private study in a great house.

Only the photographs on the wall and the two airplane models on the table signaled the occupation of the man who worked in this office. The pictures on the wall, there were three of them, were all of men in uniform. One was of Hap Arnold, commanding general of all Army Air Forces. Dixon knew and admired Arnold. But the Colonel knew that despite a genial manner, General Arnold was a demanding taskmaster who had little hesitancy in replacing officers he felt were not getting the job done. The second picture was of Eddie Rickenbacker. Rickenbacker was the top scoring American ace of World War I. He had once offered Dixon a job in civil aviation. The two men had become friends despite Dixon's decision to remain in the Air Corps. The third picture was of Dixon himself, and taken recently. In the photograph, he stood alongside a Spitfire. Next to him was Air Vice Marshal Keith Park, the RAF officer whose tactical leadership won the Battle of Britain.

The two models were wood. Unpainted, they were recognizable by shape alone. One was the twin boomed P-38. The other was a P-47. Too old to fly in combat, Dixon nonetheless was checked out in both aircraft. He liked the P-38 for its range and the safety implicit in two engines. He also liked the P-47. At high altitude, Dixon found the P-47 to be fast and maneuverable. Like all Army Air Force officers in Europe, he wished the P-38 had greater reliability and the P-47 greater range.

The job as Deputy Air Attaché called for tact and social graces, qualities that James Dixon had in abundance. Rickenbacker had helped him win the assignment as attaché to which he applied great energy and considerable intellect. These two qualities were not immediately obvious for Dixon had a soft southern drawl and a gentle manner. At West Point, where he had graduated in the top five percentile, his classmates had nicknamed him Bobbie Lee. Dixon had a successful army career. His ambition was to make general and lead an air force in combat.

Today, as always, Colonel Dixon was a busy man. Already this morning, he had cabled Barney Giles, Arnold's Deputy and Chief of the Air Staff, about fighter requirements for the invasion. He had met with two senior RAF officers about search and rescue efforts in the Channel. He had discussed short term logistics with his naval counterpart at the Embassy. And he had even found time to read an account of last week's football game between Army and Georgia Tech, a contest he considered to be the game of the week.

Now, sipping his third cup of coffee, Dixon was going through paperwork on his table, wondering whether the Luftwaffe was similarly burdened by memoranda and reports. There was a knock on the door and in walked Sergeant Howard, Dixon's secretary and office manager.

"Colonel, your 10:45 appointment is here."

"Right, Sergeant. I'm ready." Dixon stood up, pushing the paperwork to the side of the table. He then took from the stack a file marked London Advisory Committee. Dixon put on his service jacket and checked his reflection in the mirror to make sure he looked presentable. As he did so, Sergeant Howard ushered in the Colonel's next visitor.

"Colonel Dixon, I'm Helen Trent. It's a pleasure to meet you."

"Thank you, Mrs. Trent. The pleasure is all mine." Dixon was shaking hands with Helen as he spoke. He noticed immediately that she was an attractive woman, smartly dressed in a simple, but well tailored navy blue suit. Middle aged, she was probably in her late thirties. Dixon took notice of her deep black hair and pale skin, finding the contrast compelling. He observed that the woman before him had a slender figure with subtle curves that most men would notice. Since Helen Trent was wearing a wedding ring, Jimmy Dixon concluded that whoever Mr. Trent was, he indeed was a fortunate fellow. "Sit down, Mrs. Trent. Where are my manners?"

"Thank you, Colonel."

"Warren Smith spoke very highly of you."

"That was kind of him. He's a dear man."

"Warren's a good judge of people and he told me you would be perfect for the committee we're setting up. Actually, what he said was that I absolutely had to have you on this committee."

"That's sweet. If I can be of assistance, I'd like to be."

"Well, we'd love to have you."

"Colonel, I shall serve on your committee gladly, but I think perhaps you should tell me something about it. What do you envision it will do? Your army has been here for some time and I see your Red Cross clubs have been set up to make your soldiers feel more comfortable. I'm not sure I can add to what's already been done."

Helen had a point. The first U.S. soldiers to reach England arrived in January 1942. At first, they were few in number. By September 1943, thousands had sailed east across the Atlantic, but these were few in comparison to the over two million men who would arrive by May 1944, a month before the invasion of France. To acclimate these soldiers, the army issued every American disembarking in England a booklet entitled *A Short Guide to Great Britain* written by the popular novelist Eric Ambler. Of greater interest to the soldiers were the clubs established for their benefit in those cities of England most likely to be visited by U.S. troops. The first such club opened in May 1942. The American Red Cross managed these facilities, with staff from Britain and America. The clubs offered the young soldiers a touch of home, providing food and entertainment, haircuts, and hot showers. The most famous of the Red Cross clubs was called the Rainbow Corner, at the intersection of Shaftesbury and Picadilly. It was open twenty-four hours a day, and stayed in business for thirty-eight months.

"You're right of course, Mrs. Trent. We, the Americans that is, have had some experience in having our young men visit London and your other fine cities. But I must tell you that the Army Air Force is expanding. Right now, we put up three hundred, nearly four hundred bombers each mission. But that's not enough to pulverize Germany. Our aim is to saturate German air space with a thousand bombers every day we fly, while your RAF flies at night. That means more airfields, more planes, more supplies. All that is coming. It also means more young men to fly these planes and more men on the ground to keep them flying.

"So, London will be seeing more Americans in uniform."

"Exactly. There's twenty men on the ground to keep one man in the air. And our bombers carry a crew of ten. So we're going to have literally thousands and thousands of men flooding in to East Anglia."

"And these young men will go on leave."

"Yes, Ma'am. And they'll get two and three days passes as well."

"To let off steam, as you Americans say."

"Yes indeed, Mrs. Trent. These are mostly men in their early twenties, kids really, far from home in a land that's a bit strange to them."

"You mean everyone doesn't drive on the left side of the road?" Helen was smiling as she said this.

"Not in Iowa or Alabama. It's all somewhat foreign to them. But they'll have money in their pockets and be ready to raise hell, if you'll pardon the expression. And many of these youngsters will descend upon London."

Helen laughed and looked at Jimmy Dixon. "It's a good thing London is a big city."

"Yes Ma'am it is. And it's a great city. But it's about to be invaded. Not by the Germans, but by thousands of young American men either homesick or ready to have a good time, or both."

"Colonel, I'm sure you and your colleagues have thought through what needs to be done."

"Mrs. Trent, we have thought about it hard, but we don't have all the answers. Some of our people do, or think they do. But General Ira Eaker, who heads the Eighth Air Force, wants us to do some listening to people who know London and don't have the perspective of military commanders."

"What a lovely and simple idea. And if I may say, how wonderfully American. I cannot imagine English generals doing anything like this."

"No doubt. I can't say most of our generals would either. But Eaker's different. He wants to hear what others have to say."

"Sounds like a remarkable man."

"He is. You're going to meet him shortly."

"I am?"

"Yes Ma'am. The committee meets this Friday. It's the first meeting and General Eaker's going to attend."

Helen Trent and Jimmy Dixon continued talking for twenty minutes. At first, they reviewed the committee's organization and schedule, with Helen making a number of suggestions readily accepted by the American. They then discussed where the committee might meet, deciding that the initial location, the Rainbow club, would be too crowded and lacked a suitable room. Helen suggested the Royal Aeronautical Society at which she and Sir Robert recently had attended a reception. The Society's building, an old mansion in Mayfair, was both elegant and functional. Colonel Dixon replied, "It's a splendid idea, to use a phrase my English friends employ." He then called in Sergeant Howard, instructing him to track down who at the Society he needed to call. The conversation also covered what formal name the committee might have. Neither cared for London Advisory Committee, but were unable to devise a suitable alternative.

"Colonel, when do you anticipate the committee will finish?"

"Mrs. Trent, I think of this a short-term activity. The Eighth is growing fast and the young men are beginning to pour in."

"Quite so."

"I'm thinking December."

"So we have two and a half months. That should be time enough."

"Yes, although my experience tells me that committees take whatever time you give them to do the job."

"I wouldn't know about that, Colonel. I do know the task itself appears perfectly achievable. Surely we can provide a number of helpful suggestions by December."

"I hope so. Because, as the song from World War I says . . . "

TERENCE T. FINN • 113

"The Yanks are coming."

"Yes, Ma'am. We are."

"There are many in Britain extremely pleased that you are. Myself included."

"And more than a few that are not."

"I wouldn't say that, Colonel. A few Englishmen would prefer that we not have to depend on others. And a very few, to be perhaps too candid, simply don't like Americans. I think it really is a matter of pride, you see. We think of our Empire not only as grand, which it is, but also as self-sufficient, which apparently it is not. Most of the people in Britain, the common folk and the upper classes, realize that we alone cannot stop Mr. Hitler."

"Well, we intend to stop him. And, together with the Allies, we shall do just that."

The remaining few minutes of the conversation, which lasted longer than the time allotted on Jimmy Dixon's calendar, dealt with items unrelated to the advisory committee. This more personal conversation, which the Colonel welcomed, began when Helen, after complimenting Dixon on the rug, asked where he had obtained it. Dixon responded, telling Helen of the store in Paddington. She knew of the merchant and told Jimmy that the Indian enjoyed a reputation for quality, although, as she put it, "He's a bit pricey." These remarks led to others, and the two spoke a little of their upbringing and travels. They then briefly discussed what every conversation in 1943 eventually focused upon: the war and how it affected people's lives. The two then parted company.

"I've enjoyed this Mrs. Trent, and I'm delighted you've agreed to join our little committee."

"I look forward to it, Colonel."

"Good. The committee begins its work on Friday at 9:30. We'll see you then."

"I will be there. At the Royal Aeronautical Society."

"Yes. Let's assume the meeting will be there. If it's not, Sergeant Howard will phone you with the new location."

"Fine. Good-bye then."

"Good-bye, Mrs. Trent."

As Helen rose to leave Jimmy Dixon's office, she noticed, not for the first time, the two airplane models on the Colonel's desk. They reminded her of the ship model so treasured by her grandfather, which she, when visiting as a little girl, was strictly forbidden to touch. The model was of HMS *Ivanhoe,* the battlecruiser her grandfather had commanded at Jutland. He was extremely fond of that ship and of the model that stood prominently in the entryway of his home. Helen assumed that Jimmy Dixon was equally devoted to his models. She had noticed that men frequently adorned their offices and homes with models of machines. The models were replicas of automobiles, ships, or airplanes. Apparently, men identified with such machines. Helen was amused by this custom. She considered the models to be playthings. "Men with their toys" was the phrase she employed to describe this fascination men had with things that could be flown, sailed, or driven. Jane Ashcroft and Harriet Pennington shared their friend's amusement. They, too, had noticed the custom. Harriet attributed it to men wishing to proclaim their masculinity. Jane, more thoughtfully, saw the models as a man's way of expressing accomplishment and interest. Helen did not disagree with either Jane or Harriet's interpretation, but she pointed out to both that women felt no similar compulsion.

Once outside in Grosvenor Square, Helen decided to walk home. The weather was clear and, for once, rain had not been in the forecast. Helen crossed Park Lane and entered Hyde Park having decided to take a more idyllic route home.

Like the rest of London, Hyde Park was showing signs of war. Maintenance had been reduced and the flower gardens, while still blooming, had been toned down in number and arrangement. As she walked, Helen saw numerous plots of land turned to agriculture, mostly vegetables. These reflected England's need to grow as much food as possible. The more food the country could grow, the less had to be imported. Imported food had to be purchased and England was short of money. Moreover, such food ran the risk of destruction by submarine. So important to Britain was agriculture that across the entire country, playing fields and village greens had become "allot-ments," small parcels of land rented for farming. In 1943, over 3.5 million such allotments produced vast quantities of vegetables.

More ominous than vegetable patches were the anti-aircraft guns and barrage balloons Helen also saw. The army had sited several bat-teries of guns in Hyde Park to shoot at intruding enemy aircraft. Rarely did the guns strike the enemy, but their presence and noise made Londoners feel better. The balloons were more dangerous to the Luftwaffe. These were filled with gas and tethered to the ground by cable. The danger lay not in the balloon itself, which easily could be avoided. The danger lay in hitting the cable, which could rip apart those parts of the plane necessary for flight: wings, tails, and pro-pellers.

By 1943, the Luftwaffe's presence over London and Southeast England had diminished. Raids consisted of up to twenty fighters armed with a few bombs. While capable of causing damage, these planes were no threat in any strategic sense. The Blitz, in which Hitler, night after night, sent hordes of bombers against London, had occurred two years before. During the winter of 1940-41, one in six Londoners was homeless at some point. But the city held and "London can take it" became a defiant expression in all parts of the city. In May 1941, despite a raid that killed 1,436 people, the Germans abandoned hope of defeating England from the air. Not until June 1944 was the city again threatened. This time the V-1 vis-ited London. These were small, rocket-powered guided missiles. The Germans had many of them—2,340 reached the city and caused considerable damage. Later in the war, London was terrorized by the V-2, the world's first ballistic missile.

As Helen walked toward the Serpentine, many men, most of whom were in uniform, passed by her. These were soldiers, sailors, and airmen all moving more briskly than she. Each was dressed in the distinctive garb of their service. In 1943, London was a focal point of military efforts to defeat Germany. Every nation involved in the fighting had men assigned to the city. Their job was to formulate the plans of battle while concurrently protecting the interests of their service and country. Helen recognized many of the uniforms, but not all. She could identify the uniforms of Canada, the United States, and of course, Great Britain. Because Robert had once served in Malta, she was familiar with the khaki of the King's Own Malta Regiment. Because she had spent time in France with Peter, she recognized the uniforms of the Free French. She did not recognize, as many in London did not, the uniforms of men from Norway, Holland, Poland and Czechoslovakia. These men had fled to England to continue the fight once Germany had overrun their countries.

As she walked, Helen played the silly game she had taught Claire. She decided that a burly seaman of the Royal Navy was a portrait painter of the Royal Academy. A well-tailored American soldier was a jockey running an errand. And an overweight officer in the RAF was in fact a professional boxer in training for his next match.

Helen left the park at the Alexander Gate near the Royal Albert Hall. She continued south, turning right onto Cromwell Road. From there, it was six blocks to 28 Temple Court.

In one of the blocks, bomb damage was severe. This was unusual since most of the destruction in London occurred in the East End. Here, west of Buckingham Palace, damage had been relatively light. But not in this one block. A string of bombs from two Me-110s had knocked apart several buildings. Sidewalks were uprooted and the area was pocketed with three deep craters. The bombing had occurred recently as Helen noticed firemen and air raid wardens still at work sifting through wreckage. But she smiled at the sight of a sign on one of the buildings. The building, off Gloucester Road, contained a barbershop. A hand painted sign in the fractured front window read, "We've had a close shave. You should, too."

Once home, Helen went upstairs and changed clothes. She exchanged her navy blue suit for a pink cotton shirt and drab workman's pants. Then she went downstairs to the back closet and grabbed a kerchief, and headed out to the garden where her flowers still showed some color, although their peak period clearly had passed. Her vegetable garden was doing well, but was in dire need of weeding.

For the next two hours, Helen worked in the garden, tending the vegetables. The flowers she left for another day. The vegetables were mostly tomatoes, brussels sprouts, and cabbage. There were potatoes, of course, and a few green beans and carrots. Helen was not a natural gardener. Digging around in the dirt was not an activity she had done much of in her youth. But, she was determined to do her part in this aspect of British wartime life and so, armed with several booklets on gardening issued by the Ministry of Agriculture, Helen Trent had devoted a good portion of her backyard to vegetables. However, she made sure that the flowers she loved were allotted their fair share of the land. The results, to Helen at least, were entirely satisfactory. With some flowers present, the garden produced decent quality vegetables, which, on more than one occasion, she would share with Clara Harris.

While Helen had more than enough vegetables, her supply of meat, fresh eggs, butter, sugar, and cheese was extremely limited. These basic foodstuffs, and others, were rationed. The government issued ration books containing coupons that were exchanged for food. Adults were limited to four ounces of meat, two ounces of butter, and three ounces of cheese per week. Sugar, so necessary for satisfying an Englishman's sweet tooth, was restricted to eight ounces each seven-day period. People would queue in line at food shops where books would be checked meticulously to ensure equitable distribution of limited stocks. At the start of the war, experts worried that rationing might impair the health of the populace. Their concerns proved unfounded. In fact, people remained in remarkably good health throughout the conflict. These same experts later attributed this to the low fat, low calorie, nutritious diet brought about by rationing.

After working in the garden, Helen returned to the kitchen to fix herself a light noonday meal to eat. She had a dab of the potato salad she had made the day before, along with a fresh salad of cold green beans and tomatoes, plus two slices of bread. She enjoyed a cup of tea as well. Sitting there in her kitchen, she realized how fortunate she was to have sufficient food. Neither she nor Robert went hungry. Rationing was hard on everyone, but they were able to manage quite well. Helen did, however, yearn for fresh oranges, which were no longer available.

Helen was a better cook than gardener, so supper was more often than not a pleasant experience. Helen listened to the BBC's *Kitchen Front* broadcasts and collected recipes from several wartime cookbooks. The book she found most useful was the *Good Housekeeping Book of Thrifty War-Time Recipes.* With numerous recipes to choose from, Helen made a concerted effort to vary the menu and avoid the monotony associated with rationing. Sir Robert acknowledged her efforts, although at least twice a week, he would dine at his club or make do at one of the many receptions his position required him to attend.

On those occasions, Helen would have supper alone. At first, she had been lonely. But as time passed, Helen came to appreciate, even enjoy, the solitude. On those occasions she would eat in the dining room, listening to the BBC or to music on the Victrola. The dining room had a large mahogany table capable of easily seating ten people—more when leaves were inserted. Helen would sit on the side nearest the kitchen, at the chair near the end. It was her spot. There she would quietly take her meal and think about the day and what lay ahead. Often, she would remember Peter and how sweet life used to be. Always, she would think of Claire, and trust that all was well at Roedean.

After the midday meal, Helen went upstairs to take a bath. This she did at least three times a week. Usually, she bathed later in the day, but today she was having tea with Clara Harris. Tea would be in two hours, which gave Helen time to wash off the evidence of gardening and to rest a bit. As the water swished around her, she again realized her good fortune in having a life of considerable comfort. Helen knew that many in England did not. The country was at war and people's homes were destroyed and loved ones were lost. Helen faced neither hardship. How horrible it must be to hear that one's child is no longer alive. She shuddered at the thought.

All at once, sitting in the tub, having momentarily contemplated the death of her daughter, Helen Trent felt very much alone. Peter was gone. Claire, very much alive, was off at school. Robert was present, but inattentive. There was no one with whom she might share her most personal thoughts—not even with Jane Ashcroft, who was a dear and devoted friend. There was no one to listen to when she needed to talk and express what was on her mind. There was no one close by to touch to tell what was on her mind and in her heart. There was no one to hold; no one to be held by.

Once experiencing this loneliness, Helen felt ashamed. Here she was feeling lonely and a tad sorry for herself. Her face wrinkled in self-disappointment. How could she focus upon herself when others faced true hardship and grief.

"Enough of such thoughts" she said aloud, rising to towel off. Helen continued to speak, but silently and to herself. *I shall banish my loneliness away with will power and activity. I have no reason to feel sorry for myself, so I shall not. Not only do I live quite nicely, thank you very much, I am blessed with a marvelous child. Robert is at least civil and provides for us all. And I'm about to do something useful again, this time with the Americans.*

Now Helen spoke aloud again. "And I'm due at Clara's in twenty minutes, so now I shall have to hurry."

"My dear, how good of you to come." Clara Harris was opening the front door of her small house.

"It's so nice to see you, Clara." Helen's expression was heartfelt. She felt genuine affection for her neighbor.

"Please come in. You look well."

"It is good to see you. All is well with you, I hope?" Helen worried about Clara. She was all alone; her husband had been killed. There could not be an abundance of funds.

"Yes, all is fine. As good as can be expected." Clara led Helen into the small parlor where on the table, biscuits and jam were laid out. Let me get the tea."

"That would be lovely." Across from the table, upon the mantle was the picture Helen noticed each time she visited with Clara Harris. The picture was a photograph, elegantly framed, of a young woman alongside a handsome man in an army uniform. The two were standing in front of Stonehenge. The man was William Harris. He had fought bravely at Dunkirk and now was dead. Clara was left with but memories of what had been a happy marriage.

"I've no sugar, Helen dear. I'm so sorry."

"Not to mind. There's so little sugar, I'm learning to live without." Helen and Clara would learn to live without sugar for some time. The rationing continued until 1953.

"I do have some milk."

"Lovely, just a bit, thank you." Helen had sat down while Clara brought in the tea along with a tiny china creamer filled halfway with milk.

The parlor was comfortably furnished in an old fashioned way. Heavy burgundy drapes covered both windows, letting little light fill the room. A large well-worn winged chair sat in one corner next to a lamp that had a cloth shade draped about its frame. Next to the lamp was a small table. Upon the table were two large glass ashtrays. These were companions to the rack of pipes placed upon the mantle next to the photograph. Helen could visualize Colonel Harris sitting at ease in the chair reading *The Times*. He had been a particularly gentle man, surprising perhaps for one in his line of work. Devoted to the army, equally devoted to Clara, William Harris had been one of those solid, decent men upon whom England depended in time of need. He had gone to France with the British Expeditionary Force full of courage and hope. Now what little remained of his body lay in a crude cemetery established by the Germans for those not evacuated from the Dunkirk beaches.

"That was a lovely dinner party last week, Helen. And you were so sweet to invite me."

"Good. I'm glad you could come and trust that you had a pleasant time."

"I did indeed. You give such lovely parties, dear. It was all just perfect. And that nice American walked me home."

"Wasn't he a pleasant man? I hope all Americans are like him." Helen then told Clara of her chance meeting with Warren Smith along Regent Street and of the cashmere scarf, the bill for which he had insisted upon paying.

"How nice of him to do that."

"Yes, it truly was."

"And how is that daughter of yours?"

"She is well and away at school."

"Claire is such a dear little thing."

"Not so little anymore, Clara. The little girl you knitted that precious sweater for is now fourteen."

"Oh my. Time passes so quickly."

"It does indeed. I think that's how we measure time. I mean, parents do. Children grow up before their eyes and make them aware of how quickly time has moved along. When a child first rides a bicycle or goes off to school, it's a sign they're growing up, getting older. And if our children are older, how much older must we be. As our children age, we become aware that we are no longer what we were."

"I suppose you're quite correct. So Claire is now fourteen. I know it to be true and yet I remember so well the day we met. You were pushing her in the pram."

"Yes, a sweet moment, now a dear memory. For both of us."

"She'll be a woman soon."

"Oh dear, I know. And I want her to be. But at the same time . . ."

"You wish she could stay . . ."

"Cute and cuddly."

"But they don't."

"No, Claire is growing up, as she must."

"You miss her, don't you?"

"Oh Clara, I do miss her. And love her so. I think she's the reason I exist. To keep her safe, to make sure she's loved. To be there when she needs someone to turn to."

"She's a wonderful young girl. A perfect young lady."

"Not perfect, but she is wonderful. She's full of life, a flower about to blossom. I want so very much for all to be well with her."

"Mothers do."

"I suppose that's right."

"Did she know her father?" Clara had asked this question before. Helen thought that her neighbor simply had forgotten she had done so, attributing the repetition to Clara's age. Not so. Clara had noticed that Helen acquired a wistful serenity whenever she spoke of Claire's father. Helen's voice betrayed not pain, but love. Therefore, every so often, Clara would ask something of Helen that enabled the younger woman to voice her feelings and thoughts about the man she had loved, honored, and obeyed.

"Not really. Claire was four when Peter died."

Peter. The mention of his name brought to Helen's mind images and feelings she kept safely stored in her heart. For a moment, sitting across from Clara Harris, she separated from her surroundings, focusing upon the man she had married. Younger then, caring passionately for this handsome solicitor who sounded more like a poet than one devoted to the law, Helen pictured in detail how they had met and how they had become friends before they became lovers. Peter was someone with whom she felt safe and at ease. They could communicate easily and no topics were taboo or awkward. Never had she felt so connected to another human being. At first, Peter had been uncomfortable with sex. That soon changed and their physical relationship became compelling. Their lovemaking was frequent, exhausting, and satisfying. They particularly liked to make love when dressed for dining out. Peter would peel off her clothes and Helen would tremble with desire and expectation. They also liked to travel. Peter had a motorcycle and trips to the Continent were not infrequent. Helen would climb aboard the leather seat and off they would go. Holland, France, and Belgium were a few of their favorite destinations. They would ride through Germany as well.

Germany. What they saw they did not like. As they cycled about, brown shirts and economic hardships were much in evidence. Helen remembered when she and Peter had seen Adolph Hitler. He was riding in an open Mercedes being cheered by people on both sides of the street. Peter had remarked that this little man, who soon was to be appointed Reich Chancellor, seemed far more menacing in person than he appeared in British newspapers.

Their life together ended in Germany. Helen and Peter had spent the day touring the coast north of Wilehmshaven. The sun was setting as they returned to their hotel. Another Mercedes, this one a coupe at great speed, sideswiped their motorcycle. They went off the road, hit gravel, and skidded out of control. Helen landed in a marsh, which cushioned her fall. Peter was not as lucky. He flew into a stone wall. At first, only bones appeared broken, but much internal bleeding occurred and he died later that night.

"I still miss him, Clara."

"I know, Dear. And you always will. But you have the sweetest of memories and you have a child in whom he will always live.

"How true. Often I see something of Peter in Claire. It's remarkable and so very sweet."

"From what you've said, Peter was someone who delighted in life, as your daughter seems to."

"Yes, he did. Peter was one of those people who enjoyed whatever he was doing. Reading the law, riding his motorcycle, even paying the bills—he always seemed in fine spirits." As she spoke, Helen's face was aglow. She was pleased to recall memories of Peter, as Clara knew she would be. Once painful, these memories were easier to think about now. "Peter's love of life would put me in good spirits. It was contagious. I did love him so. He made me feel as though I was at the center of his universe."

"Men in love, men who are wise, do that."

"I wasn't, of course, but I felt as though I was. To have had such a man makes everything now seem slightly out of focus."

"Yes, Helen, I know that to be so." Looking up at the stack of pipes upon the mantle, Clara Harris was recalling memories of her own.

Helen stayed at Clara's for just over an hour. Their conversation encompassed more than commentary about Claire and her father. Helen told Clara about her meeting with Colonel Dixon and said she looked forward to serving on the advisory committee. Clara expressed great interest in the committee, commenting that it was just what Helen needed to feel part of the war effort. They talked about the war itself and the havoc it wreaked. They saw 1943 as another year when families were broken apart, fathers and sons killed, and civilians placed in peril alongside those in uniform. As women, they focused less upon grand strategy and more upon the war's impact upon people. Both Clara Harris and Helen Trent believed England needed to emerge victorious and would do so. But their concern was for men and women everywhere who were trapped in this cauldron of death and destruction.

Clara and Helen also talked about England and the changes likely to occur once the war was over. Each loved their country and thought it special, yet each knew that postwar England had to be different. Clara believed that more generous pensions had to be made available. She was worried about making ends meet now that William was gone. Helen, influenced by the Ashcrofts, thought a totally different approach to health care was needed.

They also discussed rationing. Helen again had brought Clara some vegetables, mostly tomatoes. The widow accepted them with thanks. She then remarked to Helen that she was about to use eleven coupons for a new dress. For not only was food rationed in England during the war, so was clothing. Beginning in June 1941, garments for men and women were hard to come by. Everyone received sixty-six coupons for an entire year, in a ration book issued by the Board of Trade. Different items required a different number of coupons. Shoes, for example, cost five coupons. A man's three piece suit required twenty-six coupons. With new clothes in short supply, many folks added to their wardrobes by making their own garments. The nation of shopkeepers had become a nation of tailors. Aided by dozens of instructional manuals and garment patterns that minimized the amounts of material needed, the women of England, and men too, took up needle and thread, and began to sew. "Make do and mend" was a slogan heard everyday in every corner of the Realm.

That evening, Helen mentioned her meeting with Jimmy Dixon to Sir Robert. She also told him of her decision to accept the Colonel's invitation to join the advisory committee. His reaction was not what she had expected.

"I suppose if you must." Sir Robert was reading a newspaper. He spoke quietly, in a voice reflecting resignation. He knew Helen would join one organization or another, so her announcement caused no surprise. In responding to her, Sir Robert had decided not to raise a fuss, as he realized she was unlikely to be dissuaded.

But there was more to his acceptance of Helen's decision. Sir Robert had reflected upon her remark of days before that her visibility in wartime work would be beneficial to his career. The more he thought about it, the more he concluded she was correct. Speaking to his Principal Assistant at the Colonial Office, Sir Robert had raised the subject of Helen's return to volunteer service.

"I should say so, Sir. A jolly good idea." Hugh Williams was a young man recently graduated from Oxford. The Deputy Permanent Secretary for Colonial Affairs had concluded his young assistant's judgment was quite sound for someone his age. "Women are accepting positions to help themselves and the war effort. And, by doing so, they bring credit to their sex and . . . " the Principal Assistant paused, "to those to whom they're married. I should say having your lovely lady out front, so to speak, would be helpful in many ways." In conversation, Hugh Williams always referred to Helen or the wife of any senior officer as "your lovely lady."

"Quite so, Hugh. I suspect you're on the mark." Sir Robert knew that obtaining an ambassadorship after the war would not be easy, but he thought it well within his grasp. A woman as attractive and convivial as Helen would make a good impression everywhere. And she would widen his circle of acquaintances.

Now, putting aside his newspaper, he spoke again to Helen. "But must it be for the Americans?"

"Robert, they are our allies. And Colonel Dixon on behalf of the Americans is asking for our advice."

"Which they most likely will not follow."

"Perhaps. Perhaps not. I think it's good form of them to ask, and rather splendid that they're here."

"God, are they ever here. One cannot walk in London without seeing Americans." Sir Robert Trent disliked both the U.S. and its citizens. In this, he was not alone. Many in Britain, particularly among the upper classes, considered Americans boorish and provincial. "Americans are terribly loud and frequently ill mannered. And, I might add, they seem rather poorly educated."

"Perhaps some are. But many are not, and you should not generalize."

Sir Robert heard Helen, but did not listen. "And they have little grasp of strategy as that American fellow Smith so amply demonstrated here in this very house."

"Perhaps they simply disagree with what the Government proposes."

"Nonsense. God help us if Roosevelt continues to act like Woodrow Wilson. They simply don't understand the realities of power."

"I doubt that's true, Robert. In any case, they're now our guests."

"Guests? I suppose so. Though they seem to have invaded our island, with their pockets full of money and their mouths full of gum. I'm not sure which is more disgusting. And they talk a great deal, mostly about themselves."

"You exaggerate. And I think you're being unkind. The Yanks are perfectly pleasant people, informal like the Australians. Though perhaps with twice the energy. Think of them as a large shaggy dog trying to be friendly with everyone in the room while wrecking some of the china with its wagging tail."

"I wish they were wrecking Germany. They seem to talk a lot, and they haven't accomplished much." Sir Robert had a point. By September 1943, the Americans had done little fighting, except in North Africa where, initially, they had been soundly beaten by the

Africa Corps. In time, their army improved and fought well, as the Germans learned in Sicily and Salerno. But in Britain, which had been fighting for nearly four years, many felt the Americans were late to the struggle and lacking in military skill. These people believed the newcomers had not yet earned the right to talk as much as they did.

"They'll do fine. I'm sure. Bravery and skill are not limited to British forces. And I understand they do rather well at supply and transport. Someone wrote in *The Times* last week that American soldiers were superbly equipped."

Here, Helen's remark was right on target. In World War II, no nation mastered logistics as well as the United States. The country produced vast quantities of equipment and deployed material and men to every corner of the globe, on a scale never before seen. In battle the British, Russian, German, and Japanese soldiers were full of courage. In logistics, they all played second fiddle to the Americans.

"They should be well equipped. Their factories have not been bombed, their homes are all intact, and their troops have shed precious little blood. Moreover, they've taken their jolly good time in getting over here, just like the last time. They let us bleed and then come in to finish the job, and take most of the credit."

"Robert, that's an awful thing to say. And you know better than that." Helen spoke sharply. Her voice expressed irritation. She disliked his tendency to cast judgment upon groups of people rather than individuals. And, in this instance, she believed Sir Robert to be totally wrong. "The Americans have their own problems. Half of them are what they call isolationists who think America should leave Europe and its politics alone."

"My dear, I'll repeat what I've said. They came over late in the hour, when the crisis is nearly over, and then assume they know how best to proceed. It's damn irritating."

"I'm sure it is, but I suspect they find our generals a bit much as well."

"They'd do much better if they listened to our chaps. Their General Eisenhower seems an agreeable fellow, but he's hardly up to leading the combined armies into battle."

"Robert, you're talking as though the U.S. is a dominion, part of the Empire. America's not like Canada or New Zealand. There's no bond to king and country."

"My dear, I hadn't realized you were so keen on the Yanks. I suspect you'll do just fine with that Colonel Dixon and his friends."

Helen remained silent for a moment. Why was she seeming to appear so pro-American? She had met several Americans, and they all seemed pleasant enough. But she had not visited the States, although she was familiar with its geography as a result of her interest in maps. Nor had she before spoken out in defense of the United States. After giving the matter more thought Helen concluded she was reacting to Robert, to his obvious dislike of America, and to his horrid habit of disparaging groups of people rather than singling out individuals for his displeasure. Helen Trent was no saint, but she found this habit extremely distasteful.

"Robert, I don't know if I'm pro-American or not. Perhaps I am. I do know that the Americans share our values. They speak our language. We come from the same stock."

"Ah, so they're our country cousins."

"Don't be flip. Values matter, particularly in today's world. They believe in the God we believe in. They believe in freedom and democracy as we do. They believe that individuals matter."

"Now I suppose you want me to admire their 'all men are created equal' rubbish. Really, Helen. I thought you knew better. The Americans want to be chums with everyone. Their beloved equality is poppycock, and you know it. What happens is that Americans bring everything down to the lowest common denominator. Refinement and good taste are lost. The Americans are rich, and sad to say, quite powerful, but they are hardly the types one would choose to be associated with."

"So you'd not have them as members of your club."

"Heavens no." For a moment, Sir Robert imagined what it would be like to have Americans at the Collingwood and he visibly paled. "The club is for English gentlemen—men of standing, men of accomplishment. It's hardly the place for Americans. Admit them to membership and next would come the followers of Abraham."

Sir Robert's anti-Semitic remark reflected a prejudice not uncommon in England. Among the upper classes, Jews were often unwelcome—this despite England's tolerance of religious diversity.

By now, Helen had heard enough. Visibly irritated, she spoke coldly. "Robert, at times like this you make me feel ashamed. Ashamed of you, ashamed of Britain. Remarks about Jewish people are uncalled for, especially now when so many have fled persecution from the Nazis. And we were talking, let me remind you, about the Americans, who certainly have their faults. God don't we all. The Americans have come to England to help us win the war. Their young men are going to die just like our young men are going to die. Instead of belittling them, I think we should be grateful for their help. To me, they are guests in our land and we should treat them as such."

Sir Robert could see that Helen was upset and he heard the anger in her voice. Deciding that little good would result by continuing to talk about Americans, he chose to steer the conversation elsewhere. In doing so, his demeanor changed. Gone was the Englishman relaxing at home expressing what he truly felt. That man was replaced by the Sir Robert Trent of Whitehall, the always pleasant civil servant who remained calm no matter how disagreeable the subject.

"Dear, let us not quarrel. You're upset and I regret having made you so." His regret was sincere. Experience told Sir Robert little was accomplished when Helen was angry.

Helen recognized the transformation. Many times before Robert had done the same thing. Usually, she would react by talking about something else, having recognized his signal. This time, sitting in the green chair in the living room, she remained silent. Still upset at his views about Americans and uncomfortable with his remark about Jews, Helen simply stared at the man across the room.

Her mind switched time and place. Images were projected upon her consciousness. She saw a younger man who resembled the now senior civil servant with whom she had just conversed. Thinner then, he was driving the SS Jaguar 100 alongside the Thames, on the road to Windsor. She was next to him, in the left front seat. A picnic basket sat in the back. He was serious, but not shy. Obviously bright, he had impressed her with his quickness of mind and determination to succeed. They drove to Windsor, finding a spot to stop where they could sit on the grass and see both the river and castle. He told her of his childhood, of his ambition, and of his loneliness. He said she was the most interesting girl he had ever met and certainly the most beautiful. She looked at this young man who promised devotion and a second start at life. He said he would protect little Claire and take exquisite care of her mother. The man at the picnic proposed marriage. She said no, but he did not accept the response. With charm and persistence, with sincerity and devotion, the young man who wanted this woman for a wife eventually got what he desired.

She was not in love, at least not as once before, but she saw much that was good and admirable in this man. He appeared neither unkind nor selfish. He was intrigued with ideas and collected books much like a Cambridge don. He mixed well with people. He enjoyed music and the theater and dressed with great care and style. If he lacked sexual energy, he provided an intellectual passion, which, with his genuine friendship, made for comfortable and rewarding companionship. And he certainly said he was in love. Most importantly, he showed affection for Claire and promised the young girl a bright future.

Over time, Sir Robert Trent changed.

The man Helen now lived with at 28 Temple Court was not the man at the picnic. He had become self-absorbed. Maybe he always had been and she had not noticed. His ambition, once admirable, had become all consuming. He also had become arrogant. As he advanced in the civil service, power and position went to his head.

Respect for the views of others declined. Faint signs of pomposity emerged. His charm remained, but to Helen, it now seemed insincere, seemingly produced for the moment at hand. Gradually, he drifted away from the woman along the Thames. Devoted to his work, he engaged less and less in meaningful conversation. To his credit, he did provide for Claire, who prospered. And he did enable Helen to live comfortably, with a circle of friends she now had the wherewithal to enjoy. But Sir Robert had pursued a life centered upon himself and his career. The woman he married was now but an adjunct to his ambition. Sir Robert enjoyed his life immensely. He was not lonely, nor did he notice nor care that the same could not be said of the person with whom he lived.

That person had tried to love Sir Robert. She had done her very best. Helen worked hard taking care of him and of their home. She supported his career and, indeed, had helped it along. She had met his friends and entertained them expertly. She had slept with him whenever he wished, though their short-lived lovemaking was neither frequent nor satisfying. Early on, the encounters in bed had disappeared altogether.

Helen was now trapped, locked in a marriage that from the outside looked fine, but in fact, was hollow. Strong in appearances, the union lacked the intimacy and friendship that can so deeply unite a man and woman.

Helen understood her situation. She always had been self aware. She knew that in many ways she was fortunate. Her daughter was safe and healthy. She herself retained a comfortable life, despite the war. Moreover, she realized that many women in England would gladly exchange their life for hers. Yet Helen Trent knew something was missing. Something Peter had provided and Robert clearly did not. And being a perceptive individual, she knew what that something was.

"Ahem. I say Helen, have you heard what I've just said?"

"Yes, Robert. Well, actually no." The images of years gone by disappeared. Helen's thoughts were brought back to the present by Sir

Robert's voice and the question it posed. "I'm sorry. I was just think-ing, do tell me again."

"Well, as I was starting to say," Sir Robert was frowning at the woman in the green chair, choosing not to inquire what Helen was thinking. He was more interested in what he was about to say. "I shall be traveling a bit in November and December. Business, of course. The Government wants to prepare an analysis of postwar politics in the Colonies and I shall be visiting several of them to hear what they themselves feel is likely to happen."

"Will you be gone long?"

"Quite likely a good bit of November and all of December."

"Oh dear. Robert that means you'll be away at Christmas."

"I'm afraid so. Don't want to be, of course, but duty calls, as they say."

"Might you not arrange a return in time for Christmas?" For Helen, Christmas was a special time of the year, to be celebrated at home with family. The Christmas spirit was real to Helen Trent. She decorated the house, played carols on the Victrola, and imparted cheer and good will to all she encountered. At Christmas, Claire would be home, so the season was especially dear. The three of them would spend Christmas Eve at church, usually St. Andrew's, although once they had gone to the midnight service at Westminster Abbey. The next morning they celebrated with presents and visits from close friends. That all was not blissful did not matter. Christmas tran-scended marital unhappiness. Helen believed December 25 was a time to rejoice in the glory of God. It meant giving thanks for all the blessings life brought, or had brought. This included life with Robert, as well as treasured memories of Peter. For this forty-three year old woman who cherished the season, Christmas was a time of friendship and forgiveness, of peace and joy to the world.

"I'm afraid not."

"I guess if you must, you must." The news of Sir Robert's trip made Helen realize she would be alone for some time. She did not mind being able to come and go as she pleased and not having to work around someone else's schedule. These were part of the pleasures of having a house all to yourself. Yet, at the same time, the solitude would produce a sense of loneliness. The house would be empty and unusually quiet.

Thus, Helen was ambivalent towards Sir Robert's news. This did not trouble her. She recognized the ambivalence for what it was. She realized the two feelings were at odds with one another. But as both feelings were genuine, she remained unperturbed and let the reactions sit side by side in her mind.

"What is your schedule, Robert? When will you be leaving?"

"The first week of November, I believe. We fly to Gibraltar and then to Africa. There is a delegation. I shall be leading it."

"That's good news, and well deserved. You'll enjoy that." Despite the less than perfect relationship they had, Helen wished Sir Robert well in his career, knowing how important it was to him. "And no doubt do a splendid job."

"Thank you, my dear. That's good of you to say. I shall have an itinerary soon, which I'm not allowed to share with anyone, although I will tell you the general outline. Hugh Williams is not going, so you will be able to get in touch with him should the need arise." Sir Robert then cleared his throat and spoke somewhat less authoritatively. "There is one other thing I wish to discuss. To ask you, really."

"And what is that?" Helen was not used to hearing Sir Robert speak hesitantly.

"I should like to have a reception here, in mid October, in the evening with a good number of people. I shall be gone for sometime and would like to see our friends and a few colleagues before I depart."

"I don't see why not." Helen's response was mostly automatic. Entertaining was a responsibility she accepted unfailingly as spouse to the Deputy Permanent Secretary for Colonial Affairs. "Though food might be a problem."

"Well, you shall have to work your charms with the Collingwood. I'd like this to be a smashing success. So we shall spend what we need to."

"I'm sure we can do something quite nice. I'll first need a firm date and idea of who's to come."

"Quite so. I shall have them for you shortly." He paused. "And thank you my dear." Sir Robert's expression of appreciation was genuine.

"You're welcome."

Eager to avoid complications about the reception that might arise from further discussion, and wishing to seal Helen's acceptance, he once again purposefully changed the subject. Again, his demeanor changed. Gone was the hesitancy in his voice. His face broke into a smile and he spoke in a friendly, slightly gruff tone.

"And now I shall retire upstairs. I've a few papers still to review tonight and I hope to read another chapter in my book." Each night, Sir Robert read before he went to sleep. Currently, he was reading R. W. Seaton-Watson's *Disraeli, Gladstone, and the Eastern Question.*

"Good night then."

"Good night my dear." With this, Sir Robert rose and left the room. No kiss went Helen's way. No sign of affection. He simply walked out of the living room, unaware that a gesture of warmth might be in order.

Helen was not surprised by the nature of his departure. Robert's nightly procedure was much the same. A few words, a pleasant "good night," and he then withdrew. Helen thought the truly sad part was that she now expected little else. Nonetheless, this behavior hurt. Helen told herself the hurt was very small, more like disappointment. Whatever the nature of her reaction, Sir Robert's evening withdrawal was something she felt, as well as witnessed.

Helen remained in the green chair for twenty minutes before deciding it was time for her to retire also. The day had been busy, but productive. Except for the after-dinner conversation with Robert about Americans, it also had been enjoyable. She had had a good first meeting with Colonel Dixon, she had worked in the garden, and she had had a pleasant visit with Clara Harris.

As always, when bedtime beckoned, she thought of Claire. Such a dear child. Helen prayed that all was well with her daughter.

Climbing into bed, she sent a bunch of hugs and kisses in the direction of Roedean.

Lying in bed, Helen pulled up the covers as a chill was in the room, reflecting the temperature outside. September meant the end of warm weather. While not yet present, winter was not far down the calendar.

Soon she began to relax and fall asleep. She thought briefly about the reception. There would be much to do. Then other thoughts came to mind, thoughts far more compelling than any reception. She saw images of Peter and recalled how it felt when they were together. So sweet were these memories, so vivid that Helen blushed. But not for long. Soon, her mind's eye and a pressing need from her body's depths directed a slow, rhythmic movement of her hand. She gasped and shuddered as the rush filled her. At the height of her pleasure, she imagined the smell and strength of a man. She remembered the sense of connection, physical and otherwise, two people in love provided each other. There, safely in her bed, Helen wondered whether Peter would be the only man to capture her heart. The answer came to her as the warmth from inside subsided. It was not what she might have produced by analysis or intellect. It was a feeling, something beyond her control, that reflected a sense of urgency from within her very being. Ever self aware, she recognized its simplicity and veracity. For the first time in years, Helen Trent admitted to herself that she would like to love again.

Six

All across East Anglia, RAF and American pilots, returning home from attacks upon the Continent, had great difficulty in landing due to bad weather. This was not so for Forester. After escorting the two Spitfires safely home, he and his three companions had encountered heavy clouds, which forced them to fly in tight formation, barely visible to one another. But a break in the clouds occurred near Ipswich. Forester, who had been conversing with himself about the discipline required for flying in such dreadful weather, was able to confirm his location and set a more precise course for Bromley Park.

A few seconds after Ipswich appeared, it was hidden again. Forester's flight had reentered the clouds, but Tom was not worried. He knew where they were and he was certain he could bring the flight down. Not all his pilots shared his confidence. Over the radio, one of them spoke up with a voice that betrayed anxiety.

"Trumpet, this is Snowflake Red 4. My fuel's pretty low, Colonel. I've got about five minutes of flight time left. Maybe I ought to hit the silk."

"This is Trumpet, Red 4. We'll be on the ground in three minutes. Keep descending and keep formation. I'll get you down, Red 4. Just stay calm."

Forester was calm and knew that they were on course. And he knew that were they not, it was far too early to abandon the aircraft. Parachuting might become necessary, but only as a last resort. Abandoning the P-47s meant losing four aircraft, which would endanger the people below. One P-47 could easily demolish a house. Through Tom's mind flashed the thought that American fighter pilots were in England to help the British, not kill them, which was likely to happen should four P-47s come falling down out of the sky.

As he spoke to Snowflake Red 4, Forester and his flight broke free of the clouds. They were now at 1,000 feet. Above, like a blanket, was the seemingly endless watery mist. Once bright white, it was now a dull color, a white that had been mixed with a touch of black. Below was the ground. This was dark green, dark brown, and dingy grey, not at all welcoming. Everything looked wet, soaked through, although the rain was but a light drizzle. Visibility was poor, but Tom could see St. Stephen's Church off to the left. The church was in the town south of Bromley Park. Its twin spires served to mark the approach to the airfield. With the spires in sight, Tom felt that he could reach the runway with his eyes closed.

Now, Tom the instructor was telling Tom the pilot to keep his eyes open and get ready to set the four aircraft down upon a 6,000 foot strip of concrete that comprised Runway 26. Landing a P-47 required total concentration. Forester knew the task to be more difficult than taking off. When taking off, the pilot merely shoved the throttle forward, kept the plane straight, and let the physics of flight do the hard part, namely lifting a 13,500-pound fighter plane into the air. Landing a P-47, or a similar aircraft, called for genuine skill. Altitude, direction, speed, wind velocity, alignment, and rate of descent all had to be integrated quickly in order to place the plane in exactly the right spot. A 6,000 foot runway might appear rather long. To an exhausted pilot, flying a heavy plane in bad weather with a fuel gauge near empty, the strip was far too short, leaving little margin for error.

"This is Trumpet to Snowflake Red Flight. Spread out a bit and follow me." To his left, Forester saw Ennis ease away while Red 3 and 4 expanded the distance between their own aircraft and Forester's. "Standard approach and touch down, but stay low on the turn."

At once, Tom remembered Snowflake Red 4's fuel situation, and the pilot's worry. "Scratch that. Red 4, you go directly in. It's clear with the tower." After seeing Ipswich, Forester had raised Bromley Park by radio and advised the field of their situation. In turn, the tower had provided navigational assistance reinforcing Tom's own calculations.

"This is Trumpet. Red 2 and 3, stay with me. We'll do the standard. Let's look sharp."

Looking sharp was important. Eighth Air Force planes, after combat with the Luftwaffe, attempted to approach their home airfields in battle formation. A source of pride, the returning formation demonstrated the professionalism of airmen and the *esprit de corps* of the squadrons involved. As importantly, the formation sustained the morale of those below, many of whom viewed the aircraft as their own. All personnel, those who flew and those who didn't, equated sloppy flying with poor performance. Forester, though not a stickler for things military, had little tolerance for anything sloppy. He wanted the 19th Fighter Group to succeed, to perform the very best it could. To Tom, this included looking sharp, both in the sky and on the ground.

Once he saw that Snowflake Red 4 had gear down and was over the runway, Forester spoke to the remaining two pilots. "This is Trumpet. Okay Red 2 and Red 3, let's go."

The three P-47s came across the field, parallel to Runway 26 at 200 feet. Forester led, with Snowflake Red 3 and 4 in echelon right. The planes were moving rapidly. Air speed indicators registered 375 mph. The noise was extreme. With engines near full throttle, the aircraft gave off a thundering and decidedly belligerent sound.

Walking to his Jeep, which was parked outside the Operations Building, Harry Collins heard the returning fighters and looked up. He had often seen Forester and others on the deck, flying low and fast. Yet every time, he found the sight impressive. To Harry, P-47s were special. He felt a kinship with them. Rain or shine, the Group Intelligence Officer never failed to watch the big planes come home. Nor would he fail to meet Forester at the end of a mission, giving him a lift to the post flight interrogation, which he, as Intelligence Officer, conducted. As Collins saw the three fighters prepare to land, he once again felt envious of those who flew P-47s. Yet, at the same time, he was thankful—thankful that his wartime service, which he realized was but an interlude in an otherwise conventional life, had brought him in contact with these aircraft and their pilots. Harry Collins was a wise man. He knew that life at Bromley Park was more exciting and more useful than anything he had done or would do.

Halfway down the runway, Forester peeled off to the left in a shallow turning climb. At three-second intervals, Snowflake Red 2 and 3 did the same. The maneuver was a bit theatrical, though not uncommon. It served to place the aircraft, after a turn of 360 degrees, at the forward end of the runway with the concrete ready to receive the descending fighter.

As Forester flew the circle, he made ready to land. Ailerons and rudder in landing trim. Oil shutters and intercooler in neutral. Propeller at 2,550 rpm. Mixture control at auto rich. Cowl flaps closed. 150 mph indicated airspeed. Flaps full down. When Tom pulled the throttle back, the P-47's landing gear warning light came on. This light went on whenever power was cut back and went off only when the wheels were down and locked. The light was a reminder to pilots to perform the most elementary of tasks, which Forester now did. He pulled the landing gear control lever and heard a reassuring thunk. The light went out as Forester's P-47 came out of the turn.

Aligned to the middle of the runway, Tom cut back on power even more. This caused the lift, provided by air speeding below and above the wing, to be progressively reduced. At 115 mph, the plane met the concrete one third of the way down Runway 26. The tail wheel then settled and Forester's P-47 was firmly on the ground rolling out. Tom the instructor told Tom the pilot that it was an average landing, not a good one. Too far down the runway. Airspeed a bit too high. And not a sweet three-point landing as the two main wheels up front in the wings had touched down well before the small wheel in the fuselage near the tail. Tom the pilot replied that they, he, the plane, and Tom the instructor were down in one piece, which meant the landing had been eminently satisfactory.

Before turning onto the perimeter track, Tom saw in his rear view mirror that Snowflake Red 2 was on the ground as well, followed by Red 3, 200 feet high in perfect alignment with the runway.

Forester pulled back the canopy and began to taxi to his hardstand, the circular concrete pad where the P-47 would be parked. He already had unlocked the tail wheel and opened the engine cowl flaps. He then retracted the wing flaps and began a series of S-turns, necessary because the pilot of a P-47, when the fighter was on the ground, could not see what lay ahead.

Taxi speed was slow, and with the turns, it took several minutes for Forester and his plane to reach the hardstand reserved for the 19th Fighter Group's commander. There, waiting for plane and pilot, was Staff Sergeant Chester McGowan.

No one, not Eisenhower, not Marshall, nor even Douglas McArthur believed more firmly in the United States Army than did McGowan. The son of an enlisted man who had served in the Philippines, Chester McGowan, in 1943, was thirty-seven years old. For nineteen of those years, he had been in uniform. Conventional in outlook, uncomplicated in character, he conducted his life according to the army manual.

Content with the rank of sergeant, for which he expected and extended respect, Chester McGowan nonetheless worked hard at whatever job the army gave him. Not without ambition, his goal, as he had told his father, was to be "the best sergeant in the outfit." This he had achieved. Throughout the 19th Fighter Group, McGowan was recognized as one of the best of the crew chiefs. Harry Collins, who had arranged his posting to Forester's aircraft, called McGowan "the very model of an army sergeant." The sergeant took pride in his work, and knew it to be important. He understood, as did Forester, that without crew chiefs to keep the planes flying, the Army's air force was unlikely to succeed.

As Forester's plane approached the hardstand, McGowan could see that its guns had been fired. The tape placed across the muzzle of the guns to keep barrels free of moisture and dirt had been broken, while the leading edges of the wing near the guns were blackened from gunpowder. The crew chief gave a thumbs up signal to Forester who responded first with a wave and then by holding up two fingers. Sergeant McGowan jumped with joy upon seeing Forester's response. The pilot of his plane had downed two enemy aircraft. That was good news. The 19th Fighter Group, McGowan thought, was better than its record. More kills to its credit and the brass would begin to appreciate Forester and the job he had done in making the group battle ready. Colonel Phillips was your average officer. Colonel Forester was a cut above.

McGowan considered Tom Forester to be one of the finest officers under whom he had served. The sergeant approved of Forester's insistence upon everyone doing their very best. He appreciated the man's genuine regard for enlisted personnel. And he admired the courage it took to confront the enemy in the skies above Europe, as Forester repeatedly did.

When the plane came to a stop and the big propeller was no longer spinning, McGowan lifted himself onto the wing, using the landing gear as a step.

'Welcome back, Colonel. Glad to have you home."

"Thank you, Sergeant. It's good to be back."

This was the first exchange the two men always employed upon Forester's return from a combat mission. The words never varied. They initiated a ritual of words and movement that brought to closure the P-47's flight and put the crew chief once again in charge of the plane.

"Colonel, how'd it go?" This too was part of the ritual.

"We scored today, McGowan. Two Me-109s. One I nailed from the rear and down it went. One just blew up. And I got pieces of two others, one of which may no longer be flying."

"That's great, Colonel. Great job." McGowan was truly excited. This was his plane. He cared for it and he wanted its pilot to succeed. As evidence of ownership, his name was painted on the fuselage below that of Forester's. Up from the wing root, close to the canopy, in small block letters, the words *Crew Chief: S/Sgt. Chester McGowan* proclaimed the man responsible for maintaining this particular P-47. The practice was widespread among the American Air Force. Crew chiefs kept the planes airworthy. Seeing their names displayed on their planes sustained a crew chief's morale. And most pilots wanted their crew chief's morale to be as high as possible.

McGowan then asked the standard question, "How's the airplane?"

"The plane flew well, Sergeant. Real well. Engine was fine. No unusual noises. And I don't think I broke anything."

"I'll take a look, Colonel. But, if you did, I'll fix it right."

As he spoke, the sergeant handed Forester Army Air Force Form 1A which, as pilot, Forester had to sign. The form indicated the condition of the aircraft. If something did not work or sounded, Forester had to so indicate on the form. The problem had to be addressed before the plane could be declared ready to go.

Sitting in the cockpit, Tom signed Form 1A and handed it back to McGowan. He then took off his leather helmet and unbuckled the canvas straps that held him tightly to the P-47's seat. Sweaty, tired, and stiff from sitting in the same position for nearly two hours, Forester just sat there acclimating to the ground and to the absence of noise. For a long ten seconds, he just rubbed his face and rested. Silently, he spoke to himself. *The Group did well today. Chalk up another mission. Another safe return. This is one bitch of a job. But I love it. Sometimes it gives me the shakes. But I do love doing this.*

Tom sighed. Rest period was over. He double checked the controls, making sure that all those that were supposed to be off were indeed off. Mixture control, magnetos, battery, and fuel selector valve. Rudder and aileron trim to neutral. Flaps were positioned downward. Generator switch off. Now there was but one remaining task to perform—to lift his weary self out of the cockpit. This he now did, stepping onto the wing. His crew chief then helped him unhook the S-2 parachute. McGowan would place the chute on the aircraft's horizontal stabilizer. Parachutes were never placed on the ground. The fear was that field mice might burrow into the chute and tear the silk.

Already, McGowan had handed Tom his service cap. With stiffeners removed, the cap had a crushed look highly prized among pilots of the Army Air Forces. The look meant the wearer flew on operations. Army regulations specifically allowed aircrew to remove the stiff circular band inside the hat to permit radio headphones to be worn while in the air. Pilots, as well as navigators and bombardiers, took great pride in their crushed caps. Regular army officers, particularly those of high rank, disapproved. They thought the look undignified. The pilots thought it separated the men from the boys.

As Tom stepped down upon the hardstand, he turned to his crew chief with an appreciative look. "She's all yours, Sergeant."

"I'll take extra good care of her, Sir."

"I know you will."

With this exchange, which never varied, the ritual was now complete. The two men, bound together by an airplane, separated. At Bromley Park, they led different lives and did not interact outside the P-47. One man was a Lieutenant Colonel, commander of a fighter group, responsible for forty-eight aircraft and over 1,500 men. The other was a sergeant, responsible for a single plane and for a pair of soldiers, both corporals, who helped to maintain it. Separated by rank, ambition, education, and social standing, the two men had little in common. Yet when the P-47 brought them together, they were brothers. Each cared for the other. Each trusted the other. And each had the same compelling desire—that the P-47 be mechanically perfect and successful in the sky.

With the mission completed and the plane parked at its hard-stand, McGowan now had to service the aircraft in preparation for its next flight. Corporals Davis and Schmitt, respectively the Assistant Crew Chief and Armourer, worked with him. Each P-47 had a ground crew of three to maintain the plane. Expected to perform normal maintenance, the crew had specialists at squadron and group levels to handle more extensive repairs. Servicing the P-47 usually took McGowan and his men about two hours. Oxygen had to be replenished. Fuel tanks refilled. The radio would be checked out, as would the hydraulic and electrical systems. The P-47's massive Pratt and Whitney engine would be inspected, and its brakes and tires examined.

One of the first tasks for ground crew was the removal of the small motion picture camera located in the right wing of the P-47. Triggered automatically when the guns were fired, this 16 mm camera recorded what damage, if any, had been achieved. The film was developed promptly and used to assess harm done to the enemy. Gun camera film also was used to verify claims of aircraft destroyed by pilots who, fresh from the excitement of battle, often overstated their successes.

In the post-flight servicing of Forester's aircraft McGowan and his crew would pay particular attention to the P-47's guns. Having been fired, the eight weapons would be removed and taken to Bromley Park's armory. There, they would be inspected and cleaned. Schmitt would then return the guns to the airplane and reinstall them. Care had to be taken in inserting the .50 calibre bullets into the ammunition belt and in feeding the belts into the magazines atop the wings. Any misalignment might cause the guns to jam, with unhappy results. So McGowan kept his eye on Schmitt who, while working, often whistled the "It's Off to Work We Go" song from *Snow White,* much to the Sergeant's annoyance.

This time, McGowan and his crew took just over five hours to finish their work. The P-47's radio kept emitting a strange buzz, which required the attention of the squadron's radio expert. The truck that delivered aviation fuel was delayed, the result of two flat tires. Then there was the small hole in the wing from Granelli's errant aim. So it was late in the day when Forester's aircraft was settled in for the night. McGowan had reminded Davis to take the Colonel's parachute to the loft before performing the final servicing task—placing a protective cloth cover over the P-47's glass canopy.

Satisfied at last that the aircraft was in tip-top shape, McGowan took one last walk around the plane. As he did so, he softly touched its various surfaces, his way of expressing affection for the now silent machine.

Hopping onto his bicycle, he steered towards his barracks, half a mile from the hardstand. After washing off the grime from hands and face, he headed to the mess for dinner. He chatted with other enlisted men as they stood in line for food, which, if bland, was abundant and hot. McGowan retired soon thereafter, wanting to get plenty of sleep as each morning he arose early to salute the flag at reveille. This action he considered a matter of pride, important to a sergeant in the United States Army.

Forester had stepped down from the aircraft by the time Harry Collins had arrived in his Jeep. The Intelligence Officer greeted the Commanding Officer of the 19th Fighter Group with a friendly wave as he parked the ubiquitous vehicle in front of the left wing, near the landing gear where Tom was stretching, still stiff from the mission.

"Hello, Colonel. We're glad to have you back. Some of our mutual friends were beginning to worry." As he spoke, Collins threw Forester an informal salute.

"Hell, Harry, I always come back." Forester said this in earnest. Like most fighter pilots, he believed neither flak nor enemy aircraft would bring him down. This was not arrogance on Tom's part. He simply was confident, in a matter of fact sort of way, that he would always prevail, returning safely to Bromley Park. Forester understood the risks involved in what he did. He just felt they did not apply to him.

"How'd you do?" Collins could see that the guns had been fired and he knew, from speaking to other pilots before Forester had landed that Tom had tangled with the Luftwaffe.

"I did fine. More importantly, how did we do?" Forester emphasized the plural pronoun. Tom realized that all three squadrons had engaged the enemy. He was anxious to learn the outcome.

"We did well, Colonel. We did real well. Preliminary reports suggest nine Jerries bit the dust. All Me-109s. It's been a good day for the 19th Fighter Group. Now we have something good to tell the brass."

At last. At last we've hit them hard and come out ahead. Just what this group needs to lift morale and do what it's capable of and trained to do. And Harry's right. Now we have something to show Harrison and his cronies that all the hard work of the summer has paid off.

Tom looked straight at Collins. "Any losses?"

"Two P-47s did not return. One went down for sure, although a chute was seen."

"Who was it?"

"Marks. Captain Richard Marks, a flight leader in the 341st."

"Damn."

"Did you know him?"

"Yeah, he was a good pilot."

"Well, he took a Jerry with him. Maybe two. Confirmed reports say he blew up a Messerschmitt with some nice shooting. There's some evidence he got another as well."

"Nine to two. I'll take that score any day. What about the other P-47?"

"Can't tell you much. It's overdue. No one saw what happened."

"Who is it?"

"The Kid."

"Oh, God."

"This was bound to happen. You kept telling Richards to stay with his flight."

"I know, but damn. Somehow he was special. Knowing him, he may still turn up. He has before."

"True enough. But I'd have thought we'd have heard from him by now."

"Any word about the bombers?"

"Yup. They came home with minimal losses. And apparently they even hit their target. We got a call from their commander, a Colonel by the name of Billings. Wanted to thank us for the escort work."

"That was nice of him."

"Yes, it was."

"Harry, I saw one of them go down. It was not a pretty sight. Left wing down and on fire. Dropping like a brick. I saw six chutes. Then the whole plane just exploded. A B-17 just vanished."

"Jesus!"

"That's not the bad part."

"What do you mean?"

"One poor bastard had his chute catch fire."

"Oh, God."

"It just torched. And down he went. I tell you, Harry, it shook me up. For a few seconds, I couldn't do anything. I didn't function. I just watched that poor guy. And thanked God it wasn't me."

"That's normal."

"I know, but it was truly awful. That poor guy must have fallen over 17,000 feet. That means he had a long time to die."

"Listen, my friend." Collins voice turned gentle. Despite differences in age and rank, he and Forester were friends. The two men liked each other and valued the other's opinion. Both men were careful to keep their personal and business conversations separate, realizing the difficulty a Commanding Officer had in having a friend among subordinates. "You and I both know that lots of men are going to die in this war. And many will check out in great pain and terror."

"You're right, of course. What troubles me is not that I sometimes see men die horrible deaths or that it hurts and sickens. I can handle that. And I do. What troubles me is that I can so easily put it aside and forget it ever happened. I just click off and go about my job like nothing ever happened."

"That's 'cause you're normal. It's a perfectly human reaction. And besides, there's one other factor."

"What's that?"

"You've no choice but to do that. You're the Commanding Officer of an Army Air Force fighter group."

"True enough, I suppose I don't."

"And you've told me, you really like the job."

"I do. I really do. I tell you, Harry, this is one great job, despite all the dying. When one of our boys gets hit, I feel just awful about it. But the feeling goes away. Leading this fighter group, flying that P-47—well, there isn't anything better."

"So you're a lucky man."

"I suppose I am."

"I see your guns were fired. And I'll get the details in interrogation, but how did you do up there?

"I did okay. I'm pretty sure I knocked down two Messerschmitts."

"Geez, that's terrific."

"One I hit close up, about 200 yards. My fire went straight into his cockpit and down he went. The other one just exploded. And I went flying through his fireball."

"What about the two Spitfires?"

Forester looked at his friend and chuckled. "How do you know about them?"

"I'm your Intelligence Officer. Mr. Roosevelt pays me a lot of money, well not actually a lot, to know such things."

"Two Spitfires were in trouble. North of Dunkirk. We helped them out. Routine stuff."

"That's not how I heard it. I heard three P-47s took on a whole bunch of Germans. Shot a few down and saved two of Great Britain's finest."

"Harry, let's not make a big deal of this. The Spits were in trouble and we got the Germans off their backs."

"Sounds more like the U.S. cavalry coming to the rescue all in the nick of time. I heard you took on half the Luftwaffe. The story is all around the squadron. It's one hell of a story. You've created quite a stir."

"You know the job I have? The one you just told me about. The one about commanding an Army Air Force fighter group."

"Yes."

"Well, I was just doing it. Nothing more."

"Perhaps, but I think there's more to it. It's one terrific story. And it's gonna do wonders for the morale of this group."

"Well that's all to the good. Maybe this is what we've needed. A big brawl with the Luftwaffe where we come out on top. No tie. No split decision. Just a nice clear cut victory."

"I think you're right, and I think that's what we've got. In my view, the 19th Fighter Group has arrived."

"I tell you, Harry, they were good up there today. We took on the Germans and did real well."

"Let Jerry now beware."

"Damn right. I think we're about to show Jerry, and everybody else, what this P-47 group can do."

As they spoke, Harry Collins and Tom Forester were driving towards the 340th Squadron's Operations complex where, in the ready-room, the post-flight interrogation would take place. After each mission, pilots would assemble in the squadron's ready room to review what they had seen and what they had done. As Forester had flown this mission with the 340th, Collins was steering the Jeep towards its Operations area, which lay on the southwest portion of the airfield.

Although important business fighter interrogations were informal affairs, coffee and donuts were served. For those who needed them, shots of whiskey were available. At these sessions, Intelligence officers asked lots of questions, attempting to glean useful information from young pilots who, still in a high pitch of excitement from aerial combat, were talkative and, occasionally, boisterous. The Intelligence staff wanted to know about enemy tactics, aircraft markings, friendly aircraft, anything that, like a piece of a puzzle, might contribute insight to the Luftwaffe and to the campaign against it being conducted by the Army Air Force.

Post-flight interrogations also saw the processing of victory claims. Pilots making such claims had to submit a written report, which would be assessed against gun camera footage.

The interrogations usually lasted forty-five minutes. Results were assembled, analyzed, and written up. These reports, as well as the footage, then went up the chain of command. Eagerly awaited, read promptly, and examined thoroughly, these reports often shaped the next day's mission.

Forester was sitting in the front of the Jeep with Collins at the wheel. Harry was driving slowly. Once, while speeding, he had rolled a Jeep. No one had been hurt, but the experience scared him. So he now drove cautiously. Tom did not mind. When Forester wanted to get somewhere more quickly, he would tell Collins to move over and take the wheel himself. Now, despite the need to get to interrogation, he was content to let Harry drive. With one foot hanging over the side, with his Mae West life jacket and oxygen mask in his left hand, he was relaxing. At times, he would light up a cigarette, which helped him relax. The drive to interrogation would be the only time he would smoke. Forester would take a few puffs and then discard the cigarette. This time, he chose not to smoke, content to sit in the Jeep and let the tension of combat dissipate. The process of relaxing, with or without a cigarette, would begin in the ride to interrogation. It would end when he confronted the fear he earlier had felt. But that confrontation would take place later, occurring after the post interrogation. Now, Tom was simply enjoying the ride, looking at the P-47s he and Harry Collins were passing on the way to the Operations area of the 341st Fighter Squadron.

"Colonel, we heard from General Harrison shortly before you landed."

"What did he want?

"Seems there's going to be a meeting. Actually, Colonel Arnie was the person who called. Said Harrison wants to meet with all the fighter group commanders."

"Did he say what about?

"No, Sir."

"I can imagine what's on his mind."

"Same old story?"

"I'm sure. Harrison wants us to stay close to the bombers. Wants us to stay above 18,000 feet."

"You've heard that before."

"Indeed we have. And it may once have made sense, but it sure doesn't now."

"Well, Colonel. The bomber boys are probably making noises again, demanding that the fighters stay close by. And Harrison is listening to them."

"Harry, the man is Director of Fighter Operations. He ought to know something about fighter tactics. Maybe he once did. He sure doesn't now."

"My Intelligence friends tell me the man is in over his head."

"What I want to know is how does a guy like that become a general?"

Collins took his eyes off the road and looked at Forester. "Generals, my friend, are like apples. There are good ones and bad ones."

"Well, I give him credit. He looks like a general. Trim, crew cut, wears his uniform nicely . . . "

"That helps him, you know."

"What do you mean?"

"Well, generals are supposed to look like generals. Colonels who don't often don't become generals."

"You're serious, aren't you?"

"Yes, I am. Take Harrison. He's not stupid. No doubt was a good flyer and is pretty good at logistics. He'd make, and probably was, an extremely competent colonel. But he looks like a general. Straight out of central casting. He's polite, outgoing when he needs to be. Dresses well, and his wife plays her role as Mrs. General quite nicely, although I hear the woman is a bit of a bitch. The total package is just what the Air Force wants to project. You are what you appear to be."

"That's crazy."

"Of course it's crazy, but it's true."

"Harry, the man is DFO for God's sake. That's a really important job. It may determine the fate of daylight strategic bombing. How can a man like Harrison get such a job?"

"That I can't answer. I would have thought Eaker would know better."

"Me too. General Eaker is a fine officer. A bit too Air Force for me, but he's smart, well organized, and fair. A true gentlemen."

"He's all of that. He's also the guy who is building the Eighth Air Force, and doing one hell of a job."

"He is that. I wonder if Arnold appreciates him."

"I hope so. They're old friends. But Arnold has a reputation for coming down hard on people who don't perform. If the Eighth Air Force falters, old Hap Arnold will pull Ira Eaker out of Wycombe Abbey so fast he won't know what hit him."

"That would be a shame."

"Yes, it would. But with the stakes so high, anybody commanding the Eighth Air Force better succeed. Including its second tier commanders, one of whom is Brigadier General Richard Harrison."

"Any details about the meeting?"

"Not really. Arnie was letting us know early on, so we could work schedules, actually your schedule. Arnie's apparently a decent guy. Does most of Harrison's work. Gets little credit."

"I've met him a number of times. He's okay. When's the meeting?"

"This Wednesday at 9:45." Harry Collins rarely used the military's twenty-four hour time format. Although a major, and a talented Intelligence Officer, he was a civilian at heart.

As the Jeep passed two P-47s parked close together, Forester saw someone he recognized. "Hold on Harry. Head over there." Tom was pointing to the second P-47 whose pilot was examining the plane's rudder from which a piece was missing. Several holes in the fuselage occupied the attention of the ground crew.

Harry turned the wheel and pulled the Jeep up to the P-47. Next to the big fighter with its massive but smooth lines, the little Jeep looked awkward and innocent. Forester spoke to the pilot who had waved as the Jeep drove up.

"Hop in Lieutenant. You did well today, Ennis."

"Thank you, Sir. I'm afraid I got my aircraft banged up a bit."

"That happens. But you were on the ball today. I owe you my thanks."

"Sir?"

"You called out in time for me to break away and not get hit by two Me-109s."

"Yes, Sir."

"Well done. You did what you were supposed to do." Forester then asked the question wingmen never wished to hear, but Tom purposely had no accusatory tone in his voice. Ennis had done well in his first combat mission, and Forester did not want to discourage the young lieutenant. "How did you get separated?"

"Well, Sir, the Messerschmitts came after me, too. There were four of them. The first two went after you. The others fired at me. That's when my radio got hit. You can see the holes in the fuselage. I broke left and dove for the deck. I finally pulled away from them at about 11,000 feet. And when I climbed back up, no one was in sight. I had lost you, Sir, and I'm awfully sorry. A wingman is supposed to stick with his leader, and I didn't."

"You did fine, Ennis. You were in a tough spot and came out of it. Just be sure to tell the Intelligence folks what you saw today."

"Yes, Sir."

"And one other thing, Ennis."

"Sir?"

"You'll be flying my wing next mission. So keep your eyes sharp and stay with me."

"Yes, Sir!" Robert Ennis was pleased. He had survived his first combat with the Germans. And, despite having lost sight of the

Group Commander's airplane, he was to fly again as Forester's wingman. The Lieutenant knew he was getting a second chance. Determined not to screw up, Ennis vowed he would stick to his leader's aircraft like glue. Still excited from the mission, he sat in the back of the Jeep, happy to be alive, and happy to fly P-47s for the 19th Fighter Group. As the three men drove to interrogation, the young pilot was trying to paint in his mind the colors and markings of the Messerschmitts he no longer feared.

The Operations complex of the 341st squadron consisted of several buildings. Foremost among them was a large, single story drab concrete structure that housed the squadron's Operations and Intelligence sections. Access to this windowless, bombproof building was restricted, as within fighter tactics were devised and reviewed. Reflecting its important functions, the building was guarded night and day by military police. Adjacent to the Operations structure was a large Nissen hut where the post flight interrogation would take place.

Nissen huts dotted the landscape of Eighth Air Force airfields. Made of corrugated metal, they were shaped like half cylinders, with sides of brick or wood. Cold in winter, hot in summer, and damp whenever it rained, Nissen huts had two virtues dearly appreciated by Air Force commanders—they were cheap to buy and easy to construct. The U.S. Army Air Forces used Nissen huts for a multitude of purposes. They served as barracks, kitchens, workshops, clubs, sick bays, armories, post exchanges, and the like. At Bromley Park, there were forty-seven Nissen huts. All were put to good use, including the one Forester, Collins, and Ennis now entered, where the interrogation already had begun.

"Ten shun!" Everyone stood as Forester entered the hut.

"At ease, everybody. Keep working. Let's do this and do it right. Pilots, let's make sure we give Intelligence solid and precise information. They've got an important job to do and it's our job to help 'em."

Harry Collins appreciated these remarks. Too often, fighter pilots talked at length about the Messerschmitts they clobbered, but provided few detailed observations to enable the Intelligence section to track specific Luftwaffe squadrons or detect new enemy capabilities. "Here you go, Colonel." This was Collins handing Forester a cold bottle of Coca-Cola. Tom rarely drank coffee after a mission and never partook of the whiskey. But a cold Coke was something he wanted each time he completed a combat flight. Forester craved the sweet taste of the soda. He enjoyed the carbonation and wanted the Coke to be ice cold. Early on, Collins had learned of his Colonel's craving. He then took steps to ensure that a cold Coca-Cola greeted Forester at each post-flight interrogation, regardless of squadron. Harry thought any colonel commanding a fighter group was entitled to a few quirks, both personal and professional. Forester had his fair share. One was the Coca-Cola. Another was his dislike of large desks. For administrative matters, of which there were many for a group commander, Forester wanted a simple table, one without desk drawers. Drawers, Forester thought, encouraged retention of paper. Better to process the paper quickly and get it off one's desk. Harry Collins rather liked formal desks. He had had one in his office prior to the war and used one now. As for Coca-Cola, he couldn't stand the stuff and was amused that Forester loved it so. Harry much preferred the mellow taste of a good scotch.

During interrogation, Forester learned that he had shot down three Messerschmitts, not two. Collins, after looking at Tom's gun camera footage, thought the Me-109 Forester had met head on was likely not to have survived. So Harry sought out Granelli, who confirmed that the enemy aircraft had broken apart after passing Forester's P-47.

"The Kraut's propeller stopped spinning, Major. Then his wing folded up. The Kraut himself hit the silk. I saw the bastard's chute open."

Inwardly, Tom felt good about this victory. The combat had been personal. Two pilots had flown directly towards each other, like jousting knights of old. Only one would survive in what had been an aerial game of chicken. Forester had kept his airplane straight and his aim true. The German had not. Hence, Forester triumphed. Tom felt no remorse, nor did he even consider that a man similar to himself might be dead. He simply wanted to take the 19th Fighter Group into combat, and lead by example. This victory, and the others, would help him do so.

Counting the one enemy aircraft he had destroyed in August, Forester's score now stood at four. Others had done better but, in September 1943, four victories were extremely respectable. Later, in the great air battles of early 1944, American pilots would shoot down large numbers of German aircraft. Eventually, a small number of aces would tally twenty or more victories. Yet as the summer of 1943 drew to a close, most Army Air Force pilots in England were still learning their trade. So Forester's score, while not spectacular, suggested he had a bright future as commander of the 19th Fighter Group. That General Harrison did not think so only underscored the importance of Wednesday's meeting. Indeed, the meeting was to alter Tom's life, but in a way neither he nor the General could imagine.

"Excuse me, Sir." One of Collins' Intelligence officers was speaking to Forester. "There's a phone call for you. The phone's in the next room, on the desk to the left."

"Thank you, Lieutenant. Excuse me, Harry. I'll be right back." When Forester picked up the phone, he heard a familiar voice."

"Hi ya, Colonel. It's me."

"Richards, where the hell are you?"

"I'm at an RAF station, west of Dover. You gotta speak up Colonel, the connection's not too good."

"How'd you get there?" Dover was considerably south of Bromley Park. "Oh, never mind." Forester was about to yell at the Kid, but thought better of it. His voice changed when he said, "Are you okay?"

"I'm fine, Colonel, just fine."

"And your airplane?"

"Well it's not so fine. But the Limeys say they'll patch it up and gas it up—they call it petrol—and I should be back late tomorrow. Is that okay?"

"Yes. That will be all right. Just call ahead when you know your ETA."

"Say Colonel." Richard's voice sounded like a son of the South. "Yes?"

"I got one, Colonel. I hit a Jerry 109 and down she went."

"Well done, Richards, well done indeed. I'm glad you scored, but I'm more glad you're alive."

"Hell, Colonel, don't worry about me."

"Richards, get some rest. Get your plane fixed and get yourself back here." Tom paused for just a moment. "Assuming you can find Bromley Park."

"Shucks, Colonel. I can always do that. I'll be seeing you soon."

Amused by Richard's unmilitary bearing, and happy to have the youngster safe, Forester put down the phone and went to find Harry Collins.

"Well, Major, it seems you'll have to add one more to our score today."

"Sir?"

"It's the Kid. He's okay. Landed at some RAF field far from here. Says he got a German."

Collins's face brightened, showing the same pleasure Forester felt in having Richardson turn up. "If the Kid said he scored, he probably did. I'm just glad he's alive."

"Me too."

The interrogation continued. Both Harry Collins and Tom Forester were more upbeat than usual. Richard's safe return had buoyed their spirits. Both men knew they had to accept the loss of pilots. They also knew that they should not have favorites. But both men liked the Kid and wanted the youngster to complete his combat tour. A tour was 200 hours, after which a pilot was transferred to a safe occupation. Nowhere near having 200 hours of combat flying, Leroy Richards had many missions ahead of him.

With the interrogation over, Harry Collins gave Forester a lift back to his quarters. As Tom was stepping out of the Jeep, Collins remarked that he had forgotten to mention a phone call that had come in while the group was airborne.

"Arnie's phone call? You told me about that."

"No, another one."

Anybody interesting?"

"I don't know. A bit odd actually. Do you know a Roger Baldwin?"

"Name's not familiar."

"Well, he's a colonel on Eaker's staff. Does storms. Wants you to call him before you speak with General Harrison. Says it's important."

"That's strange. What's a met officer want with me?"

"I don't know, but do talk with him. It may be important."

"I will. I'll be driving up to Harrison's headquarters . . . "

"General Harrison's not to be trusted. Be careful, my friend."

"I will Harry. I always am." Forester then said good-bye to Collins and went into the small Nissen hut that served as his lodgings.

Immediately upon entering the hut, Tom sensed the presence of his inevitable post flight companion. Forester's legs went limp, his stomach churned, and he nearly fell to the floor while laying down upon his cot. With his clothes still on, Tom lay there for twenty minutes, sweating profusely. He felt extremely hot, and momentarily wondered what his body temperature might be. Unable to do anything and shaking inside, but not crying, Forester was thankful for the privacy he enjoyed at Bromley Park. Rank does have its privileges and a hut to himself was one of them. Fear remained with Forester for the entire time he lay on the cot. Fear meant impending death. Death meant the end of all he cherished. He saw himself burning inside a P-47, which sat on the ground, billowing black smoke. Then he was inside a pine coffin, looking through the wood and through the American flag that draped the box. From within, Tom could hear a bugler play taps. A eulogy was being given, but the words were not in English. They were German and Forester had no idea what they meant. Strangely, his father was present, dressed in a blue pinstriped suit, head bowed in prayer. Next to him was Mrs. Hale, Tom's fifth grade teacher. She was passing out homework assignments. Nearby was a Catholic priest who said nothing and did nothing. To Tom, inside the coffin and drenched with sweat, the man of God appeared to be enjoying himself. As the bugler's trumpet went silent, a young woman appeared. Dressed in a white gown and wearing an elegant hat of lavender and white, she glided to the side of the coffin. Tom could see her pale skin and dark hair. Then the woman aged. Now she was fifty, but still beautiful. With great care, she placed upon the coffin an enameled box. The box contained Forester's Army Air Force wings. Tom noticed that of all the people present, only one individual was crying. That was the Lady in White. She whispered words of love as the pine box was lowered into eternity.

For a moment when Tom awoke, he was uncertain whether the dream was reality and his Nissen hut surroundings imaginary. This uncertainty quickly sorted itself out, and Forester wandered off to take a shower, knowing that rushing water swiftly would convey him back to the tangible world of Bromley Park.

Two days later, at 9:30 A.M., Forester was at Wycombe Abbey, standing outside the small office belonging to Roger Baldwin.

"He said you should go right in, Sir," remarked the sergeant at a nearby desk.

"Thank you." And Forester, after knocking gently on the door, walked into the office.

"Come in, Forester. I'm Roger Baldwin."

"Tom Forester." As he spoke, the two men shook hands. Both seemed comfortable with the other.

"You're probably wondering why I asked to see you."

"Yes, I am," responded Tom.

"Well, I just wanted you to know beforehand that a certain general is out to get your ass."

"Harrison?"

"The very one. I don't know what you've done, but Harrison is on the warpath."

"Thanks for the warning. I'll be on guard."

"What's your sin?"

"I'm not fond of General Harrison's rules of engagement."

"Figures. You probably want to go out and shoot down German fighters wherever they are."

"Indeed I do."

"Well, I don't profess to be Clausewitz, but that seems to me to be what air warfare is about."

"You'd think so, wouldn't you? Listen, I really appreciate your giving me this heads up, but I have to ask you, why'd you make the effort?"

"Two reasons, Forester. One is Harrison. He's not a very nice fellow and I hate to see him screw one of our better group commanders, which I'm told you happen to be. And two, I hear you went to Dartmouth."

"I did. Class of '38."

"I'm Class of '25. It's a great school."

"Go Indians," chanted Forester. Both men were now smiling and completely at ease with the other. They then spent the next few minutes conversing about Dartmouth and student life in a small New England college town.

The meeting called by General Harrison took place in what had once been the school library. Now it was a conference room used frequently by Eaker and his senior staff. In attendance were the other commanders of fighter groups then in England. Several bomber group commanders were present as well. After very brief opening remarks by Harrison, a number of bomber group commanders spoke, all emphasizing the need for close in fighter escort. Colonel Arnie then discussed specific fighter tactics. Hubert Zemke, commander of the 56th Fighter Group, pointed out that tying the fighters to bomber formations hindered rather than helped escort work. Zemke's remarks irritated Harrison, who went up to the lectern that had been provided for his use. He praised the efforts of the B-17 and B-24 groups, calling them heroic, which they certainly were. He was less generous with the fighter commanders. He said that they were not doing the best possible job. They were not strictly following the rules devised by him and his staff to ensure the safety of the bombers. As he spoke, Harrison's tone became increasingly less pleasant. He concluded his remarks by threatening court martials for fighter pilots who, as he caustically put it, "Went chasing after Germans all over Europe."

As General Harrison left the room, he spoke to Forester. "Colonel, I need to talk to you in my office. Now."

Tom acknowledged General Harrison's command with, "Yes, Sir." He accompanied General Harrison out of the conference room.

"I don't care for you, Forester, and I don't like the job you're doing."

Tom remained silent, correctly concluding that the General had more to say.

"We're trying to win a war and you're off on a wild goose chase trying to knock down Germans."

"General, with respect, knocking down Germans is what P-47s are designed to do."

"*Colonel,*" Harrison emphasized the rank, "Let me remind you that we're here to escort strategic strike forces to and from their target."

Forester realized there was nothing to be gained in debating fighter tactics with Harrison. The General's mind was made up and his experience was ill-suited for understanding the realities of commanding P-47's in combat. So Tom kept silent, expecting Harrison to hammer him again. It came almost immediately.

"I'm not satisfied with the 19th Fighter Group. They're under performing."

To this comment, Tom took umbrage. He was about to respond harshly until he heard his own voice speaking to him. *Stay calm Forester. This guy's a general. Nice and steady. Keep your cool.*

"General, two days ago the 19th downed ten Me-109s for the loss of just two P-47s. That's one fine score and shows all our training and hard work has paid off. And we kept the Germans off the backs of the bombers. You might ask Colonel Billings about that."

"You're disobeying the rules."

"General, my P-47s stay with the bombers even though I think the tactics are wrong. We do not go below 18,000, except in a dive when we're being chased. But we always come back up. We do not, repeat do not, go chasing after the Germans, although we should be."

"Forester, you'll be hearing more about this from me. In the meantime, I have a special assignment for you."

Tom, who had been standing at attention, again said nothing.

"The Army Air Force is forming a committee of Londoners to help us figure out what to do with the thousands of Americans descending upon the city. More of us are coming and London's going to be filled with American boys. Well paid boys, full of energy. The Eighth Air Force Fighter Command has a representative on the committee. And you're it."

Forester knew such a job meant less time in the air. He also knew that Harrison meant it as punishment, so protesting would be futile—and unwise. Tom understood that the General was waiting for him to step out of line in order to come down on him harder.

"When does this assignment begin, General?"

"Day after tomorrow. The Committee meets somewhere in downtown London. Be there. You're dismissed."

Forester saluted, did an about face, and walked out of General Harrison's office. He was thinking to himself as he did so. Some silly advisory committee. Just the sort of job a group commander didn't need. Clearly, the General was out to get him. But he would lead the 19th Fighter Group as he had done in the past and let the chips fall where they may. And knowing that aspects of life cannot always be sequential, he would do this committee at the same time, and give it his very best. London was a city he did not know well. Now he would spend time there. That was not likely to be a hardship, for the city was full of interesting people.

SEVEN

Late on Thursday evening, Ira Eaker was comfortable, almost cozy, as he sat in the wing chair reading *Scaramouche*. The room was dark, except for a soft light on both the General and his book cast by a tall brass lamp, which stood next to the chair. Eaker enjoyed the serenity of the moment. During the day, officers came and went, seeking answers and advice from the Commanding General of the Eighth Air Force. The intense daily routine left little time for relaxation. Now that the plans for tomorrow's mission had been formulated, Eaker had a small window of time in which to escape the pressures of leadership. He did so with anticipation—to Ira Eaker, few things were as enjoyable as reading a good book.

Forty minutes later, the General had finished *Scaramouche*. Much like a child, he felt guilty for having read past his normal bedtime. Amused by this reaction, he set the book down upon the table and, bringing his hands to his head, rubbed his eyes and face, attempting to erase the weariness he now felt. It didn't work. Eaker was tired and he knew the time had come to go to bed.

Before retiring to his private quarters, he remained in the chair, conscious and appreciative of the silence around him. For a moment, he wondered what the world would be like once the war was over, and what he would do. Then his mind returned to the subject of books. General Eaker looked at the two novels upon the table. Knowing he shouldn't, he nonetheless picked up the Stevenson story and contemplated starting the book. At that moment, he heard a number of aircraft flying overhead. RAF bombers. Probably Lancasters. On a training mission or perhaps on their way to Germany. Round the clock. That's what he had told Churchill. Together, the Eighth and Britain's Bomber Command were going to pulverize Nazi Germany. His mind started to ignite with thoughts about the air war. No longer was he concerned with the exploits of Lord Durrisdeer. Ira Eaker was thinking about the business at hand.

Foremost among his thoughts was the letter from Barney Giles he had received two days before. The Chief of the Air Staff had penned a personal note, indicative of their long friendship, which dated back to when both men were young pilots in the fledgling Air Corps. Giles had told Eaker that Washington was not satisfied with the progress of the Eighth Air Force. "Washington" meant Hap Arnold. General Arnold, wrote Giles, was unhappy with the numbers of aircraft sent into battle and the results being achieved. Hap wanted more sorties and better bombing. At meetings of the Joint Chiefs, Arnold consistently had to make the case for daylight precision bombing. He had to demonstrate that the Eighth was inflicting decisive damage upon Germany. So far, Eaker's command had not done so.

The stakes were enormous. Were the Eighth Air Force not to succeed, the core doctrine of the U.S. Army Air Forces was at risk, as was the central role aviation would play in America's military strategy, now and after the war.

"We can absorb moderate losses," Giles told his friend, "for more planes and air crew are coming. But we need better results. Ira, I'm not going to tell you how to run the Eighth, but I will tell you things need to change."

Eaker also wanted better results. He believed greater numbers of B-17s and B-24s in tighter formations would make the difference. Together, these bombers would constitute a strike force the Luftwaffe could not stop.

Sitting in the chair, Eaker pondered what else was needed to achieve what Arnold wanted. The list was neither long nor difficult to make. Weather forecasting, navigation, formation flying, and aerial gunnery all warranted improvement. Deception of German air defenses also had to get better. So did bombing accuracy. Too often, the bombers simply missed the target or scattered their loads far from the aiming point. Already, Eaker was making changes. He believed the results would soon be evident, not only to Hap Arnold, but also to all who doubted the efficacy of strategic air power.

In early autumn, despite substantial losses, the Eighth Air Force was growing. Eaker could now dispatch three hundred bombers to attack Germany. Germany, he knew, was the key. For most of September, following a disastrous raid upon Stuttgart in which forty-five bombers were lost, the Eighth had concentrated upon softer targets in France and Holland. The General understood that such raids would not win the war. The primary target of the Eighth Air Force was Germany. And Ira Eaker intended to send his bombers there. Plans were being drafted to hit a number of targets inside the Reich. October would be the month when once again the Eighth struck the enemy's homeland.

With that thought in mind, Eaker stood up and turned off the light. He was tired, but at peace with himself. He knew what had to be done and he was determined to have it happen. Pipe in hand, the General walked to his quarters. Once there, he brushed his teeth and put on his pajamas, uttering the word "Germany" as he climbed into bed. Ira Eaker then fell asleep without difficulty.

The next morning, he was at his desk at 7:45 A.M. A quick breakfast of coffee, powdered eggs, canned pineapple juice, toast, and marmalade had fortified him for the day ahead. Eaker first read an intelligence memorandum prepared for him during the night and received a briefing by Roger Baldwin on weather conditions. That was followed by a status report on the day's mission by Major General Frederick Anderson. Anderson also briefed Eaker on the progress in planning the upcoming air campaign against Germany. When General Anderson left the room, Eaker sent for Major Hull.

Harris Hull was already outside Eaker's office when Anderson departed. The Major saluted the General and stepped inside the room as he was being summoned.

"That was fast, Harris. Good morning."

"Good morning, Sir. A good rest last night?

"Yes, thank you. I slept well."

"One change in today's schedule, General. Air Vice Marshal Sidney has asked for fifteen minutes of your time this morning. And I've put him on your calendar."

"That's fine. Do we know what he wants?"

"Not exactly. He seems very nice; they all do, really. Said he would not try to convince you to have the Eighth fly at night."

Eaker laughed in response to this last remark. "That's good. We'd probably run into each other up there at night. It'd get pretty crowded."

"Air Vice Marshal Sidney did mention the subject was medals, although more than that he didn't say."

"Well, the RAF are our good friends and allies, and they've gone out of their way to be helpful to us. So I'm available whenever an Air Vice Marshal wants to see me."

"Yes, Sir."

With a twinkle in his eye Eaker, spoke to Hull. "They don't have too many Air Vice Marshals, do they, Harris?"

"No more than we have major generals, Sir."

"Oh dear." Both men were now smiling. Hull, who had accompanied Eaker to England early in 1942, knew that his boss considered the rapid expansion of the Air Corps to have resulted in too many general officers, some not qualified to hold such high rank.

Eaker sighed, recalling how long he had awaited promotion in the 1930s. Quickly, he brought himself back to the present, and reached for a pipe. "Back to the business at hand. What else do you have, Harris?"

"Nothing, Sir. But I did want to remind you that the Advisory Committee we're establishing to help London and other cities deal with the influx of American airmen meets today. It's on your schedule."

"Oh yes. What time is that?" Eaker had agreed to speak at the first meeting of the Committee. He realized, as perhaps others did not, that there was more to running the Eighth Air Force than planning combat missions. The General never forgot that the Eighth, indeed all the American forces, were visitors in England and that every effort had to be made to mix well with the Brits.

"It starts at noon. I'll have a car ready for you, General, at 11:15."

"Fine. Where is it?"

"At the Royal Aeronautical Society, in London, Sir, off Park Lane."

"Sounds like an appropriate place. We still don't have someone from the bombers sitting on that committee, do we?"

"No, Sir."

"Let's see." Eaker leaned back and puffed on his pipe. "Ask Keith Davenport to come see me. That will be all, Harris. And thank you."

"Yes, Sir." Harris Hull saluted and walked out of the office in search of Colonel Davenport. The colonel had been the commander of the 918th Bomb Group, based at Archbury, which had performed poorly while suffering heavy losses. Davenport, a decent man who could not stomach the loss of life, was relieved of his command. Assigned to Wycombe Abbey, he now served on General Anderson's staff. Despite the experience at Archbury, he was showing himself to be a capable officer.

Davenport soon reported to Eaker. "You wanted to see me, Sir?"

"Yes, Keith." Eaker was paging through one of the black binder notebooks. "How are you getting along?"

"I'm fine, General. Thank you for asking."

"Good. I'm glad to hear it. Fred Anderson treating you well?"

"Yes, he is. General Anderson's a tough cookie."

"Learn from him Keith and maybe you'll get another chance. How's the planning for Germany?"

"Coming along. But I'm still worried."

"Why is that?"

"We're taking heavy losses, General. Stuttgart cost us 450 highly trained men. The weather was lousy and most of the planes couldn't find the target."

"That simply tells me we need better navigation. The crews we can replace." Eaker tapped on one of his black notebooks. "We're building up a powerful force, Keith. The Eighth is a strategic weapon. To fulfill its mission, it's got to strike at Germany."

"I know that, General. I just worry about our boys. Most of them are just kids."

"Listen, Keith, war's a lousy business. And men are going to get killed. But the Eighth can make a difference. And probably shorten the war. Your job, my job, Fred Anderson's job, is to get on with it."

"Yes, Sir, I know that."

"And that means hitting Germany, which is what we're going to do."

Davenport nodded in agreement, but kept silent. General Eaker then asked what targets had been identified.

"It's preliminary, General, but we're looking at Emden, Bremen, Munster. And some possibilities exist in Poland and Czechoslovakia. There are some armament plants we want to hit there."

"Good."

"The problem is fighters, General. And frankly, I'm worried. They can't escort our bombers into Germany. They don't have the range."

"We'll do it without the fighters, Keith. I know we do better when the P-47s are around, but the B-17 and B-24 are designed to fight their way in and fight their way out."

"I hear you, Sir. I just worry about our boys over Germany without fighter escort."

"You worry too much, Colonel. Now I'm going to change the subject and ask you to take on a special assignment."

"I'll do whatever you want, General."

"I know that, and I appreciate it. You'll still be working for Fred Anderson. This is just an extra job. Shouldn't be too hard."

A slight smile appeared on Davenport's face. "I always worry when a job is said to be not too difficult."

Eaker smiled in return. "Don't. There's a committee I want you to serve on. We've set it up to get some advice from the English on how to handle the large numbers of Army Air Force personnel who will spend their leave in London and the other cities. We've asked some knowledgeable people who know London and who are sensible and intelligent to be on the committee. And I want to have two combat flyers on the group, to show our English friends we take the effort seriously. I also want them to meet some Americans who have been in combat. The Americans they tend to meet are either old farts like myself or administrative warriors, not real ones. It will remind them why we're here and that our blood is being spilled as well as their own."

"And I'm one of the flyers?"

Eaker nodded in response, and then worked on his pipe. "You're my bomber rep. I've got a fighter pilot on the committee too."

"May I ask who that is?"

"Of course. His name is Forester, a lieutenant colonel. He was General Harrison's selection. Do you know him?"

"Not directly, but I've heard of him."

"And?"

"He's topnotch—good pilot. He's got a few kills. But more than that, his fighter group is really coming on. Apparently, he's the reason."

"Well, he and you are the combat flyers on the Committee. Just come up with some good ideas about how we can keep our troops happy in London without wrecking the place."

"I'm sure we'll get a good list together, Sir."

"Good. See that portrait up there?." Eaker was pointing to the picture of Miss Eleanor Steeples.

"Yes, Sir. She seems a bit unfriendly. Who is it?"

"A certain Miss Steeples, once the headmistress of the school whose building we now occupy. I'm told she was quite a woman, in more ways than one. Anyway, she reminds me, her picture does, that we're all here as guests of the British and I want us, all of us, from general down to private, to behave accordingly. That's why I formed the committee. Incidentally, Jimmy Dixon, one of our air attachés at the Embassy, is running it. We need to make sure that our men don't cause trouble while they're having some fun. The English can help us figure out how to do that. So pay attention to what they have to say."

"Yes, Sir. I'll do that for sure."

"General, I do have one question. When does the Committee next meet?"

Eaker was working on his pipe again. Half the fun of smoking a pipe was the fiddling necessary to light the tobacco and keep it burning. The other half was the smell and taste of the tobacco itself. The General enjoyed both halves. When he responded to Davenport, for a moment, Ira Eaker looked more like a university professor than the commander of the Eighth Air Force. "Oh yes, I knew there was something else I needed to tell you about this. It's today. We leave at 11:15. Gives you an hour to prepare."

Davenport was thinking that things just got a bit sticky since General Anderson had scheduled a meeting for 11:15 to review possible target routes for the mission to Munster. Not attending was likely to irritate Anderson. "General Eaker, any chance I might be excused from this . . . "

"Not to worry, Keith. I'll speak to Fred. I need you in London."

A soft knock on the door caught both men's attention. "Come in," said the more senior of the two.

"Excuse me, General Eaker." Standing by the now open door was Major Hull. "Air Vice Marshal Sidney is here for his appointment and Colonel Baldwin wonders whether he might have two minutes of your time."

"Okay, Harris, I'll be with the Air Vice Marshal momentarily. Keith, go introduce yourself to our RAF guest. Tell him what it's like to bomb Germany in daylight. Harris, tell Colonel Baldwin he can have ninety seconds, but they need to be a quick ninety seconds."

"Yes, Sir." Harris Hull left the room, as did Keith Davenport. In doing so, they nearly collided with Roger Baldwin who was entering Eaker's office.

"Good morning, General Eaker," said the meteorologist.

"Good morning, Roger. What's up?"

"I wanted to give you the latest update on conditions. They're getting worse." Baldwin then crisply ticked off a series of technical data before summarizing so it made more sense to Eaker. "May make the return trip a bit sporty." Roger was referring to the planes dispatched earlier in the morning.

Eaker noticed his weather man was standing in front of the fireplace He appreciated being kept informed, yet he suspected Colonel Baldwin had something else on his mind. "Anything else?"

"Actually there is, Sir. I'm going over to RAF Hadley for lunch and shop talk with their weather people and I was hoping I could tell them something about whether or not we might be interested in their Mosquitoes."

"Not yet, Roger, although I did mention it to Air Marshal Harris and he reacted positively. I suspect it will work out."

"That's good news, General."

"I suppose so, but don't say anything about it just yet."

"No, Sir, I won't." Baldwin was pleased that his suggestion to employ Mosquitoes might actually result in the wherewithal to gather data over the Continent before, during, and after a mission. In fact, he was very pleased, although his face showed no emotion.

"Good. Now, Colonel." Eaker paused to let the use of Baldwin's lower rank sink in. Yet the sparkle in his eyes and a slight grin on his face ran counter to the tone in his voice. "There may be a price to pay for this very sensible suggestion of yours."

"Sir?"

"If we end up with Mosquitoes for weather reconnaissance, I may assign you to fly them."

Baldwin, who did not at first realize that Eaker was teasing, visibly paled, but he recovered quickly. "I have but one life to give for my country, which probably does not care where exactly it is given."

"It would do you good, flying that is. Broaden your experience. You might even like it. Besides, Roger, we are the Eighth *Air* Force."

"Best damn outfit in the Army."

"That it is, Colonel, that it is. Now go help Keith Davenport make conversation with Air Vice Marshal Sidney for a few minutes. I need some time by myself. You could tell our guest how much you admire their little wooden airplane."

Immediately after the meeting with the RAF officer, Eaker would be speaking to General Harrison. Before doing so, he wanted to take another look at the report on auxiliary fuel tanks Harrison had prepared. He also wanted to sort out in his own mind questions about fighter escort he intended to ask the Director of Fighter Operations. General Eaker expected Keith Davenport and Roger Baldwin to entertain the British visitor for the next few minutes.

As the two colonels spoke with Air Vice Marshal Sidney, Richard Harrison sat in a nearby office conversing with Colonel Arnie.

"Colonel, where are the production numbers for the British-built fuel tanks?"

"There in your folder, General."

"What about their distribution to our fighters?"

"Going well. A few hiccups, but nothing serious."

"And the P-47s can go how far with the 108 tanks?"

"About 325 miles. About three hours of flight time, depending on the power setting. I've got a chart in your folder updating the one in the report. With the 108 tanks, the P-47s can cross the border with Holland and reach into Germany."

"Good. Eaker will want to hear that." General Harrison then made a mental note to mention this to Eaker at some point in their conversation.

"General, the subject of fighter tactics may come up."

"I don't think so, Colonel. General Eaker wants to talk fuel tanks and how they'll extend the range of our fighters. Besides, tactics are pretty much firm. We've told the escort groups to stay close in and protect the bombers. Eaker agrees with that. He's a bomber type and thinks they can do the job with or without the fighters."

"What do you think, Sir?

"I think whatever General Eaker thinks. He's the man in charge."

At that moment, Eaker was greeting Air Vice Marshal Sidney. Keith Davenport had been describing the August mission to Schweinfurt when the Eighth Air Force commander came out of his office. Eaker outranked the RAF officer, who thus saluted the American. The General responded in kind and welcomed his visitor to Wycombe Abbey.

"Thank you, General. You're most kind. Actually, I've been here before."

"Oh?" Eaker's voice did not hide his surprise.

"Yes, quite. My daughter went to school here a number of years ago. We'd visit when term began and fetch her when it ended."

"Well, we've made a few changes, although the building itself is still intact."

"The school was comfortable here. I trust you are as well."

"Yes, it's working out nicely. When we're gone, I hope the girls come back."

"I expect they will."

Eaker stood by the open door to his office and gently motioned the Air Vice Marshal to enter. The General then spoke to Baldwin and Davenport. "Thank you, gentlemen. I'll now take care of our guest."

The two colonels departed as Sidney and Eaker stepped inside. Once there, Eaker guided the British officer to a cushioned chair next to the large globe. The General sat in his winged chair. Eaker had reasoned this visit was not to debate strategy. Had it been so, he would have remained at his desk or met the Air Vice Marshal at a conference table. No, this was to be an informal meeting. No formal agenda. Nothing contentious to discuss. Sidney, whose first name was Philip, seemed relaxed, so Eaker expected little more than pleasant conversation, but he admittedly was curious why the RAF had sent such a high ranking officer to Wycombe Abbey.

"Cigarette?" Eaker had opened a small pewter case he kept filled for occasions like this.

"Yes, splendid. Thank you. Your American cigarettes are quite fancied over here." Philip Sidney removed a lighter from his pocket and lit the cigarette. Inhaling, he blew the smoke away from Eaker. "Splendid indeed."

"As you can see, I prefer a pipe." Eaker was eyeing the rack of pipes next to his books on the table beside him.

The General did not wish to appear abrupt, so he refrained from asking Sidney his purpose in coming. He chose instead to begin with the Air Vice Marshal by mentioning Berlin.

After a summer campaign against the industrial Ruhr Valley and a number of German cities, most notably Hamburg, the RAF had targeted the German capital for repeated visits by Bomber Command. Preliminary strikes had taken place in late August and early September, but success had not been achieved. Bombing accuracy was poor. Losses were high. Yet Air Marshal Harris, like Eaker, was determined to strike Germany and intended to hit Berlin hard and often. Air Vice Marshal Sidney, though attached to Fighter Command, would be familiar with this strategy.

"Let me ask you about Berlin. Are you going to go ahead with the raids?"

"Most definitely, Sir. Bomber Command is convinced we can defeat Germany from the air, or so weaken the country that they will not put up much of a fight once our armies engage."

"I think you're right. I just wish we could join you. We're not quite ready for such deep raids into Germany, but we're going back into Germany soon, and we're going to make them wish they never started this war."

"Together we can crush the Nazis."

"Indeed. I admire the RAF and the courage of its crews."

"There's no lacking for courage, General Eaker. Both in your Eighth Air Force and in Bomber Command."

Eaker welcomed the compliment, yet let it pass without comment. "And though I'm extremely fond of B-17s and B-24s, I must admit you have one fine aircraft in the Lancaster."

"She's a splendid airplane. Better than the Halifax and infinitely better than the Sterling, although I've never been in one."

"Fighters?" Eaker's question hinted at preference.

"I'm afraid so. Give me a Hurricane to fly and I'm a happy man."

"It's a good little airplane." Eaker knew about the Hawker Hurricane, as did everyone in England at that time. Designed by Sidney Camm, the Hurricane was the RAF's first mono-wing fighter plane. A sturdy eight-gun aircraft, by 1943 it was becoming obsolete. But in 1940, when teamed with the newer, more glamorous Spitfire, the Hurricane had brought the Luftwaffe its first defeat, in the process gaining immortality for the few who piloted these two airplanes.

"Yes it is. The Spitfire gets more attention, perhaps deservedly so. But Sidney Camm's little airplane shall always be my favorite flying machine."

"Well, your air force has done wonders with them, and with the Spitfires."

"That's kind of you to say. And that's why I'm here today. Spitfires, that is. General Eaker, I do not wish to appear rude, but let me, if I may, use an expression I've borrowed from you Americans, and come straight to the point."

"Go ahead, please."

"General Eaker, the long and the short of it is that we, the Royal Air Force, that is, would like to give one of your pilots a medal. Actually we would like to award him the Distinguished Flying Cross. And in doing so, we'd like to make a bit of a fuss about it."

Eaker relaxed. This meeting indeed was problem free. No hard decisions to make. No one likely to be killed as a result. "It sounds fine to me. And very generous of you. Tell me what did this pilot do?"

"He saved the lives of two Spitfire pilots."

"Wonderful. How did this come about?"

"Your pilot, with two of his comrades, took on a large formation of Mersserschmitts that were about to attack the Spitfires, one of which was damaged. Just like in one of your western films, this American came to the rescue. In the engagement that followed your pilot, he was flying a P-47, downed three Jerry aircraft, and completely frustrated the German attack. Apparently, it was a splendid piece of flying—quite courageous. The chap didn't hesitate. Flew right into those buggers. Took on a good portion of the Luftwaffe. Our pilots, who were able to put down in an emergency airfield, witnessed the entire episode."

"Sounds like a happy ending. The kind we like."

"Quite so. It most certainly was a piece of distinguished flying and we'd like to recognize the pilot. Quite a gallant lad."

"You certainly have my permission, and my thanks."

"General Eaker, there's more. We'd like to honor this American in a ceremony that receives widespread public attention. We've spoken with the BBC and they have agreed to broadcast the event. The two Spitfire pilots would attend and make a few brief remarks, thanking your pilot and such. Then we'd award the DFC to your chap and he'd say a few appropriate remarks. All this in front of a radio microphone."

"That's a terrific idea." Most generals disliked such public relations events. Eaker, however, was not one of them. He understood the value of putting forward your story to the public at large. Indeed, much earlier, he and Hap Arnold had co-authored a book promoting air power as a weapon of war. So when Air Vice Marshal Sidney mentioned broadcasting the award ceremony, Eaker immediately saw benefit in what the British officer was proposing. "This would show that our two air forces can help each other out, and work together. And I guess just as importantly, it will demonstrate the respect we have for one another."

"Exactly so. For our side, it will serve to remind the British people of the great benefit in having the American forces on our soil. We need the value of cooperation expressed in human terms, something everyone can understand."

"You'll have my full support. When do you propose having the ceremony?"

"Soon. Certainly within a fortnight."

"Let me know when you set the date, and I'll make sure you have from us whatever you need."

"Thank you, General. There is one additional aspect of this I should perhaps mention. It's by no means certain and it may not come to pass, but we've talked with the Palace and there's a chance, albeit small, that Her Majesty the Queen might honor us with her presence at the ceremony."

Eaker was taken aback by what he had just heard. His mind quickly began to list what would need to be done were the Queen of England to attend an event the focus of which was an Eighth Air Force pilot. The list was very long. "That would be something."

"The possibility is real, though again, it's small. From what I gather, schedules may not permit. She is, of course, frightfully busy. I thought I should mention this to you nonetheless. Though we must, for now, keep it among ourselves—hush, hush, so to speak. You do understand?"

"Of course, but you'll keep me posted?"

"Absolutely, Sir." Glancing at his watch, the Air Vice Marshal rose from his chair, having decided he had taken up enough time from the commander of America's Eighth Air Force. As Philip Sidney stood, General Eaker shook his hand.

"We're delighted about this award; it's quite good of you. The ceremony's a fine idea and has my full support. You'll get from the Eighth whatever you need." Eaker was now escorting the RAF officer to the door. "I do have one question I should have asked earlier. What's the name of the P-47 pilot?"

"Ah, yes. His name is Forester, a lieutenant colonel I believe. Do you know him?

"No, but I've heard a few things about him."

"Well I suspect he's one splendid fellow. Quite what we need in fighter pilots, don't you think?"

Recalling Keith Davenport's remark, Eaker chuckled to himself. "I'm certainly beginning to think so."

As Ira Eaker accompanied his visitor to the room outside his office, he saw Roger Baldwin and General Harrison sitting together engaged in a conversation that appeared unusually animated. Next to him was an RAF Wing Commander, obviously assigned to Sidney. All four officers rose when Eaker and the Air Vice Marshal entered.

"Well, good-bye," said Eaker to Philip Sidney. "Stay in touch and thank you once again."

"Good-bye, General." This time, no salutes were exchanged. The atmosphere was more like one of a family gathering than a military headquarters.

That atmosphere vanished when the Air Vice Marshal and his aide had departed. General Eaker beckoned Harris Hull. "Come in, Major. I need you for a minute"

Once inside, the General spoke again. "Harris, I want you to get me the most recent data on our fighter groups—sorties, kills, that sort of thing. And anything you can get your hands on about a Lieutenant Colonel Forester. He commands the 19th Fighter Group. Also, see if you can get Mike McCready on the telephone. I'd like to talk with him."

"Right away, Sir,"

"By the way, what were General Harrison and Colonel Baldwin talking about? They seemed somewhat agitated."

Major Hull paused. He knew exactly what they were talking about. Hull had little respect for Richard Harrison and felt he thus needed to compensate in responding to Eaker. Harris carefully considered his words and spoke without any emotion in his voice. "General Harrison was expressing his views about one of our fighter commanders."

"I see." Eaker recognized the tone. Major Hull sounded like that whenever he was striving to be diplomatic. "Well, no matter. I'll be hearing his views soon enough myself. Go get the data I requested and track down General McCready."

"Yes, Sir." That Hull understood the urgency behind these orders was revealed in the haste with which he left Eaker's office.

But before the Major was completely gone, the General spoke once again. "One last thing, Harris. I may be attending an RAF award ceremony fairly soon. Consider that a heads up."

"Yes, Sir." And Harris was out the door.

Eaker then turned round to his credenza, reaching for the binder notebook labeled *Escort Groups*. After briefly reviewing its content for several minutes, he switched on his office intercom. "Please have Colonel Baldwin come in."

"Yes, General?" Roger Baldwin's face reflected the question he had just asked. He stood at attention, or what in his mind passed as attention.

"Sit down, Roger. I'm going to ask you a question. The answer's important and I want you to give me a straight answer. And no, it's not about the weather."

"Sir." This response was Baldwin's acknowledgement that he understood fully Eaker's remark. Nonetheless, he was puzzled. Occasionally, the General would ask his views on a variety of subjects, none of them having to do with meteorology. Roger Baldwin never understood why Eaker did so. Baldwin was unaware how much the commander of the Eighth Air Force valued his judgment.

"Tell me what you think, and what you've heard, about Colonel Tom Forester, commander of the 19th Fighter Group."

"Well, General," Baldwin gathered his thoughts, "I should tell you first I have met him, but just once. He and I went to the same college, so I might be a bit biased."

"Dartmouth, yes?"

"Yes, Sir."

"Fine school. Just tell me what you think."

"Forester seems solid and bright—doesn't bullshit you. Not the military type, if you'll pardon the expression. Scuttlebutt is that he's a hot pilot and an excellent group commander."

"I see." Thumbing through the black binder notebook, Eaker continued. "The records would indicate that as well."

At this moment, Harris Hull appeared in the doorway. "Here's what I could gather quickly, General. Seems Colonel Forester is doing a good job."

"I've just heard the same thing. And General McCready?"

"He's going to call you shortly."

"Good. Major, tell Keith Davenport he can ride with us to London. And let me have a few minutes alone before you send in General Harrison. Thank you, gentlemen."

This last remark meant Hull and Baldwin were dismissed As they departed, General Eaker examined the folder Major Hull had given him. He then returned to the black notebook.

Five minutes later, Harris Hull announced via the intercom that, "General Harrison is here for his appointment."

"Show him in, Major."

"Yes, Sir. Did you get General McCready's call?"

"I did. Thank you."

Eaker was stoking his pipe as Major Hull brought General Harrison into the office. As Harrison walked in, Hull discreetly left.

"Good morning, General Eaker."

"Good morning, Dick." The culture of the Army Air Forces permitted the senior officer present to address his subordinates by their first name. Rarely, if ever, did junior officers reply in kind.

Brigadier General Richard Harrison stood in front of Eaker who now sat at his desk. Eaker's eyes took in the Director of Fighter Operations. What they saw was a trim, smartly dressed, forty-one-year-old man with a touch of grey in his hair, which was cut short. He wore aviator glasses behind which blue eyes focused sharply. Adorning his dark greenish brown service jacket were two rows of campaign ribbons. Silver aviator wings were pinned above the ribbons. The wings contained both a star and a wreath, identifying Harrison as a Command Pilot, which meant he had at least ten years of service with a minimum of 2,000 flying hours. To himself, Eaker remarked that Harrison certainly looked the part of an Army Air Force general.

"That was a good report on fuel tanks. Thorough, understandable, and I found the charts most helpful."

"Thank you, Sir." In fact, Colonel Arnie had prepared the report. Harrison edited the piece, making the report smoother and easier to read, though not altering its substance. However, the DFO had read the report several times, so by the time of this meeting with Eaker, he was well versed in its contents.

"Any distribution problems? Are we getting the tanks out to the fighter groups?"

"That's going well, General. A few hiccups, but nothing serious." Colonel Arnie would have been amused to hear Harrison use his exact words. Harrison was not aware he had done so.

"And range? How far can they take P-47s?"

Richard Harrison knew Eaker would be pleased with the answer. "Across into Germany. Not as far as we'd like, but we'll no longer have to turn back at the German–Dutch border."

In his mind, Eaker recalled the cities in Germany that Keith Davenport had listed. Now Eighth Air Force fighters would accompany the strike force to at least some of these targets.

Though the meeting with General Harrison had started well, Eaker found the remainder unsatisfactory. He had turned their discussion to the subject of fighter tactics, for which the Director of Fighter Operations seemed unprepared. Moreover, Harrison appeared uncomfortable with the subject. With ease and expertise, he could discuss logistics and training, two areas where he had performed well. But in reviewing operational tactics, the man seemed unable to grasp essentials. On a topic most fighter pilots could expound ad infinitum, the Brigadier General displayed neither imagination nor flexibility. On how to more quickly assemble the escorts, on how to better integrate RAF capabilities with those of the Eighth, on how to improve radio communications between airborne commanders, Harrison had little to say. To Eaker, Harrison focused entirely too much on keeping the P-47s close to the bombers and above 18,000 feet. No doubt, that was important, but it was hardly the complete story. General Harrison, Eaker concluded, believed fighter tactics were fairly straightforward. The Eighth Air Force commander knew better. Nothing about war in the air was simple.

Later, as Eaker was being driven to the meeting of the Advisory Committee accompanied by Keith Davenport and Harris Hull, the last few minutes of his conversation with the DFO came to mind. For Eaker, they had an element of humor that he was certain Harrison had failed to see. Just as Eaker was leaving for London, Harrison had brought up a new subject.

"General Eaker, there is one other item I should like to mention. One, unfortunately, I feel forced to bring up."

"Go ahead." Eaker was looking at his watch. "However, I'm due downstairs in three minutes."

"It concerns one of our group commanders."

"Which one?"

"Forester, the CO of the fighter group at Bromley Park. Actually, he's the acting Commanding Officer."

"What's the problem?"

"In my opinion, the man is not up to the job. He doesn't follow orders. We've laid down strict directives to the fighter groups about escort work. They're to stick close to the bombers. The 19th apparently doesn't do that. And Forester's going down below the prescribed altitude chasing German fighters."

"I understand the 19th is now doing well. Out of their slump, so to speak."

"They are doing better, General, but I've concluded the group is poorly led. Forester sets a poor example."

"Dick, that's not what Mike McCready tells me." An old friend of Eaker's, Lieutenant General Michael McCready was Deputy Commander of all Eighth Air Force fighter aircraft. "I spoke with General McCready just before you came in, and he told me that, next to Zemke, Colonel Forester was one of the best group commanders we have."

Actually, McCready had spoken somewhat more directly than suggested by Eaker's comment. "Listen, Ira we're going to win the war with men like Forester, so we better stick up for them. Forester's a good man and he's doing a hell of a job with the 19th. His only fault is that he wants to shoot down Krauts, which is why the hell we're here. I wish we had more like him."

Eaker then told McCready he suspected General Harrison wanted to relieve Forester as commander of the 19th.

"Figures. That guy doesn't know diddly-doo about combat flying. Why you still have him as DFO I'll never understand. Ira, leave Forester alone. He's doing a first rate job and the 19th is one of our better groups."

"But is Forester disobeying orders? Leaving the bombers and all that?"

"Hell no. That's just Harrison and his screwed up ideas as to how to do escort work. The 19th stays plenty close to the formation. When Jerry shows up, the group is there. Harrison wants to keep them too close. Fighters need room to fight. Forester knows what he's doing. He and his group are also starting to shoot down Germans, which, in my book, is what the hell they're supposed to be doing."

"So we keep Forester?"

"Absolutely. He's one of the best we've got. Wish I had more like him."

"Thanks, Mac." Eaker began to laugh. "As always, you've held back and not told me what you're really thinking."

"Don't mention it, Chief. How you doing up here in your girls' school?"

"I'm fine. Just wish I could fly and drop a few bombs myself."

"We're too old for that, Ira. Now, we're just generals."

General Harrison had no intention of backing off, despite Eaker's response "I respect General McCready, Sir. He's a fine officer. But, in this instance, I have to disagree with him. Colonel Forester sets a poor example for the men. He's not proper military and he's not obeying orders I personally gave to all group commanders."

"So, what do you wish to do?"

"I regret having to say this." Harrison was not speaking truth-fully. He had absolutely no regret in what he was about to say. "I'm going to relieve him of command."

Eaker heard this remark with a touch of sadness. He was truly disappointed in his DFO. General Harrison's grasp of fighter tactics was demonstratively weak and he now seemed to have a vendetta against Forester whose only crime, as far as Eaker could tell, was to have success with the fighter group he commanded. Forester proba-bly bent some rules, but Eaker told himself that long ago he and Mike McCready had done the same thing.

For a moment Eaker worked on his pipe, which he held in his left hand. After taking a puff and then exhaling, he spoke to Richard Harrison. "That would be somewhat awkward."

"Sir?" The DFO was puzzled by Eaker's response. *Awkward? How could removing Forester be awkward?*

"Seems our English friends want to give Colonel Forester a medal for what they consider some distinguished flying."

Surprised, General Harrison stood where he was. Then, gauging Eaker's voice and body language, he spoke, "General, I don't wish to complicate matters, and certainly the British can do as they see fit, but Forester needs to be disciplined, and possibly court mar-tialed."

"Which would send exactly the wrong message," Eaker fin-ished the sentence for him. "Dick, do us a favor, yourself included, and drop this matter."

"Sir?"

"We can't go around court martialing someone the RAF has just decorated. We'd all look pretty silly, wouldn't we? And we can't relieve a group commander who, by most accounts, is doing an out-standing job."

"But General . . . " Harrison began to protest, but saw Eaker raise his right hand to signal silence. The DFO paused. The Lieutenant General before him did not want to hear more. Quickly, he changed his tone of voice. "I'll do what the General wishes."

Richard Harrison was angry. Not furious, but more than a little displeased. Wisely, he showed no emotion. Eaker was the boss and nothing would be accomplished by challenging the Eighth Air Force commander. General Harrison had advanced in the Army Air Force by pleasing his superior officer. He intended to continue to do so. This clearly was a step backwards. So Harrison willed his anger to subside, replacing it with a calculation that what might have been gained no longer was worth the cost. To make this thought more palatable, he reduced Forester's importance, dismissing the episode as minor. After all, the issue involved nothing more than a lieutenant colonel. Harrison went on to reason that other steps would present themselves. These he would take to forward his career. The goal remained the same—two stars and the rank of major general.

"Good." Eaker was now speaking. "Let Forester get on with his job. I'll have General McCready keep an eye on him. If there's a problem, I'll know about it." Eaker had no intention of asking Mike McCready to do any such thing. The problem was not Forester. The problem, apparently, was Harrison. This, Eaker decided, he would deal with later. Presently, he had to leave for the meeting with Jimmy Dixon's committee. "Now, I need to do my job, which, at the moment, takes me to London. Good day, General."

Harrison was still standing in front of Eaker's desk as the more senior officer, pipe in hand, departed. Noticing the two books on the nearby table, the General examined the titles. He then opened *Scaramouche* and *The Master of Ballentrae*. Quickly, he skimmed through a few pages. Richard Harrison, who rarely read for pleasure, found the text strange. Why, he wondered, would someone in command authority read such trivial works?

—◆—

The drive to London took thirty-five minutes. Traffic was light, given the near absence of private vehicles, and the 1942 Dodge sedan carrying the three officers moved at considerable speed. Eaker sat in the rear seat as did Colonel Davenport. Harris Hull sat in the front along with the driver, a Corporal Lewis, who frequently drove the Commander of the Eighth Air Force.

As the car sped down the road, Hull became nervous. He thought Lewis was driving too fast, especially given the weather. A light rain had begun to fall, and many leaves sprinkled the road now that fall was arriving. The road had numerous curves, which Lewis navigated in spirited fashion. Because the Corporal had, more than once, forgotten that traffic in England kept to the left, Harris Hull was extremely anxious. For his part, Lewis remained calm. With both hands on the steering wheel and eyes on the road, he resembled a professional race car driver. Such an appearance was not surprising as, prior to joining the army, the Corporal raced automobiles in North Carolina. The Dodge continued to speed. Indeed, its speed increased, at which point the Major ordered the Corporal to slow down. Lewis complied, although he gradually pushed the accelerator down and the Dodge resumed its original speed. Hull conceded and decided to seek support from higher authority—not Eaker, who trusted Lewis and seemed oblivious to the high speed, but to someone with even greater rank. There in the front seat of the Dodge, Harris Hull prayed, hoping that God might see them safely through to London.

As the Major prayed, Ira Eaker and Keith Davenport chatted informally. They put aside the war and spoke of life back in the United States. Each mentioned what they missed most. Davenport said he missed America's expansiveness. To him, everything in England was small. In a land where automobiles, roads, and farms seemed tiny in comparison to those in the States, Keith Davenport felt confined. The Colonel added that, from what he had seen, fences seemed to be everywhere. Built of stone, wood, or metal, they delineated spaces and helped give England its tidy appearance.

Eaker said he missed the warmth and sunshine that seemed to have passed by England. When the sun did appear, the country was breathtakingly beautiful, particularly the gardens, which were tended with great care and skill. But the sun appeared to be a precious commodity in this land, rare and unpredictable. Jokingly, he told

Davenport that after a few more years in England he most definitely would retire to Florida or Arizona so that his tired old bones would never be wet again.

Both men laughed awkwardly when one commented that neither had said they missed their wives most of all. They were both happily married and completely faithful. In truth, Eaker and Davenport did miss their wives, but they would admit it only to themselves. Their business, the business of the Eighth Air Force, to which they also were married, was war, which the two officers felt necessitated compartmentalizing their person life. The two men had placed other pieces of their existence in storage.

God answered the prayers of Harris Hull and delivered the Dodge sedan intact to the Royal Aeronautical Society. The Society was housed in what once had been a private home. Elegant and well tended, the building sat in Mayfair, north of Picadilly. In front of the building's large wooden doors, a doorman stood ready to greet visitors and shoo away those who did not belong. The doorman was Milton "Taffy" Edwards. He was an imposing figure, physically strong with a military bearing ingrained from a long career in the ranks. Taffy knew the city of London better than the Lord Mayor. He also knew much about the military including that of the United States. Hence, he snapped to attention when the big American sedan pulled up, noticing immediately the small red flag with three white stars attached to the front fender. Before Major Hull could get out of the car, Edwards, umbrella in hand, opened the rear door, barking a welcoming, but nonetheless severe, "Sir!"

"Thank you" responded Lieutenant General Ira Eaker in a much softer voice.

"Sir!" Taffy bellowed again, no doubt rattling windows as far away as Buckingham Palace. This response was Edward's standard comment, but served as a variety of messages. In this case, it conveyed an additional word of welcome as well as a mark of respect.

Davenport and Hull were about to follow Eaker up the steps when they saw the General return to the Dodge and speak to Lewis.

"Thank you, Corporal. We made good time."

"Nah, General. We did only okay. Six minutes off our best time to Marble Arch."

"Must have been the rain."

"We'll do better next time, General. I promise."

Edwards held open the front door as Eaker sprinted up the steps and went inside, followed by Davenport and Hull. As they did so, another American officer, unnoticed, came walking up the street, having watched the arrival and departure of the big sedan. This man also belonged to the Eight Air Force, but, as a lieutenant colonel, he had not been driven to London. Instead, he had taken a train from the village of Bromley Park, then hailed a taxi, which had carried him to Piccadilly Circus. From there, despite the rain, he had decided to walk, wishing to get a better feel for the city he now expected to visit more often.

"Morning, Colonel!" Taffy Edwards again was bellowing.

"Good morning. Could you tell me if this is the Royal Aeronautical Society?"

"Yes it is. Can I help you?" Edwards's voice remained loud.

"I'm here for a meeting, an advisory committee."

"Good show that. Well, in you go, Colonel." Taffy was easing the American towards the door. "We don't want to keep the General waiting, nor the ladies."

Once inside, Eaker, Davenport, and Hull found themselves in a large foyer, dominated by a grand curved staircase. Above them hung a lovely crystal chandelier that enhanced an already elegant decor. The walls were an off white, although one side was painted a light rose red, which stood in attractive contrast to a burgundy carpet that covered most, but not all, of the hardwood floor. Near the staircase, set in brass holders, were three flags. One, placed to the left, was the Stars and Stripes. Next to it stood the Union Jack. The third flag, which the Americans did not recognize, represented the City of London. It was white with a large cross of red. Opposite the flags, a wooden sign, also white, faced the wooden doors to be seen immediately by anyone entering from the outside. Stenciled neatly in black block letters on the sign was *Advisory Committee for Visiting*

Americans (ACVA). An arrow on the sign pointed to the right. In the upper left hand corner of the sign, an insignia had been painted with considerable skill. Eaker and his colleagues did recognize this. The insignia, identical to the colorful patches these men wore on their uniforms, was a gold number eight, the bottom part of which had wings, set in a circle of blue.

Colonel James Dixon greeted General Eaker as soon as the three officers entered the room. "Good morning, General," said Dixon, saluting as he spoke.

"Hello, Jimmy. What's the drill?"

Dixon explained how the meeting was to proceed. Lord Rawlins, the Vice Chairman of the Royal Aeronautical Society, was to begin with a few words of welcome. Then, Dixon would make some appropriate remarks, to be followed by Lord Mayor of London and then General Eaker. Dixon would then introduce the members of the Committee.

"That's when Colonel Davenport shows us his speaking skills?"

"Yes, Sir," responded Dixon with amusement as he saw a sudden strained expression on Keith Davenport's face.

"Forester, too. I assume he's here."

"Haven't seen him, Sir."

Eaker frowned. "Well, we won't wait for him."

"Yes, Sir. General, we'll be sitting at a number of small tables. You're with Lord Rawlins and His Honor the Mayor. Colonel Davenport, you're with the General. Major Hull, you're at Table 4. There's a lectern from which you can speak and see everyone in the room. Microphone is good, though the room doesn't really need one. Acoustics are pretty good. Lighting is good. Everything looks in order, although I can't vouch for the food."

"Sounds easy enough." Eaker looked at the three men, and then at his watch. "Well gentlemen, we begin in four minutes. Let's circulate."

Jimmy Dixon was listening as the General spoke, but was looking elsewhere. He had noticed an attractive woman standing alone near the flags. She was wearing a forest green suit, smartly tailored, with a large silk scarf draped over her neck and shoulders. Unlike the other women in the room, she wore no hat. Her black hair, somewhat long, but shining in the light from the chandelier, set off her pale skin, which, like the room itself, was white, but with hints of soft red.

With a practiced hand, Dixon guided General Eaker towards the flags. "Come with me, General. I'm going to introduce you to that lovely woman in front of us."

The two men moved forward. The woman was still alone, but seemed completely at ease. She was admiring the room, although aware her solitude was about to be broken.

"Hello again, Colonel." The woman had spoken first.

Jimmy Dixon responded to Helen Trent with a smile. "Mrs. Trent, permit me to introduce General Ira Eaker, commander of the Eighth Air Force. General, this is Helen Trent, a member of our Committee."

"Mrs. Trent, my pleasure." General Eaker took Helen's right hand in his, shaking it firmly, but not hard. "Let me thank you for agreeing to serve on our committee."

"My pleasure. I hope I can help."

"I'm sure you will. And I hope it's a pleasant experience for you."

Looking straight at Eaker, Helen saw a man whose face projected determination and dignity while somehow retaining an American informality. "I'm sure it will be, General."

EIGHT

Jimmy Dixon had suggested to Helen that she sit at Table 7. Located in a corner of the room not far from where General Eaker was seated, the table afforded Helen an unobstructed view of the proceedings. The room itself, to the right of the entryway and facing the street, contained eight tables. These were round and placed near one another, giving the room the appearance of a small private dining room. Actually, the Royal Aeronautical Society used the room for stand-up receptions. But as the Society's regular dining facility was rather large, Dixon had convinced the day manager to use the smaller space, contending that the larger room would overwhelm the Advisory Committee. "In this case," Dixon had told Mr. Elliot, the manager, "the blue reception room is more intimate, and will encourage conversation and camaraderie."

The room most definitely was blue. Helen thought the colors worked, although she herself would not have chosen such a scheme. Three of the walls were painted sapphire blue. The fourth wall, which opened to a large reading room populated with numerous winged chairs, was papered with a pattern of wide alternating stripes of shiny and matte gold. Alongside the walls were several elegant wooden tables above which hung two large mirrors, both in gilded frames. The table linens also were blue. These contrasted nicely with the off-white Royal Doulton china bordered in navy. Complementing the walls and table settings was a large oriental rug. It featured beige and blue, sprinkled with yellows and traces of grey. Helen found the look created to be attractive, but perhaps a bit too much.

Positioned at Table 7, Helen faced a large fireplace that was surrounded by an elaborate and lovely marble mantelpiece. Atop the mantel were two large brass candelabras. Each contained six candles. No illumination was provided as the candelabras were purely decorative. Light came from a central chandelier. More elaborate than the one in the entryway, this fixture was a magnificent example of Venetian artistry, having been made in Murano expressly for this reception room. Helen marveled at the delicacy of the design and of the many crystal attachments. She was less impressed by the large rectangular painting placed above the mantelpiece between the two candle holders. This was an oil on canvas, in a carved wooden frame, of two men pulling a fabric and frame contraption out of a shed onto what appeared to be a sand dune. Helen thought the image to be bleak and noticeably stark in color and form. The artist had mastered his paints, but the work lacked a richness Helen believed great paintings required. Only later would she learn of the subject whose significance she was well aware. The painting, a gift to the Society from the Aviation Club of New York, portrayed Orville and Wilbur Wright at work in North Carolina the morning of their epic accomplishment.

Sitting next to Helen, on her right, was John Bigelow. Mr. Bigelow was a trade unionist. He represented transport workers in London and throughout the country. A gruff, not altogether friendly person, Jake Bigelow had accepted Colonel Dixon's invitation to serve on the Advisory Committee with reluctance. He saw little need to assist the Americans and wished to focus solely on efforts to improve working conditions for members of the Transport Workers

Union. Only a telephone call from the number two man at the TWU brought Jake on board. Jimmy Dixon wanted Bigelow or someone like him on the Committee because Army Air Force personnel, when off base, were dependent upon public transportation. Dixon also wanted the Committee's composition to reflect Britain's political diversity. Because the Labour Party served in Winston Churchill's national coalition government, someone from the left needed to be a Committee member.

Chemistry between Jake Bigelow and Helen Trent was nonexistent. The trade unionist was not rude, but made little effort to engage in conversation. He looked at this well dressed lady to his left and judged her to be upper class. She was a person with whom he had nothing in common. How could such a woman understand the hardships he and his mates faced everyday? With her expensive clothes (the green suit she was wearing probably cost more than his wife's entire wardrobe) and her fine hands, hands that showed no signs of hard work, this Mrs. Trent was not someone whom he wanted to know. Let her sit with her rich friends and fancy clothes. He would mind his own business and hope she did the same.

She did not. Ever the diplomat, Helen attempted to strike up a conversation. Aware of their differences and sensing hostility, she sought common ground on which they might communicate. Helen asked Bigelow about his family, about the war, and about the Advisory Committee. Jake responded with little enthusiasm and few words. Helen Trent kept trying, but was unable to overcome the man's reticence. Finally, she decided to respect his desire to remain silent, so she turned her attention elsewhere. With the seat to her left empty, Helen watched quietly as the room filled. Before her eyes, the men and women who comprised the Advisory Committee took their places.

Most everyone was seated when Helen noticed an American officer standing alone in the doorway. In search of a seat, the man's eyes scanned the room. He seemed not at all uncomfortable that a number of people were watching him.

Helen thought the officer was particularly well dressed. She did not know that because American army officers had to provide, and pay for, their own uniforms, many went to private tailors who made the clothes according to standard specifications. The result was that uniforms often looked good and fit perfectly. Such was the case with the officer in the doorway. Before going overseas, his father had insisted his son purchase a new set of uniforms from the family tailor on Madison Avenue. English tailors also benefited from this American practice. Many Eighth Air Force uniforms were hand-crafted in London, bringing welcome revenue to shops throughout the city.

The officer in the doorway wore what in the army was called "pinks and greens." The winter service jacket, dark brown with a tint of forest green, covered an olive shirt worn with a brown tie. His trousers and shirt were a color officially designated "drab No. 54 (light shade)." This was a brownish grey, which in certain light had a decidedly pinkish cast. The combination of colors worked well. American officers, at least those with custom tailored uniforms, looked sharp.

Helen found herself staring at the man, whom she considered rather good looking. He was of medium height, more stocky than skinny, with dusty brown hair that matched a well trimmed moustache. His head was oddly angular, with a nose on the small side. But what drew Helen's attention were the eyes and the expression on his face. Although Helen couldn't tell their color, his eyes, from where she sat, penetrated deeply whatever they focused upon. They conveyed a determination, a forcefulness of character, even perhaps a hint of arrogance. Someone looking at him, as Helen was, saw in the man's face kindness, as well as confidence. A sense of humor was also apparent. This manifested itself in a look of bemusement the Lieutenant Colonel, for that was his rank, conveyed as he surveyed the now crowded room. Helen was not sure how all these traits could coexist in one person, or why she was so certain that they did. But she was convinced this American possessed these qualities, and in abundance.

As he walked into the room where the meeting was to be held, the American officer recalled the doorman's comment about not keeping the General or the ladies waiting. The general in question he noticed immediately. Eaker was sitting at the most prominent table, near the middle of the room. General Eaker acknowledged his presence with an approving nod. The Colonel interpreted the gesture as awareness on Eaker's part that the Committee's fighter pilot had arrived on time. How the General was to know the identity of this pilot the Colonel did not contemplate. In fact, Eaker recognized the officer because Harris Hull had included a photograph in the files he gave the General prior to the meeting with Richard Harrison.

The Colonel also noticed the large number of women in the room. For reasons he did not stop to consider, this surprised him. He had expected the Advisory Committee to consist mostly of men. But here in a room so blue that it reminded him of the skies above France, he saw at least fifteen women. Some were old; a few were young. Some appeared well dressed; several were in plain garb. All were talking to people at their tables, save one woman.

As the officer scanned the room, this woman came into focus. Sitting silently, alone with her thoughts, she was simply watching the other people in the room, appearing to enjoy being apart from the activity around her. The woman wore a simple green suit, which, on her, looked extremely elegant. While she was no youngster, the woman was not old. He estimated her to be in her late thirties, maybe forty.

He was neither prepared for was how lovely she looked, nor for the impact she had upon him. Literally, his breath was taken away. He forced himself to continue to scan the room so as not to stare. He could hear his mother speaking sternly to him in a restaurant. "Thomas, do not stare. People will think you have no manners." Yet, he could not help himself, nor did he really wish to. Willingly, his eyes went back to the woman in green. She was striking, one of the most beautiful creatures he had ever seen. At Bromley Park, he had seen few women and interacted with none. There was, after all, a war to be fought and there was neither time, nor any real desire to get involved with members of the opposite sex. This woman made him realize his folly. Suddenly, unexpectedly, and powerfully, she inflicted upon his being a desire so strong that little else mattered. Women can do that to men. And when they do, the effect is total. The man unravels. The walls of his compartmentalized life tumble and merge. Priorities are reset. Attention is redirected. The man aches with longing for the company and pleasure of the woman involved.

Situationally aware, as fighter pilots must be, the Colonel understood what had happened. Like a P-47 racked by bursts of ground fire, he had been hit hard. His balance was upset. In the air, he would concentrate his energies to recover. Now, in the blue room of the Royal Aeronautical Society, he did the same. Looking at tables to his right, he fought to regain his composure, and did so. As he continued to glance about the room, he hoped no one had noticed what had just occurred.

The officer saw that, besides Eaker, a number of people had seen him come in, but they seemed unaware of his distraction. Soon, they had looked elsewhere, continuing to talk with those at their table.

Except for the woman. Still silent, she was now looking at him. His composure was about to fly apart again when he saw something that until now had escaped his attention. The chair to the left of the lady was empty.

Helen Trent found herself again focusing upon the American officer. He was indeed good looking, but the more she looked, the more she thought him intriguing rather than traditionally handsome. His expression had now changed. No longer seemingly amused by his own presence at the Royal Aeronautical Society, the officer appeared flushed and ever so slightly distraught. What a strange metamorphosis. What could have caused the man to change his expression? He was still glancing about when the thought occurred to Helen that in addition to assessing his whereabouts, the poor fellow was looking for a place to sit. Thereupon, with her left hand, Helen slid back the empty chair causing it to be more visible. She wanted the American to sit next to her. Helen Trent rationalized her action on the basis of politeness. The man needed somewhere to sit and the chair next to her was empty. But she knew customary polite behavior was not the reason. Quickly, very quickly, she pondered her motives. Was it vanity? The need to control? Loneliness? A desire for excitement? Or was it something sweeter, yet more earthy, with all sorts of implications a woman of forty-three best not pursue?

A veteran of air battles where indecision cost lives, the officer had chosen his course of action. Stepping into the room, he headed toward the empty chair and the woman who had so jarred his composure. He saw she was looking straight at him.

Helen watched as the man approached. *God what am I doing? I'm acting like a schoolgirl. Gain control of yourself.*

The American was also talking to himself as he made his way towards the empty chair.

Stay calm. Don't walk too fast. Remain focused. This is just a woman, not an Me-109. Above all, do not, repeat, do not, say something stupid.

The officer followed his own advice. He did not say anything he later regretted, though his first remark, for someone so taken with a woman, was hardly memorable.

"Excuse me, is this seat taken?"

"No, it's not." Helen moved the chair out further, blocking forward progress by the American.

"May I?" The officer took hold of the chair, claiming the seat for himself.

"Please do." Helen's voice betrayed none of the emotion she felt.

"My name is Tom Forester."

"Hello. I'm Helen Trent. Please do sit down."

Tom did so, pulling out the chair and placing himself next to Helen. With body language she welcomed his presence and found to her surprise that she was perfectly relaxed. Any girlish anxiety was gone. She remained fascinated with the man. Indeed, her interest had grown for, in seeing him up close, she verified those contradictory traits she first had perceived when looking at him across the room. This man seemed to have a gentle side, a kindness uncommon in the male species. Yet his eyes conveyed a capability for decisive, even harsh action. Not in years had Helen come across someone so instantly appealing.

Forester was also relaxed. Now just inches away from Helen, he could see that she was truly lovely, maybe more so than he first had noticed. Her hair was lustrous and abundant. Deep black, it contrasted with creamy skin for which English women were noted, but few possessed. Helen's mouth was large, her eyes a deep green that sparkled as she spoke. Not classically beautiful, Helen Trent had individual features others might not envy, but which together formed a package that was striking. Forester found the lady sexy, but his attention went beyond carnal appeal. She was elegant and dignified, with a captivating presence.

To Tom, Helen Trent seemed completely at ease. This, in turn, made Tom more comfortable—so much so that he let down his guard, allowing Helen, if she wished, to meet the real Thomas Forester. Being a man, as well as a group commander, Forester kept a shield about him to retain privacy and control. That he withdrew the shield upon first meeting Helen was remarkable. Rarely did he do so. The shield enabled Forester to keep his distance. Few people were permitted access. Harry Collins was one. Now Helen Trent was another. She would meet the person Tom really was. Despite having more than a full measure of self-confidence, Forester was suddenly concerned that she might not like what she encountered.

Both individuals had wanted to meet the other. Sitting side by side, proximity no longer an obstacle, they each privately hoped their instincts had been correct and that first impressions would endure. Much, they knew, depended on their conversation. Each expected an awkward moment or two. Happily, none occurred. In the minutes before the meeting began, Helen and Tom found conversation easy and interesting. Both the English lady and American officer were pleased by this. They were enjoying the other's company, though neither gave any hint of their pleasure beyond what good manners would permit.

At first, their topic of conversation was a safe one. They spoke about the Advisory Committee. Helen told Forester about Warren Smith and his insistence that she be a committee member and about her meeting with Jimmy Dixon. Tom explained to Helen how General Harrison had given him the assignment to Dixon's committee. Forester was truthful. He told Helen his involvement with the Advisory Committee was a form of punishment.

"That's awful. Why should he be so spiteful?"

"Generals are not always nice people."

"What are you going to do about it?"

"Absolutely nothing. I'm under orders and, being in the Army . . . "

"I thought you were in the Air Force."

"Well, I am. The Air Force is part of the army. It's not like in Britain where the air force is a separate organization. In the States, it's a branch of the army, although it functions separately, just like the RAF." Forester was correct. There were no "airmen" in the Eighth Air Force. They were "soldiers" even though everyone expected, once the war was over, that the Army Air Forces would become an independent service. "Anyway, I'm under orders, so here I am in this blue room."

"'Tis blue, isn't it? Would you rather be flying?"

Tom was about to say yes when he stopped himself. Tom realized that telling a woman sitting next to you that you'd rather be somewhere else was unwise. Even if true, which in this instance he was not sure it was, such a remark would be ill advised if not rude.

"Well, I'm here in Britain to fly and fight, which is what I've been trained to do. But this committee can be useful, and, hopefully, I can be as well."

"Should I believe you? Pilots, I'm told, love to fly."

"Yes, Ma'am, we do. The challenge for me is not only to fly, but to also win and lead a team effort. I am supposed to turn a bunch of men and their flying machines into an effective fighter group, something they and I can be proud of. Sometimes, I think flying is the easy part."

"But you cannot do that if you're here at the Advisory Committee."

"No, I can't. But I'm here . . ." Tom was about to say "and need to make the best of a bad situation" when once more he stopped himself. Explaining to a woman that her company was "a bad situation" was extremely poor form, unlikely to encourage any interest in him she might have. Moreover, Helen Trent's company was particularly pleasant. Contemplating such pleasant company, Forester's attention began to wander. This Helen Trent was certainly an attractive female, and a very interesting lady. *I wonder what she'd be like to spend a day with. Not in bed. Just with . . . Focus Forester. You're just sitting next to this woman and hardly know her.*

"And?" Helen was amused by Forester's obvious departure and return. She wondered where in his mind the American had just visited. And she admitted to herself that she also wondered whether Tom Forester had traveled alone.

"And I'm going to give it my best. Try to enjoy myself a little, get to know London." Tom's eyes then turned away from Helen's. "And meet some nice people."

"That sounds like a sensible strategy. Have you been to London often?"

"Not really. Most of my time is spent at Bromley Park."

"Bromley Park?"

"That's my airfield."

"I see. Well, London is a wonderful city, despite the war and all the hardship. It's full of fine things to see and do. You should set some time aside and, as they say, see the sights."

Helen thought about adding that she would be delighted to show him about. However, she remained silent. She was not concerned Forester might decline the invitation. Intuitively, she knew he would accept. Rather, Helen's silence was the product of constraints. The first related to Sir Robert. Mindful of the marriage contract, she was concerned that escorting the American around London might be considered improper. Married women were not supposed to be seen alone with other men, although Helen wanted to believe that their common membership on the Advisory Committee might permit her to skirt this behavioral expectation. The second constraint, unlike the first, neither related to external perceptions nor to vows of fidelity. It existed totally within Helen's mind, originating with her upbringing, maintained by norms of feminine behavior. As a proper English lady, Helen Trent did not wish to appear too forward. In 1943, women did not initiate a relationship with a man, be it innocent or not. They waited to be asked.

Forester wanted to ask, but did not. "You're quite right. I should take advantage of my being here in London and see at least some of the city."

Forester thought about continuing the sentence. He wanted to add words to the effect that perhaps she'd be kind enough to show him the sights. But Tom also remained silent. Like Helen, he was conscious that she was married, having seen the ring on her left hand. But that alone would not have stopped Forester. Normally, he respected the tenets of accepted behavior and would not pursue someone else's wife. At Dartmouth, he had declined a tempting offer from a woman married to a psychology professor, but he no longer felt bound to such conventions. He believed situations had changed, thus altering permissible norms. In 1943, life could be brutally short. Alive today, he could be dead tomorrow. So a woman's company might be enjoyed whenever and wherever it might be found. Nonetheless, Tom Forester did not make a request of Helen Trent. He said nothing about seeing London in company with her. Why? Because he thought she might possibly take offense. And Tom did not wish to offend this woman whom he hoped to know better.

Helen was about to make an additional remark about London when the sound of silverware gently tapping against a glass drew her attention, and Forester's, to the lectern. The wooden stand was set to one side of the room, but positioned so that everyone might see who was speaking. At the lectern was an older gentlemen that Helen did not recognize. He had been sitting next to General Eaker with whom he had struck up a friendly conversation.

The man was Archibald Rawlins. A former director of Imperial Airways, he was a benefactor of the Royal Aeronautical Society, well known and admired in aviation circles. Now a spry seventy-seven, Lord Rawlins was dressed impeccably and spoke with ease and confidence. Only a loud voice betrayed the deafness with which the old gentlemen was inflicted. Rawlins welcomed everyone to the Society and expressed his wish that the Advisory Committee use its facilities whenever possible. He spoke graciously about the Americans, pointing to the portrait of the Wright brothers saying that from the dunes of the Carolina coast had originated a device that had and would continue to serve men of vision in peace and war. He then told an amusing story about Imperial Airways to which this audience responded with genuine laughter. Rawlins closed his remarks by praising Eaker and the Eighth Air Force.

"Your air force is a proud and powerful force for freedom," said Archibald Rawlins. "Know that whenever it takes to the sky, I along with your many friends in Britain, wish pilots and crew Godspeed and a safe return."

Jimmy Dixon spoke next. He thanked Lord Rawlins for the hospitality shown the Advisory Committee, which he said would happily use the Society's rooms and services. Dixon then read a short word of welcome from the Lord Mayor of London. Minutes before, Jimmy had learned that the mayor literally was speechless, having the night before caught a severe case of laryngitis. Explaining the mayor's predicament, Dixon threw a salute to the man who acknowledged with a friendly wave the polite applause that greeted the Colonel's words. The note itself was brief, yet artful. In it, the Lord Mayor remarked that London and its citizens looked forward to hosting young Americans who had come so far to aid the cause of freedom. "This city is our home," read Jimmy Dixon in a southern accent the Brits found charming, "and we hope, General Eaker, that you and your intrepid men will consider it yours as well."

The next speaker was Ira Eaker. Under explicit instructions from the General, Dixon kept his introduction of the Eighth Air Force commander brief and straightforward. "Just a few words, Jimmy, and a few facts. Don't pile on the sugar."

Dixon did as he was told. First explaining that the meal would be served soon and that he would speak about the Advisory Committee afterwards, he introduced General Eaker in only three sentences. The first summarized Eaker's career in the Army. The second outlined the role of the Eighth Air Force and its place in the military structure of the United States. The third sentence, too sweet perhaps for Eaker, stated that no man in America was more qualified to lead the Eighth than Lieutenant General Ira C. Eaker.

Ample and heartfelt applause accompanied Eaker as he strode to the lectern. Gripping its flat, slanted top with both hands, he acknowledged the presence of the Lord Mayor and thanked Lord Rawlins and the Royal Aeronautical Society for assistance rendered and to be rendered the Advisory Committee. With a few well crafted, words he then explained the need for the Committee. He urged Committee members to work hard at their task, promising that he would personally read every word of their report.

Helen Trent and Tom Forester listened intently to Eaker. As the General explained the Advisory Committee's importance, Helen turned to gaze upon Forester who, intrigued by Eaker, did not notice. Still aware of what General Eaker was saying, but with her eyes focused elsewhere, Helen came to realize that having Tom as a member of the committee ensured further encounters. Pleased by this conclusion, which she later realized was obvious, Helen looked away, returning her complete attention to the speaker.

Ira Eaker was about to finish his short speech. Somehow sensing that the General would conclude with words worth listening to, the audience became hushed. The silence was complete as even the waiters stopped bustling about. Eaker did not disappoint.

"From across the Atlantic, from every state in the Union, we have come to join with England to destroy the evil now residing in Germany. The battle has begun, but is far from over. Danger remains in the skies over Europe where the Luftwaffe, although bloodied, is not yet broken. Men, brave men in British and American uniforms, are dying and will continue to do so. But the Eighth will fly and fight for as long as is necessary.

"One day, down the road in our common future, the engines of our aircraft will be silent. Aircrew and ground personnel will have departed for the long journey home, and the American airfields of East Anglia will be empty. No longer will the city of London host the boys who in battle became men before their time. As years go by, these men will recall with affection this city and its people. They will remember the kindness and goodwill that greeted them everywhere they went, especially in your homes," here Eaker paused, "and in your pubs." These last words produced the intended laughter.

But the laughter quickly subsided as Ira Eaker, in a gentle voice that made his presence all the more commanding, brought his remarks to a close.

"It is my deepest hope, that as months and years go by, you here on this island kingdom will remember us and say to your children, and later to their children, that yes, the Yanks were here. They came in 1942 and fought hard and well, helping to defeat the Third Reich. But they won another victory as well. For while here, they conquered our hearts as they, with us, met the call of duty."

For an instant, no one spoke. The silence conveyed respect for the man and for the power of his message. The English in the audience were particularly impressed for the American general had taken note of Britain's sacrifice and courage. Eaker never failed to do so. Other Americans would mention the subject, but frequently without passion. They believed the war with Germany was now an American enterprise. Eaker knew better. He was aware not only of Britain's pivotal contribution to the forthcoming victory, but also of the strategic role being played by the Soviet Union.

Upon completing his remarks, General Eaker returned to his table where he was greeted warmly by Lord Rawlins. The Lord Mayor, voice cracking and sounding like a broken fog horn, congratulated him as well, uttering the phrase "jolly good" several times.

With Eaker seated, the meal was served. Waiters, once spellbound by the General's eloquence, went to action stations and were busy bringing plates of food to the men and women assembled in the blue room.

Forester found the food not at all to his liking. Sautéed calves liver with onions, fresh brussels sprouts, and sliced boiled potatoes sprinkled with parsley were the featured attraction. He ate little, knowing full well that food was not plentiful in England. Essentially, Forester picked at his meal and felt like a little boy as he attempted to make the plate appear more empty by rearranging the food. Tom was pushing three brussels sprouts to the top of his plate when he heard Helen's voice.

"Colonel, you don't care for brussels sprouts?"

"No, Ma'am." Tom's face was turning red. He felt caught in the act. "I do like vegetables, but I'm afraid brussels sprouts are not among my favorites."

"Nor, it would appear, is liver." Helen's face reflected her amusement.

"Back home, my mother served liver and onions every Thursday night. My parents loved it, but I never developed a taste for it, nor did my brother."

"Well today is Friday, so perhaps your body just assumed it was safe for another week." Helen's attempt at humor did not succeed. She could see that Forester remained embarrassed. Time to change the subject. Time to make this man feel more comfortable. "Parents are like that. They assume their children will like whatever they like. Mothers in particular worry about how well their children are eating. Mine did, and I suppose yours did, too."

"I guess that's right. I never thought much about it."

"Well, trust me, as a mother, we do. Tell me, Colonel, is your mother still alive?"

"Yes, she is."

"Well, no doubt she's been worrying about you eating properly here in England. How about your dad? Is he still living?

The transition worked. Forester forgot about the liver and brussels sprouts and told Helen about his parents and brother. Mostly he talked about his father, whom Helen soon realized had played a large role in his son's life. She then asked Tom about his childhood. He replied by speaking of their home in Port Washington and of the nearby private school he attended until the age of eighteen. Now relaxed, Forester found conversation with Helen easy and interesting. More questions came. They were polite, but probing. Tom responded in full, providing detail and color to the description of his youth on Long Island.

"And then what? Helen had additional questions to ask.

"Pardon me?" Tom did not understood what Helen meant.

"What happened next? You finished grammar school, what I think you in the States call high school, and then went off to university?"

"Yes, Ma'am."

Helen was not sure she liked Tom Forester calling her "ma'am", but she decided to say nothing. For now. She told herself that later she would encourage this man to call her by her given name.

Forester continued, "I went to school in New Hampshire, at a college called Dartmouth."

"Which you enjoyed?"

"Yes, Ma'am. Dartmouth's a fine school. It's a small college, not a large university. There's a sense of community at Dartmouth. It's academically strong, but still a place where one will not get lost. A number of schools are like that. Bates, Williams, Haverford . . . "

"I'm afraid I've not heard of them."

"Most people haven't, even in the States. Back home and here in England, too, people know about Harvard and Princeton and Yale, but the small liberal arts schools are nowhere near as famous."

"And what did you elect to study at Dartmouth?"

Tom responded by telling Helen of his interest in European history. He also told her of his desire to pursue graduate studies, aiming eventually for a Ph.D. His father, he said, had urged a career in banking, but Tom had resisted, hoping to become an academic. In the event, neither career path was followed. Now speaking more earnestly, Tom related to Helen how his plans had changed, telling her about his trip to Germany in the summer of 1937. "I was still in college, but what I saw convinced me that a second war in Europe was inevitable."

"And such a war would involve the Untied States?"

"Absolutely. America would not stay on the sidelines when the Nazis assaulted the democracies of Europe. So I junked plans to attend graduate school. I was planning to go to Cornell or Syracuse, but after Dartmouth, I enlisted in the Army Air Corps instead. And here I am, several years later."

"Somehow, I think there's more to tell. A career that's made you a colonel just a few years from university seems rather extraordinary."

"Not really. It's a long and not terribly interesting story. Let's just say I was in the right place at the right time. And besides, it's not really a career. Once the war is over, my army days are over. Someone else can fly P-47s. I'm going back to school."

"Colonel Dixon tells me you're in charge of a large number of aircraft. That's quite a responsibility."

"I suppose it is, although lots of guys have much more to worry about than I do." As he spoke these words, Forester realized that so far, the conversation had centered upon himself. Warning bells went off in his mind. *Poor form, Forster. You're talking about yourself again. Soon, no doubt, you'll be describing the 19th Fighter Group and life at Bromley Park and bore Helen Trent to death. Find a subject that will interest the lady. Now. Change the subject now. No need to be subtle.* "Enough about me, Mrs. Trent, tell me about yourself."

"Not much to tell, really."

"Come now. I've told you most of my life story. Now it's your turn. It's only fair."

Helen was pleased that Forester had had the presence of mind to stop talking about himself. In her experience, few men did. They seemed to assume that women found compelling conversation that both started and ended with themselves. Helen thought most men tended to be self-centered. She accepted this as fact. But she expected common sense and good manners to prevail. Men need not have their own activities monopolize a conversation. Those who knew this and acted upon it fascinated Helen Trent. To her, they were men worth getting to know. How intriguing that this American was such a man.

Much to her surprise, Helen found herself wanting to tell Forester her life story. Never had she felt this way. She wanted this man to know of her successes and disappointments, of the people she had encountered along the way. To Helen Trent, life was a journey of immense diversity, filled with pleasure and pain that was exciting to experience and observe. She hoped that Forester would find her story of interest so that he and she then might have common ground upon which to build future conversations.

Helen began by telling Tom about her parents. She spoke warmly about her mother and father and of the loving household they had created. She told Forester about her father's career in medicine and how he had encouraged her to be inquisitive. "From Mother," she said, "came a sense of style and things beautiful. From Father came an awareness of the world and a desire to grow intellectually." Helen also spoke of her grandfather, relating to Tom the old gentleman's devotion to the Royal Navy and his delight in recounting the clash of dreadnaughts at Jutland. She then mentioned Peter and her decision to leave school early in order to be with the man she eventually would marry.

"He sounds special."

"He was. A dear and wonderful man."

Tom took notice of Helen's use of the past tense, and used it himself. "You were lucky."

"Yes, I was. Only later have I come to realize how rare it is to find a man who truly captures your heart." Unexpectedly, Helen became aware that she did not want to talk about Peter. Not now. Not with this man. Peter resided safely in her heart. Nothing ever would cause the memory to leave, but now was not the moment to recall his presence. This realization surprised Helen. She had not felt this way before. Momentarily, she wondered whether the time to move on had forced itself upon her consciousness. Helen Trent looked straight at Forester. Her eyes focused on the American, but her mind was elsewhere. *Is something happening here? Why do I not want to talk about Peter? Why am I reacting this way? What do I feel for this man my eyes see?* No answers came. So Helen switched to her favorite tactic of asking a question. "Do you have someone special in your life? A wife? A girl back home?"

"No, Ma'am. Neither."

Helen was pleased by Forester's answer. "Surely there's someone."

"No, there really isn't." Tom was telling the truth. He had had a few girlfriends and a few passionate encounters, but no girl had won his heart. "It's not that I'm unwilling. I do rather like the opposite sex. It's just that I've not met a girl I'm nuts about."

Nuts about. Helen had not heard this phrase before. It sounded typically American. But she understood its meaning. "Life is much sweeter when you do."

"I'm sure that's true. I think of it as the difference between a movie that's black and white and one that's in Technicolor."

"That's a good analogy. I shall have to remember that. May I borrow it?"

"Please do." Yet Forester did not want to talk about girlfriends or movies. He wanted to know more about the man for whom Helen Trent had thrown away a college education. Before speaking, he imagined what his father would have said had he come home to tell John Forester that he was leaving Dartmouth to be with a woman. The resulting explosion would have destroyed Port Washington. Vividly, Tom imagined the town erupting in streams of smoke and fire. "So you left school and married this fellow?"

"Yes, I did." Helen then quickly told Forester about Peter and Claire. She spoke with feeling, especially when describing the accident in Germany.

"I'm very sorry." His face expressed sympathy, reflecting the words.

Helen observed, and appreciated, his reaction. "Thank you. It was a dreadful experience, but I've learned that life goes on."

"Life is very fragile, isn't it?"

Helen realized the context in which Forester spoke. American pilots were being lost in combat. No doubt, some were this man's friends. "You're quite right, and yes, I'm sure you understand it all too well."

"And now you're remarried?" Tom changed the subject. He was looking at the wedding ring on Helen's left hand.

"Yes, I am." Helen then narrated the story of her life after Peter. She spoke of the hardship early on and of her employment at the dress shop. She explained how Sir Robert had courted her and described their relationship in positive terms, portraying the union as more successful that it actually was. But Tom noticed that in speaking of her second husband, Helen Trent conveyed little emotion. Neither excitement nor signs of affection were much in evidence as Helen talked. This contrasted with the account of her first marriage and with her description of Claire. In both instances, Tom saw gestures and heard phrases that indicated deep feelings. No such signals were given when the lady spoke of her current situation.

At age twenty-six, Forester possessed no special insight into women, but he was sensitive to people and had been listening carefully. Having heard Helen speak, and she had talked for at least ten minutes, he concluded that the lady was trying hard to convince him that she was happy being the wife of Sir Robert Trent. He wondered if she was attempting to convince herself as well.

Helen, too, was aware of the contrast. She had sensed the shift in mood as she went from Peter to Claire to Robert. Helen purposefully had tried to paint a bright picture of her relationship to the Deputy Permanent Secretary. This she did instinctively, though later she reflected that her intent was to discourage Forester from showing an interest in her, all the time hoping that he would nonetheless. The words Helen had employed were appropriate for her purpose. Only her delivery hinted at their insincerity. Helen had recited the words as though reading a script. She realized the sentiments expressed were not true. Still looking at Forester, she wondered if he did as well. Her mind, conscious of propriety, hoped he did not. Her heart wished for a different reaction.

Later that evening, at home after dinner, Helen replayed the events of the day. She recalled meeting General Eaker, deciding the man was a true gentleman who spoke with a forceful eloquence. She pictured the room at the Royal Aeronautical Society where the Advisory Committee had met. She took note of the specific tasks set forth by Colonel Dixon who, in speaking after a dessert of lemon custard had been served, gave instructions as to how the Committee was to function. Helen was pleased that Dixon appeared to have accepted several of the suggestions she had made when they had first met in his office. She also recalled the speeches that had been given. One in particular stood out. This was made by a Colonel Davenport who, though clearly uncomfortable at the lectern, had spoken impressively of the B-17 and of the warm welcome he and his fellow soldiers had received whenever they visited London.

But mostly, Helen Trent recalled Tom Forester. Sitting in her living room, Helen relived the experience of meeting and getting to know this man. He seemed to have several qualities she much admired. Forester was serious, but not pompous. He was good looking, but his physical appearance was secondary to a personality Helen found both engaging and intriguing. Well dressed, he also was well educated and appeared to have been brought up well. The man had been greatly influenced by his father, although his good manners suggested that his mother had been ever vigilant, as Helen knew mothers must. She wondered what Forester's mother was like. No doubt the lady would disapprove of her grown son's practice of rearranging food he did not like on his plate.

In picturing Forester, Helen was struck by the man's self confidence and comfort with himself. He seemed to know who he was and be unperturbed by those around him. She reminded herself that pilots tend to be cocky and self-centered. Yet Tom Forester was neither. Nor did he exhibit the bombast and arrogance so often associated with men who fly.

Helen conjured up Forester's face, and closely examined the image created. Thick, short sandy hair, but nicely combed and cut. The moustache that made him look older than he probably was.

Angular features that either enlarged the smile or enhanced the frown. Slightly tanned skin, suggesting a robust health and energy that the Americans seemed to have brought with them to England. But the eyes were the man's most captivating feature. Helen again saw in them a sparkle and a kindness that complemented his soft, but earnest voice. But she also saw the capacity for decisive action.

Contemplating whether she would ever witness this side of Forester's character, Helen sipped her tea. She was alone in the living room, enjoying the solitude that comes at the end of an eventful day. Sir Robert was upstairs, at work in his study. All was quiet in the house. When the telephone rang, its jarring sound broke apart the images of Forester Helen had created. She wondered who could be calling at this late hour.

"Hello, Colonel Dixon. No, not at all. I was just sitting here with my tea, thinking about the day."

Jimmy Dixon knew evening was not the best time to be making business calls. Still at his office with much to do, he hoped to catch a few members of the Advisory Committee at home before turning his attention to the pile of correspondence that sat on his desk. Dixon was pleased that Mrs. Trent has answered the phone. "I see you met our Colonel Forester."

"Yes, he seems awfully nice." In using the phrase awfully nice, she knew she sounded terribly British. She wondered whether the Colonel had noticed.

He had, but Dixon said nothing. "Well, Mrs. Trent, the Colonel is one of our best fighter pilots and it's about him that I'm calling. Again, I hope it's not too late."

"Not at all, Colonel." Helen was intrigued by Dixon's reference to Forester. The images of the man returned. *I wonder what I'm about to hear.*

"Turns out the RAF thinks he's a splendid chap, to borrow a phrase I've heard a lot here in England. Seems Forester's rescued two Spitfire pilots from a nasty situation over Dunkirk and took on half the Luftwaffe to do so. Apparently he did some first-rate flying, shot down a few Germans, and got the Brits home safely."

Helen said nothing, so Jimmy continued.

"Well, the RAF is most grateful and wants to use the rescue as an example of British-American cooperation. They're going to give our Colonel Forester a medal, the Distinguished Flying Cross actually, and with General Eaker's approval, make a bit of a fuss over him."

"That sounds splendid." The sentiment was genuine. Indeed, Helen was pleased that Tom Forester was to be publicly commended for his skill and bravery. She found herself proud of the man, and, in some undefined way, already involved with him. Yet, in responding to Jimmy Dixon, her voice reflected uncertainty. Helen did not understand why the Colonel was telling her this.

Dixon quickly explained. "We thought it might be appropriate to have a few members of the Advisory Committee attend the ceremony—to build up team spirit and show support for something that represents close cooperation between you Brits and us Yanks." Dixon, a southerner, never would describe his team as Yankees. "The ceremony is to be next Tuesday at eleven o'clock at the BBC building. I'm hoping you might be able to attend."

"Colonel, it's kind of you to think of me."

"I apologize for the short notice, Mrs. Trent, but we just learned of the award. I thought that since you met Tom Forester at the meeting today, you might like to see him receive the DFC."

"Tuesday morning seems fine, Colonel. Yes, I think I can be there." Deliberately, Helen did not respond to Dixon's remarks about a desire she might have to see Tom get his medal. Her wish to be in Forester's company again was considerable. Helen realized this, but she had no wish to admit it to anyone or to appear eager.

"That's great, Mrs. Trent. Thank you." The Colonel was glad he called, despite the hour. He had snagged Helen Trent before she made other commitments. Her attendance at the ceremony would be helpful. He needed a few live bodies, preferably British. They would give visibility to the Advisory Committee, and, in Helen Trent's case, add color and a touch of class.

Jimmy Dixon had no idea how Helen really felt about his invitation. He also was unaware that he need not have called this evening. He could have invited her much later. If necessary, Helen would have rearranged her schedule in order to see Forester on Tuesday.

Ten minutes later, extremely content, Helen still was sitting alone in the room, sipping tea from her mother's chintzware. She was thinking about Tom Forester, pleased that she would be seeing him sooner than expected. Tuesday was just three days away. Helen wondered whether they again would be able to converse at length, given he was to be the center of attention. She also wondered if he would show an interest in her. Might he consider their meeting today of little consequence? Might he think she was but a member of the Advisory Committee, and one of many at that? Quickly, she answered these questions, dismissing the possibility that Forester had been unaffected. Helen felt the two of them had connected, that they had enjoyed each other's company. She felt this in her heart where instinct told her they both realized something out of the ordinary had occurred.

Helen Trent was perceptive about people. She believed, correctly so, that she understood how and why men and women behaved as they do. But Helen knew that, in affairs of the heart, judgment easily could be misplaced, especially when the heart in question was your own. Sitting in the living room, she considered the possibility that, in regard to Tom Forester, she had misread the situation. For several minutes, Helen reflected. Then her patience with herself snapped while, at the same time, her confidence reasserted itself. *Enough! I did not imagine what took place today. I saw it with my own eyes. I felt it inside. It lingers and fills me with anxiety and expectations. I am as sure as I can be that Tom Forester and I created something today. Call it what you may, and it may be simply lust, infatuation, or a mixture of both. But it exists.*

Who was that on the telephone, my dear?" Once again Helen's solitude was interrupted. Sir Robert had come downstairs.

"Ah, hello, Robert. That was Colonel Dixon from the American Embassy. He wanted to discuss some Committee matters. Nothing urgent, though it's a bit odd he'd call so late."

"Remember my dear, Americans are odd. I gather all is well?"

"Yes, things are fine."

"And your meeting went well?" The question was superfluous, a kind of verbal filler meant to maintain a conversation. No answer was required, as Helen already had told Sir Robert about the meeting.

Actually, Helen had not related the complete story. She had remained silent about Forester as she did now about the award ceremony. Later that night, she would think about why she had done so. Usually, Helen kept Sir Robert informed of her whereabouts and mentioned the people she had met during the day. Not this time. Helen kept Forester to herself. As she pondered why, a sense of guilt emerged. Helen Trent recognized the feeling for what it was. Yet guilt did not stop her from wishing Tuesday would come quickly.

"My dear," Sir Robert continued, "I do have the particulars of my trip." Purposefully, the man was changing the subject. He had little desire to inquire further about the Advisory Committee. While pleased that Helen's participation might provide welcome visibility, Sir Robert had shown only moderate interest at dinner as she related to him the day's events at the Royal Aeronautical society. In fact, he had come downstairs to talk about both his planned trip and the large party preceding his departure.

"I have left an itinerary in the library. It appears we leave on November 4, by plane, to Gibraltar. Then we head to North Africa and again by air to the Caribbean. Christmas day, I'll be on Tortola. We then fly to Washington for a round of meetings, and will be back in England on January 3.

"That sounds like a terribly busy trip. Do get your rest. Have you got all the things you'll need?" By things, Helen meant light clothes for warm weather.

"Yes, I've got plenty—a few items from our days in Malta. And I'll purchase next week whatever else I'll need."

"Good. I wish you would not be away at Christmas."

"I know, my dear. But I'm afraid I must."

"Well, I'll plan to come down to the airport and see you off."

"That's sweet of you, Helen, but not at all necessary. At the moment, I'm not sure what airfield it is. The RAF is flying us out and I believe we're leaving dreadfully early in the morning."

Helen's marriage was not a success, but she tried hard to perform those functions expected of a wife. "Well then, I shall arise early myself and fix you a fine breakfast."

"Most kind of you, my dear. I'll look forward to it." For just a moment, Sir Robert had a warm feeling for Helen. But the emotion soon passed. He had little need or desire for her to prepare breakfast, having planned to spend the night at his club. Wisely, he said nothing at this moment, deciding to inform her at a later date. "We can go over the itinerary in detail at another time. And do remember that Hugh Williams will be remaining here should you need to contact me."

"Yes, I'll remember."

"I've left something else in the library as well. It's the list of people to be invited to our party. I'm afraid the list is rather long. I've come up with eighty-two names."

"That is a large number. Our house will be filled, but I'm sure we can handle it. And possibly a few more."

"No doubt." There were a few additional people Sir Robert hoped to invite.

"Good. I thought I might invite a few members of the Advisory Committee."

Sir Robert could hardly object. Helen was about to organize a large affair for his benefit. He knew she would work hard and make the affair a huge success. So letting her add to the invitation list was the least he could do. Moreover, hosting a number of committee members might be advantageous. "Quite so. The more the merrier, so to speak."

"I've already spoken with the Collingwood and they've given me a number of ideas as to food and drink."

"Splendid."

"But I will need two things from you."

"And they are?" Sir Robert was beginning to frown.

"Do relax, Robert. We need a specific date and an idea of how much you wish to spend."

"Ah, well that's a relief. I thought there might be a problem. As to money, spend what you need. I would like this to be a memorable affair with fine wine and good food. I leave the food to you and our friends at the club. But then I will choose the wine and liquor. I suppose we'll spend a great deal, but no matter."

"And the date?"

"Ah yes, the date. I've scheduled the party for October 19. That's a Tuesday.

Helen was annoyed, but said nothing. She believed Sir Robert might have consulted with her regarding the date, especially since the party was to be at their house. "I'm sure that will be fine."

Sir Robert soon went back upstairs, unaware that he had displeased the very person upon whom a successful party depended. At times, men can be remarkably insensitive to the feelings of women. Because men believe their role is to find solutions and make decisions, they frequently do so without first seeking advice or concurrence from the woman whose involvement makes consultation advisable. In this instance, Sir Robert had set the date for the October party without thinking to speak first with Helen. He did so not from malice, but from a simple belief that he knew best how to make a decision that was his to make. Helen had seen Sir Robert act this way before and knew he would do so again. She also had seen other men do the same. Herbert Ashcroft frequently made solitary decisions, much to Jane's annoyance. Even Peter, who could do little wrong, on occasion would charge ahead and decide something that affected them both. Thus, Sir Robert's action did not surprise Helen. It just disappointed her. Why could men not stop and think before making a decision that involved others? Alone in the living room, Helen Trent wondered if Tom Forester were equally insensitive. Would he disappoint her as well?

Forester. She smiled as the image of the American came back into focus. He was much younger than she. Helen wondered if their difference in age mattered to him. It did not to her. She wanted very much to see him again, and soon.

As Helen Trent pictured Tom and herself in conversation, she realized something startling, but encouraging as well. Not once in the blue room of the Royal Aeronautical Society had she and Forester talked about the war. Helen considered this a good omen for the future.

The hour was now late and Helen Trent decided the time to retire for the evening had arrived. Amused that the thought of bed had coincided with images of Forester, she went upstairs and undressed.

Once under the covers, having turned out the light and blown a kiss to Claire, Helen imagined she and Tom alone together. They were in a cottage by the sea. Night had fallen and only a candle enabled shadows to be cast upon the small bedroom's walls. Outside, waves fell gently upon the sand. Inside, the two caressed.

NINE

To the east of Bromley Park, the early morning light appeared as a thin line of blue set down across the horizon. Expanding slowly, pushing the black night westward, the light signaled the arrival of a new day. For the 19th Fighter Group, the day would be relatively quiet. No missions were scheduled. No aircraft were primed for battle. Not because it was Sunday, but simply because Eighth Air Force planners, aware that their men and machines occasionally required rest and repair, had scheduled a short respite from the daily grind of war.

Forester was up early nonetheless. He had risen at 5:30 A.M., as he did each day. Tom dressed quickly since his quarters were cold, despite the tiny coal-burning stove that was present wherever personnel of the Eighth were located. As ubiquitous as Nissen huts, the devices were messy and inefficient, rarely warming the cold air that appeared increasingly as summer departed.

Bromley Park had a small, two story cottage near the southern perimeter of the field, part of a large estate owned by the dowager Countess of Falmer. The Countess, with both a son and grandson in the Royal Marines, detested the Nazis. Wanting to assist the Americans, she leased the cottage to the Eighth Air Force for an annual fee of ten shillings. Forester lived in this small house along with Harry Collins, Wilbur Williams, and several other officers assigned to the Group's headquarters contingent. The arrangement was entirely satisfactory. An English woman from a nearby village cleaned the cottage and did the men's laundry. She was happy to receive the twenty dollars each week that enabled her to live far more comfortably than she had in years. Sergeant Edward Dobbs lived in the cottage as well. He manned the telephone, kept track of messages, and made sure coffee and donuts were always available. When on duty, Dobbs served as secretary to the Group Adjutant.

While still dark outside, Forester had grabbed two donuts and a mug of hot coffee, politely acknowledged Sergeant Dobb's salute, and gone outside to his Jeep. Wearing his Army flight jacket and service cap, Forester confronted the morning chill, glad to have the coffee, which he sipped while starting the Jeep.

With a cough and a sputter, the Jeep's engine sprang to life. With one hand holding the coffee and the other handling the gearshift and steering wheel, Forester began his morning drive around the field. He did this at least once a week on days he was not scheduled to fly. Forester wanted to see for himself the condition of the field. He also wanted time to think, which he could do best when alone. As the Jeep made its way about the airfield, Tom would both think systematically and let his mind wander. Somehow the process worked, and Forester's mind was at its most creative in these morning interludes. Moreover, Tom relished the solitude. At times, his thoughts would turn to subjects having nothing to do with the business at hand. This morning, however, he was not thinking much about anything. Forester simply was enjoying the drive, watching the sunlight creep skyward, marveling at the serenity early morning brought to Bromley Park.

Bromley Park. An airfield at war. Property of the U.S. Army Air Forces. Forester's mind shifted into high gear. Not just any airfield, Bromley Park. *His* airfield. He led its aircraft into battle. He commanded its troops. Tom Forester was proud of Bromley Park, both its pilots and ground personnel. He had trained the pilots of the 19th Fighter Group and now was responsible for everyone at the base. He worked hard and expected the nearly 1,500 stationed there to do the same. Above all, he wanted the enterprise at Bromley Park to succeed. Competitive by nature, Tom was spurred on by the realization that for both Americans and the Eighth Air Force, the stakes in 1943 were enormous. Success had to be achieved. Hence the airfield, despite an occasional stand down, exhibited a work ethic that was evident even to first time visitors. Not that Forester was a martinet. He wasn't. Nor that Bromley Park did not see its fair share of parties. It did. Indeed, the men of the 19th Fighter Group became somewhat wild at times. Often, Tom would join in the fun. But for him, the burden of command meant that work came before play.

Bromley Park was one of 122 airfields allocated to the Eighth Air Force. Built by British contractors in the summer of 1942, the field originally had been earmarked for B-24s. Designed for heavy bombers, Bromley Park thus met Class A specifications. This meant the airfield had three runways placed at sixty-degree angles to each other. The main strip, aligned SW-NE, was 6,000-feet-long. The others were 4,200 feet in length. Runways were concrete, six inches deep, laid down upon a crushed rock base covered with a thin layer of macadam. Connecting the three runways was a perimeter track from which at various points numerous hardstands were placed to enable aircraft to be parked.

Forester pulled onto the perimeter track as he began his morning drive. Steering the Jeep towards the control tower, Tom watched the thin blue line of dawn give way to a red band as the emerging sun reflected off the ever present clouds. Gradually, the red disappeared, becoming a soft orange and yellow, which in minutes became patches of blue sky among grey clouds. Sunrise was over, its colors tucked away until next time.

The control tower was the signature feature of Bromley Park. Constructed of a rustic red brick, square in shape, the structure was two stories high with a flat roof and balcony, which, facing the runways, ran around two sides of the square. Atop the building was a smaller closed-in glass facility affording an unobstructed view of the field. In addition to directing air traffic, the tower housed weather and signal equipment. During operations, when the P-47s were either taking off or returning home, men would crowd the balconies to view the progression of aircraft.

Next to the control tower were two large Nissen huts. Painted dark brown, they served as garages for the three ambulances kept at the ready whenever aircraft were operating. The ambulances themselves were modified Dodge command cars. Easily identified by the large red cross set against a panel of white, the vehicles were ever present reminders of the danger inherent in wartime flying. The ambulances at Bromley Park had seen but few instances of blood and broken bones. This was in contrast to bomber bases where the Dodge "meat wagons" awaited damaged B-17s and B-24s returning home with dead and wounded aboard.

To Forester's left were two buildings traditionally associated with airfields. These were the hangers, specifically in the case of Bromley Park, Type T2 hangers. Capable of comfortably accommodating six P-47s, these large structures were built of corrugated steel and painted in a camouflage pattern of green, black, and brown. They provided a welcome shelter from the elements, enabling maintenance and repair to take place practically twenty-four hours a day.

The level of maintenance and repair at Bromley Park was extremely high. Backing up an aircraft's individual crew chief and assistants were specialists at squadron and group level, located at the airfield's Technical Site. This site was a collection of buildings, mostly Nissen huts, housing workshops, and warehouses. Engines, radios, cameras, control systems, guns—indeed almost every component of a P-47 could be taken apart and made to work again. If it could not, the plane was flown or trucked to one of two air depots established by the Eighth Air Force. Located in Lancaster, at Burtonwood and Warton, these facilities performed complete overhauls of P-47s and other American aircraft.

The primary reason for the superb engineering support was the expertise and ingenuity of Colonel Myron Tuttle. Tuttle was the Group Engineering Officer, commanding his three counterparts at the 340th, 341st, and 87th fighter squadrons. At age fifty-three, Tuttle was the oldest serving officer at Bromley Park. With degrees from Purdue and Michigan, Tuttle, known to one and all as "Colonel Tee," had enjoyed a successful career in civilian life managing aircraft operations for the Western Oil Company. Shortly after Pearl Harbor, Colonel Tee signed up with the Army Air Forces. At first assigned to Wright Field, home of the Army's aeronautical research and development program, Tuttle had talked his way into a combat posting. Given the choice of a P-38 outfit in the Southwest Pacific or a P-47 group in England, he chose the latter, commenting that he preferred rain and cold to malaria.

There was hardly anything associated with an airplane Myron Tuttle couldn't fix. He was particularly skilled at detecting malfunctions and diagnosing problems. Crew chiefs held the man in awe. Specialists at the Technical Site marveled at how much Colonel Tee knew about their own particular business. "That man knows more about propellers than Mr. Hamilton Standard," remarked a sergeant in the Propeller Shop who believed, incorrectly, that a single individual had founded the Connecticut company. Tuttle was something of a father figure at Bromley Park. Moreover, he worked hard. And he worked generously, always finding time to teach a mechanic a better way to approach maintenance and repair.

As Forester drove towards the Technical Site, he thought of Myron Tuttle. Smiling, Tom realized that Colonel Tee would still be asleep in his room at the cottage. Tuttle was one of the officers quartered at the Countess of Falmer's little house. No doubt, the Colonel had gone to bed well past midnight, having stayed up late to assist someone confounded by a P-47 component. As always, Forester would let Tuttle sleep. Like Forester himself, Myron Tuttle was not altogether comfortable with military life. He resisted the structured existence upon which the Army thrived. Tuttle liked to work his own schedule, at his own pace. Tom didn't mind. He knew how lucky he was to have Colonel Tee at Bromley Park.

Forester's coffee was no longer hot, so he turned off the perimeter track and drove the short distance to one of Bromley Park's communal sites, where, despite the early hour, he was sure to find a fresh pot of fresh coffee. Communal sites consisted of several buildings, many, but not all of them, were Nissen nuts where soldiers ate and where, when not in their barracks, they spent their off duty time. The sites had clubs for officers and enlisted men, the Post Exchange, a library, barber and tailor shops, and the mess hall. At Bromley Park, the mess halls were, except for the T2 hangers, the largest buildings on the airfield. They were made of wood and painted grey, a welcome contrast to the brown Nissen huts, brown uniforms, and brown mud that seemed to dominate the base. The mess halls contained well equipped kitchens that could serve three meals a day for 250 men. Breakfast was available from 6:30 A.M. to 9:30 A.M., the late cutoff time mandated by Forester to allow Colonel Tee to sleep late and still eat. Dinner, or "lunch" to many of the soldiers, was served from 11:45 A.M. to 1:30 P.M. while supper was ready at 5:30 P.M. with mess hall doors closing at 6:30 P.M. Food at Bromley Park was served cafeteria style. It was plentiful and nourishing, though variety was not a strength of army cooks. More than one soldier had vowed never, upon returning home, to eat Spam or brussels sprouts again. Yet despite the grumbling and the inevitable long lines, the U.S. Army was the best-fed army in the world. More than once, Harry Collins had remarked to Wilbur Williams, the Group Adjutant, that, "It the GIs could fight as well as they eat, the invasion of Europe was a sure thing."

Forester brought the Jeep to a halt in front of the communal site's mess hall. Two minutes later, he emerged, hot coffee in hand, pleased with himself that he had declined a mess sergeant's offer of fresh donuts.

After fetching Forester his coffee, the sergeant had thrust a plate of glazed donuts in front of the Group Commander. "Just made them myself, Colonel, so I know they're good."

"I'm sure they are, Sergeant, but I've had my fill. Forester loved donuts, especially with his morning coffee, but purposefully he limited himself to two per day. "Too many donuts and I won't have room in the cockpit for my parachute. But thanks. If we run out at the cottage, I'll send Dobbs over for more."

"Any time, Colonel. You just let me know."

"I will, and thanks for the coffee."

Once again armed with hot coffee, Forester started up the Jeep, and driving with one hand, moved out onto the perimeter track. His destination this time was a series of hardstands nearly a mile away. Parked there were sixteen P-47s. Twelve of those belonged to the 341st Fighter Squadron. The remaining four were assigned to the Group itself. One of the four was Forester's. He visited this P-47 on each of his morning drives.

The morning sky was now a blanket of blue and grey. This day the sun was making a concerted effort to shine through to Bromley Park. However, the clouds as they did so often in England, were mounting a strong defense. To the west the clouds appeared in control. Extended miles skyward they were continuous streaks of gloomy mist not particularly foreboding in appearance but substantial in coverage. To the east blue predominated. The sky there looked innocent and welcoming, as if to say to Forester "Come fly with me this morning, my friend, and enjoy the beauty I've provided." But weather in England moved west to east. So Tom knew that by noon the blue sky most probably would disappear. Grey clouds would cover the airfield. And once again the sun would be hidden from view. More than likely rain would accompany the clouds which meant that the men at this Eighth Air Force field would find the day dreary and wet.

As Forester steered the Jeep towards the P-47s he looked up. The rain, he figured, would not come for several hours. The sky was remarkable, divided, as once his country had been, between blue and grey. To him, it seemed as though the blanket above had two separate pieces.

A sky such as this he had seen but once before. He was on *Reward,* early in the morning off Shelter Island. His family, with John Forester in command, had sailed from Port Washington along the northern shore of Long Island, around Orient Point, into Gardiner's Bay, mooring across from Greenport. The voyage was one of the few times they had been aboard the sloop for more than a day. This was a long weekend trip. Marjorie Forester enjoyed the time they had together, watching her three men work the boat. Tom and Will were capable and hardworking deck hands. At the helm, the boys' father managed the sailboat as expertly as he managed the bank's business in Manhattan.

On Saturday morning, with the boat anchored in a small cove, Tom had come up on the deck early. The sun was just rising, though his father was already up. John Forester gave his son a cup of hot coffee and a gentle hug. The two then had talked for at least an hour. With Will and Marjorie below deck, the hour belonged to them alone, which they both appreciated. Their conversation was meaningful. The quiet that engulfed *Reward* and the majesty of the dawning day discouraged trivial talk. John Forester was being philosophical, explaining to his son the importance of a life well lived.

"I believe, and I hope you believe, that to be happy a man must do something useful with his life."

"I do Dad, but to tell the truth, I'm just enjoying the summer."

"Fair enough. But next month you go off to Dartmouth and sooner than you think you'll be making decisions that will shape the rest of your life."

"I suppose that's so. Although four years at Dartmouth or anywhere else seems like a long time."

"Youngsters always think that. Trust me, the four years will go by in no time."

Tom was genuinely interested in what his father had to say. He wanted to know what made John Forester feel useful. Tom did not have to ask. Sitting against the main mast, holding his own cup of coffee, his father continued speaking.

"Three things, Tom. Three things have given me great satisfaction—made me feel useful. One is my family—my life with your mother and raising two fine boys. That's been enormously satisfying, and I think useful."

"Mother would think that's enough."

"Yes, she probably would. But she'd be wrong. There's more to life than home and hearth. To feel truly useful, a man needs to accomplish things out in the world. You'll learn that as you get older."

"That would be the *real* world?" Tom, emphasizing the adjective, was smiling as he spoke. Many times he had heard his father speak forcefully of the world beyond school and home. This world the elder Forester had found to be demanding and harsh though not without gratification.

"The very one." John Forester was returning the smile, full of affection for this boy he was proud to call his son.

"Well, if Mom and Will and I are one thing, what are the other two?"

"The second is my time in France with the army. That was a useful time in my life, although not always pleasant. Everyone ought to do something for their country. It doesn't have to be in the army. It can be somewhere else, in some other way, but people ought to contribute to this land we call America."

"Dad, you sound like an announcer on radio recruiting for the government."

"I know, and I don't mean to. But in this country, we enjoy a way of life many people don't have. This is a great country, Tom, a democracy where a Bill of Rights guarantees our liberties and a written Constitution outlines a form of government that's worked well for over 150 years. People need to care about this country and keep it strong and make it function the way it's supposed to. I have and I feel good about that."

Never before had Tom realized his father felt this way about the country. John Forester had spoken with obvious emotion. This surprised Tom who had assumed that his father, despite wartime service in France, was largely indifferent to patriotism. From Tom's perspective, John Forester had spent most of his time at the bank, never mentioning his strong feelings for America.

"The third thing, Tom, that's made me feel useful is something you're not aware of, nor could you be. I've never spoken to you or Will about it, although now is as good a time as any. On occasion, I've tried to help someone in need or in distress. One's life, Tom, can't be focused just upon yourself, although Lord knows I've met men in Manhattan who do just that. To feel useful, to be able to sleep at night, you need to give something to a person less fortunate or to an organization that's trying to make this world a better place. The something can be money, or a gift, or just your time. But you can't march through life concerned solely with yourself, particularly if, as we have, you have a comfortable life full of nice things and good fortune. Do you understand what I'm saying?"

"Yes, Sir."

"Good. It's important. It doesn't mean you can't have a career and work hard at your job. It doesn't mean you can't have fun or that you should feel uncomfortable with success. There's nothing wrong, especially in this country, with making money and leading the good life. This is, after all, the land of opportunity, where Wall Street is better known than Main Street. It's just that with success and with wealth comes an obligation to help those in need. I trust that you and your brother will embrace this idea and, when the times comes, act upon it."

"I will, Dad. And I suspect Will will do the same."

"That's good to hear, Tom."

"Can I ask you, Dad, what you've done in this regard?"

"You may. It's not something I like to talk about. But you're my son, so I will tell you what I do, prefacing my remarks by saying I've tended to give money to groups rather than gifts to individuals. Perhaps that's the easy way, but the bank seems to require most of my time and, when it doesn't, I want to spend it with your mother and you and Will."

Tom was listening intensely. At this moment, his father seemed more human, less distant than ever before.

"There are two organizations, three actually, if you include our church, that I've helped out each year and will continue to help out. One is the Salvation Army. The other is the National Association for the Advancement of Colored People. Do you know what they are and what they do?"

"Yes, Sir."

"Good. One helps people who are down and out. The other helps those who suffer simply because their skin is black. I try to help both groups. They both help people who need assistance, who've been locked out of the American Dream. I try to be useful, though not with any fanfare. Sometimes a chunk of dollars can be helpful, so I provide them and believe they are well spent."

Useful. The word left an indelible mark upon Forester. His father had reemphasized the importance of being useful, of living a life that at least in part benefited others. Tom never forgot what John Forester had said that Saturday morning. Driving the Jeep toward the P-47s, he could see and hear his father speaking, envisioning again the conversation aboard *Reward*. The key to a satisfying life, his father had declared, was to enrich the lives of others. The concept was profound, though remarkably simple. It's validity Tom had accepted immediately. Henceforth, he had assumed that as an adult, he would pattern his life so as to be useful to others. Not all of the time. He was not aiming to be a saint. But at least part of the time. That's what his father has meant. To be useful, one needed occasionally to focus on others. John Forester had, concentrating upon his family, his country, and three organizations that served people in need. Tom intended to do the same. Thus, the elder Forester had achieved what all fathers wish to accomplish—instilling in their offspring a core value of their own that shapes the child's future. Tom had listened to his father and, over time, had adopted the concept as his own. He too now believed that a life well lived required at times being useful to others. Just as John Forester, that Saturday morning at the end of Long Island, hoped he would.

In September 1943, Tom Forester felt particularly useful. He commanded a fighter group that was becoming increasingly effective. The group was part of an air force that was pounding the Nazi war machine. Forester rarely debated the pros and cons of the war against Germany. He believed, as did most people in America and Britain, that Hitler was evil and that the Nazis had to be destroyed. One way to do that was by daylight precision bombing, as practiced by the Eighth Air Force's fleet of B-17s and B-24s. Forester's job, using the P-47s of the 19th Fighter Group, was to protect these bombers. Forester had little doubt that his present line of work was useful. What could be more worthwhile than leading his group into battle? Forester could not think of anything, nor could he imagine anything more exhilarating.

The sixteen P-47s now were not far away. Up ahead, the perimeter track curved slightly to the left. Where it did so, a paved taxiway, 42-feet-wide, went off to the right, perpendicular to the track. Along this taxiway, jutting out on both sides, were hardstands where P-47s were parked.

P-47s were built by the Republic Aviation Corporation of Farmingdale, New York. The initial order for the plane was placed in September 1940. So anxious was the Army Air Corps to have a front line fighter, the order was placed before the prototype had flown. Despite early technical difficulties, the Thunderbolt was a success. More P-47s were built—15,683 in all—than any other U.S. fighter aircraft. To meet demand, Republic opened a second factory in Evansville, Indiana.

In 1943, the Thunderbolt was the principal fighter of Ira Eaker's Eighth Air Force. The more exotic P-38, with its longer range, was performing poorly in the harsh climate of northern Europe. The P-40 Warhawk, the Army's standard fighter in 1940 and 1941, was outclassed by German Me-109s and FW-190s. The P-39 Aircobra, General Harrison's favorite, had been banished from England. Victory in the air thus depended upon the P-47.

Forester liked the P-47. Tom appreciated the size and strength of the Thunderbolt, unlike many pilots who scoffed upon first seeing the big airplane. He thought the plane to be much like the country from which it emerged—generous in proportion with noticeable shortcomings eclipsed by undeniable superlatives. True, the P-47 climbed slowly and was limited in range, but at altitude, the plane performed extremely well. Moreover, no aircraft could out dive a P-47, nor could any fighter absorb more damage and still return home. The Thunderbolt's ruggedness was considerable. So was its firepower. Eight .50 caliber M2 Browning machine guns unleashed awesome destruction. Each "point fifty" shell, the P-47 usually carried 2,136 rounds, was propelled through the muzzle at 2,550 feet per second. Contributing to the effect was the stability the plane retained while the guns were firing, enabling pilots to stay on target.

Later in the war, the Eighth Air Force replaced the P-47s with the P-51 Mustang. These newer aircraft, though armed with only six machine guns, had much greater range than the Thunderbolt, enabling the bombers to be escorted deep into Germany. As the fighter groups of the Eighth in 1944 reequipped with the Mustang, the P-47 found a new role. It became the Ninth Air Force's weapon of choice. The Ninth was a tactical air force, based initially in England, providing support to ground troops as they invaded France and advanced into Germany. In this role, the Thunderbolt excelled. Structurally strong, the plane could be loaded with bombs hung beneath its wings. It also could take the severe punishment the enemy inflicted upon low flying aircraft. By war's end, the Ninth Air Force had over one thousand Thunderbolts in service. The plane had become a premier ground attack weapon.

The P-47 was not a glamorous airplane. Unlike Britain's beloved Spitfire, it was big and ungainly, and never the subject of a Hollywood movie. Unlike Lockheed's P-38, it was plain looking and lacking in glamour. Unlike the P-51, it did not become the favorite fighter of the Eighth Air Force. But in 1943, when the Army Air Forces needed a plane to challenge the Luftwaffe, Republic's big bird was available and up to the task.

Nearing the taxiway, Forester pulled off the perimeter track and brought the Jeep to a halt. Sitting there, enjoying his coffee, he looked about the airfield. To his right, the sixteen P-47s were parked, awaiting crew chiefs to make them mission ready. Beyond the aircraft was a line of trees that marked the south end of Bromley Park. Ahead, some distance away, stood a collection of dark brown buildings, mostly Nissen nuts. These served as quarters for men of the 341st Fighter Squadron. Close by, within Forester's line of sight, was Bromley Park's infirmary. This was a larger than usual Nissen hut, also painted brown. Upon its roof and one of its sides, the one facing the runways, was the customary red cross made visible by its white background. The Nissen hut housed a twenty-bed hospital, plus offices for the medical staff. Bleakly, the site also included a mortuary and isolation ward.

Several Jeeps were parked in front of the medical building. Forester assumed one of the vehicles belonged to Major Norman Horwitz, the Group's senior medical officer. The major was a fine doctor and a brilliant flight surgeon who believed the world had gone half mad in 1939, with doctors and nurses consequently now responsible for healing people no longer protected by norms of civilized behavior. Tom appreciated the job Horwitz did. He minded not at all that the man marched to his own tune. At most every Eighth Air Force establishment, the medical officers were called "Doc." Not so at Bromley Park. Among his fellow officers, Dr. Horwitz insisted on being called Norman, and so he was.

Tom felt relieved at having such capable men as Harry Collins, Colonel Tee, Wilbur Williams, and Norman on duty at Bromley Park. They made his life as Commanding Officer much easier. Each did his job extremely well, enabling Forester to concentrate on leading the Group's three squadrons of P-47s.

Tom was enjoying the solitude and silence of the moment, sipping his coffee, surveying all that lay before him. Parked off to the side of the perimeter track, he was thinking about how good it was to be alive, to be among humanity, present at a particular time in history. There in the Jeep, Forester was not pondering his responsibilities at Bromley Park. He simply was focusing upon being alive. He was cherishing the scene before him as an aspect of human activity, conscious of its existence and his own, hoping he would never forget how he felt this morning, or what he was seeing.

The moment was ephemeral. At first, he heard the sound. Coming from one of the P-47s, it interrupted Forester's contemplation. Before Tom saw the propeller spin, he heard the big Pratt and Whitney engine cough and roar into life. A crew chief had begun work early despite the absence this Sunday of a scheduled mission. Perhaps the plane needed a test flight. Perhaps the engine itself needed maintenance. The sound was loud, but not shrill. It had a richness, a fullness and depth that was unmistakable. When a squadron of P-47s were assembled, engines running up before takeoff, the result was extraordinary. Sound reverberated all across Bromley Park. The sky itself seemed to shake.

This morning there was but one P-47 running up. Forester listened. Something sounded not right. In the cockpit, the crew chief heard the anomaly. He cut the throttle and the engine sputtered, then stopped. Concurrently the propeller became stationary.

As it did so, two trucks drove up to the P-47s. About twenty men piled out, fanning out to the planes. The daily tasks of checking, testing, maintaining, and fixing P-47s had begun. It never really ended. Complex and sometimes temperamental, Thunderbolts required constant attention.

Forester thought about what else required constant attention. Boats did. They needed to be scraped and painted, retooled, and repaired. The *Reward* spent as much time in dry-dock at the Port Washington Yacht Club as she did on the Sound, although Tom sensed his father enjoyed the maintenance as much as he did the sailing. What else? Houses. Houses required a great deal of work. This, Tom admitted to himself, was speculation, as he did not own one. Anything else? Forester smiled to himself, amused as the next candidate for constant attention came to mind.

Women. Women needed constant attention. He was no Romeo, but Forester did have sufficient experience "with the ladies," his father's phrase, to know that the female of the species disliked being ignored. His roommate at Dartmouth once had been inattentive to his girlfriend. The girlfriend, an art history major at the Rhode Island School of Design, had reacted poorly, at times sulking and at other times ranting. Tom was relieved when they made up, as was the roommate. In Forester's experience, all women, in this regard, were the same. Pretty girls, young girls, plain Janes, and older gals all required their male companions to be constantly attentive—if not all the time, then certainly most of the time.

Forester's musings had taken him to a realization that women were similar to his beloved P-47. The analogy appealed to him. Both the airplane and the female were complex. Both required daily attention. Both were expensive to maintain. Yet, to be sure, both were things of beauty.

Tom asked himself whether there was a girl he knew as compelling as the airplane he flew. The answer was immediate and positive, even though the lady in question was no girl. She was, most decidedly, a woman. Regrettably, unlike the Thunderbolts at Bromley Park, she belonged to someone else. Forester told himself he would deal with this complication later. Did he love this woman? No—at least, not yet. But he wanted to be with her, to get to know her better, and to enjoy her company. He also wanted to make love to her. Tom wanted to touch her, smell her, caress her, lay down with her. She was the most lovely of creatures whose age intensified her appeal. Forester imagined her as he had seen her only two days before—lustrous black hair, pale white skin, a face alert and alive that projected intellect and passion. And a body men were eager to explore. There in the Jeep, not far from sixteen P-47s, Tom reaffirmed a decision he had made on Friday in the blue room of the Royal Aeronautical Society. He would pursue and win the heart of Helen Trent.

Daydreaming about this English lady was very pleasant. She indeed was someone special. Forester imagined how enjoyable a few days alone with her might be. Long walks and easy conversation would fill the day. A museum might be visited, an old churchyard explored, or they might see a film or browse through antique shops. Nights would be a different matter. Tom thought about how sweet Helen would be in bed, how compelling their lovemaking would be. He was painting in his mind an erotic encounter. That he was sitting in an Army vehicle off the perimeter track at Bromley Park made no difference. Forester was envisioning a dining room where he and Helen were having dinner in a small hotel by the sea. The room was small and dimly lit. Other couples were present, but not close by. Outside, the wind was whistling, rattling windows through which the water could be seen, but not heard. Helen was wearing a red evening gown. He was in uniform. Dinner was over and a momentary silence had occurred. He was about to suggest more tea or coffee or an after dinner drink when Helen said she wished to go upstairs. They did so, walking past the hotel clerk without embarrassment or notice. Once inside the room, she turned off all the lights but one and gently pushed him up against the closed door. She then pressed her body into his, kissing him hard. Her lips were wide apart, her mouth was warm and wet. As Tom felt her breasts against his chest, she told him she loved him and suggested he unhook her dress. He did so, and watched as she slowly slipped off the red gown and tossed it aside. Helen again moved up against his body. Speaking softly, she whispered that tonight belonged to them and them alone. He was about to reply, but she held her hand across his mouth. She said words were unnecessary.

Once again, Forester heard the sound before he saw what caused it. This time, the noise came from a Jeep heading towards him from one of the hardstands. The vehicle was moving at great speed, splashing through puddles on the taxiway and perimeter track. Reluctantly, Tom expelled the image of Helen Trent from his mind. Time to get back to business. Reality was P-47s at Bromley Park, not a hotel room by the beach.

The Jeep pulled up next to Forester's and out jumped Major Kenneth Browne. Browne was commander of the 87th Fighter Squadron. Two days ago, he had shot down two Me-109s west of Ghent. In addition to being a fine pilot, the Major was a first rate

squadron commander. Likeable and easy going, Browne had a formidable intellect behind a cheery smile and sense of humor. After a
slow start, the 87th was becoming a crackerjack outfit. Forester
believed Browne was the reason. Tom assumed that if Browne could
stay alive, he would someday get a group of his own.

"Good morning, Colonel."

"Good morning, Major."

"Another quiet day at Bromley Park. Weather's nice, although it
looks like we'll get some rain this afternoon. If I didn't know, I'd
swear I'm in England."

"Too much sun and we'd all be spoiled. Besides, everybody can
use some rest, including you."

"My plane's been having radio problems, so I was going to give
it a test hop. Now the engine's not right. Doesn't sound right, to me
or my crew chief."

"Nor to me."

"Colonel, can I do anything for you? I saw you parked out here."

"No, Ken. Thanks. I'm fine," Forester replied.

"Like a doctor with his patients."

"Something like that."

"Well, let me know if you need anything."

"I will, and thanks.

Browne threw his Group Commander a salute and hopped back
into the Jeep which then went racing back to the parked P-47s.
Forester always worried when pilots drove Jeeps at high speed. As
Harry Collins had discovered, the vehicle rolled easily when turned
abruptly. One of these days Ken Browne was going to hurt himself
if he didn't slow down.

Forester continued his morning drive. Stopping again, this time
just near the end of Runway 26, he got out to walk and reflect. No
longer cold, for the coffee and morning sun had erased the chill, Tom
moved toward the concrete strip, standing on grass that was now
more brown than green. Forester noticed the color, a clear sign that
summer was departing. England was noted for the lush greens of its
parks and gardens, yet brown was the predominant color at Bromley

Park. Forester wondered whether all Army Air Force bases looked so brown. To him, it seemed a bland color, without much character or brightness. Maybe, he reasoned, that's why the Army chose it. To blend in better, to emphasize conformity.

Standing where 26 ended, Tom looked down the runway. How peaceful it seemed. And quiet. There were no P-47s to break the silence with their loud engines or squeal of rubber when tires came down hard upon the macadam.

Before him, the panorama of Bromley Park stood out with clarity. Much was flat. Not just the runways and perimeter track, but the fields in between and all around. Outlined against the sky were the identifying features of the air base. Hangers, Nissen huts, and the control tower all were easily visible. Few trees were present, save for the line to the south. What Forester saw as he surveyed all before him had little charm. It was largely utilitarian in design, undistinguished in color or architecture. Nevertheless, Bromley Park had a presence, a strength that could be seen or felt by anyone. Out by Runway 26, on this quiet Sunday morning, Forester could feel this strength. From it, he derived comfort and courage.

Two hours later, Tom was in his office. It was in a small, square wooden structure not far from the control tower. The building was divided into five rooms, one of which served as the group commander's office. This room was furnished with standard Army furniture. Forester had two tables, one of which he used as a desk, the other was used to stack official papers. There were several chairs and one large table at which Tom held small meetings. By the window stood an American flag. Its red, white, and blue contrasted sharply with the ever present brown. On the wall was a large map of England and northern Europe. On the desk table was a brass lamp, an intercom, and a small sign that read *Commanding Officer, 19th Fighter Group.* The office was largely impersonal save for a framed picture of Forester and his family taken aboard the *Reward.*

Tom understood that a group commander had administrative responsibilities that of necessity could not be ignored. While he preferred to lead the 19th from a cockpit rather than a desk, he took these responsibilities seriously, finding a certain bureaucratic satisfaction in carrying them out sensibly and correctly. He thus spent considerable time in this office, ably assisted by Wilbur Williams, whose own office was next door.

The Adjutant was speaking to Forester, reviewing some items that required the Colonel's attention.

"There's some paperwork that needs your signature, nothing special. I've flushed out the ones I can handle, but I'm afraid the rest need your John Hancock. They're on your table ready to go."

"Good. I'll have them back to you this afternoon."

Williams nodded his appreciation. "Major Collins is outside and wants to see you. So does a Lieutenant Ordway. He's a pilot with the 340th."

"Don't know the man. What does he want?"

"I don't know, Colonel. But he's insistent. Says it's important. Says his squadron C.O. has no objection."

"Okay, I'll see him. What else?"

"Some locals from Sedgewick have been complaining about the noise."

Sedgewick was a town south of Bromley Park, where St. Stephen's church was located. "They're going to ask us to reroute our flight paths. They're quite insistent, although I must say they've been most polite about the whole business."

"Wilbur, you know we can't do that."

"I know that, Colonel, and that's what I've told them,"

"Well, tell them again. Nicely of course. But it's yours to handle. Keep me out of it."

"Yes, Sir. I'll do that." There's another item I need to mention, Colonel. It concerns Lieutenant Oscar Perkins."

"What's he done?"

"You're not going to like this, Colonel."

"I'm ready. Let me have it."

"Well, Lieutenant. Perkins was on a test flight and decided to have some fun and buzz Lincoln Manor, which I've learned is a fancy home near Ipswich. Seems the Lieutenant misjudged his distances. In roaring past the house, which has, or I should say had, several large chimneys, Lieutenant Perkins managed to have the left wing of his airplane clip one of the chimneys, which crumbled into a zillion pieces, apparently quite spectacularly. The owner of the house, Sir Richard Wilson, saw the entire episode. His description of it is quite graphic."

"I'll bet. And the P-47?"

"Let's say it was damaged. Perkins got it home okay, but Colonel Tee says it will take at least a week to fix, maybe more."

"That bloody idiot. I swear, he's got no brains in his head. Doesn't he realize P-47s are hard to come by—and they cost a fortune, nearly a hundred thousand dollars." Actually, Forester did not know how much a Thunderbolt cost. His was a guess, but a good one. In 1943, a P-47 was priced at $96,475.

"Hold on, Colonel. There's more."

"Go on."

"Well, the chimney's gone, and Perkins' P-47 has a bent wing. But it seems Sir Richard breeds race horses, some of which are stabled at Lincoln Manor. Well, Perkins flies low over the stables, scaring the horses, which bolt. One of them, Golden Arrow by name, trips and has to be destroyed. Sir Richard is livid. Not about the chimney. About the horse."

"Does the Army allow commanding officers to draw and quarter people, to tar and feather them?"

"I'm afraid not, Colonel."

"Too bad. Have Harry come in and let's decide what to do."

Major Collins soon entered the room, saluted Forester, and took a chair at the large table where Tom and Wilbur Williams were already seated. Forester began to explain to Collins about Oscar Perkins's aerial antics when the Major interjected.

"Colonel, I know about Lieutenant Perkins. Wilbur's told me. I guess Golden Arrow won't be winning any blue ribbons now."

"We can't do anything about the horse. What do we do about Perkins?"

In answering Forester, Major Williams suggested a court martial. Tom was reluctant because the Group needed pilots and Perkins was a good one. Harry Collins proposed a reduction in rank. Then Williams suggested Perkins be made to pay for the chimney and the race horse. "Even with flight pay, Colonel, it will be some time before Lieutenant Perkins has any money in his pocket."

"I like that Wilbur. Let's do it. But I have a feeling neither of these will induce Perkins to mend his ways."

"So what do we do?"

"I propose," Forester was speaking, "to put the Lieutenant in jail for two days. We do have a jail in this place, don't we?"

"Yes, Sir" responded the Adjutant, "but I don't think Army regulations permit an officer to be jailed without a trial."

"Just watch me, Wilbur. Stick Perkins in a cell and leave him there for two days. Feed him, but that's all. No visitors, no nothing. We can't have pilots beating up the countryside, or banging up P-47s. Everyone needs to be reminded of that. And jail might just do that."

Forester turned to Collins. "Harry, why don't you have an off-the-record chat with the Lieutenant and explain the facts of life here at Bromley Park. Let him know that one more screw-up and he'll be a corporal in the infantry, if he's lucky."

"Will do, Colonel. I'll make sure he gets the message."

"Good. Everyone around here gets a second chance, but I don't give third chances. Screw up twice and life will become extremely unpleasant."

Tom turned back to the Adjutant. "Now, Wilbur, I'm changing the subject. I've got an idea about our neighbors in Sedgewick—something to make them happy."

"I'm for that, Colonel, especially since we're not changing our flight paths."

"No, we're not, but maybe we ought to introduce them to Bromley Park. Give them a close-up look at P-47s and show them what we do and how we do it. Let's invite a bunch of them to spend half a day here. We'll feed them and have a parade and let them climb around a Thunderbolt. Maybe we'll do a few low level aerobatics for them to watch." Tom now smiled. "Though not with Lieutenant Perkins at the controls. We'll show them the control tower and explain how we operate. All in simple terms, of course. Not state secrets, just simple stuff."

"Colonel, that's a great idea." Wilbur Williams's enthusiasm was genuine.

"Well, you're the Adjutant. And, as I said, you're in charge. Go figure out the details. Work out a plan and all that."

"How many people, Colonel?"

"You decide. Just make sure the mayor comes, and the leading town folk. We'll show them a good time and maybe they won't complain as much."

"I'll have you a plan in three days."

"That's fine, Wilbur. Take the time you need to do it right. Now, Harry, you wanted to see me?"

Before Collins responded, Wilbur Williams spoke up. "If you'll excuse me, Colonel, I'll leave you two and go attack my paperwork."

"You're excused, Major." Tom returned the Adjutant's salute. You're doing a great job. Keep it up."

"Thank you, Sir." Major Williams left the room. As he did so, Tom turned to Collins. "What's up, Harry? You have that look on your face that tells me I'm in for a surprise."

Collins was enjoying the moment. "Colonel, I'm just here to make a simple request of my commanding officer."

"Now I know I should be worried."

"Really, it's just a simple request, and . . . " here Collins paused, "it won't cost a lot of money."

"Now I am worried. Okay, Harry, let's hear it."

"Let's go buy an ice cream factory."

"Harry, I could have sworn you just said we should buy an ice cream factory."

"Colonel, you heard right. There's a small plant that's closed down about twenty miles from here. The equipment's in pretty good

244 • THE BEST OF TIMES: A NOVEL OF LOVE AND WAR

shape and what isn't we can fix. It's an ice cream factory and it's for sale."

"Why would we want to buy an ice cream factory?"

"To make ice cream." Collins was grinning.

"I shouldn't have asked that."

"Colonel, I know it sounds crazy, but we could buy the plant, move the equipment here to Bromley Park, set it up, and provide fresh ice cream to the men."

"That part I like. How do we get the money?"

"From either our mess budget or we could take up a collection, or both. I've done some arithmetic and it will work. In fact, if we charged Stateside prices for the ice cream, we could turn a profit."

"Where do we get the supplies—the milk and cream?"

"Our quartermaster people are very resourceful. There's milk and cream around, you just have to know how to get it. They do. And we can requisition the sugar and that's really all we need."

"What about running the equipment? Do we have anyone who knows how to run an ice cream plant?"

"Actually, we do. Two sergeants in the motor pool worked at the Breyer's plant in Philadelphia before joining the army. And, besides, we have Colonel Tee. He can make anything work."

"That's true. I don't suppose our beloved Army regulations address the subject of ice cream factories?"

"Surprisingly, they're silent on the subject."

"Which means we can do it." Forester was warming to the idea. "Besides it's for the well being of our troops—their health and morale. America's soldiers need their ice cream."

"Exactly. I should tell you our Adjutant thinks it's a terrific idea."

"Well, if Wilbur thinks it's okay, I guess I have no choice. McCready's going to love this."

"We'll send him a quart."

"Indeed we will. Okay, Harry, go buy the plant. Just make sure to give the Brits a fair price. More complaints from the locals we don't need."

"Will do, Colonel. Uncle Sam will treat 'em fair and square."

"Major, there's one thing you should know, however."

"Sir?"

"I like chocolate chip. Keep that in mind."

Collins was about to respond when the intercom on Forester's table buzzed. The voice belonged to Wilbur Williams. "Colonel, Lieutenant Ordway is here. Should I send him in?"

Tom went over to the intercom and replied in the affirmative. Moments later, the door to Forester's office opened and Lieutenant Samuel Ordway entered.

Forester did not recognize him. Ordway walked up to Tom, stopped, and saluted. "Lieutenant Ordway, Sir. Thank you for seeing me."

"Stand easy, Lieutenant." Ordway's voice had a familiar ring to it but Forester could not place it. "You know Major Collins."

"Sir." Ordway respectfully acknowledged the Group Intelligence Officer.

"Lieutenant." The Major responded agreeably.

"What can we do for you, Lieutenant?" Forester had no idea why Ordway was in his office, nor did Collins.

"Well, Sir, to get right to the point, I wish to be relieved of flying duties."

At once, the mood in the office changed. Gone was the informality brought about by talk of an ice cream factory. Forester knew he had a problem on his hands. A pilot of the 19th Fighter Group wanted to quit.

Yet something else clicked inside Tom's head. He recognized the voice. Ordway was Snowflake Red 4, the nervous pilot who was low on fuel the day the Spitfires were rescued off Dunkirk. "Why, Lieutenant, what's the problem?"

"I just can't do it anymore. I don't want to die, and I will if I keep flying missions." Ordway was speaking calmly. There was no hesitancy or embarrassment in his voice.

"Lieutenant, none of us want to die."

"But I'm gonna die, Colonel. Maybe not the next mission, or even the one after that, but it'll be soon enough. I want to live."

"Lieutenant, listen to me." Forester was speaking earnestly, although without harshness. His eyes focused solely on Ordway. "You've been trained to fly and fight, like all the other pilots here at Bromley Park. They're scared, but they go and do their job."

"Colonel, I just can't do it any longer. I want out."

"Son, if I grant your request, you'll have to live with this the rest of your life. The British call it LMF, lack of moral fiber. It's not something you want on your service record or as part of your past."

"Colonel, I'm not brave like you. I'm just a guy, an ordinary guy. My nerves are shot, I don't sleep anymore. I shake when I get near a P-47."

"Ordway, I can't grant you your request. Your country has trained you to fight and that's what you must do." Tom's mind sought and found an option that might work. "Let's do this. Fly the next two missions and come back and see me. If you still want out, I'll send you down to the Central Medical Bureau and they'll check you out. I promise I'll listen to what they have to say."

Forester turned to Collins. "Major, do you have any suggestions?"

"Actually, I do, Colonel."

"Let's hear it."

"Lieutenant, how many missions have you flown?"

"Twelve, Major."

"Good. Well how 'bout flying the next two as the Colonel suggested, after which we'll send you over to Keythorpe for some rest. Spend ten days there and you'll come back rested and ready to go."

Keythorpe Hall was one of sixteen rest homes established by the Eighth Air Force. There, battle weary and shell-shocked aviators got a short reprieve from combat. Good food and plenty of sports were provided in a casual environment. These were intended to restore the spirits of young men dazed by the hardship of aerial warfare.

"Thanks, Major, but I don't know. I think I'd just like to stop flying and live."

"We all do, Lieutenant." Forester was speaking. "I understand your fear. I really do. But you can't just quit. You can't walk away from your fellow pilots."

"But, Colonel . . . "

Forester had raised his hand to silence Ordway. "Let's take the approach suggested by Major Collins. Fly the two missions and you can have ten days at Keythorpe to get yourself back together. That's it, Lieutenant. That's the best I can do for you. You're dismissed."

"Yes, Sir." Ordway saluted, turned around, and left the room.

"Well, Harry, what do you think?"

"I think he's one scared kid, Colonel."

"But if we let him off the hook after only twelve missions, what happens to discipline? If pilots can quit just because they're scared, we may not have a fighter group six weeks from now. These men have been trained to fly and fight, and they've got to do it."

"I don't disagree with that."

"Let's hope your approach works. Maybe two weeks at Keythorpe will do Ordway some good."

"And if it doesn't?"

"Then he flies and may indeed die. The reality is that even fighter pilots die in wartime, not just foot soldiers or sailors. Hell, you know that, Major. Just ask Carl Phillips."

Harry Collins leaned back in the chair. He took a moment before speaking, looking reflective. "Colonel, Bromley Park is one interesting place. One minute we're talking about ice cream, the next about a young kid who doesn't want to die, but might."

"And before that, about our friends in Sedgewick who don't like the noise we make in P-47s."

"Not to mention Golden Arrow."

"Poor old Golden Arrow. And the crazy Lieutenant who killed him. You're right, Harry. This is one fascinating place."

Major Williams, knocking on the door as he waked in, interrupted the conversation. The Adjutant seemed extremely pleased. He was holding two messages in his hand.

"Excuse me, Colonel, for barging in, but we've just received a message you'll be interested in. It's really great news. Let me be the first to offer congratulations."

"For what, Wilbur?"

"You've been awarded the Distinguished Flying Cross by the British." Williams handed Forester one of the messages. "This is a teletype from an Air Vice Marshal Sidney at Fighter Command. It says the RAF is pleased to recognize the skill and courage of Lieutenant Colonel Thomas Forester."

"What did I do?"

"According to the Air Vice Marshal, your impeccable flying near Dunkirk resulted in the rescue of Spitfires at the expense of several Messerschmitts."

"Well done, Colonel. Let me add my congratulations." Harry Collins had stood up and thrown Forester a salute."

"Thank you both." Although he was showing no emotion, Tom was pleased.

"There's another message you should read, Colonel. It's a telegram from Pinetree." Wilbur Williams handed Tom the second message. Pinetree was the code name for the headquarters at Wycombe Abbey.

Forester read the message out loud:

To: Lieutenant Colonel Thomas Forester
   Congratulations on receiving the DFC from the British. Award is most deserved. Gratifying to me that today's Army Air Force pilots confront the Germans head on and triumph. Award symbolizes cooperation between England and U.S. vital to final and inevitable victory.
Lt. Gen. Ira Eaker
Commander, Eighth Air Force

"Colonel, that's one terrific message. We're real glad for you, and proud."

"Major Williams is right. This is a feather in your cap, Colonel."

"Thank you, gentlemen, but, as you know, I didn't do anything that any other commander wouldn't have done. I think it's simply a case of right time, right place."

"Perhaps, Colonel, but you were there and you did it. That's what counts. The RAF is happy. And the Lieutenant General who commands the Eighth is pleased."

"Maybe now they'll think more highly of Thunderbolts," said Forester.

"And the brave men who fly them," added Harry Collins.

Tom addressed the Adjutant. "I assume there'll be a small ceremony. When will the RAF be coming down to Bromley Park?"

"Actually, it won't be here, Sir."

"Where then?"

"Seems they're going to make a big deal of this," replied the Adjutant, "and in my view, rightly so. Colonel, the award will be presented to you in London, and will be broadcast by the BBC."

"Good Lord! When does this all take place?"

"This Tuesday, Sir, late morning."

"Which means I won't be flying that day, so someone will need to lead the Group."

Forester was considering certain candidates. "Let's do this. Let's have Ken Browne do it. We'll find out if he's as good as we think he is."

Wilbur Williams and Harry Collins then began talking about Forester's award. Both men were genuinely pleased for their Commanding Officer, whom they believed richly deserved such recognition. They also were pleased by Eaker's message. Now, perhaps the Eighth Air Force brass would take note of the 19th Fighter Group.

Tom wasn't listening to either Williams or Collins. He was thinking about London. Tuesday morning would be taken up with the award ceremony. But the afternoon would be free, if he chose not to return immediately to Bromley Park. A few hours to explore the city might be fun, but doing so alone was not what Forester had in mind. There was one individual he was intent upon seeing.

Tracking her down should not be too difficult. If he could navigate in the skies above Europe, he could certainly find Helen Trent in London.

TEN

The Queen did not attend the RAF's ceremony for Forester. Her Royal Highness, consort to George VI, mother of two princesses, had come down with a nasty cold. Her doctors insisted she remain inside Buckingham Palace, pointing out that attending any public gathering was sure to aggravate her condition. Elizabeth resisted. She was a conscientious woman who captivated her subjects by a devotion to duty she performed with dignity and charm. Early Tuesday morning, the Queen announced her intention to carry out a full day's schedule of appearances. The doctors were horrified. They appealed to the one person in the country who could, and would, command the Queen to do otherwise.

The King of England, after conferring with the doctors, spoke to his queen. A decent man who had come to the throne unexpectedly, the King entered the sitting room where Elizabeth was preparing to dress for the day. George VI was a shy, reserved individual. Rarely did he raise his voice when speaking. Nor did he now.

"My dear, the doctors say it's best you remain inside."

"I know, my dearest, but there is much to do today and we must not disappoint those who expect to see us."

"Of course, you're right, but your health is precious to me and I would not want to make it worse."

"I shall not, my dearest." Elizabeth could see the look of concern in George's eyes. The man before her was a gentle individual whom she had married without reservation and now loved more than ever.

"So you'll do as the doctors order?"

"Yes, my dearest, but only because you wish it so."

"Elizabeth, I speak to you as your husband, not as your monarch."

"I know that and I love you for it." Gently she pressed his hand in hers. Not wishing to kiss him for fear of spreading germs, Elizabeth gave the King a smile that radiated warmth and spoke of love.

Thus, the Queen stayed home on Tuesday. Her doctors were relieved. And George VI felt much better, knowing that his beloved Elizabeth would rest a bit, thus helping to shake the cold she had caught. He reflected that ample opportunities existed for future visits to ceremonies involving the RAF.

Also relieved by the Queen's decision was Ira Eaker. The General had intended to attend the ceremony, having heard from Air Vice Marshal Sidney on Saturday that the Queen would be present. Eaker was at Wycombe Abbey this Tuesday morning. When he received word of the Queen's last minute cancellation, his first reaction was one of regret. Her presence would have ensured a worthwhile audience to whom he might speak about daylight precision bombing. He might also have preached the importance of cooperation between his air force and Britain's.

Further reflection caused General Eaker to reconsider his regret. If the queen were not present, he need not be either. The telegram to Forester, Keith Davenport's idea, met any obligation he had regarding the Colonel's DFC. So, if he wished, he could have the morning free, unencumbered by scheduled appointments. Free mornings were getting few in number for the commander of the

Eighth Air Force, so Eaker seized the opportunity. He wanted to review with General Anderson the plans for the upcoming attacks upon Germany. Instead of talking about daylight precision bombing, he would shape its implementation. He also wanted to think further about the new letter he had just received from Barney Giles.

His friend, Hap Arnold's Deputy and Chief of the Air Staff, had written again to advise that Arnold was displeased, and getting more so each week. The Luftwaffe, Giles said, had to be destroyed as a prelude to the invasion. More enemy fighters had to be destroyed. Already Arnold had pressured Eaker to relieve several senior officers. Among them was General Richard Harrison whose removal would reflect poorly on Eaker who had placed the Brigadier in the DFO position. More importantly, Giles told Eaker that the Commanding General of the Army Air Forces was dissatisfied with the results being achieved by the Eighth's bomber force. Arnold wanted more planes dispatched and more bombs on target. He was demanding that Eaker put forth a continuous maximum effort to inflict decisive damage upon Germany. Eaker believed his force was too small to achieve that, but, in October 1943, with four hundred bombers at his command, he thought he could strike hard at the Nazis, thereby providing tangible evidence to Arnold and the admirals in Washington that the Eighth, if given sufficient resources, could pound Germany into submission.

Eaker intended to increase the attacks upon Germany this week. He knew General Anderson had the plans near completion, and he was eager to review and approve them. In responding to Barney Giles, Eaker said the skies above Germany would soon witness the destructive force of American air power.

The General called for his aide, Harris Hull.

"Major, I'll not be going into London this morning. Tell Corporal Lewis to put his race car back into the garage. The Queen isn't going to the ceremony, so I'm going to stay right here."

"Yes, Sir."

"Advise the RAF of my decision. Give my regards to Air Vice Marshal Sidney and tell him I'm sorry. Also tell him I'm going to finalize our plans for the air assault upon Germany. He'll understand, I'm sure.

"Yes, Sir."

"Then tell Keith Davenport he's to attend the ceremony in my place. He's on that advisory committee with Forester, so it's appropriate he's there. Have him read a message on my behalf. After his speech at the Royal Aeronautical Society, I have no doubt he'll say the right thing."

Unlike General Eaker, Air Vice Marshal Sidney was extremely disappointed upon hearing that the Queen would not be attending the ceremony. Her presence would have been a great honor. It also would have elevated the entire affair, bringing recognition at the highest level to the RAF. Yet, despite the Queen's absence, Sidney was convinced the ceremony would be useful. The award to Forester would highlight the cooperation between the RAF and the Americans. Like Eaker, the Air Vice Marshal had quickly grasped the symbolic value of the ceremony. Indeed, he had approved the idea immediately upon its suggestion by a young Wing Commander on his staff. However, Philip Sidney's primary interest in involving the Palace had been strictly parochial. He wanted to have Fighter Command bask in the limelight of the Queen. He wanted newspapers around the world to publish pictures of the Queen in company with fighter pilots, and the BBC to broadcast her remarks to every corner of England. In the Air Vice Marshal's mind Bomber Command and its single minded leader, Air Marshal Arthur Harris, were receiving far too large a share of public acclaim, thereby shortchanging the men who flew Spitfires and his beloved Hurricanes. Fighter Command, Sidney had concluded, needed to ratchet up its campaign against the Bomber Boys. Queen Elizabeth would have been a useful, if unwitting, ally in this effort.

Upon hearing from the Palace that Her Majesty was not coming, Philip Sidney quickly made adjustments to his plans. However, he was surprised to learn than General Eaker would not be in attendance. He thought the American would find the event a useful forum to advocate bombing in daylight. The Yanks seemed commit-

said, "No reason to have him deal with the crap before he leaves. Tomorrow's a special day for him. Let's let it get off to a good start and hope he enjoys himself. The problems can wait 'til tomorrow."

The train from Bromley Park took a little less than an hour. Forester had boarded the train at exactly 9:20 A.M. and quickly found an empty compartment. Unlike trains in the United States where the aisle ran down the center of the coach with rows of seats to each side, British trains had the aisle along one side. Doors opened to walled-off compartments seating eight people. Compartments were first or second class with the former more comfortable and costly yet less crowded. Forester had walked toward the end of the train locating an empty second class compartment which he entered.

The compartment remained empty until the next stop. There, a middle aged man and his wife along with two children joined Forester. The adults uttered polite, yet guarded greetings whereupon they fell into silence. No conversation took place. Tom attributed the silence to typically British reserve. Gradually, he took no notice of his traveling companions and began to enjoy the quiet. Forester had begun to daydream about Helen Trent when a tug on his trousers and a small voice grabbed his attention.

"Are you a Yank?"

"Yes indeed, young man."

"Ronald, we do not talk to strangers." The boy's mother had spoken, looking sternly at her son, whom Tom guessed was eight or nine years old. As children of that age often do, the boy ignored his mother.

"Are you a pilot?"

"That too." Tom had a smile on his face, and had spoken pleasantly.

"What do you fly? A B-17?"

"No, I fly little planes." Amused, Tom realized he had never so described a P-47. "It has only one engine and seating for just one person."

"Like a Spitfire."

"Yes, just like a Spitfire."

"I think Spitfires are the best airplanes in the world."

The thought passed through Forester's mind that a number of Luftwaffe pilots might agree. Tom looked at Ronald's mother. Her expression, once distant, even cold, was softening. With her eyes, she signaled Forester that once her son began to ask questions, he was unlikely to stop. Nonetheless, Forester answered the child.

"I think they're pretty wonderful myself."

"Have you ever flown one?"

"No, I haven't, but I'd like to. I fly a P-47 Thunderbolt."

"My daddy says the Yanks don't have very good airplanes."

Instantly, a silence filled the compartment. Not even the noise of the train overcame the embarrassing halt in conversation. Ronald's mother was mortified. Her husband looked acutely uncomfortable, but was obviously cowardly and said nothing, leaving his wife to make amends. Awkwardly, she began to stammer out an apology.

"No need, Ma'am." Forester raised his hand and gently shook his head. He was smiling as he spoke, hoping to relieve the lady's obvious discomfort. "The admirals in our navy feel the same way."

With this remark, her face brightened and the embarrassment she felt gradually dissipated. She introduced herself as Sarah Graves while poking her husband, whose name was Phil, to acknowledge and greet Forester. Phil Graves did so, them mumbled an apology, which Tom said was not at all necessary. Graves went on to introduce the two children. He first introduced Ronald, age eight, describing the boy as "an inquisitive lad." The other child, also a boy, was named Richard. Much younger than his brother, Richard had been asleep when the Graves first entered the compartment. He remained so throughout the train ride.

Before long, the three adults were chatting comfortably. They spoke mainly about the war and the difficulties the average Englishman faced in daily life. Forester was sympathetic, aware that Americans back home had not been exposed to comparable hardship. As they talked, Ronald, living up to his father's description, peppered Tom with questions about flying. These Forester answered in turn, careful to make the response understandable to the youngster.

"You have an easy manner with children, Colonel." Sarah Graves commented.

Tom responded silently, simply by smiling.

"You seem to like children."

"Yes Ma'am. I guess I do. Probably because I used to be one and can remember how frustrating it was to be ignored by adults."

"Quite so. But I do say that Ronald's questions can become very tiring."

Forester laughed out loud. "That's what my mother used to say about me."

Before long, the train had pulled into the Liverpool Street Station. After saying good-bye to the Graves family, Tom soon found himself outside the station among the bustle of midmorning London. The big overhead clock near the ticket windows had indicated 10:35 A.M., which left plenty of time to get to the BBC. Forester realized he had left behind the slip of paper upon which had been written the BBC's address. Annoyed with himself, Tom shook his head in disbelief. How could he have been so forgetful? *Poor form, Forester, to be late to your own award ceremony.*

Tom was about to phone Bromley Park and track down the address when common sense told him no such call would be necessary. He simply walked along Bishopsgate until he saw a taxi.

"The BBC, please," he told the driver.

"Right you are, Guv'ner."

Ten minutes later, Forester was at 200 Oxford Street, where Britain's national radio service broadcast news and features around the world. In fifteen minutes, it would carry the story of the RAF awarding its DFC to an American fighter pilot.

This Tuesday morning, Helen Trent also rose at 7:30 A.M. She got out of bed and contrary to her usual routine, promptly took a warm bath. She also washed her hair, using the last of her favorite shampoo that no longer was available at Fairfield's, a shop she had patronized since childhood. With clean hair and a clean body, Helen then went downstairs to fix a bit of breakfast. She was feeling particularly chipper, looking forward to seeing Tom Forester. Helen splurged on the morning meal—canned grapefruit juice, oatmeal with a touch of brown sugar, and toast thinly spread with blackberry jam, all accompanied by tea served in her mother's chintzware. The food was delicious and Helen savored it all as she ate and listened to music on the radio.

Alone in the kitchen and in the house, she also enjoyed the peace and quiet occasioned by Sir Robert's absence. He had spent the night at his club. The Collingwood not only had dining and reading rooms, but it also had lodgings for members and their guests. Lately, Helen had become aware that Robert had spent considerable time at the club, both dining and remaining overnight. She attributed this to the lateness of the hour and general fatigue when he and his friends finally finished their cigars and brandy.

At this moment, Helen was not thinking about Sir Robert Trent. Her mind was on Forester. She was hoping they would have at least some time together at the ceremony. Not for a moment did she consider that they might not get on well together. Helen was confident that she and the American colonel would connect as they had at the Royal Aeronautical Society. The challenge would be to carve out time when they could focus upon one another. That might require concerted effort given that he would be, and properly so, the center of attention.

In fact, Helen was hoping that she and Forester might have lunch together after the ceremony. More than likely, their time in company with the other would be limited. She would not ask him to lunch. That would be inappropriate. But she could, and did, hope that he might extend such an invitation. Hopefully, he would not have to return to his airfield immediately upon conclusion of the ceremony. For this reason, she had suggested afternoon tea to Clara Harris when her neighbor had mentioned the possibility of dining together at noon on Tuesday. So her calendar at midday was free. She would be due at the BBC at 11 A.M., but was then free until 4:00 P.M. There would be ample time for lunch with this intriguing man.

Sitting in her kitchen, a cup of tea in hand, Helen brought Forester into sharper focus. Masculine, confident, intelligent, even heroic and certainly compelling. The man was a warrior, yet seemed unimpressed by things military. Moreover, he retained a child's sense of wonder at what he had seen and done. There was in Tom Forester a softness and kindness that Helen perceived and found most attractive.

Thinking of Forester, imagining their forthcoming encounter, led Helen to consider what she would wear. Her clothes needed to be appropriate for the occasion, which was neither formal nor an evening affair. She wanted something simple, yet Helen also wanted Forester to notice her, which meant she needed to look feminine, although not too much so.

Helen ran through her mind various ensembles. Several she rejected as too dressy; several were too severe. Finally, she settled on a smartly cut, tailored dark blue suit. The jacket had a v-neck with tiny pearl buttons leading down to a fitted waistline and attached peplum. It accented her still slender waist while complementing her no longer twenty-year-old hips. Under the jacket she wore a softly elegant white blouse that nicely hid, but hinted at, her full bosom. The short skirt with a buttoned kick pleat exposed and flattered her legs. This was perfect. She wanted to remind Forester she was a woman.

The room at the BBC where the ceremony was to be held was a small auditorium on the third floor. At one end was a stage upon which sat a plain wooden table and five chairs. Not far from the table was a podium. Above the podium hung an electric sign that, when lit, read "On the Air." Several other signs requesting "Quiet Please" were placed around the room, visible to anyone in the audience. Behind the audience and facing the stage was a closed-in glass booth where BBC engineers monitored equipment and signals. These engineers had set up microphones on the table and at the podium.

At 10:50 A.M. this Tuesday, the engineers were finishing preparations for the RAF ceremony. Speaking to Air Vice Marshal Sidney and Colonel James Dixon, the BBC director had explained how the program was to proceed.

"I do not see any difficulties," said the director. Addressing the Air Vice Marshal, he continued, "I've followed the sequence of events outlined by your staff, so all should proceed smoothly."

"Yes," Philip Sidney replied, "all seems very much in order."

"Piece of cake."

"Hmm." Air Vice Marshal Sidney frowned, displeased with the director's use of RAF slang. His annoyance quickly disappeared as he spoke to Jimmy Dixon. "Well Colonel, you're comfortable with this, I trust?"

"Indeed I am, Sir. It should go off without a hitch. Assuming of course that Colonel Forester shows up."

Tom did arrive on time, but just barely so. Once inside the building, he had been directed to a studio on the second floor. When he finally took his place on stage at exactly 10:58 A.M., Jimmy Dixon breathed a sigh of relief. So did Helen. She was sitting in the audience, in the fifth row of seats. At first disappointed by Forester's absence, she had become worried when he did not appear.

A man wearing earphones was at the podium. At precisely 11:00 A.M., the electric sign went on and the director brought his right arm down pointing at this individual who began to speak in a deep, rich voice. "Good morning, everyone. I'm Richard Bloom of the BBC's Home Service. To our listeners who are tuned in for our regularly scheduled program, *Music for the Home Front,* let me assure you that the program will air immediately following this brief, but very special broadcast. This morning we will listen to a ceremony at which the Royal Air Force will award its Distinguished Flying Cross to an American pilot, Lieutenant Colonel Thomas Forester. The BBC is pleased to carry this ceremony, which we believe you will find most enjoyable."

Several miles away, at home in their parlor awaiting the broadcast of their favorite BBC program, a man and woman were surprised at Bloom's mention of Tom's name. Tea cups in hand, Sarah and Paul Graves turned and looked at each other. The American with whom they had shared a train compartment this very morning was a genuine hero. Recounting how they first met, the two felt slightly embarrassed. This gave way to pride in knowing Forester as they recalled the American's friendliness and the pleasant conversation they subsequently had shared.

—⁓—

"It is now my pleasure to introduce Air Vice Marshal Philip Sidney of RAF Fighter Command. He will serve as moderator of today's event."

With the word "event," the director motioned to Philip Sidney, sitting at the table, that he was on the air.

"Thank you, Mr. Bloom, and good morning ladies and gentlemen." The Air Vice Marshal then gave a succinct summary of the air war against Germany. He mentioned the importance of strategic bombing, but paid greater attention to the role of fighter aircraft. Praising both British and American pilots, Philip Sidney spoke with admiration of the men who flew the single engine planes. "One such pilot the RAF will honor this morning."

Sidney then introduced the two officers at the table who would speak next. The first was Keith Davenport. The second was Squadron Leader Ian Packard who commanded the Spitfires at Chase Hill.

Colonel Davenport remained at the table while speaking. Careful to talk into the microphone, he read a message from the Eighth Air Force Commander that he himself had written that morning. The message was brief. It conveyed Eaker's admiration for Forester's fighting spirit. It expressed high regard for the RAF, as well as appreciation for their recognition of an American pilot. And it emphasized the necessity of cooperation between England and the

United States represented so well by "this small action above Dunkirk."

Colonel Davenport then offered a few words of his own.

"Ladies and Gentlemen, before going upstairs to Air Force headquarters, I commanded a group of B-17s, which, as most of you know, is a big, four engine bomber. With these we bring the war home to Germany. Our job in the skies above Europe is dangerous, but it is much less so whenever Spitfires and Thunderbolts are about. They are "Little Friends" and I can tell you from first hand experience that the young men in the bombers, brave boys all of them, are deeply indebted to RAF Fighter Command and to our own groups of P-47s."

At the mention of Fighter Command, Philip Sidney beamed with pleasure.

When Keith Davenport finished speaking, the BBC director pointed to Squadron Leader Packard. This RAF officer carefully explained what had occurred near the French-Belgian border when, low on fuel, he and his wingman were about to be jumped by a large formation of Messerschmitts. Speaking into the microphone, but addressing Tom, who was sitting next to him, Packard expressed gratitude for the timely arrival of the P-47s. These aircraft, he noted, were flown with great skill and tenacity. "Dispatching the Germans, they saved two of His Majesty's Spitfires and their pilots."

Packard continued speaking, although now sounding less rehearsed. "The situation was rather bleak at the point in time when Colonel Forester showed up, after which things got rather bleak for the Messerschmitts. It was a jolly good show by this American and I now have a new respect for those formidable Thunderbolts he and his men fly."

At this point, Squadron Leader Packard turned to Forester and saluted, a mark of respect that Tom promptly returned. "The last time we did that, said Ian Packard, "we were in two aircraft some 1,500 feet above the white cliffs of Dover."

"Now let us get down to the business at hand." This was Philip Sidney speaking. He was at the podium, motioning for Forester to come forward. Tom did so, and saluted the Air Vice Marshal. Squadron Leader Packard accompanied Forester.

"It is now my great pleasure and high honor to award the Distinguished Flying Cross to Lieutenant Colonel Thomas Forester of the American Eighth Air Force. For those of you listening in, Colonel Forester is standing next to me."

Reaching into his pocket, Sidney withdrew a sheet of paper that was neatly folded into quarters. Opening up the paper and putting on a pair of spectacles, he began, with a rich baritone voice, to read the citation. This began with another account of the air battle, extolled Forester's courage and skill, and expressed the RAF's pride in having Lieutenant Colonel Forester as a comrade in arms. "Thus," concluded the Air Vice Marshal, "it is with gratitude that we of the Royal Air Force present you with our Distinguished Flying Cross."

Philip Sidney carefully refolded the paper and returned it to his pocket. From beneath the top of the podium, he took out a small blue velvet box. He then took the medal out of the box, and, waiting for two photographers to set up, pinned the DFC on Forester's chest. The cameras flashed and the Air Vice Marshal beckoned Tom to the microphone. "Well, young man, now it's your turn to speak."

In his mind, Forester had prepared brief remarks for this occasion. As he stepped up to the microphone, he forgot them totally. There, out in the audience off to his right, was Helen Trent. His surprise was complete, as was his delight. She looked terrific, as beautiful as he remembered. Forester made eye contact with Helen and she in turn smiled. Tom nodded slightly, wanting to smile back, but choosing not to for fear of calling attention to Helen. He just stood at the platform, remaining silent. His heart and mind were focused solely on this English lady, *his* English lady. Random thoughts raced through his head. *What is she doing here? Is she alone? Please let her not have plans later on. Now I don't have to waste time traipsing around London trying to find her. She's right in front of me! Waiting for me to speak. As is everyone else, including the BBC director who is frantically rotating his right hand urging you to speak. Don't disappoint them. More importantly, don't disappoint Helen. Make this good.*

As Forester stood at the podium saying nothing, he distinctly heard Air Vice Marshal Sidney cough, though the sound was artificial.

Helen had become anxious. Was he going to just stand there? She could have sworn they made eye contact and had been amused at his obvious surprise. More important, Helen was pleased that he knew she was present. Her mind, too, was filled with thoughts. That man up there, that American officer, was someone she hoped to know better. She hoped too he might be interested in her. *That all could come later. Now, dear Colonel Forester, it's time for you to speak.*

So Tom did. Without notes and from the heart, he found the words to express how he felt.

"Mr. Bloom, Air Vice Marshal Sidney, Squadron Leader Packard, Colonel Davenport, Colonel Dixon, ladies and gentlemen. Let me first say how grateful I am to receive this award. Brave men, men who are far braver than I, wear the distinctive ribbon of the Distinguished Flying Cross. I am honored now to be in their company.

"Honored in large part because the Royal Air Force is itself distinguished. With courage, skill, and sacrifice, the RAF has defended freedom. Now it carries the war to wherever the enemy is cleared for takeoff. Those of us in the Eighth Air Force are proud to share the sky with the Royal Air Force. Together, Spitfire and Thunderbolt, Lancaster and Flying Fortress, we will destroy the Luftwaffe. Nowhere will the swastikas of the German Air Force be safe.

"Victory is not yet at hand, but I believe victory is certain. Surely, with Great Britain and the United States pulling together, we simply cannot be beaten, for we fight for all that is decent and true. Thank you very much."

Tom then returned to his seat, amidst polite applause. As Forester sat down, Keith Davenport leaned over and congratulated him.

"Nice little speech, Tom."

"Thanks, Keith." The two officers had become friendly now that they were both serving on the Advisory Committee.

"Eaker would have approved."

"How so?" Tom queried.

"Short and sweet. General Eaker dislikes long speeches, especially ones given by Americans. But I have to tell you that I was worried at first. You sort-of took your time in getting started."

Tom smiled, and lied, "Stage fright. It hit me when I got up to speak."

As the two Americans exchanged words, Air Vice Marshal Sidney was bringing the ceremony to a close. As he did so, Richard Bloom approached the microphone. When Philip Sidney had finished, Bloom, on cue from the BBC director, spoke to the radio audience.

"Ladies and gentlemen, this concludes our special presentation. The time now is 11:27 A.M. We turn to *Music for the Home Front*. Here is your host, Clyde Harper."

Harper, located in a different studio, began his broadcast. As Bloom mentioned Clyde Harper's name, the director drew his hand across his throat at which point the "On the Air" sign went off. "Well done everyone, the broadcast is over."

Tom stood up and chatted briefly with Squadron Leader Packard. Anxious to intercept Helen before she might leave, he made his way towards the side of the stage where steps led to the audience. However, Philip Sidney blocked his path. Both good manners and military protocol dictated he acknowledge an Air Vice Marshal. So as Tom approached Sidney, he saluted, once again thanking him for the DFC. After two minutes of polite conversation, Forester was able to break away. Richard Bloom had joined the group, wishing to speak to the RAF officer.

Tom stepped down from the stage and went in the direction of Helen Trent. Damn. Jimmy Dixon was speaking to her.

"Hello, Colonel. Nice speech."

Forester recognized the voice, but did not see a face. The person speaking was off to the left, near the first row of seats. Tom turned and greeted Roger Baldwin.

"Hello, Roger. Good to see you. What are you doing here?"

"Come to see my Dartmouth chum receive the DFC. Drove down with Keith Davenport." Baldwin shook hands with Forester. "Well done, you've made us proud."

"Thanks." Tom was genuinely pleased to see Baldwin, and flattered that Eaker's meteorological officer had made an effort to attend the ceremony.

"You're in good company, you know. A DFC is a DFC, and do you know who won America's first Distinguished Flying Cross?"

"I haven't a clue."

"Fellow by the name of Lindberg. Flew over a large body of water, all by himself."

"So I'm in good company?"

"Indeed you are."

"Well, I'd rather be in her company." With his eyes and head Tom was pointing towards Helen.

"The one talking with Colonel Dixon?"

"Yes. Her name is Helen Trent and I need a few minutes alone with her. Can you help?"

"By getting rid of Dixon?"

"Exactly."

"Say no more, my friend. Give me half a minute."

Roger Baldwin walked over to where Helen and Jimmy Dixon were conversing. After being introduced to the lady, Baldwin whispered in the ear of Dixon. The Deputy Air Attaché then shook hands with Helen, and escorted by Colonel Baldwin, walked past Tom towards Richard Bloom. As they passed Forester, Roger winked and spoke discreetly.

"She's all yours. Go Indians."

Forester approached Helen who now was standing by herself.

"How nice to see you, Colonel." In friendly fashion, Helen extended both arms, which Tom gently grasped, holding them slightly longer than necessary. Helen noticed, but was not displeased. "Let me offer my congratulations."

"Thank you. This is a pleasant surprise. Seeing you, that is."

"Colonel Dixon invited me and others from the Advisory Committee. Anyway, I wanted to attend and here I am."

"I'm glad, very glad. It really is nice to see you again." Tom wanted to say, more but felt it prudent not to. He began to converse with himself, silently. *Not too fast Forester, or you'll mess this up. But you're going to have to say something. Silence here is not golden. God she looks good.*

Finally, Forester did speak, passing on a compliment he truly meant. "You're looking lovely today, Mrs. Trent."

"Helen, you must call me Helen." She had a soft, but earnest tone to her voice. "And thank you." *Well, he seems to have noticed I'm female. That's a start. But the sweet man seems befuddled as to what to say next. Time to help Tom Forester.*

"The ceremony was splendid. Simple, yet quite dignified and pleasant. But what happens next?" *I shall have to make this easy for the dear boy.* "It's almost time for lunch. That's what you Yanks call the noon meal, isn't it?"

"Yes, it is" Forester spotted the opening, and responded accordingly—just as Helen had intended. "Helen, I've some time before I must get back to Bromley Park. And, if you're free as well, I'm hoping we might have lunch together."

"Why Colonel, I'd . . . "

"Tom." Forester interrupted, speaking now with ever so slight a tone of command in his voice.

"Tom it is. I'd like that. And, yes, I'm free."

"Wonderful." Forester's face reflected his pleasure. "You don't suppose we could leave now, do you?"

"I'd love to, but you're the star attraction at the moment. So you need to circulate a bit. Appearances and all that."

"Okay, but you won't leave without me, or with someone else, will you?"

Helen looked Forester straight in the eyes. "No, I'll be here, waiting for you."

"I'm glad."

Helen felt good inside, pleased at how this encounter had gone. "Me too."

As Forester moved about the auditorium, conversing with members of the audience, Helen slipped off to the ladies room. There she ran a comb through her hair and checked her appearance. All seemed in order. Indeed, Helen was pleased by what she saw. No longer youthful at forty-three, the person Helen saw in the mirror nonetheless was attractive, still able to make men look twice.

Helen took from her purse a small piece of pink paper, about the size of an index card. Upon it she wrote her telephone number. She then returned the paper to her pocketbook. With one final check in the mirror, Helen returned to the auditorium where she found the crowd to be diminishing.

Ten minutes later, Helen and Tom left the auditorium together. By then, most people in attendance at the ceremony, including Air Vice Marshal Sidney, had departed. So the exit by the American officer and English lady went unnoticed, except by Roger Baldwin and Jimmy Dixon. The former, perceiving Forester's interest in the woman, wished them well. *Life,* mused Baldwin, *at times can be full of pain and sorrow. Best to enjoy a little happiness if and when opportunity knocks.* The latter, unaware of Tom's intentions, simply was envious. Standing by the stage, Colonel Dixon watched as Forester escorted Helen Trent out of the studio. He too mused. *Some guys have it all— youth, the company of a pretty lady, and best of all, three squadrons of P-47s to command.*

Helen and Tom walked out onto Oxford Street and headed west, towards Marble Arch. They had gone only two blocks when Tom turned to her. "Helen, I need to tell you something."

Helen braced herself, afraid that she was about to hear something she clearly did not want said. Something sad, something that would ruin their time together.

"Yes?" Hesitancy had invaded her voice.

"I have no idea where we are going."

Helen turned towards Tom and burst into laughter. Her foreboding vanished, replaced instantaneously by amusement and relief.

Her eyes sparkled as she responded. "How terribly funny. You certainly fooled me. You were walking with a sense of purpose as though you seemed to know exactly where you were going."

"I'm afraid not. It's my job. Sometimes I need to look like I know what I'm doing, even when that's not the case. Like now, for example."

"This really is most amusing.

"Yes it is." Tom was smiling. He too saw the humor in the situation. "I feel like I should be embarrassed, but I'm not. I just don't know where to take you to lunch."

"Not to worry. I do. This is my city and I am, after all, a member of a committee your air force established for advice on how to get on in London. As it happens, I know just the spot."

"Sounds good to me."

"Follow me, my boy." Helen steered Tom to the right and they walked up on a small lane that flowed into Oxford Street. Coming up to a cross street, they stopped at the curb. Instinctively, Tom looked left, saw no traffic coming, and stepped onto the street. An automobile, coming from the right, screeched to a halt just as Helen pulled Tom safely out of the way.

The automobile, a taxi, moved forward slowly, drawing even with Tom and Helen. The cabbie leaned across to them both, but spoke to Tom. "Careful, mate, you're not in America now. We drive on the left, we do."

Before the cab had moved away, Helen exclaimed, "Good heavens Tom, do be careful." She was genuinely worried.

"Yes, I must. That was much too close. I keep forgetting where I am."

"Here." Helen wrapped her arm around Tom's and drew herself close to him. "I'll hold on to you. That way you'll be safe."

The two of them continued walking, with Helen leading the way. Neither of them spoke. They both were still shaken by the incident with the cab. But their silence in no way was awkward, for they were now connected, physically touching. Both Helen and Tom were acutely aware of this connection, of their close proximity to one another. A barrier had come down. No longer were they separate and apart. Each felt a tinge of excitement.

The couple soon arrived at Fogarty's where she was warmly greeted by the proprietor. Helen introduced Tom to Mr. Fogarty, who escorted them to a table.

"How good to see you again, my dear." Henry Fogarty's voice reflected the genuine pleasure he felt in seeing Helen Trent. "You are looking lovely, as always."

"You're too kind, Henry, as you've always been."

"Nonsense. And little Claire? She is well?"

"Yes, she is. Thank you for asking. She is away at school."

"And growing up, yes?"

"Indeed, she is. She's getting to be quite the young lady."

"That is good." Fogarty turned to Tom. "She will be as beautiful as her mother. He then handed menus to them both. "Today we have lamb stew. It is excellent. Now I return to the kitchen."

"As Fogarty moved away, Tom spoke to Helen. "He seems very fond of you."

"Yes, and I him."

"Why do I sense the two of you have known each other for some time?"

"Because, my perceptive friend, we have."

Tom's expression encouraged Helen to continue.

"After Peter's death, when times were tight, Henry Fogarty took me in when I needed a job. Father had died and money was scarce. Henry owned the dress shop I told you about. It was right here, before this was a restaurant. This is where I worked as a seamstress and as a sales clerk. His wife helped me with Claire. I don't know what I would have done without them."

"Somehow I think you would have survived." Tom found Helen's story of the dress shop interesting. He encouraged her to tell him more about those years, which she did. Helen enjoyed doing so for the years, despite the hardship, had been satisfying and pleasant. As Helen recounted her experiences, Tom saw in her a strength of character he greatly admired. She had been alone, without much money and with a child to care for, and she had managed. Indeed she had flourished. Forester wondered if he would have done as well.

"Looking back," said Helen with a sigh, "it was a happy time."

Tom thought Helen might add the comment "unlike now." But she did not. Yet Forester got the definite impression that Helen had implied the thought. He concluded that in her present circumstances, Helen Trent was unhappy. So, there and then, Tom decided he would try to change that. He felt this woman deserved a full measure of happiness. Yes, he was going to pursue Helen Trent. He already had decided that. And he hoped to bed the woman. But in Henry Fogarty's restaurant, on the day he received the DFC, Forester vowed to do something more. He was going to do his best, his very best, to bring some joy into the life of this very special lady.

Helen was watching Tom closely as he made this resolution. The man had remained quiet, intent, lost in thought. She wondered what he had been thinking.

Forester had not yet uttered a word, so Helen continued speaking. "But that was then, and now is now."

"To be sure," replied Tom, rejoining the conversation.

"But someday, now will be later. The war will be over and life will be different."

"Then what?"

"Then, Tom, we get on with our lives. You, me, everyone."

"We'll never be the same."

"No, we won't. But life moves on. You'll see. The day will come when this war is over and you'll need to decide what it is you wish to do with your life."

"I hope I see that day."

"What do you mean? Helen was truly puzzled.

"I may not live. People get killed in wars and my number may be up."

"Don't say that!" For a moment, Helen contemplated what she had never before considered—that Forester might die, that what could be might never come about. Images of Peter and the motorcycle came to mind. *Please God, not again.*

"Well, not to worry," Tom was speaking lightheartedly. "I don't intend to die, or expect to. I plan to be around when this war is over."

"Are you afraid?"

"Truthfully?"

"Yes. Surely you must be."

"Well, I do get afraid. Right before we engage the Luftwaffe, for a very brief moment, I realize I might soon be dead. Sometimes when I'm going out to my plane, my whole lower body goes limp and I want to run away. Imagine playing a game of tennis that if you lose, you will die dead. That's what it's like."

"It must be awful."

"It keeps you alert, that's for sure. The good part is that when it happens I'm too busy to think about it. At 28,000 feet I've got a lot on my mind with Thunderbolts and Messerschmitts all shooting at each other."

"So what do you do?"

"I postpone my fear. That's what most of us do. We put fear aside and get on with our jobs. The fear returns later on, often with a sense of true terror."

"How awful."

"It's not pleasant or pretty, nor particularly heroic. Just a poor human being, alone and trembling. Glad that he's alive today. Worried that he might not be tomorrow."

Hearing Forester speak, Helen felt the urge to hold him close.

Unaware of what Helen was feeling Tom continued speaking. "The flying part of the job is really fun. I don't know any pilot, at least any good one, who doesn't love to strap in and head upstairs. But every so often, you realize it's a serious business. Like when someone you know doesn't come back. In the sky, death is one's constant companion."

At this last remark, Forester laughed. "How melodramatic. 'In the sky death is one's constant companion.' Sounds almost literary, or something like you'd hear in a movie."

"It's no joking matter."

"No, it's not." Then Tom's expression changed, becoming more serious. "Actually, Helen, it is. Otherwise, we might not continue. Death is less real if it's treated lightly. So that's what we do. All of us. I expect the German pilots do the same. We try not to dwell upon the possibility of death or acknowledge its presence. We know it's there and we've seen it up close. I guess what we do, at least what I do, is to try to contain fear and set aside the thought of death."

Helen looked across the table at Tom, noting the ribbon of the DFC upon his chest. How handsome he looked, yet how vulnerable. She saw in his face youth, maturity, and the strain of commanding men in combat. Again, she felt like taking him in her arms to comfort, even caress.

"You're very brave, Tom Forester."

"No, Mrs. Trent, I'm not. And it's important for you to realize that."

"It's Helen, and why?"

"Because I don't want to appear to you to be something I'm not. I'm just a guy, trying to do something useful, fighting for something worthwhile. I do enjoy what I do. I'll admit that. Not the killing, but the flying—leading the Group. But I'm no Captain of the Clouds." Forester was referring to a James Cagney movie about a heroic bush pilot who joins the Royal Canadian Air Force. "I'm just a guy, one guy like a thousand others who have come over to help win the war."

Tom believed what he had just said. He did feel ordinary, one of many Americans in uniform fighting an enemy of freedom. But, at the same time, Tom felt special. He flew a P-47, commanded a fighter group, and was the man in charge at Bromley Park. These two opposing feelings existed in Forester's consciousness. To him, they posed no dilemma or created any tension. Each was genuine. Each was heartfelt.

"You're wrong, Tom Forester. You're very brave." Helen reached across the table and boldly took Tom's hand in hers, squeezing it gently.

Forester put his other hand upon hers. He focused upon this woman whom he now desired. "I'm just glad to be here with you."

The two of them spent the next three hours at Henry Fogarty's eatery. They talked and laughed, and continued to hold hands, oblivious to their surroundings. They told each other more about their childhood and how the experiences of youth had shaped their lives. Tom recounted his experiences at Dartmouth and expressed his hopes for a career in teaching once the war was over. Helen told Tom about school and voiced regret, as her father had predicted, at leaving early. Helen also spoke of her life with Peter and related to Tom her situation at 28 Temple Court. When Tom delicately asked about Sir Robert, Helen responded in full, telling the truth. Never before had she done so. But in telling Forester, she felt neither shame nor embarrassment. Indeed, she wanted him to know the truth. Because it was the truth, and because, she later admitted to herself, she wanted to encourage this man to pursue a relationship with her. Along these lines, with a degree of premeditation, Helen invited Tom and some of his officer friends to the party for Sir Robert planned for October 19. Tom accepted and told Helen he would be there, to which she replied, "Good, although I shall probably have to ignore you for much of the evening."

As they talked, the chemistry between them grew. Words and ideas fueled a reaction that grew in intensity as additional ideas and words propelled their conversation. In part, the reaction was intellectual. They found each other to be interested in ideas, comfortable with concepts. They shared a love of history and could speak intelligently about current events. To their mutual satisfaction, they again made no mention of the war, finding much to talk about beyond the event that now shaped their lives.

The reaction also was physical. As they conversed, intellectual compatibility fostered a more basic attraction. Already, they had found the other pleasing in appearance. Now this appeal was heightened. They became aroused, aware of the other's sexuality. Both Helen and Tom were in need of emotional support and a bedtime partner. Each felt they were sitting across from the person who could meet both needs. Helen found Tom handsome and intriguing. Tom found Helen fascinating and beautiful. Moreover, beneath the surface, each was an extremely passionate individual. Helen hid her sexual desires behind a sense of propriety and a reserve typically associated with Britain's upper class. Tom, whose desires were less camouflaged, contained them by adherence to good manners instilled at childhood. In addition, he was restrained by the military's requirement that officers in the United States Army Air Force be gentlemen.

As lunch progressed, so did their awareness of the other's physical charms. Increasingly, Tom and Helen felt an urgency neither had experienced in some time. These desires were enhanced by their proximity to one another and by the singular pleasure each took in holding the other's hand.

The two of them realized something special was happening. They were becoming involved. They were experiencing the magic that can exist between a man and a woman. Wisely, they did not attempt to analyze this phenomenon. Nor did they even discuss it. They simply allowed the first signs of romance to flourish, praying that it would survive the rigors of reality.

As Helen and Tom sat at the table and became something more than two acquaintances, only one person in the restaurant took notice. And he wholeheartedly approved. Henry Fogarty stood at the entrance to the kitchen observing his old friend and her new companion. Fond of Helen, he was aware she did not have a special man in her life. But he sensed she soon would. "Love needs not explanation or apology," Fogarty said aloud to no one in particular, "and lovers have to find whatever time and space they can."

Shortly after Henry Fogarty spoke, Helen looked at her watch. To her surprise, the time was 3 P.M. She told Tom reluctantly, "I'm having tea with my neighbor at four o'clock, so I must be on my way."

"Is it three o'clock already?"

"Yes, somehow it is. This has been just wonderful. I'm sorry to have to go." Helen looked about the restaurant, which was now largely empty.

"I don't suppose you could postpone tea? You could telephone your neighbor and say something's come up."

"I could, but shouldn't. Clara Harris is a dear friend and I must keep this engagement."

"So you must." Tom squeezed Helen's hand, acknowledging the correctness of Helen's response. He then went off to pay the bill while Helen walked back to the kitchen to say good-bye to Fogarty. When she returned, he escorted her outside. There they headed towards Oxford Street where Helen was to catch a bus. The two of them walked in silence, aware that their time together was about to end.

At the bus stop where a short queue had formed, Tom broke the silence.

"Helen, there's so little time and much still to say. Dear lady, please forgive me, and please don't take offense, but I want—" Here he paused. "I need to see you again. And soon."

Helen hesitated, but only for a moment. Her bus had arrived and there was no time to weigh consequences or debate right or wrong. She had to respond quickly and she did so. Conscious that her choice was full of danger, she nonetheless took from her purse the slip of pink paper. As she stepped onto the bus, Helen handed it to Forester. "You will. You will."

ELEVEN

By early October, the Eighth Air Force was ready once again to strike at Germany. During September, the bombers had hit targets in France and the Low Countries. With poor weather over the Nazi homeland and the need to support the ruse of an invasion near the Pas de Calais, only two missions in September had targeted Germany. One, against Emden, produced mixed results. The other, against Stuttgart, had been a complete fiasco. A force of 338 B-17s had struck the city, or tried to. Because of heavy clouds, most could not find the target. Moreover, the opposition was fierce. Thirty-three bombers were shot down. Another twelve ditched in the North Sea having run out of fuel on the way home.

Under pressure from Hap Arnold to produce better results and eager to demonstrate the effectiveness of daylight precision bombing, Ira Eaker called for a maximum effort in October. Every B-17 that could fly would be sent aloft. The Eighth Air Force was going to pound German industry, particularly those factories that produced fighter aircraft. Eaker aimed to close off the flow of planes to the Luftwaffe. This would ease the threat against his own force and make possible the invasion of France now scheduled for the coming spring.

General Eaker also hoped that the forthcoming attacks would weaken the morale of people in Germany, sapping their will to continue the war. People who once had cheered Hitler might now have second thoughts. At the very least, they would share with the people of Warsaw, Rotterdam, Antwerp, and Coventry the terrifying experience of having bombs fall from the sky.

"Are we ready, Keith?" The General was speaking to Colonel Davenport.

"Yes, Sir. General Anderson has thought of damn near everything and the plans have been checked and rechecked. Jerry's about to be hit very hard."

"Good. I want to blow the German war machine apart. And, in the process, put the Luftwaffe out of business. That will give General Arnold something to tell the Joint Chiefs."

"And their British counterparts."

"Them too. The Nazis may be constructing Festung Europa, but the Fortress has no roof. How many planes can we expect to launch each day?"

"A few less than four hundred."

Eaker frowned. "I wish we had more. I need more, but it's a start."

Davenport then raised the subject most on his mind. "General, be prepared for casualties. Germany's going to be a hard nut to crack. Stuttgart showed us that. We're going to lose some of our boys."

"I know that, Keith." Eaker's voice reflected no sign of irritation. "A lot of good men are about to die, but nowhere near the Stuttgart numbers. We can do much better than that, with tighter formations and better escort work. We'll probably lose ten, maybe fifteen planes a mission. Perhaps a few more. But that's acceptable. We can and will replace them, both the planes and their crew. You can't fight a war and not suffer losses."

Reluctantly, Keith Davenport agreed with his boss. "No, Sir. You can't."

At this point, both men heard a gentle knock on the door, after which Roger Baldwin entered the room. He walked to the fireplace, then turned towards Eaker.

"I've got the latest weather report, General, as you requested.

"What's it look like, Roger?"

"Well, Sir, the heavy cloud cover that's been hanging over the Continent should be pushed east by tomorrow. There's a high pressure system coming off the Atlantic, which should give us clear to scattered conditions over Germany for the next three, maybe four days. We'll have some early morning fog here, but it should burn off by half an hour after sunrise. So as far as weather is concerned, General, it looks like the Eighth can fly to Germany and back."

With his pipe clenched between his teeth, Eaker spoke to both Davenport and Baldwin. "And so it will, gentlemen, and so it will."

—⚬—

The October campaign of the Eighth Air Force began with a strike against Frankfurt. Of 361 aircraft dispatched, 16 were lost. Eaker's estimate seemed right on target. Yet no one at Wycombe Abbey, not even Keith Davenport, expected the slaughter that followed. On October 8, 30 planes were shot down when 399 bombers visited Bremen. The next day, 28 bombers failed to return. On October 10, Eaker sent 274 B-17s to Munster. Only 244 made it back. In three days, the Eighth lost 88 aircraft. More importantly, 880 highly trained men were either dead or prisoners of war. Statistically, in 1943, the most dangerous place for an American was in a bomber on the way to Germany.

Keith Davenport was appalled at these losses; Ira Eaker less so. Clearly dismayed, the General understood that out of necessity military commanders must send young men to their deaths. Eaker accepted responsibility for the October losses, but he persevered. He believed, as did most everyone in the Army Air Force, that the Eighth, despite the aerial carnage, was whittling down the Luftwaffe. German fighters rising to oppose the bombers were being destroyed in record numbers. German aircraft factories were being blown

apart. The effort to destroy the German Air Force appeared successful. Hence, the losses were acceptable. Yet Eaker and his fellow
generals were wrong. The Luftwaffe, though stretched thin, was far
from broken. The claims of American gunners aboard the bombers
were exaggerated. The damage to factories, while substantial, was
limited, at no time were the Germans short of fighter aircraft. In
October 1943 the Luftwaffe remained a formidable adversary. Aware
of the threat to the Reich now posed by American bombers, the
Germans had repositioned their fighter force. About eight hundred
planes, well armed and ably flown, awaited the Americans. These aircraft were supplemented by numerous gun batteries. They were
assisted by effective early warning and control systems. Thus, on
October 14, when Ira Eaker sent the Eighth Air Force back to
Schweinfurt, the Luftwaffe was ready.

Forester did not fly on the mission to Frankfurt. Major Browne
again led the Group. According to Harry Collins, he did well. The
Group made its rendezvous with the bombers and, in one giant free-
for-all with the Luftwaffe, shot down five Messerschmitts. Two P-47s
were lost.

However, Tom was back in the cockpit for the missions of
October 8, 9, and 10. Of these, the trip to Munster was the most
eventful.

Although October 10 was a Sunday, there was little time for
church services as the mission meant the men at Bromley Park were
extremely busy. For Forester, the day began at 5:30 A.M. when, having just awakened, he sat on the side of his bed and rubbed his face
and body. With grogginess dispelled, he then marched through his
early morning ritual. Once dressed, he went downstairs where
Dobbs had prepared a pot of coffee. He poured himself a cup,
grabbed a donut, and walked outside the cottage to his Jeep. He then
drove to the Operations Office, which was situated not far from the
control tower. There, Harry Collins greeted the Commanding
Officer of the19th Fighter Group, presenting him with a summary
of the scheduled mission.

Earlier in the morning, Collins had received word of the upcoming mission from General McCready's staff. This was soon followed by a Field Order signed by McCready as Deputy Commander of Eighth Air Force fighters. The Field Order provided the key parameters for the attack upon Munster. It specified targets and routes for the B-17s, rendezvous points for the P-47s, composition of both the strike force and escorting fighters, radio frequencies to be used, and the all important time lines around which the mission was to be flown.

From this information, the Bromley Park staff put together a more detailed operations plan geared to the 19th Fighter Group. This plan designated the individual airplanes to be used, the pilots who would fly, the schedule for take off and assembly, the relative position of the three squadrons once in battle formation, and the exact routes to and from the rendezvous. The plan also contained information about the weather and expected opposition from the Luftwaffe. All this and more had to be established before the order to "Start Engines" could be given so that Forester had a well conceived plan to execute.

Tom listened to Harry Collins review both the Field Order and the operations plan. He asked several questions, but made only two changes to what the staff had prepared. One benefit of having competent subordinates was that Forester rarely had to alter the Group's ops plan that invariably awaited him the morning of a mission.

"Okay, Harry. It looks pretty good to me."

"I think we're in good shape, Colonel. Hawkins has done his usual thorough job and Ken Browne came by and made some helpful suggestions."

Major Fred Hawkins was the Group Operations Officer. Thus, he was responsible for mission planning. Like Collins, Colonel Tee, and the other senior staff, he was a talented individual. Unlike them, however, he wore a set of wings above the left breast pocket of his uniform. But Hawkins had not flown in several months. He was grounded due to a heart murmur that Norman had been unable to cure. So the Major made his contribution to the 19th Fighter Group by piloting a desk rather than a P-47.

Having absorbed and then approved the operations plan, Forester drove over to the nearest mess for breakfast, accompanied by Hawkins and Collins. Tom quickly devoured scrambled eggs, spam, and another donut. With a mission about to start, he thought of breakfast as fuel. He would not eat again until well after lunchtime.

"Ten shun!" Wilbur Williams's voice exploded as Forester entered the Nissen hut that served as the briefing room. All fifty-nine men in the room stood to attention.

The briefing room was drab since brown was the predominant color. A strictly utilitarian space, no effort had been made to enhance its appearance. Lighting in the room was barely adequate. Heating was even less so, being supplied by two small, overtaxed coal-burning stoves. With fifty-four pilots and five staff officers present, space was at a premium. And with at least half of them puffing cigars or cigarettes, the Nissen hut had a smoky, dingy ambiance. It looked more like a gambling parlor in a cheap nightclub than a room essential for Bromley Park's success.

Most of the briefing room was filled with collapsible wooden chairs of the kind usually found in a school auditorium. At one end was a raised stage on which rested the room's most prominent feature. This was a large map of southern England and northern Europe. On the map was a piece of red yarn stretching from East Anglia across the North Sea to Munster and back. This represented the route the 274 B-17s would take. A blue piece of yarn intercepted the red well out on the North Sea at a point just before the bombers turned south on a line straight to the city. The blue yarn traced the path the 19th Fighter Group would take to meet up with the B-17s. Forester and his Thunderbolts would be escorting the strike force down toward the target before breaking off to return home. Marking their route back, the blue yarn ran northwest from Munster across Holland directly to the spot on the map representing Bromley Park.

At one side of the stage was a school-sized blackboard on which, carefully lettered, were painted critical mission milestones. These included Start Engines, Take Off, Rendezvous, and Return to Base. Next to each of these was space on which, in chalk, the particular time and navigational headings could be filled in. All of the pilots were copying down the information. A few were writing on paper. Most, using fountain pens, were writing on the back of their left hand where the data more easily could be referenced.

Stepping up to the stage, pointer in hand, Tom spoke to the men in the room.

"Thank you, gentlemen. Please be seated. Major Collins, why don't you start?"

Harry, who had followed Forester into the briefing room and onto the stage, walked to the center of the platform. Speaking without notes, he explained the importance of Munster as a target for the Eighth Air Force. He then described the bomber force and outlined its plan of attack. He also identified the known locations of enemy antiaircraft batteries and discussed the likely response of the Luftwaffe to this particular raid.

"You may see some Messerschmitt 110s. Intelligence reports that Me-110 crews have been brought back, retrained, and told to stop the Forts and Liberators. Some of them are armed with rockets, which can blow a B-17 apart with a single strike. So, keep a lookout for these guys and remember," here Collins paused, wanting to have everyone's attention, "where there are 110s, there will be 109s and 190s nearby looking for you."

The 110 was a well armed, twin engine aircraft with a crew of two, not dissimilar to the DeHavilland Mosquitoes Roger Baldwin wanted to borrow from the RAF. Sturdy in construction, with ample range, the Me-110 was a mainstay of the German Air Force. It flew wherever the Luftwaffe fought, from Norway to North Africa, from the British Isles to the Soviet Union. The plane was designed to destroy enemy aircraft. Hence its nickname, *Zerstroer.* However, in the Battle of Britain, the Messerschmitt fared poorly. Throughout the epic struggle, Me 110s were outclassed by both Hurricanes and Spitfires. In North Africa, the German plane frequently fell prey to Allied aircraft. Midway into 1943, Me-110s were withdrawn to

Germany for defense of the Reich. In this role, they did well, particularly at night. Although when confronted by P-47s, the *Zerstroers* almost always came off second best.

After the Intelligence Officer had finished, he took a seat on the stage next to Forester. Next up was the Group's weather officer. In a dry monotone, he spelled out the weather conditions along the entire route the P-47s were to take. Conditions over Germany were normal, which meant intermittent clouds would greet the strike force. Sometimes the weather in England would simply shut down the Eighth Air Force's bombers, as well as fighters. When that occurred, morale went down, particularly among the crews of the B-17s and B-24s. Bomber crews went through lengthy preparations for flight with tension building as the time for Start Engines drew near. An order to scrub the mission meant not only that the stress had been for naught, but also that no progress would be made towards the twenty-five missions needed to complete a combat tour.

The meteorological officer soon completed his forecast. As Harry Collins had done, he returned to a chair near Forester. When Major Fred Hawkins took center stage the pilots in the room became particularly attentive. Hawkins spoke clearly. His voice had a distinct no nonsense tone. He reviewed procedures for take off and assembly, and, with a pointer pressed to the yarn, discussed the routes both the B-17s and P-47s would take. He then pointed to the blackboard.

"Gentlemen, Start Engines is set for 08:40. Six minutes later, Colonel Forester will commence his run down Runway 26. Rendezvous with the bombers is at 10:15. You arrive back at base at 12:06," Hawkins face broke out into a big grin, "give or take a minute or two.

"It's a long trip today, but you'll be carrying the 108 drop-tanks, so you should be able to make it to Munster and back. But it will be close, so keep an eye on your fuel gauge."

The next step in the briefing was for all pilots to synchronize their watches. In most fighter groups, this was done by the officer who that day was leading the Group. Forester had chosen a different procedure. He had Fred Hawkins perform the task, in order to maintain a bond between the Operations Officer and the pilots. Major Hawkins appreciated the gesture.

"On my mark, gentlemen, it will be 8:05 exactly. With his thumb and index finger on the knob of his wrist watch, Fred Hawkins began to count down, "Five . . . four . . . three . . . two . . . hack!" In unison, the pilots set their watches. Now they would be working off the same clock.

"It's yours, Colonel." Hawkins was looking at Forester, who rose and walked to the center of the stage.

"We're going to Germany today, so everybody needs to be extra sharp. For some strange reason, the Germans don't like it when we come to bomb their cities, so we can expect to see the Luftwaffe come up and try to stop us. They'll come out of the sun on us, so keep your head out of the cockpit." This last remark was an instruction combat pilots had been told over and over again. It meant the pilots were constantly to search the sky about them and not have their head down looking at their aircraft's instruments. Forester continued speaking.

"Stay with the bombers and don't go below eighteen thousand feet. That order still stands, courtesy of General Harrison. But if you're on the tail of a 109 and he's diving through eighteen thousand feet, I want you to follow him down and blow him to kingdom come.

"I'll be flying with the 87th this morning in the Cowboy Red 1 position. Call sign, as always, is Trumpet. Red 2 on my wing, that's you Lieutenant Conrad, will be monitoring the bomber's radio channel.

"I want you guys to exercise discipline on the radio. No chatter, gentlemen, no chatter. Speak only when you must and then keep it short.

"Start Engines is at 08:40. Let's get airborne quickly and make the rendezvous on time. The return home heading is 276 magnetic. That will take us real close to some flak concentrations near the

Hague, so keep weaving. If you get separated, find another P-47 to come home with. Fly smart and we'll all get back safe and sound.

"Okay, let's go get 'em."

Forester eschewed fancy speeches or pep talks. He thought a low-key approach was more useful, particularly given that fighter pilots were fairly cynical. Besides, with missions on tap practically every day, there was just so much he could say before repetition set in. Once, in August, as the 19th Fighter Group was beginning operations, Forester had given a rousing speech just after Fred Hawkins had completed his part of the briefing. Tom thought the speech was hokey. He later asked Harry Collins what he thought.

"Honest, Harry, tell me. Was the speech okay? I thought it was a bit much."

"Colonel, truthfully? It was pretty good. Knute Rockne would have liked it and I suspect many of your pilots actually enjoyed it. But a few more like it and the men, myself included, will start to think you're practicing to be a politician."

"There's a dreadful thought. I think I'll stick to the basics."

"Good idea, Colonel."

"But, Harry, when I say 'Let's go get 'em,' I really mean it."

"No one doubts that, Colonel, not for one minute."

When Forester completed his remarks, the briefing was over. It had lasted twenty minutes. Scraping their chairs along the concrete floor, the pilots stood up and began to file out of the Nissen hut. With the door now open, fresh air entered the room, dispersing the smell of tobacco smoke. Most everyone was talking. A few were making jokes. Many were double-checking time schedules or navigational headings. One or two were either silent or speaking in an abnormally loud voice. Among the quiet ones was Lieutenant Samuel Ordway.

Ordway was about to fly his first mission since spending twelve days at Keythorpe Hall. The time there had been wonderful, totally relaxing. The Lieutenant had come back reluctantly to Bromley Park. He dreaded his return to combat operations and now hated the sight of P-47 Thunderbolts.

Major Norman Horwitz attended the briefing to watch for signs of physical and mental exhaustion among the pilots. This was standard practice at Bromley Park, as well as other Eighth Air Force fields. Despite the bravado these men exhibited, a few were close to cracking. Ordway was such a man, minus the bravado. Norman noticed him and spoke to Forester.

"We've got a pilot here who looks in terrible shape."

"Which one?"

"That fellow over there, behind the pilot with the cigar." Norman was pointing to Ordway.

"I know him. His name is Lieutenant Samuel Ordway. He just got back from a nice rest at Keythorpe. He should be ready to fly."

"I'm not sure he is."

"Norman, we can't coddle these kids. This guy has just had a lot of time off, which no one else has. It's time for him to get back to work." Forester realized he sounded harsh, and felt sympathy for Ordway. But discipline and Group integrity came first. "He flies to Munster, unless you ground him."

"I need more data to do that, Colonel. Flight surgeons are supposed to base decisions on facts, not hunches. But I'm worried about this man."

"Norman, he'll be okay. Take a look at him when we get back, and I'll do whatever you want. Deal?"

"Do I have a choice?"

"Not really. At least not now. But later, we'll send him over to you and you can do what you think best."

"Fair enough, Colonel." Horwitz then changed demeanor. What followed was truly heartfelt. "Do well up there today."

"Thanks, Norman." Tom waved his hand across the room pointing to all the pilots. "I'll try to bring 'em all back."

Once outside the briefing room, Forester and the other pilots walked the short distance to three adjacent Nissen huts. Each hut was assigned to one of the Group's three squadrons. Tom went to the building belonging to the 87th Fighter Squadron. In these rooms, the pilots were given their gear. They received helmets, oxygen masks, Mae West inflatable life jackets, coveralls, which many did not wear, gloves, and a parachute. Before this gear was issued, the pilots had turned in any personal items still in their possession. Were the pilot shot down and captured, these possessions unwittingly might be of intelligence value to the enemy. The men were also given navigational cards, maps, and escape kits.

Loaded down with flight gear, the pilots were transported out to their aircraft. The goal was to get the pilots to their planes fifteen minutes before Start Engines. Some would ride in a Jeep, stacking their parachutes on the hood of the little vehicle. Others would travel in the GMC 6x6 trucks that were found in every motor pool of the Eighth Air Force. Still others would use a Dodge command car. These were similar to Jeeps, though larger and with a more powerful engine. Unlike the Jeeps, they would fade from view and memory.

Forester always rode out to his P-47 in a Jeep. And Harry Collins always drove. The pilots of the 19th Fighter Group respected this tradition. Upon posting to Forester's command, new pilots were immediately told not to hitch a ride with the Colonel whenever a combat mission was scheduled.

Neither Tom nor Harry Collins spoke on the way out to the plane. Collins correctly sensed that Forester needed to be alone with his thoughts. Tom used the silence to prepare, as an individual, for the upcoming flight. Since rising that morning, Forester's focus had been upon the mission as a collective endeavor of men he was charged to lead. But, as one person about to participate in this endeavor, Tom needed to get himself mentally ready. The few minutes of the drive was all the time allotted for Forester's own preparation. On the way out to the P-47, he focused on what he had to do to fly the plane and fight the enemy. During this time, the mission became an intensely personal experience.

Fear rode in the Jeep as well. Ensconced in Forester's mind was the inescapable thought that within three hours, he might well be dead. Tom could sense the presence of this fear. He could feel it in his legs and lower body as they turned to mush. In his mind, he could see treasured images that might disappear forever. Then, as the Jeep drew near to the P-47, his training, self-discipline, and courage came into play—and prevailed. With Forester, this was as inevitable as the fear itself. The anxiety he felt and the nervousness he exhibited was put aside, relegated to later. Tom concentrated solely on the task ahead. What he had to do as an individual combatant merged with his responsibilities as Group Commander. By the time Harry Collins brought the Jeep up to the Thunderbolt, the fear had gone. Forester was ready to fly.

Tom's Thunderbolt was a P-47D-1-RE. The letters "RE" indicated the plane had been built at Republic's home factory in Farmingdale. Aircraft manufactured at the wartime plant in Indiana carried an "RA" designation. The letter "D" identified the model type. Models represented major changes to the plane. The first production Thunderbolts were P-47Bs. The last were P-47Ns. The number following the model designation was termed the block number. Aircraft built in large quantities over several years had numerous improvements. Those aircraft incorporating a specific improvement or set of improvements were given a block number.

Block 1 P-47Ds had additional cowl flaps, improvements to the fuel system, and more armor for the pilot. There were 105 P-47D-1-REs constructed before Republic made further changes warranting the Block 2 designation. Aircraft with these changes were called P-47D-2-REs. Changes over the plane's lifetime were many. The last Thunderbolts built were P-47N-25-REs.

The P-47s at Bromley Park were painted a flat, grayish brown on the upper surfaces. Flat gray was used on the underside. The purpose of the paint was to make the aircraft more difficult to observe from above and below. Effective as camouflage, the color scheme was drab in appearance. However, pilots often had colorful personal markings displayed on the left side of the forward fuselage.

To aid in aircraft identification, early in 1943, the Eighth Air Force ordered a wide white band be painted around the forward portion of the P-47 cowlings. Also ordered were white stripes on the tails and horizontal stabilizers. Each side of the P-47 carried the national insignia, which also was found on the wings. The insignia was a large white star on a circle of blue from which two white rectangles extended. Initially, the entire insignia was outlined in yellow, then red. In August 1943, the order came through to have this "surround" painted in blue. The decorative effect of these orders was negligible. The P-47s at Bromley Park and elsewhere in East Anglia remained dull, artistically uninteresting.

Forester's P-47 carried no personal marking other than his name and McGowan's painted in small letters near the cockpit. At one time, he had considered naming the plane *Marjorie's Boy*. He decided not to when his mother, in a letter to her son, expressed discomfort that a machine designed to kill was to be named after her. "Mothers," she wrote, "tend to nurture and respect life. I'm not sure it's appropriate to place my name on an aircraft that does neither." Tom took the hint and dropped the idea.

Fighter planes of the Eighth Air Force had two letters on the side of the fuselage identifying the squadron to which the aircraft belonged. These were painted just forward of the national insignia. Aft of the insignia was a single letter assigned to an individual aircraft. The P-47 Forester flew belonged to the 340th Fighter Squadron whose squadron code letters were "TT." Exercising a prerogative of the Group Commander Tom had the aircraft identification "F" painted on his plane. Thus the aircraft Forester flew, even when flying with the other two squadrons, bore the letters "TTF" which were Tom's initials. His middle name was Tyler, which was Marjorie Forester's maiden name.

Waiting for Forester at the P-47 was Chester McGowan. The Sergeant said good morning to Tom and Harry Collins, saluting them both as he spoke. McGowan then reported to Forester that the aircraft was in tiptop shape.

The Sergeant had risen early this Sunday. After dressing, he stood at attention as the Stars and Stripes were raised over Bromley Park, enjoying the accompanying sound of reveille. McGowan then hastily ate a breakfast of creamed chip beef, toast, and coffee. Afterward, he bicycled out to the hardstand where Forester's aircraft was parked.

To be joined thirty minutes later by Corporals Davis and Schmitt, Chester McGowan immediately began to prepare the P-47 for flight. He first walked around the plane searching for leaks. Finding none, he removed the cloth cover from the canopy and inspected the landing gear and tires. Sitting in the cockpit, he tested the flight controls and gun sight. When the two corporals arrived, he had them "pull through" the engine. By hand, they rotated the propeller to remove any surplus oil from the cylinders. Once this was done, the big Pratt and Whitney R 2800 power plant could be started. McGowan soon got the engine running. After several minutes, he was satisfied that it was warmed up and would operate normally. He then shut the engine down and climbed out of the cockpit. Corporal Schmitt was attending to the guns. Davis was assisting the crew of a fuel truck that had arrived to top off the tanks. McGowan carefully watched this latter operation, reminding the crew not to forget the 108-gallon drop tank slung beneath the aircraft's fuselage.

When the truck had departed, the Sergeant and the Corporal replenished the P-47's oxygen supply. Above 10,000 feet, the air is thin so oxygen must be supplied artificially. Because the P-47's cockpit is unpressurized, its pilot wore a mask to which oxygen flowed from two steel oxygen bottles carried in the fuselage. It was these bottles that the two men filled. By the time they had finished, Corporal Schmitt had armed the guns. He also verified that the ammunition belts would feed smoothly and not jam. Schmitt then told McGowan that the guns were in working order. The Sergeant replied that he and Davis could now go get some breakfast.

"But come back when you're finished. I'll continue to check things out and may need your help. We want this ship in perfect shape for Colonel Forester."

As the two soldiers departed, McGowan gazed at the P-47. To this hardworking crew chief, the aircraft was a thing of beauty, a perfect mixture of raw power and aerodynamic grace. He was proud of this machine. He considered it his airplane, on loan to the pilot for several hours each day. When Forester and Harry Collins drove up,

McGowan was stepping down from the plane's wing, having cleaned for the fifth time the glass surfaces of the Thunderbolt's ribbed canopy.

When the Jeep came to a halt, Forester broke the silence, turning to Collins.

"I'll see you when I get back. Thanks for the ride."

"Anytime. Have fun up there today."

Both men had spoken casually. They purposely kept their words brief. Forester was concentrating on what he had to do to fly the airplane and to lead the Group into battle. He was in no mood for extended or melodramatic conversation. Collins also preferred few words. He wished his friend well and he truly hoped the mission would succeed, but these were not his primary thoughts. Rather, Harry was thinking about himself, focusing on his own desires to fly and fight alongside Forester.

The feeling was not new. Each time Harry Collins saw the P-47s lift off the runway, each time he heard the thunder of their engines, he wished that he was a pilot. Collins knew this would never be. He was an Intelligence officer, not a flyer. But as Tom's plane started up, as Bromley Park came alive with the sound of aircraft, the Major's disappointment turned to awe as one by one, the Thunderbolts taxied along the perimeter track to Runway 26, where two at a time, with throttles pushed forward, they would speed down the concrete strip and take to the air.

At exactly 08:46, Forester's P-47 was in position for takeoff. His wingman, Lieutenant Conrad as Cowboy Red Two, was off to the left, slightly behind.

Quickly, Tom went through the preflight check—tail wheel straight and locked, trim tabs set for take off, mixture control to auto rich, propeller control to maximum rpm, fuel selector valve to main tank, flaps up, and cowl flaps open. He was ready to roll.

Forester then saw a green flare shoot into the sky. This was the signal to proceed. Tom the instructor told Tom the pilot to move flaps to half, ease the throttle forward to thirty-two inches HG, yet hold the brakes.

"Cowboy Red Two, this is Trumpet. Here we go." Forester released the brakes and advanced the throttle to 52 inches. Power to the engine was measured as manifold pressure—52 inches was full power. The big Pratt and Whitney, with eighteen cylinders and a turbine supercharger, roared, and the P-47 began to move. Down the runway she went, gaining speed. The airplane weighed 14,000 pounds but accelerated rapidly. More than once, Colonel Tee had told Tom that the engine could haul a freight train up the Rocky Mountains. Now it easily pulled the Thunderbolt forward. Halfway down the runway, the tail wheel lifted. Ten seconds later, obeying the laws of physics, but seeming to defy common sense, the plane became airborne.

Tom raised the landing gear and began climbing to 1,500 feet. A glance leftward confirmed that his wingman was in position. Forester flew straight ahead. The practice was to initiate a slow 180 degree turn to the left once 3 miles out. This enabled the remainder of the squadron to catch up and take position.

In less than four minutes, the 87th Fighter Squadron with Forester in the lead flew back past Bromley Park. Eighteen planes were in formation. Two were spares. Should a P-47 need to abort the mission, a replacement was available. If all sixteen aircraft ran smoothly, the spares would return to base.

Tom led the squadron north heading for the coast. By now, weather conditions had worsened. Visibility was less than two miles. Clouds extended upward from 1,300 feet. Only occasionally could Tom see the ground through breaks in the clouds. In the States, cross country flying was prohibited if visibility was below 3 miles horizontal with a ceiling less than 1,500 feet. Had this cautionary rule been applied in England, the P-47s at Bromley Park would have spent most of their time on the ground. Thus, Forester was pleased that the 87th's aircraft had formed up nicely despite the weather.

Through one hole in the clouds, Tom could see the ground below, with farms clearly outlined by hedges and roads. Often, Forester could tell where he was by the shape of the woods below. From the vantage point of 1,500 feet, the land looked like a patchwork quilt with blocks of green, yellow, and brown. East Anglia covered 8,000 square miles, but nowhere was it 400 feet above sea level. Although flat, the land was fertile. To Forester, it looked much like Connecticut. By American standards, the farms were small. And in 1943, there were fewer of them. In constructing its airfields, the Eighth Air Force had removed 40,000 acres of prime English farmland.

Tom flew slowly toward a prearranged point just off Lowestoft, the eastern most tip of Great Britain. By cruising at well below top speed, the 19th Fighter Group's other squadrons would be able to reach the rendezvous point at the same time Forester did. So when the fighters headed out over the North Sea to escort the B-17s, all forty-eight P-47s would be in formation.

This morning, however, the two squadrons did not meet up with Forester at the appointed time. On taking off, two aircraft of the 340th Squadron collided. Both pilots were killed, and the runways at Bromley Park remained closed for several minutes while the wreckage was cleared away.

Notified of the accident, Tom had to decide whether to take the 87th to the rendezvous with the bombers or wait until the other aircraft arrived. One choice left him with too few P-47s for escort work. The other choice meant being late, leaving the B-17s unprotected. Forester easily made the decision. He chose the first option, reasoning some escort was better than no escort.

"Cowboys, this is Trumpet. We're on our own. Course is now zero six two. Let's go find the Big Friends."

Forester pushed the throttle of his Thunderbolt forward and pointed his airplane in the direction of Germany. Fifteen P-47s did the same, each now in its combat position.

For thirty-five minutes, Forester and the 87th Fighter Squadron flew east, climbing to 28,000 feet. High above the North Sea, despite the strike force consisting of 274 B-17s, Tom saw not one Flying Fortress. Then, sixty miles out from the German coast, they saw the contrails that marked their flight path. The contrails were highly visible streaks of condensed moisture, streaming behind the engines of the bombers. They formed whenever the warm exhaust mixed with extremely cold air. Beautiful, even majestic, the contrails were unwelcome for they pinpointed the location of the B-17s. Luftwaffe pilots merely had to follow the contrails to find their prey.

"Cowboy aircraft, this is Trumpet. We'll all fly top cover. Red and White flights will take the center. Blue to the left. Green to the right. Keep you eyes open, we'll have visitors shortly."

The sixteen aircraft accelerated and soon were in position. Forester could see about sixty B-17s. No B-24s were going to Munster. Perhaps that was just as well. Though its bomb load was greater than a B-17's, the aircraft flew at lower altitudes where flak was more concentrated. And, because the B-24 was less aerodynamically stable, it flew in looser formations, which made its defensive fire less effective.

Still over the North Sea, the B-17s churned forward. Bristling with guns, tucked in close together, with engines at full power and controls streaming, the bombers looked unstoppable. Forester admired the courage of their crews. He knew, as they themselves did, how vulnerable the B-17s really were. Late in 1943, the average life expectancy of an Eighth Air Force B-17 was eleven missions. Many of the planes flying to Munster this Sunday had flown more. They were living on borrowed time and their crews knew it.

On course, the bombers soon turned southwest heading directly to Munster. Sixteen P-47s turned with them.

Crossing the coastline, they were now over the Third Reich. No welcome mat was visible. Instead, a gaggle of German fighters, guns at the ready, awaited their arrival. Among the fighters were twelve Me-110s. Slung beneath their wings were the deadly rockets. At 8 inches in diameter and 7 feet long, a single rocket on target could wreak havoc.

Forester spotted the Germans.

"This is Trumpet. Okay everybody. Time to earn our pay. Blue Flight, come on top and wait for the second wave. Green Flight take on the 109s. Red and White, follow me. We're after the 110s. Let's go get 'em."

The Meserschmitts were at the same altitude as the B-17s, but a mile in front. The twelve *Zerstorers* were themselves escorted by eight single engine Me-109s. Together, the twenty aircraft were about to utilize their most deadly tactic—a head on attack to which B-17s, and their pilots, were particularly vulnerable. None of the Germans appeared to have seen the P-47s.

That would soon change. Tom took the eight Thunderbolts of Red and White Flights directly towards the enemy. With throttles pushed forward, the planes approached 410 mph. There was nothing subtle about Forester's attack. He was flying straight at the Messerschmitts.

The Germans saw the fast approaching Americans too late. The Me-109s attempted to block the attack, but could not do so. The geometry favored the P-47s whose guns erupted. Two Me-110s blew up. The others broke formation, making impossible their intended attack upon the B-17s.

So far so good. Forester's plane was the first to rip through the 110s. Tom had fired his guns and missed As he pulled the trigger, Tom heard a voice speaking to him. The voice was his. *Stay calm. Contain your fear. Ignore the odds. Get in close. Fire!*

As Forester's eight machine guns exploded in anger, the Me-110 bore to the right. The bullets sailed wide of the mark. The German then dove to gain speed, hoping to come around again for either a shot at Forester or a rocket attack against the bombers.

Tom flew through the scattering Germans. Once past, he banked left and turned downward, tracing an arc in the sky. He saw the Me-110 as it circled back.

Tom's P-47 was approaching the German from above. Forester could clearly see the top of the entire aircraft with its signature two engines and twin tail assembly. At this angle of attack, the *Zerstorer's* rear gun could not be brought to bear, nor could the plane's forward firing guns, two 30 mm cannon located in the nose of the plane. Tom waited until the Me-110 flew to a point just before the spot where it would converge with his line of fire. Once again, he heard his own voice. *Steady. Let him come down. Now.*

Forester squeezed the trigger. All eight machines guns roared. Tom held the trigger down for four seconds during which time 960 .50 calibre shells spewed forth. Several of the shells were tracer bullets. These glowed red, enabling a pilot to see the flight of his gunfire. Forester's fire struck the right wing of the 110, outboard of the engine. Tom pulled the trigger again, this time for three seconds. At the same time, with a light touch to the rudder, he realigned his plane, bringing the striking bullets up across the engine to the wing-root, the juncture point of the wing and fuselage.

The result was devastating. A flash of brilliant red engulfed the Messerschmitt. As the flash subsided, black and white smoke emerged as the aircraft tilted to the right. Then the wing broke off. For an instant, it formed a V with the rest of the craft. The wing then separated from the fuselage and disappeared as the rest of the plane, still on fire, began to tumble. No longer a flying machine, the *Zerstroer* was a mass of disjointed metal and smoke.

The pilot of the Me-110 was alive, but unable to escape. The forward canopy of the aircraft did not slide back and forth. Rather, it opened to the top and side. Forester's gunfire had wrecked the hinges. Thus, the pilot, whose name was Hans Faber, was trapped inside. Faber pushed as hard as he could, but the canopy would not budge. Frantically, he pounded the glass. He also began to scream, hoping the desperation in his voice would somehow help release the canopy. It did not. Faber could not get out. He lived for another thirty-five seconds. They were moments of pure terror. Mercifully, they ended when the wreck crashed into a wheat field.

Forester felt no remorse for the German. To him, the pilot was not a human being. He was simply the enemy. He was a component of the Messerschmitt, devoid of any personality or life. Had the German been in Tom's position, he would not have hesitated to pull the trigger, so Tom had no qualms in destroying the pilot along with the plane. On this Sunday in October, he and the German had played a lethal game at 28,000 feet. The simplicity of its outcome matched the severity of its consequences. Tom won. The German lost. Forester lived. Faber died.

The gunner of the Me-110 was more fortunate than his pilot. Tom's guns had not struck the rear of the aircraft where the gunner sat. As the plane began to break apart, the gunner quite sensibly decided to abandon ship. Quickly, he undid his harness, opened the canopies, and jumped. Wisely, he did not pull the ripcord until well clear of the aircraft. He eventually glided to a soft and safe landing in the garden of a country inn whose owner, an admirer of the Luftwaffe, plied him with sausages and beer.

Tom's sense of triumph was short lived. Almost immediately, he was planning his next maneuver. Diving past the tumbling wreckage of the Me-110, he headed back towards the B-17s.

What he saw was not a pretty sight. Numerous Fortresses were on fire. Several were spinning out of control. There were gaps in the bomber formation. The sky was full of American parachutes.

As Forester approached the B-17s, one plane began to fall back, smoke pouring from its number three engine. Without protection afforded by the other B-17s, the plane was extremely vulnerable. It soon drew the attention of two Me-109s. The fighters attacked, one after the other. The Fortress had little chance of survival. Yet its guns fired back. As the Messerschmitts came in a second time, the B-17s crew took to the silk. All ten men jumped. Apparently, the two German pilots did not notice for they continued their attack. The guns pummeled the now empty aircraft. Remarkably, it continued to fly. Then slowly, after a third attack, the battered plane raised its right wing as if giving a final salute. It then rolled on its back and headed downward. It crashed at full speed, shaking the ground and creating a crater that would be filled in only after the war.

Initially, Forester's P-47s had done well. Red and White Flights had broken up the first attack by the Me-110s. As ordered, Green Flight had tangled with the Me-109s, downing two of them. But Blue Flight, flying top cover, was too few in number to deflect a second wave of Zerstroers. These hit the B-17s from the side, where the bombers presented a larger target. Blue Flight's P-47s downed one of the Me-110s, but the rest launched their rockets. Several missed, but four struck home in quick succession. As though in planned sequence, four B-17s exploded in huge fireballs. Where forty men and four machines once flew, nothing remained. Shattered pieces of metal and human tissue rocketed into the surrounding sky. Some of the debris hit nearby Fortresses. The rest fell to the ground unnoticed.

"Break left, Trumpet!" The voice was Lieutenant Conrad's and to Forester, it sounded extremely urgent. Flying wing to the Group Commander as Cowboy Red 2, the Lieutenant saw a lone Me-109 dart from a cloud. Conrad had shouted the warning as the plane turned towards them. Two seconds later, he saw explosive sparkles of light at the middle of the aircraft. The German was firing his guns and seemed to have them in his sights.

Upon hearing Conrad's warning, Forester rolled his plane to the left and headed downward. As he did so, he noticed tracers zipping by his right wing and heard a crunching sound. More work for McGowan. A quick check of instruments revealed nothing abnormal. Wasting no time, he rammed the throttle forward and felt the straps of his harness tighten as the Thunderbolt gained speed. The next voice he heard was his own. *Stay calm. Zig and zag to throw Jerry's aim off. Watch your altitude. Dive faster than this guy and you'll be okay.*

At 19,000 feet, the P-47's airspeed indicator pointed to 440 mph. The plane was hurtling to the ground, and gaining speed. Soon, Forester was less concerned with the pursuing German than with the vertical distance he would need to pull the aircraft out of its dive. A look in the rear view mirror revealed no sight of the Me-109. Good old Thunderbolt. Nothing can stay with it when the nose is pointed down. Now to the task at hand. Tom began to pull back on the control stick, at the same time easing off the throttle. Not much of a response. The P-47 was still going too fast. Forester then gripped the stick with both hands and pulled harder.

The control stick was connected to cables that moved elevators at the rear of the plane. These elevators controlled, along the plane's lateral axis, the pitch of the aircraft. Like all planes of the day, Thunderbolts had no power assisted or electronic controls. Force was exerted manually. In high-speed dives, the force required was considerable. Hence, Forester had to employ all his strength to have the P-47, still traveling at high speed, change direction.

Tom now pulled as hard as he could. The P-47 responded slowly. The nose of the Thunderbolt started to rise, but the plane's altitude was now 11,000 feet. Forester knew he would need all of it to clear the ground.

Forester continued to pull, his muscles straining. Gradually at first, then more noticeably, the nose moved upward, reducing the distance from the ground to the horizon. Forester checked his altitude and airspeed. Three thousand feet and 360 mph. This was going to be close.

The plane leveled out at 600 feet. Below the P-47 was a forest and several small lakes, a quiet piece of countryside now rudely violated by the thundering roar of an American fighter plane. While many people heard Forester's plane, few actually saw it. One who did, a thirteen-year-old boy in a small sailboat, waved and cheered. The boy thought the plane belonged to the Luftwaffe.

Looking down at the trees and water, Forester could make out details of the German landscape not normally seen from the air. While he did not see the young boy in the sailboat, he did see several youngsters at a campsite. The scene looked completely normal, as though he was over flying a lake in New Hampshire.

Six hundred feet was unusually low for a P-47. The plane was skimming along the terrain. Forester realized his recovery from the dive had been what his British friends would call "a near thing." But, self confident as fighter pilots tend to be, Tom simply remarked to himself, "Room to spare, piece of cake."

Forester knew 600 feet was not a safe altitude for an American plane over enemy territory. Moreover, he was anxious to rejoin the fray. Tom pushed the throttle forward and pulled back on the control stick. The P-47 responded and began to climb. Twelve minutes later, the plane was at 22,000 feet. All the while Tom was searching for the B-17s, but he saw none. What once had been a space filled with flying machines was now empty. No aircraft. No gunfire. No smoke. No parachutes. The scene was peaceful, although without color. The sky remained grey, filled with scattered wispy clouds that stretched over much of Germany.

Forester continued to climb. He concluded that the dive had taken him further west than he first thought. He pointed the Thunderbolt in the direction most likely to cross paths with the bombers. Still he could find no B-17s.

But he did spot a single P-47.

"This is Trumpet. To the lone P-47 at 22,000. I'm waggling my wings. Form up on me."

Surprisingly, there was no response. Tom flew closer to the other plane. No damage was visible. Strangely, the P-47 was flying slowly in a wide circle. Forester noticed the plane's canopy was open. Its pilot was looking at him.

"This is Trumpet. To the lone P-47. Are you okay?"

Still no return communication.

"This is Trumpet. Rock your wings if you can hear me."

"I can hear you, Colonel."

"Identify yourself."

"It's Lieutenant Ordway, Colonel. Snowflake Red 4."

"Red 4, are you hit? What's going on? Where are the others?"

"I'm not hit, Colonel. And I don't know or care where the others are."

Forester ignored the last remark, not wishing to consider where it might lead. "Snowflake Red 4, form up on me. We've got a war to win."

"It's your war now, Colonel, not mine."

Tom remained silent, stunned by what he just heard. He then chose to issue an order. "Lieutenant, this is Colonel Forester. Form up on me." Instinctively, Tom knew this was the wrong approach. Wrong because it wouldn't work, because Ordway wasn't going to respond to military discipline. Using a different tack, Forester spoke again. "Ordway, fly my wing and I'll get you home."

"Sorry, Colonel. Like I told you, I can't do this anymore." Ordway then rolled his P-47 slightly to the left and began to climb out of the cockpit."

"Son, don't do this. You'll regret it later. I can get you home. Don't . . . "

Forester stopped in mid sentence. He watched as Lieutenant Ordway bailed out. For six seconds, he fell free. His chute then opened and the young man floated to the ground. Offering no resistance, he was soon captured and transported to a prisoner of war camp. There, far from Bromley Park and its P-47s, he no longer had to fly. At long last Samuel Ordway felt safe.

Forester was upset, mostly with himself. He had failed to stop the Lieutenant from jumping. He had not listened to Norman whose instincts always were sound. He had lost a perfectly good P-47. And he would have to report the incident and file charges against Ordway. He wanted to be angry with the man. He certainly had reason to be. The Lieutenant had left the field of battle. He was a deserter. He had abandoned his buddies who experienced identical fears, yet stayed on to fly and fight. But to his own surprise, Tom felt little anger. He thought he should, yet he didn't. Forester was saddened, full of sorrow for a young man who simply had reached his limit. Ordway, like most of the men who actually fight in wars, was just a kid. And, as all men do, he had a point at which he could go no farther. The Lieutenant had reached his point, and snapped. Tom believed the boy had taken a step that would haunt him the rest of his life, assuming he survived. For a moment, Forester considered not mentioning what had happened. Ordway would be listed as Missing in Action, but the commanding officer for the 19th Fighter Group knew he should not and would not do that. People, Forester believed, are responsible for their actions. They must live with the consequences. No one is exempt. Tom was convinced that in due time, Samuel Ordway would be held accountable for what he had just done.

Forester put the incident out of his mind and resumed his search for the B-17s. Within minutes, he saw another aircraft. Again, it was a single machine, although not a P-47. The aircraft was Me-110.

Forester followed the enemy in the hope the Messerschmitt might lead him to the bombers. The tactic worked. When he saw the B-17s in the distance, he began his attack.

The rear gunner of the Me-110 opened fire before Forester was in position to shoot back. Tom ruined his aim by taking the P-47 down beneath the twin-engine craft where the gunner could not track the plane. The German then dove to the right, hoping to pick up speed and evade the American. The maneuver was foolish. No Me-110 could out dive Republic's fighter. Before firing, Tom took a careful look at the enemy plane. Its undersides were grey. Topsides also were grey, although mottled in black. The scheme was drab, but effective as the primary color of the skies over Germany was grey. The only bright spot on the Me-110 was a yellow band around the fuselage adjacent to the ever present black cross. The cross, outlined in white, was the national insignia of all German military aircraft. The band was painted on those *Zerstroers* assigned to the defense of the Reich.

In but four seconds, Germany lost one of its defenders. For that brief period of time, Forester held down the trigger of the P-47's eight machine guns. These spit forth a barrage of bullets. All struck home. The bullets ripped into the Messerschmitt's right engine and undercarriage. Immediately, the engine caught fire while the wheel dropped into place. Before the fire could spread, the power plant exploded. The plane tipped over and began to spin. Forester's gun camera recorded the kill, which Harry Collins later confirmed.

Tom now had six enemy aircraft to his credit. With number five, he had become an ace. Forester thus joined an elite group of men. By war's end, the Eighth Air Force had 261 aces. Leading the list was Colonel Francis Gabreski of the 56th Fighter Group who brought down twenty-eight German planes. Top scorer of the entire Army Air Forces was Major Richard Bong. Flying a P-38 in the Southwest Pacific, Bong destroyed forty Japanese aircraft.

Many German aces greatly exceeded these scores. Unlike American pilots who were taken off combat flying once completing their tour of duty, Luftwaffe pilots flew continuously throughout the war. They thus could gain an extremely high number of victories. Twenty-six shot down over 200 Allied airplanes.

Forester's six was thus a modest score. But in October 1943, well before the great air battles of the next spring, his tally placed him among the leaders of American pilots stationed in England. Several generals would take notice of Tom's score. One of them was Eaker's friend, Mike McCready. Already impressed with Forester's leadership of the 19th Fighter Group, he had earmarked Tom for a senior job at Wycombe Abbey. "We'll let Forester complete his tour and then bring him upstairs," the General told an aide. "I think I know just the job for him."

Forester was aware he had become an ace. He also was pleased, for he believed in leadership by example. What better way to inspire and teach the pilots at Bromley Park than have the Group Commander himself down German airplanes? But Tom's satisfaction was not altogether altruistic. He knew he would enjoy the recognition that came with the destruction of enemy aircraft.

Certainly, McGowan would be pleased. The crew chief now could brag that "his pilot" had become an ace. The sergeant would want to display six victory crosses on the side the P-47. Up to now, Forester had instructed McGowan not to do so, despite the common practice in the Army Air Force of indicating kills by painting near the cockpit, in miniature, the national insignia of the planes destroyed. Upon returning to base, Tom intended to let the crew chief do as he pleased.

Forester did not dwell for long on his new status. He needed to rejoin the bomber formation and take charge of the escorting fighters. Shortly after he did so, the time arrived for the P-47s to take leave of the B-17s. The fuel gauges of the fighters registered one-third, so Tom issued the call to regroup and head home. The bombers continued to Munster, soon joined by other P-47s whose job was to continue the escort.

Forester's planes set a course that mimicked the blue yarn on the map at the briefing room. The Thunderbolts flew east across Holland and the North Sea touching down at 12:09.

Forty-two P-47s returned safely. Three had been shot down. Two had crashed on take off. One P-47, piloted by Lieutenant Ordway, crashed near the German coast once its fuel ran out. Against these six losses, the 19th Fighter Group shot down eleven of the enemy. The Americans claimed eighteen fighters destroyed, but postwar Luftwaffe records indicate eleven planes lost to Forester's fighters on October 10. Of the eleven, seven were Me-110 *Zerstroers*.

After Forester landed, he had made a point of speaking to Lieutenant Conrad. He told the Lieutenant that he had done well and before long would have a section of his own to lead. Tom then went over to the post flight interrogation. Coca-Cola in hand, he related mission highlights to Harry Collins. Queried about the Me-110s, Tom recounted their tactics and markings. He also asked about the Kid, who had failed to return. Collins reported that Richardson was fine, having landed at a B-24 base south of Bromley Park.

"The Kid can fly and shoot. I just wish he could navigate," said Tom.

"Colonel, he can certainly shoot. Says he got a 109 and I tend to believe him.

"Me too. But just once, Harry, I'd actually like to see him land at our airfield."

With the interrogation over, Forester grabbed a quick lunch and retired to his quarters. He intended to take a short nap before attacking the paperwork he knew Wilbur Williams had waiting for him in the office.

Before lying down to rest, Tom walked over to a small table in the room. Upon the table was a telephone next to which lay a piece of pink paper on which was written a telephone number. He picked up the phone and, holding the paper, spoke to the base operator.

"This is Colonel Forester. Give me an outside line please. I want to place a call to London."

Ten minutes later, he hung up the phone and lay down upon his bed.

The nap was not a success. Upon closing his eyes, Tom began to tremble as fear, now released, crept upon him. His body went limp and he began to sweat. The thought of death began to occupy his consciousness. In this form, death was not an abstraction. Nor was it merely an intellectual construct. It was vivid, and like a guardian angel, it hovered close by. Deviously, its presence caused Forester to fall asleep. Tom felt drugged.

Once again, Tom could see his coffin. This time it was empty. Then, smoothly, he felt his body and mind transported to the coffin, and placed within. He fit snugly as though the pine box was custom made. The coffin rested in an open field. The field was flat and full of freshly cut grass, save for a concrete strip that ran parallel to the wooden box. The strip was a runway. Airplanes, stacked with silver coffins, were taking off, yet Tom heard no sound. Despite the activity, all was quiet. Then, without fanfare, the Lady in White appeared. She was alone, standing in the grass. Still wearing her hat of lavender and white and dressed in a white summer gown, she approached the coffin. She was speaking to him, but Tom could not hear, for now the field was ringing with aircraft noise. Engines were starting up and straining at full power. The sound was deafening—the wind swirled as planes taxied and then took off. The lady's hat blew off and Tom could see her face more clearly. She was lovely as before. Not young, but elegant and distinctive. As beautiful a creature as he had ever seen. She was still speaking. He saw her mouth move—her expression. But he heard not a word. Oddly, the wind did not disturb the flag she draped over the coffin. The flag, which was the Union Jack, posed no barrier as the Lady in White leaned over Tom's body. He was dressed in his best uniform, which was clean and freshly pressed. She removed the wings from his jacket and gently kissed him. Again, she spoke and again, to his great frustration, he could not hear what she was saying. Then he spoke. He pleaded with her not to leave. In response, she smiled and ran her hand lovingly across his face. Then she answered him in words that suddenly he could now hear. *I will love you until the end of time.* Rising skyward, her image began to disappear among the clouds. As it did, Tom saw the lid to the coffin come down. Then he heard it nailed shut. His final sensation was the sense of being placed in one of the airplanes.

—ww—

Four days after the raid upon Munster, Ira Eaker sent the Eighth
Air Force deep into Germany. The target was Schweinfurt, home to
the German ball bearing industry. Because the city lay beyond the
reach of P-47s, the 291 B-17s dispatched were on their own for
much of the trip. The results were catastrophic. Sixty bombers were
shot down. Another twelve were junked upon their return. Known
to military historians as "Black Thursday," this second attack upon
Schweinfurt was a decisive defeat for American airpower.

Keith Davenport was shocked by these losses. After reporting the
grim statistics to Eaker, the Colonel had spoken to Roger Baldwin.
"We can't go on like this. Six hundred men are gone. Something's
got to change."

Eaker's reaction was similar to Davenport's. The Eighth's commander had not expected such casualties. Publicly, he called the raid
a costly victory. In private, he sounded less convincing. While he
truly believed the attacks were crippling the Luftwaffe, the General
knew his fleet of bombers could not sustain losses of the kind
October had seen. Clearly, the B-17s and B-24s could no longer fly
unprotected. Therefore, for now at least, the Fortresses and Liberators
would strike at targets in France and the Low Countries. Germany
was out of bounds. Truth be told, daylight precision bombing had
failed. What the RAF had feared would happen had happened. The
concept of strategic airpower so championed by Ira Eaker lay among
the charred wreckage of American aircraft. Thus, the air campaign
against Germany was put on hold.

"Okay. Keith, we back off and lick our wounds. Tell General
Anderson to find some easy targets, where we can do some damage,
but not get shot up so bad."

"Yes, Sir."

"We'll blame it on the weather. We'll tell the press boys the
clouds have kept us out of Germany. Given the lousy weather
around here, they'll believe that."

"All right, General." Davenport paused a moment and then spoke of the subject on his mind. "The Luftwaffe shows no sign of weakening. Despite their losses, they keep coming up in force."

"They're good pilots, Colonel, and they're hurting us more than I thought they would. But we're not giving up."

"Sir?"

"We'll hit some close-in targets for now, and wait until we get a fighter that can fly to Berlin and back."

"The P-51?"

"Yes, the P-51. If we can provide escorts all the way, we can get this train back on the tracks. And when the Mustang arrives, we'll have twice as many bombers as we have now. Then we go back to Germany and do the job right."

"What about your letter to General Giles?"

"I'll have to rewrite it. I need to better explain the situation we're facing over here. Barney knows what's at stake. If the Eighth fails, daylight strategic bombing is dead."

"I'm worried, General. The brass back home may be looking for a scapegoat. We've been hurt pretty bad. Some squadrons have been decimated. At Bremen, the 381st lost seven out of eighteen B-17s. At Munster, the 390th lost eight out of eighteen. Today at Schweinfurt, the 305th Bomb Group sent sixteen aircraft out and only three returned." Davenport's accounting was accurate. The October raids decimated several Eighth Air Force squadrons. "Washington isn't going to like these numbers."

"No, they won't. And if they want someone's head, they can have mine. But keep one thing in mind, Keith."

"What's that, Sir?"

"I didn't come over here to fail. And I have no intention of seeing the Eighth Air Force go down in flames. First, we regroup and then we go back to Germany. This battle isn't over yet, and I intend to win it."

TWELVE

"I will be at the club this afternoon and will remind Eaton." Sir Robert was addressing Helen, sitting across from her in their dining room. They had just finished a late Sunday breakfast, having decided not to attend church. Eaton was the day manager of the Collingwood. "I'm certain there will be no problem. What's this chap's name?"

"François. François Sabotier."

"Fine. The club will be happy to oblige, especially since part of the man's fee will end up in the Collingwood treasury."

"Well, it is essential we get François."

"And why is that?" Sir Robert's question reflected genuine curiosity.

"Because he's very good at what he does. Remember how successful our party for Anthony Eden was? He was in the kitchen that night and everything went splendidly."

"Quite so."

"We'll also need Hoskins."

"Yes. I've already mentioned this to Eaton and, in passing, to Hoskins himself. He said he'd be most pleased to help out."

"Good. I still wonder how your club can find all the food we need. Rationing seems not to have affected the Collingwood."

"Actually, my dear, it has. But money and influence carries the day, and the Collingwood has ample supplies of both."

"I suppose that's so. Let's see, today is Sunday, the tenth. The party is Tuesday after next. Just nine days away," Helen commented.

"There's still much to do, though at least the invitations have been posted. I gather you've asked several of your Committee members to attend?" Sir Robert was asking a question, the answer to which he already knew. His voice hinted at the irritation he felt. Sir Robert's displeasure came not from Helen having added a few names to the guest list. He was simply annoyed that the individuals selected were Americans.

"Yes, I have, as I mentioned to you that I would. This is, of course, a sort of farewell party for you and you will certainly be the center of attention. But it's an opportunity for me to entertain a few Committee members I've gotten to know, which I cannot do once you're gone."

"How many do you expect?"

"About five or six." In addition to Forester, Helen had invited Jimmy Dixon and two other officers, although, as she admitted to herself, she had done so in order to draw attention away from Tom. "I've told one of them, a pilot, to bring one or two of his chums along."

"I suppose I shall have to put on my diplomatic smile and pretend they're welcome in my house."

"Which, Robert, they are," Helen spoke sharply. Then she softened her tone. "Do remember they're a long way from home and are here to help us win the war."

"How can I forget? Wherever I go in London, I see Americans. One cannot get away from them. It's enough to make you appreciate the French."

Helen chose not to allow Sir Robert's antipathy towards the United States to divert their conversation from the subject at hand. Because she disagreed with his views about Americans, she often challenged them, but she did not this morning. Helen had something else on her mind. And she wanted Robert to focus upon it, not upon the alleged flaws in the character of England's most important ally.

"There is someone else I think we should invite."

"And who might that be?"

"Claire."

"Claire?" Sir Robert was genuinely surprised. "Why, she's in school."

"Of course she is, but she could come up late Monday morning, dine with us in the early afternoon, and attend the party in the evening. I know she'd love to say good-bye to you and you really ought to see her before you leave. Besides, it would be good fun."

"Well, I . . . "

"Oh come, Robert. It would do Claire some good to be among adults and I'd like to have our friends see her."

Helen's last sentiment was heartfelt. Mothers enjoy showing off their daughters and Helen was no exception, but she knew something deeper was at work in this instance. For reasons she could not quite explain, Helen wanted Tom Forester to meet Claire. And the party seemed a safe way to do so.

"I could put Claire on the train back to Brighton the next morning. She'd miss but a day of school."

"What would Miss Evans say?" Margaret Evans was the headmistress of Roedean. She was very strict with "her girls," so Sir Robert was confident Claire would not be given the day off.

He had not reckoned with Helen's determination. Anticipating Miss Evans's objections, she had written to the headmistress. In the letter, Helen explained the circumstances behind the request that Claire be allowed to come up to London. "It would be just one day," the letter concluded, "and I would be most grateful and indebted to you for permitting the child to join us on this special occasion."

Upon reading the letter, Margaret Evans felt the sincerity with which it had been written. She also understood the importance Helen placed upon Claire attending the party. Moreover, unlike other requests for preferential treatment, this one was modest, and unlikely to set an unfortunate precedent. So Miss Evans granted Helen's wish, writing back the same day she had received the letter. "Please return Claire to us by 11:00 on Wednesday morning so that the interruption to her studies will be held to a minimum."

Then Margaret Evans penned a more personal thought. "Claire is a lovely child and we are so very fond of her at Roedean. I'm sure you are proud of her as you have every right to be."

"Actually, Miss Evans has given permission for Claire to join us. I wrote her last week, and, to my surprise, she responded positively. So Claire can come."

"Which pleases you?" Sir Robert's remark hid his surprise.

"Yes, I'm glad she'll be here." Helen's expression reflected the great pleasure she felt.

Sir Robert's face also displayed pleasure at the prospect of having Helen's daughter attend the party, but the man was not being honest. He was not pleased Claire was coming. Nor was he annoyed. In truth, he felt no emotion at all. To Robert Trent, Claire had become an adjunct to Helen, much as a cream might accompany a cup of coffee. True, Claire was a perfectly pleasant young girl whose company Sir Robert at times enjoyed, but the child was not a presence in his life. He fulfilled what he considered to be his responsibilities toward her—he provided a home, he underwrote her education, and he gave Helen sufficient funds to otherwise sustain her. This pleased her mother, who in turn provided him with companionship and with the accoutrements of marriage that he required to support a successful career.

To foster this career, the Deputy Permanent Secretary for Colonial Affairs cultivated the image he thought would best serve his ambition. This meant he portrayed himself as a happily married family man. To promote this image, Sir Robert carefully placed on his desk at the Colonial Office a large photograph taken early in 1941 of himself, Helen, and Claire.

"Well then, it's settled. Claire will come and spend the night with us." Helen's face exuded happiness. "It will be such a delight to see her."

"Quite so."

"Let's see. I shall write her this afternoon and let her know of our plans. She'll be thrilled. She can come up by train and I will meet her at Victoria. Perhaps I shall telephone her as well. She'll need time to arrange her studies and make sure she has proper clothes to wear."

Helen then paused, turning her thoughts to Roedean's head-mistress. "And I must write Miss Evans to thank her and let her know when Claire will be away, and when she'll return. Wasn't it dear of her to allow Claire to join us?"

Sir Robert answered the question with silence, which Helen ignored.

"Sometimes I do believe Miss Evans isn't quite as awful as she's made out to be. Claire has told me of some of the names the girls call her behind her back, and they're just dreadful."

"I'm sure they are." Despite responding, Sir Robert was unable to hide his disinterest. He cared not a shred for what Roedean students thought of Margaret Evans. Helen knew this. Indeed, she knew he divorced himself from any activities related to the school other than paying tuition. So, having established that her daughter would be attending the party on October 19, she voiced no objection when he changed the subject.

"I shall be in the office this afternoon, my dear. There's a bit of a problem at Gibraltar that requires my attention. Seems the Spaniards are misbehaving. And then I'll be dining at the club."

"Oh? Surprise painted Helen's face. Her voice registered disappointment. "I thought we might dine in tonight, together."

"I wish we could, but there are some people I must see and we've arranged to have dinner at the Collingwood." Sir Robert had spoken without his customary self-assurance. He seemed to have

316 • THE BEST OF TIMES: A NOVEL OF LOVE AND WAR

told something other than the complete truth. Helen noticed, but said nothing. Sir Robert recovered by moving to more favorable terrain. "Besides, I need to speak to Eaton and remind him about our French chef."

"François."

"Yes, I remember. François Sabotier."

"Robert, you've been spending a great deal of time at the club lately. I do wish you might . . . "

"Quite so, my dear." He was now his confident self. " I shall do better, but today, duty calls."

Helen was not a suspicious person. She had always trusted Robert, who never had given cause to doubt his marital fidelity. The man spent most of his time at work. On occasion, he flirted with other women, but only in very public and appropriate social situations. Yet Helen sensed something odd in the way he had just spoken. He had been ill at ease, even awkward. This was most unusual, for Sir Robert, by training and constant effort, was extremely self-confident. Just now he had not been. Instantly, Helen's mind processed the thought that a reason had to exist for this exception. The reason, she concluded, was simple. Sir Robert had a romantic attachment. This afternoon or evening he was meeting someone surreptitiously. Helen was stunned. Never before had this idea occurred to her. At first, she had no idea who this woman might be. Then the thought occurred to her that he might be seeing Edna, Lady Roberts. Of course, that would explain his insistence that she be included at their recent dinner party.

Quickly, Helen's mind generated still another thought, one even more explosive. Contemplating its significance, she felt as though lightening had struck. Perhaps she was attributing to Robert what she herself was contemplating. Tom Forester had become part of her existence. She thought about him. She even dreamed about him. Marital fidelity at 28 Temple Court was at risk, but Helen realized that the principal threat did not involve the man in residence.

Forcing herself to think neither of Forester nor of Robert's awkward explanation, Helen returned to the conversation at hand.

"Well, I am disappointed." Helen deliberately spoke with feeling. Half of her believed what she had said. The other half did not. Briefly, she wondered what the man across from her believed.

Sir Robert offered no clue. He spoke as though nothing had occurred. "My dear, I shall make it up to you. Tomorrow we shall dine together here or wherever you might like. Now, I must get ready."

He stood up and walked out of the dining room. As he reached the stairs, with one arm on the banister, he turned towards Helen. Then with complete sincerity, as though nothing of consequence had taken place, he said, "Do have a pleasant afternoon."

Four hours later, Helen was dressed and sitting in the living room. Listening to a BBC program of music by Berlioz, she felt comfortable and relaxed. Much had been accomplished since Robert had left for the Colonial Office. Helen had telephoned Jane Ashcroft to confirm their lunch on Tuesday with Harriet Pennington. The letters to Claire and Miss Evans had been written. Clara Harris had accepted an invitation to tea for later in the day. A list of items still to do for the party on October 19 had been devised, as had a menu for discussion with Monsieur Sabotier. An interim draft report for the American's advisory committee had been reviewed. Clothes that needed to be laundered had been washed and dried. A small cottage pie using leftovers from the icebox had been prepared for supper later that evening. Only the garden, now sprinkled with leaves, required her attention. But the garden could wait, at least for ten minutes or so, as she enjoyed her surroundings and experienced the satisfaction of having spent a productive four hours.

As the radio played *Harold in Italy,* one of Berlioz' lesser known works, Helen looked about her and reflected that she had much to be thankful for. She enjoyed good health, and despite rationing, did not lack for clothes or food. No German bombs had fallen on her home, nor had she, like Clara Harris, lost a loved one in the war. She had several good friends, particularly Jane, who were loyal and dependable and in whose company she found great fulfillment. She and Sir Robert had a circle of acquaintances, many of whom were prominent in government and business, thus making for frequent and interesting gatherings. Financial worries were few as Sir Robert's income from investments and the civil service more than matched their obligations. Her work for the American advisory committee was rewarding. Most importantly, Claire was safe and healthy and receiving a first-rate education.

For Helen Trent, life was very good. No one realized this more than she. Helen remembered times not too long ago when her situation was far from comfortable. Then she had little money, neither a job nor a university degree, and a young child to raise alone. What would have happened without Henry Fogarty's generosity made Helen shudder. How different her life now was. Safe and comfortable, in good health, and without financial worries, she was this Sunday, and every day, very much aware of her good fortune.

Relaxing at home, contemplating the pleasant life she led, Helen abruptly became conscious of an intruding thought. Alarm replaced serenity as the idea jolted her afternoon respite. She realized that she would be putting at risk most of what she had by becoming involved with Tom Forester. More disturbing was the realization that she had intended to do just that.

For years, Helen had told herself that to be happy, she did not require a man's company. Peter was gone, which meant that her expectations regarding her and the male species were low. Robert was present, yet he no longer stirred Helen's heart, if in fact he had ever really done so.

Truth be told, Helen now wanted to touch and be touched by a man. How conscious she was of this desire is uncertain. However, memories can be jogged, tender moments realized. Perhaps one day she simply recalled how wonderful it was to be in love. Whatever the reason, Helen felt a need to experience again the excitement and passion that accompany an affair of the heart. Before Tom Forester, the right person had never appeared. Now, unexpectedly, in the form of a twenty-six-year-old American, he had arrived.

But what price was Helen willing to pay for romance? She was not a reckless person. Full of common sense, she more often than not exercised extremely good judgment. *I can't risk all of this for a man I hardly know. Besides, it's wrong and I've always tried to do the correct thing.*

Helen enjoyed the world she knew. She fit within it and from this world derived comfort and pleasure. If this world were not perfect, well, few things were.

Slowly, Helen calmed herself. No doubt, an affair with Forester would be sweet. She recalled his face and words when they had dined at Fogarty's after the award ceremony, then walked together down Oxford Street. He was intriguing, thoughtful, funny, decent, brave—involved in something that mattered. Helen imagined how good they would be together.

Within Helen Trent a war was being waged. Short in duration, it occurred in the moments Helen sat in the living room just before deciding to go into the garden. Economic well-being fortified by propriety fought desire and won. Forester's cause was vanquished. *He's the man I need and want, but I just can't tear my life apart.* Thus, Helen concluded she would not become involved with Tom. Convention and security were to carry the day, not romance and passion. She then decided that she would separate herself from this man. She would do so at the next meeting of the Advisory Committee. That would be a safe and sensible place, free of temptation.

The world that might have been was not to be allowed to topple the world that was. The war was over. Or so she thought, for Helen had forgotten a simple truth about love.

Love foils analysis. Science does not understand it. The theater only pretends it does. Poetry comes closest, though in the end it captures only the peripheries of love. The reason for such ignorance is clear. Love is a mystery. It is pain and pleasure. It is fleeting, yet eternal. It is both uncertain and predictable. Love is life's triumph. Not to love is not to live.

Helen should have known this. With Peter, she had found love as it is meant to be. Now older, she reasoned such feelings to be no longer obtainable. But romance is not exclusive to the young. Nor it is easily denied.

Helen believed she had acted in a mature fashion. She had considered the possible consequences of her action, weighed them against benefits, and made a decision. In this she was foolish, for decisions regarding love are not so straightforward. She had made her decision clinically, as though she were choosing an appliance. She also had acted out of fear. She had, or thought she had, much to lose in becoming involved with Tom Forester. Slowly, gradually, Helen calmed down. The tempest within, caused by the conflict between her recognition of risk and her attraction to Forester, subsided. Now, once again, she relaxed, comfortable with her decision. She sat quietly for several minutes listening to the music of Berlioz. With the conclusion of *Harold in Italy,* Helen rose and walked to the garden.

She was about to step outside when the telephone rang. As she returned to the living room, Helen thought the call might be from Clara Harris. It wasn't.

As she sat down upon the blue sofa, Helen spoke normally. "Hello."

"Hello, Helen. It's Tom. I've just paid a visit to Germany and needed to hear your voice."

Though surprised, a sense of warmth and pleasure enveloped Helen. Realizing she was home alone, she felt at ease. She would be able to devote her full attention to the call, and the caller. Forester's words and the sound of his voice sent pinpricks of excitement through her. Holding the phone, she could feel his presence. She felt physically connected to him, as though the distance between then had collapsed.

"Are you all right? You've not been hurt?" This last remark was as much a plea as a question.

"No, I'm fine. I've just had some exciting moments in an airplane after which I realized the only person in the world I wanted to talk to was you."

"I'm so glad. I'm glad you're safe and that you've called." Helen was relieved to know that he had not been hurt and was pleased, very pleased that he had taken the initiative and telephoned. Hearing his voice, picturing his face rekindled the excitement she felt whenever she thought about Forester. In an instant, Helen abandoned her earlier resolution. She cast aside her fears, pledging to accept whatever might happen as a result. Sir Robert and his world would have to do as best they could.

With this pledge, Helen felt remarkably free, suddenly conscious of being alive, deeply aware of the joy life can bring. The thought occurred to her that she had not felt this way in a long time—not since Peter. She hoped he would approve.

Then a second thought struck Helen, one she found amusing. She and Forester had never kissed. Their eyes had connected. Their hands had locked together. Words had flowed back and forth with ease as they embraced conversation. Yet their lips had not yet touched.

"Helen, are you there?" Tom was concerned by the silence following her remark. He had expected Helen to continue speaking. She had remained quiet because she was thinking of Forester, and of the world they might create. It would be a safe haven, a place where love might flourish in a time of war.

"Yes, Tom, I'm here."

"Forgive me for not calling, but in truth, I've been thinking of you a lot. You're not upset, are you?

"Oh no. I'm very glad you called. What a treat it is to hear your voice." Now it was Helen's turn to ask a question. "Where are you?"

"I'm at my airfield."

"Oh." Helen's voice reflected her disappointment.

"But I can come down on Tuesday, in the afternoon. I thought somehow we might see each other, if you're free. I know we have a committee meeting on Friday, but that's too far away."

In answering, Helen did not hesitate. She was ready to run the risks she had earlier identified. "Yes, I'm free, and would like that very much. Let's not wait until Friday."

"Terrific. Where shall we meet?"

"Not here, for obvious reasons, but I know where," Helen said.

"Where?"

"At Westminster Abbey. I'll meet you just inside."

"That sounds good. Is three o'clock okay? I fly in the morning, but should be able to get up there by then."

"Splendid." Helen realized there would be ample time to dine with Jane and Harriet and then meet Tom at the Abbey. "That will work out just fine."

"Three o'clock then."

"Yes, at the Abbey."

"I'll be there and I' m looking forward to it. Very much so," Tom responded excitedly

"I am too."

At the conclusion of the conversation Helen, shook with excitement, although outwardly she appeared calm. Anticipation and more than a touch of apprehension made her mind reel with questions that competed for her attention. Would she and Forester actually link up at Westminster Abbey? Did he feel about her the way she felt about him? How did she feel about him? Would this relationship— Helen would not use the word "affair"—last any reasonable amount of time? Would they be found out? What would Jane and Harriet think? How often might she and Tom be able to see one another? Would their differences in age and background matter? Where might they spend time alone? When was he going to kiss her?

Answers to these questions were not forthcoming. This was of little concern, for Helen did not seek answers, nor would her state of mind allow them. The woman was too excited. Her heart was throbbing, her mind was skipping from one subject to another. She felt a bit giddy and recalled the first time she had been asked to a dance.

That she had just talked with Forester continued to surprise her. More amazing was the recognition that she had done so at home— in the living room, no less. She felt as though her future had just met her past.

As the questions whirled about her, Helen felt as if her five senses had been recharged with potent elixirs. Gradually, two separate but related thoughts came into focus. The first was a belief that she was about to embark on something that would alter her life. How she lived and how she felt was going to change. Nothing ever would be quite the same. The second was the conviction that a liaison with Forester was the right thing to do. There would be no regrets. Thinking about him and being with him made her happy. Importantly, he made her smile, which men, particularly those who expressed interest in her, rarely did. Life, Helen realized, offers few opportunities for happiness. So the wise person will grasp them whenever possible. Helen was pleased she had done so. Having once before experienced true love, she now was willing to risk much to have a special someone again take hold of her body and soul.

Delighted by the prospect of Tuesday's rendezvous, Helen went out into the garden. Left inside were the uncertainty and fright that earlier had swayed her. Now she looked forward to working hard with her hands for thirty minutes. Then she would need to get ready for tea. As she knelt down to pull weeds and sweep aside the leaves, she remembered that she had had a smashing good time at that first dance.

On Tuesday, the sun took pity on London and cast its rays upon the entire city. While rain and clouds took the day off, the temperature hovered at 72 degrees Fahrenheit. The result was a glorious day, the kind of day that made everyone feel slightly more cheerful, despite the dreariness that came from four years at war.

Helen interpreted the weather as an omen that on this particular day, all would go well. Her spirits were high as she entered a small unpretentious restaurant near Covent Garden where she and Jane had agreed to meet. The restaurant was close by St. George's Hospital. The time was 12:25 P.M. Aware that she was five minutes early, Helen sat down at a small table set for four.

Alone at the table, Helen paid no attention to the activity about her. Instead, she thought about Forester. They would spend the afternoon together. She had no idea what they might do, but she had little doubt that it would be extremely pleasant. A glance at her watch revealed she would see him in exactly two and one half hours.

"Hello, Helen. You're looking lovely today." Jane had arrived and spoke in a cheerful voice. She, too, was affected by the sunshine, appearing to be even more cheerful than usual. "It's nice to see you and here we are both on time."

Helen did look lovely. She had selected her clothes this morning with considerable care and paid particular attention to her hair. The goal was to have Tom take notice. Not for some time had Helen dressed so purposely, save recently when she had attended Forester's award ceremony. Twice now she had chosen outfits with Tom in mind.

Helen wondered if he realized how much effort she made in fixing her hair and picking out her wardrobe. She concluded he did not. After all, Forester was a man, and men, Helen had learned, have no conception of what is required for a woman to become satisfied with her appearance. They think females should be able to bathe, fix their hair, choose apparel, and apply cosmetics in twenty minutes. She was convinced that, in this regard, men were hopeless, oblivious to the time consuming demands imposed by style and beauty. To Helen, the disparity of effort in dressing seemed to be a great injustice, as though God favored one sex over the other.

For today's meeting with Forester, Helen wore a long black skirt with a nicely cut long sleeved deep purple blouse. The skirt had been purchased before the war. To conserve fabric in wartime, England fashion dictated shorter lengths while encouraging women to wear pants. Helen did not mind the skirt lengths. They flattered her legs. But she thought pants looked dreadful on women, including herself. Complementing the blouse and skirt was a cardigan sweater, also black and, like the blouse, buttoned down the front. Her hair was pulled back on one side, making more visible handsome earrings that complemented a pearl choker. Hinting at possible future pleasures available to Forester, Helen had left open the top two buttons of both blouse and sweater. The effect was to highlight her skin while focusing the man's eyes downward to the first sign of cleavage.

"Jane dear, how good to see you." As Helen spoke, she stood up and gently kissed her friend's cheek. "You're well, I trust."

"Yes, I'm fine, but our friend Harriet is not."

"Oh dear."

"Nothing to worry about, at least that's what she tells me. Harriet rang me up this morning to say she was feeling poorly. She is afflicted with a bad cold, so the doctor has advised her to stay at home and get some rest."

"Poor Harriet. I do hope she feels better soon. I shall write her a short get well note first thing."

"That's a good idea. People do not write much any more. The telephone has made us all lazy."

"How true. I write Claire once a week, but have to confess that's about all. Letter writing seems to be a lost art."

"Sad, but true." Jane then spoke what was obvious. "So, it will be just you and me."

"Jane dear, there's no one I'd rather be with."

"How sweet of you. I feel the same way."

"Well, we shall toast Harriet and hope she's well again soon."

"Indeed we shall."

"Shall we move to a smaller table?"

"Good idea."

The two women then found another table, near the front of the restaurant. A waiter came by and, while handing them menus, recited the specials of the day. The plate du jour was corned beef fritters. These struck both women as unappetizing, so they put down the menus, ordering instead two glasses of sherry. Food could wait. The two friends had come to converse, not to eat. As the restaurant was less than half full, neither felt uncomfortable in occupying the table for a lengthy period of time. When the sherry arrived, they clinked their glasses in honor of Harriet and began to chat. As always, they greatly enjoyed the other's company, much as they had done at Roedean many years before.

Helen and Jane talked about Claire and the Ashcroft's two children, both boys. They spoke about mutual friends and acquaintances.

"Where does he live?" Jane realized she had improperly phrased the question. "Where is this man stationed? London, I presume?"

"I wish he were, but his airfield is somewhere in East Anglia. Despite an assignment to the Advisory Committee, he's on operations. He's a fighter pilot."

"Oh dear." Jane was now concerned for Helen. This new friend of hers not only was not close by, but he was also in combat where he might be hurt or killed. "You must be worrying yourself sick."

"I do. I didn't at first. But now I've started to, and I've started to think about it often. I get frightfully worried."

"Let's hope and pray he'll be safe."

"Yes, but there's more that I should tell you. It's all a bit sticky. And I don't mean because of Robert. Tom, his name is Tom Forester. Well, Tom is twenty-six years old."

"Oh." Jane had a slightly devious expression as she spoke.

"It's not what you think, you wicked woman." Helen was grinning. We've not yet even kissed."

"That's so very sweet. I assume you will soon."

"I certainly hope so."

Jane now posed a question she felt necessary to ask. "Is he married?"

"No, thank God."

Relieved at the answer, Jane asked a few more pertinent questions. "Are you happy?"

"Yes, I am. At least I think I am. It's happened all so suddenly. And I didn't plan it, it just happened. I feel like I've been swept away. I just want to be with him. Though in truth, I haven't. But when I am, it seems so right. I haven't felt this way since Peter."

"That's a telling sign."

"I think so, too."

"Then, Helen dear, you should see this man as much as you can."

"You don't think it's wrong, do you?

"No, I don't. Besides, I've learned not to judge other people's behavior. Especially now with the war. Everyone's life is special and unique. And all I want is for you to be happy. If this American brings you what I believe you need and deserve, then I'm all in favor."

"Really?"

"Yes, really. I just do not want you to be hurt." Jane felt protective towards Helen. She knew her friend was vulnerable.

"Nor do I. But I don't think I will. Tom is a very decent person. And I'm going into this with my eyes open."

"Good."

"I know this is a bit mad. Here I am, at forty-three, and this man is just twenty-six."

"It doesn't sound at all mad. Because, Helen dear, what counts is not years, but what's in your heart, and in your head."

"Of course, you're right."

"He sounds special."

"He is, Jane, and I can't wait for you to meet him."

"I suspect that won't be too soon."

"Actually, it will be."

"How so?" Jane was puzzled.

"He's coming to Robert's party next week. I've invited some other Americans as well."

"Good heavens. Was that wise?"

"Probably not. But I wanted him to meet Claire and you, and for me just to be able to see him."

"This party, Helen, has just gotten considerably more interesting."

"I thought you'd think so. And since I will have to play hostess and ignore this wonderful man . . . "

Jane finished Helen's sentence. "I shall be in charge of looking after Tom Forester."

"Exactly so. You're my best friend, the only person in the world I could entrust with this task. You will do it, won't you?"

"Of course I will." Jane looked fondly at Helen. "What are friends for?" Jane paused and then added another thought. "And, besides, I'll have an opportunity to meet this man and see if his intentions are honorable."

"I'm certain they are. At least, I hope so."

"I'm sure they are." Jane wanted to believe what she had just said, but admitted to herself that she had an element of doubt. However, Jane Ashcroft most definitely believed the words she next spoke. "And, if they're not, I shall wring his neck and make him wish he had never come to England."

—〰—

The west facade of Westminster Abbey features twin towers that, in true Gothic style, soar to the sky. Encased in the northernmost tower is a large clock that read ten minutes before the hour as Helen walked through the small plaza opposite the Abbey's main entrance.

As she entered the church, Helen was full of excitement, and slightly nervous. She had not felt this way for years. Excited by the prospect of seeing Forester, she nonetheless felt a tad uneasy. Not everyday did one embark upon an adventure whose origin and end point were romance.

Inside the Abbey, as her eyes adjusted to the darkness, Helen expected to see Tom at once, and was disappointed when she did not. The church was largely empty. Given the time of day, this was not surprising. Forward in the nave, a few people were seated, engaged in prayer. A few others were looking upward, admiring the vaulting. Of those remaining, only one might be the person she was seeking. Dressed in an American military uniform with a raincoat slung over his arm, this man had his back to Helen. He was standing at the grave of Britain's Unknown Warrior. The tomb was a sacred spot. In 1920, the body of an unidentified British soldier killed in France during World War I had been laid to rest in Westminster Abbey. Escorting the body were one hundred recipients of the Victoria Cross, England's highest military award. The American was standing at attention, yet with head bowed.

For a moment, Helen remained motionless, honoring the American's privacy as he stood by the grave. Then the soldier brought his head up and took a small step forward. He now was standing directly in front of the tomb. Helen watched him closely. As she did, the organ of Westminster Abbey began to play. Helen did not recognize the music, but found the sounds of the pipes to be rich and majestic. She thought the music trumpeted both the glory of God and the righteousness of England's cause. Though deeply affected by the organ music, she kept her eyes focused on the American. Helen watched intently as the soldier again brought himself to attention. He then slowly raised his right hand in formal salute. Bringing his hand down to his side, he stepped back. A soldier of the present had paid homage to a warrior of the past.

Helen then saw the American look at his watch. She did the same. The time was exactly 3 P.M. Uncertain of the man's identity, Helen walked slowly towards the soldier. He remained still, continuing to gaze upon the Unknown's Tomb. As she came up next to him, he turned his head towards her. Simultaneously, he placed her arm upon his. It was Tom. Before she could say a word, he grasped her hand, squeezing it gently.

"I'm glad you're here," Forester said. Although he was smiling, his demeanor was solemn. The respect he felt for the sanctity of the Warrior's final resting spot was obvious. Helen was deeply moved, more so when, with Helen close to him, he read out loud part of the tomb's inscription. "For God, for King, and Country, for Loved Ones Home and Empire, for the Sacred Cause of Justice and the Freedom of the World."

As he recited these words, Helen could feel him next to her. Hearing his voice, touching his hand with hers, she felt her anxiety depart. Her sense of excitement remained, but unexpectedly, it mellowed. She felt confident, secure. Reacting strongly to these emotions, Helen moved closer to Forester, who responded with a smile and another squeeze of the hand. She felt connected to him.

"I'm so glad you're here." Forester repeated. He also realized the moment was special. As he squeezed her hand, he processed the thought, much as Helen had done on Sunday, that he was embarking on a course that would alter lives, if not disrupt them. His future, he now knew, was about to change.

"You dear, dear man." Much affected by the moment, Helen was close to tears.

Forester wanted to embrace Helen, and nearly did so. However, he heard his mother's voice tell him that kissing a woman inside a church was not acceptable behavior, so he held back. Instead, turning to face her directly, he took both her hands in his and fixed his eyes upon her face. These were eyes that could spot German fighters at great distance. Helen felt they bore a hole straight through her.

"You are lovely to look at, and lovely to be with, and I am at this moment the luckiest man alive."

Before she could answer, Forester spoke again. Although his voice was gentle, his manner was firm. This was an individual comfortable with command.

"Helen Trent, come walk with me and show me the wonders of Westminster Abbey." As Tom continued the sentence, Helen noticed a sparkle in his eyes not evident before. "Before I do something the clergy, not to mention my mother, would disapprove of."

In response, Helen started to laugh. Tom pulled her close, back to his side. Their arms stayed locked together. Then he turned serious again.

"I've been looking forward to this."

"Me too."

Impulsively, yet without regret, Helen leaned forward and quickly placed a kiss upon his cheek. "Now it's my turn to say I'm glad."

Pleasantly surprised, Tom showed no outward response, save an expression that told Helen all she needed to know.

"Take me on that tour, dear lady, and we shall walk together, here in this Abbey, and elsewhere too."

Tom and Helen spent the next hour wandering through Westminster Abbey. During their wanderings, they visited Poet's Corner. Helen examined the tomb of Geoffrey Chaucer. Tom found a bust of Henry Wadsworth Longfellow and wondered why an American poet was honored in an English Abbey. Grinning widely,

Helen answered that on occasion, Americans spoke English entitling them to space next to the likes of Tennyson and Dickens.

Tom's favorite section of Westminster Abbey turned out to be the Chapel of Henry VII, noted for its magnificent circular and fan vaulting. Tom appreciated these features, but found most appealing the color banners that hung from the walls. These belonged to the Knights Grand Cross of the Bath who consider the chapel their own. The Order of the Bath, next to the Garter, England's most honored knighthood, was founded in 1725. Standing in the Order's Chapel, not far from the tomb of Elizabeth I, with light streaming through the arched windows, Forester sensed the grandeur of Britain's past. He felt proud that as a member of the Eighth Air Force, he was helping to safeguard Britain's future.

South of the Houses of Parliament, and but a short distance from Westminster Abbey, is a park that sits aside the Thames. A pleasant place to be, Tom and Helen walked to the park upon leaving the Abbey. Tom led the way. Despite concern over being seen, Helen had her arm tucked into his. The walk was satisfying to both. Their conversation never lagged. Each was at ease with the other. Neither of them wanted to be with anyone else.

At the park, they went over to the river's edge. Forester leaned against the railing and then turned to face Helen. Slowly, he brought both his hands up along the side of her body until he touched her cheeks and chin. Brushing back a few strands of hair, he focused his eyes upon this woman. Forester found her irresistible.

"You are one terrific lady, Helen Trent."

With these words, he leaned forward and kissed her. She did not resist. Indeed, she responded by pressing her body up against his as he wrapped his arms around her.

The kiss continued until Helen gently pushed Forester away.

He spoke first. "Is anything wrong?"

"No. I'm just not used to this sort of thing." Helen was somewhat flustered.

"Nor am I. But truth be told, I'd like to kiss you again."

"I would like you to, but we'd better not."

"Probably this is not the proper time or place."

"I think not."

"You're not angry?"

"No, I'm not angry. I'm rather pleased actually."

"You're a wonderful woman, Helen Trent. I think I'm in love with you."

"Those are sweet, yet dangerous words, Tom."

"Yes they are. And I'm going to show you that they're true as well, if you'll let me."

"I will let you, but not here and not now. This is all much too soon. I'm not sure what we do next."

Forester misinterpreted her remark. He thought she meant at this very moment, as they stood in the park. Helen was referring to the long term. She assumed they would now see each other, but had no clear picture in her mind of where and how often.

"I suppose we might walk."

"Yes, we could do that." Helen stopped pondering the future and responded to Forester's suggestion. Future arrangements, she decided, would take care of themselves.

Aware that more than one passerby had noticed them, Helen felt a need to avoid further attention. "Yes, let's walk, and away from here."

Forester also had seen several people in the park take note of him and Helen. One, a young man in a bowler had found their embrace amusing. So, too, had an older woman, although her companion had not.

"What time is it?" Although she and Sir Robert were not dining together this evening, Helen thought it best to be home by 6 P.M. She was not sure why she felt this way. Perhaps it was just a habit. When she did arrive home, Helen immediately wished she had stayed longer with Tom.

"It's half past four o'clock. Just a few minutes before."

"I have one hour before I must go."

"Then we'll walk and I'll tell you how much I enjoy your company and why."

"And I will listen to every word and enjoy them all."

For the next hour, arm in arm, Helen and Tom strolled along the Thames, despite concerns about being seen. They passed the Tate, eventually reaching Pimlico at a point opposite the Battersea power station. When the time came to part, they agreed to spend Friday afternoon together. Friday morning would be spent at the Royal Aeronautical Society where the Advisory Committee was to meet.

—ɯ—

At this meeting, Tom and Helen were unable to sit together. Two empty seats next to Helen were taken before Tom arrived, and Helen felt uncomfortable in asking the two individuals, one an American and the other an aide to the Lord Mayor, to sit elsewhere. Later, they agreed that perhaps the arrangement turned out for the best.

"I don't think I'd have paid much attention to the task at hand," said Tom.

Helen shared Forester's view, but spoke of another concern. "I suspect Colonel Dixon would disapprove. He seems quite keen on sticking to business." Jimmy Dixon, responsible for ensuring the committee's report was completed on time, was turning out to be a stern taskmaster who rarely let discussion get off subject.

"Dixon?" He'd be jealous," replied Tom, exhibiting a bit of cockiness. "He'd wonder how I got so lucky."

"And how did you?" Helen was amused by Tom's attitude.

"It's simple, my dear. By speaking the truth and not holding back."

"You're throwing me a line, Yank." Helen continued to be amused.

"Actually, I'm not." At which point Forester took Helen in his arms and kissed her. The kiss was long and sweet. Helen's amusement evaporated as she responded with willing lips.

By Friday afternoon, the sun had gone back to its old ways and disappeared. Most of Southeast England, and all of London, were covered with low clouds from which a light rain fell.

Tom suggested they go see a movie. Helen said she enjoyed the cinema, but rarely went. Tom asked if there were a movie she would like to see. He had in mind, in case Helen had no preference, *Gone With The Wind,* which was playing at Leicester Square. The movie had opened in April 1940 and ran for four straight years proving enormously popular in an England receptive to a story of the human spirit in triumph over tragedy caused by war.

"Actually, I've never seen *Gone With The Wind.*"

"Really?" Tom was surprised, both that she had not seen the film and that she had selected the one he was prepared to suggest.

So Helen and Tom spent the afternoon at the movies. Like teenagers on a date, they held hands and exchanged occasional kisses. They had a wonderful time, thoroughly enjoying the story of Scarlet and Rhett, and each other's company. However, more than once, Tom commented to himself that his life was a rollercoaster ride of contrasts. Yesterday he had flown to Schweinfurt where several times Me-109 pilots had tried to kill him. Today, he was at the movies in London with a beautiful woman who seemed to care for him.

Outside the theater, when the film was over, they parted company. Tom was returning to Bromley Park and the P-47s. Helen was returning home. They were both sad.

"I will try and call you soon." Tom was holding Helen's hands as he spoke.

"Promise?"

"Yes, I promise. I'm not about to say good-bye to you." From his pocket, Tom withdrew a small box inside of which were a set of aviator wings. "Here, hold on to these for me."

Helen opened to box, expressing both pleasure and surprise at its contents. "They're lovely, but don't you need them?"

"No, I have others. But these are the wings I won when I first learned to fly. They're special and I want you to have them. Will you hold on to them for me?"

"Yes, of course, I will keep them safe and hold them close to my heart."

"Good, that's what I'd hoped you'd do."

"I worry about you, Tom Forester." Helen now had someone in her life who faced danger. Her natural response was to worry, which she did. "The sky is such a dangerous place."

"Not to worry. I'm going to be fine. The German doesn't exist who can bring me down." This Forester truly believed. As any good fighter pilot would, he thought himself invincible. Tom also believed he was lucky and luck, he knew, counted more than skill.

Tom's confidence did little to assuage Helen's concern. She could not help but worry. Each time Tom flew, he would be in harm's way. Helen was now afraid. Once before, the man she loved had been taken from her. Now death again might intervene. That night, alone in bed, she thought of Peter and of Tom, and cried herself to sleep.

THIRTEEN

During the walk from Westminster Abbey to the park alongside the Thames, Helen had again mentioned the party she was giving on October 19, expressing the hope that Tom still planned to attend. When Forester replied that he was, she reminded him to bring along several of his fellow officers. Tom said he would do so and, upon returning to Bromley Park, spoke first to Harry Collins and Wilbur Williams. Receptive to the idea of a party in London, particularly one in which women were to be present, both men readily accepted the invitation.

"Besides," added Harry Collins, "it's a chance get away from army types and meet some interesting people."

"That it is," said Forester.

"I suppose we'll have to mind our manners," joked Wilbur Williams, "and dress in our Sunday best."

"Yes indeed," Tom replied, "we'll need to look sharp and act like proper gentlemen."

"Just think, a chance to mix with the upper crust," remarked Williams.

Harry Collins ignored the Adjutant's remark and addressed Forester. "Well, I think it was mighty nice of the lady to invite us, don't you?"

"Yes, I do." Tom started to think about Helen. "No doubt, the evening will be most interesting."

Later that day, Forester invited Fred Hawkins and Colonel Tee. Hawkins said he would love to go. The Engineering Officer begged off, saying that the P-47s were keeping him busy night and day.

"That's not all that's keeping Colonel Tee busy," said Hawkins with a grin while winking at Tuttle who in response simply frowned.

Tom did not understand Hawkins's remark, nor did he attempt to do so. If Colonel Tee wanted to remain at Bromley Park, that was his business. Forester made people fly and fight. He did not make them attend parties.

—⁂—

The farewell for Sir Robert took place five days after the mission to Schweinfurt. In that time, Tom twice led the 19th Fighter Group into battle. Both flights were escort missions to France. Neither encountered much opposition from the Luftwaffe. On the first mission, no German planes appeared. On the second, four Me-109s attacked the B-17s, but fled upon being challenged. Tom fired his guns at one of the 109s, but failed to score.

He did better at the plate. That afternoon, Forester participated in a softball game at Bromley Park. The officers of the 87th Fighter Squadron played the squadron's enlisted men. Invited to the game, Tom took a turn at shortstop. He fielded three ground balls and at bat went two for two. The first hit was a pop fly single, the second was a solid double to left center. Forester felt good about his time at bat, but not about the outcome of the game, which the enlisted men won 14–8. Tom enjoyed playing, but later admitted to himself and Harry Collins that he would have had a better time had they won.

Forester was intensely competitive. He disliked losing and played hard at games, expecting to win even when victory appeared unlikely. Softball and sailing were favorite sports, although he cared most about tennis. Hitting a forehand crosscourt or returning a strong serve for a winner gave Tom enormous pleasure. He thrived on competition and believed that, as a result, he was a better person.

Late in the afternoon on Tuesday, October 19, Forester was on the train to London. With him in the second class compartment were Majors Collins, Williams, and Hawkins. Their destination was 28 Temple Court. Despite the informality that occurred when on leave, Tom paid scant attention to them. His mind was on Helen Trent.

He was wondering if she were competitive. Certainly, she was intelligent, attractive, and as Harry Collins later would describe her, "a very classy lady." But competitive? Probably not. In his experience, Tom had found females to be more interested in playing than in winning the game. True, there were women tennis players who focused on winning, but they seemed the exception rather than the rule. Women tended to be soft, often delicate. At least they appeared that way to Forester. He noticed that they found pleasures in simple things whereas men required less subtle entertainment. Tom observed that women were highly sensitive to emotions and perceptive in ways that men were not. No doubt, these traits added to their charm. They also underscored how very different men and women were.

He and Helen were replete with differences of which Forester was well aware. Most obvious was age and nationality. She was forty-three and British. He was twenty-six and American. He was less reserved. She was more sophisticated. He had been educated in excellent schools. She had left university early, obtaining an education through experience rather than by books. She believed Britain still ruled the world. He assumed America did.

All these differences could be overcome. At least, Forester thought so. One that might not was marital status. Tom was well aware that Helen was married. Unhappily so, but married nonetheless. He felt no guilt in pursuing Sir Robert's wife. In Forester's mind, Robert Trent had forfeited both respect and sympathy by ignoring Helen's emotional needs. Because Sir Robert had laid no claims upon Helen's heart, he himself had violated the marriage contract. Moreover, the war had made less binding the bonds of matrimony. In London and elsewhere in 1943, the presence of death placed a premium on the present. Often the future was simply ignored. Tom understood this and accepted it. He knew, to use Helen's own words, that the sky was a dangerous place. Several pilots Forester had known had no future. They already were dead. Better to grab hold of life wherever, whenever possible. If this was selfish, so be it. Besides, a married woman was not forced into adultery. She could always say no, rejecting a man's advances. So far, Forester pointed out to himself, Helen had not.

Tom found Helen Trent to be enormously appealing. She was lovely to look at and he wanted to make love to her until they both collapsed in exhaustion. Yet Helen's appeal was more than physical. Tom found her genuinely interesting. She had a sense of humor he appreciated and intelligence he respected.

Helen's humor was quick and perceptive. A reserved individual, she rarely laughed hard, but she did laugh often. Forester enjoyed watching the process. First came a smile, followed by a casual remark that often was clever, but never mean. Then the smile would break loose and her eyes would dance as she laughed.

Helen's intelligence was obvious. She was well read and a keen observer of people. Tom found conversation with her stimulating. He enjoyed her habit of asking questions. Her insights about England he considered fascinating. In times past, at Dartmouth and in the Air Corps, Forester had challenged people intellectually. He would test their logic and see how deeply beliefs were held. Without malice, almost by habit, he had done so with Helen. She did not take offense nor did she disappoint. In fact, she more than held her own. Someone with less confidence than Tom might have disengaged, for men often are uncomfortable with bright women. Not Forester—he found Helen's intelligence compelling. To him, it made her even more appealing.

As the train rolled on towards London, Forester thought he understood why he was attracted to this woman. In his mind, the reasons were simple and, like the parts of Caesar's Gaul, three in number. Helen was beautiful, witty, and intelligent. Singly, they would have made Tom take notice. Together, they formed a captivating package. Yet the American was unaware of another perhaps more compelling reason. Simply stated, Helen Trent provided Tom Forester with companionship unavailable at Bromley Park. In Helen's company, Tom could rest easy. He could put aside the burden of command. He could find relief from the stress of combat. Helen was Forester's connection to a softer, more personal world where he, as a human being, could find warmth and friendship.

That Helen was considerably older than he did not trouble Forester. He was aware of her age and noticed that her skin was not free of wrinkles. Once he had calculated that when he was her age, she would be sixty. He knew that, should they become involved, people would notice the difference in years. No doubt some would disapprove. Tom had decided he would ignore them, and their snickering. They would not realize that Helen was the most intriguing female he had ever met, far more interesting than the girls he had dated in college or met while in the army. The years, Forester had decided, had been kind to Helen Trent. Age enhanced her appeal. Her appearance now had a regal dimension. Experience had made her wise, while the passage of time had made her appreciate what life has to offer.

Ordinarily, Tom thought a great deal about the future. John Forester had drummed into his son's head the importance of setting up goals, of planning next steps, and of laying out a course to reach one's objectives. "Tom, he would say, "always be thinking of where you wish to go and how best to get there." Tom and his brother had heard this advice a hundred times. Both boys had come to accept it.

In high school, Tom thought about college. At Dartmouth, he thought about graduate school. Once deciding upon a career in academia, he thought about what he would like to teach, and where. Then the winds of war intervened. Instead of a Ph.D., Tom pursued a commission in the military. Once in the Air Corps, he chose to concentrate on the present. He learned to fly and later how to fight.

Tom neither forgot his father's advice nor his own plans for graduate school. He just put them aside. The future had to wait. Forester focused on the here and now, which, in October, 1943 meant P-47s and the men at Bromley Park.

To these he devoted complete attention. What might take place once the war was over, a subject discussed by soldiers and sailors around the globe, held no interest to Forester. He was immersed in the air war, in how to gain advantage over the Luftwaffe, in how to lead the 19th Fighter Group to victory.

Enter Helen Trent. Would she, Forester wondered, be consigned to the present? Was she a mere episode in his wartime service, a woman who would play no part in the future? As Forester sat on the train, he stared out at the passing countryside, continuing to ignore his companions. Yet his mind did not process the sights he saw. Tom was doing what his father had instructed him to do. He was thinking about what comes next, discarding for the moment his resolve to focus exclusively on Bromley Park and its Thunderbolts. He now thought about Helen and what she meant in the context of his future.

Clearly, he told himself, she was a special person. Last week he had told her that he thought he was in love with her. But he had lied, and he knew it. He did love her. He was just reluctant to tell her. Tom knew that if he rushed Helen Trent, she would back away. He therefore intended to proceed slowly.

True, he had known her but for a short time. Yet wartime accelerated emotions. Forester was certain the feelings he felt constituted love. There was between him and Helen chemistry, a comfort level along with a desire for each other's company that went beyond simple friendship and mere lust. Tom believed that the two of them had connected in a way explainable only by love.

Forester had no doubt that in time they could be happy. But for how long, he wondered. Would they make it to war's end? Tom thought they would. What then? Would they seek to marry? Was marriage even feasible? If so, would Helen be able to secure a divorce? If not, would they continue on nonetheless? Did he wish to become an instant father? Would the child even like him? Did he wish to remain in England once hostilities ceased? Would she, could they, come to the States? Was it realistic to plan a future with Helen Trent?

As Forester raised these questions, he knew he did not have the answers. Tom simply did not know what would happen. He believed, correctly, that he was in love with Helen. He was determined to win her heart, and having done so, to take exceptionally good care of her. Still young, Forester had a romantic view of life and love. Helen was his lady and he her knight in shining armor. There on the train, Forester vowed to conduct himself honorably with this woman. He would not treat her as a wartime fling, but what their future might be, he had no idea.

Forester decided to let events happen as they might, undisturbed by strategy and plans. He and Helen would enjoy the present. Their end point would remain uncertain. What took place in the months ahead would be left to fate. That his father would disapprove of this approach he had little doubt.

Once in London, the four officers decided to have a drink before proceeding to Helen's residence where the party was to be held. It was only 5:15 P.M., too early to hail a taxi for the ride across town. They also decided to have supper, as they were uncertain how much food would be available at the party. Like most Americans in Britain, they knew that in English homes food was not abundant.

"Let's eat early, at one of our clubs," said Harry Collins who was somehow confident that the Trents would provide ample quantities of liquor, "and then we can drink on a full stomach."

Hawkins and Williams suggested they go to the Rainbow Corner, which Williams said was both convenient and cheap. Collins thought the Red Cross club would be too crowded as did Forester. So the four, all intelligent and articulate men, spent the next fifteen minutes standing outside the train station debating where to go. Eventually, they realized how ridiculous they were, at which point Harry turned to Tom.

"Okay, democracy clearly does not seem to work in this instance. Colonel, you're going to have to decide."

"I was waiting until the three of you came to your senses." Tom was laughing. "Follow me, gentlemen, I will not lead you astray."

Forester took his companions to the VanDyke Club in Kensington, a place he had heard Jimmy Dixon recommend. There, in an officers-only setting, they spent a pleasant two hours. Dinner was simple, yet good, and cost but two shillings per person. Drinks also were inexpensive, although only Fred Hawkins had more than one. No women were present, so when Forester suggested they leave, no one objected.

Collins, Williams, and Hawkins all looked forward just to being in the presence of women. Finding one to make a move on would be a bonus. Forester understood that his situation was different. He already had a female to pursue and she would be present at the party, but Tom reminded himself that tonight this woman was off limits. Helen had told him that she was going to ignore him. That made sense, and he had no doubt that she would do so. He, in turn, would have to keep his eyes off her, not to mention his hands. The temptation both to stare at and to touch her would be great. Yet he realized it would have to be resisted. As Tom walked out of the VanDyke Club and into a taxi, he spoke silently to himself. *Stay calm. Do not get in close. And for God's sake, remember where you are.*

From the outside, Helen's house was completely dark. No light emerged from the windows, which on each floor, were draped with heavy blackout curtains. Temple Court also was dark as streetlights no longer were turned on. The darkness made finding one's way more challenging to visitors on the ground, especially to Americans unacquainted with London.

"Are you sure this is the house?" Fred Hawkins was speaking to Forester.

"No, I'm not sure. I've never been here before," replied Tom who spoke to all three of his companions. "Look for the number 28."

"I can't see a thing," chimed Wilbur Williams.

"Here it is. Two nice brass numerals," said Harry Collins who fingered the numbers as though reading Braille. "We're at the right spot."

"So the taxi driver knew all along where he was. I wonder how he did it." There was a hint of admiration in the Group Adjutant's voice.

"He probably wonders how we fly to Germany and back," said Tom.

"Yes, but we don't have to do it in the dark," replied Fred Hawkins.

Major Collins was about to knock on the door when, without warning, it opened. The emerging light caused Harry to shield his eyes.

"Do come in gentlemen." A butler in a well worn tuxedo addressed the four men. "But step lively. We mustn't give Mr. Hitler any assistance."

Forester and his companions entered the house, finding themselves in a large entry hall. Hoskins took their coats and service caps. Then in a polite yet commanding voice, he continued speaking.

"I shall put these upstairs, gentlemen. The guests are in the living room. There is food in the dining room and drinks can be had in the study. I shall tell Sir Robert you've arrived." Hoskins walked to the stairway, turned and spoke again. "Please let me know if I can be of service."

Between forty and fifty people were in the living room. Most of them were standing, cocktail in hand. Many were female. All were nicely dressed, several in formal attire. A few uniforms were evident, although Forester saw that most everyone appeared to be civilians. The mood in the room was festive. Music emanated from a Victrola while conversation flourished, aided by an abundance of spirits.

As Tom stepped from the entryway into the living room, he searched for Helen. He could not find her, although he did notice an attractive woman in a stylish green gown standing off to the left. She was talking to an Army Air Force officer. Upon closer inspection, Forester identified the officer as Jimmy Dixon. The woman, further examination revealed, was extremely good looking. Tom had to make himself stop staring at her. The woman's hair was piled high and the gown fit tightly around her body save for one shoulder that was totally bare. Dixon seemed entranced. Tom could understand why, but decided he best continue his search for Helen.

Forester did so, moving slowly about the crowd. Helen was not to be seen.

"Colonel Forester, how do you do." A woman had come up from behind Tom. She, too, was attractive, but in a more wholesome way than the woman in the green gown. "My name is Jane Ashcroft. I'm a good friend of Helen's. She's out in the kitchen at the moment, attending to hostess duties, but she told me to be on the lookout for you. Now that I've found you, let me be the one to say welcome."

"Thank you. That's most kind."

"You've not been here long, have you?"

"No, we just arrived."

As they continued talking, Jane assessed the man with whom her best friend was so taken. Her first reactions were positive. Tom Forester seemed polite, well spoken, and comfortable with himself. He had offered to get Jane a drink, talked sensibly about England, and was completely at ease in a room full of strangers, most of whom were older than he. Jane thought Forester looked more than twenty-six, although the man clearly was youthful in both appearance and outlook. Regarding the latter, Jane found Tom to be typically American in that optimism was deeply rooted and easily expressed. His physical appearance she found pleasing. Wearing a smartly tailored uniform, the American looked decidedly handsome. Jane concluded that, while Tom was no Tyrone Power, women young and old would gladly be seen in his company.

"Helen has told me all about you."

"Oh?" Forester's voice and expression registered surprise. He had told no one about Helen Trent.

"Not to worry. It's all been positive." Amused by Tom's reaction, Jane guessed that Forester assumed she knew more than she did.

However, Jane decided not to pursue the matter. Her job tonight was to watch over this boy, not make him wonder how much she knew. At another time, when circumstances allowed, she would make sure his were only the best of intentions. "Now come with me, Colonel, and I will introduce you to some of our more distinguished guests."

"Lead the way, Mrs. Ashcroft." Tom had noticed Jane's wedding bands.

"Jane, you must call me Jane. I have a feeling that we're going to get to know each other this evening."

Forester had no idea what this last remark meant. No matter. He took hold of Jane Ashcroft's arm and followed her into the crowd.

They met several interesting people and a few who were not. Among the latter were a retired Brigadier who talked incessantly about India and a barrister who had little to say about anything. More successful were conversations with Peter Balfour and Harold Ascot. Balfour was a Member of Parliament. Ascot was a classics professor at the University of London. The M.P. gave Jane and Tom an entertaining view of Parliament as dominated by Winston Churchill. Ascot spoke glowingly of ancient Greece, yet made his remarks relevant to the present.

Earlier, as Forester and Jane had made their way into the living room, Hoskins had asked whether they might like a drink. Mrs. Ashcroft responded in the positive as did Tom who really did not wish to imbibe, but said yes in order not to appear impolite. Jane ordered a dry martini, shaken not stirred. Forester requested a gin and tonic, changed his mind, and asked for a glass of ginger ale. He and Jane then walked to one side of the room.

"You don't drink?" Jane was truly surprised.

"Not really. I may be the only graduate of Dartmouth College to go through school and not get tipsy."

"Heavens, that makes you sound a bit of a square, which I'm sure you're not."

"Well, I try to have fun in other ways."

"And what might they be?"

Tom was carefully considering how to respond when Hoskins returned, drinks in hand. Forester received the surprise most Americans receive in Europe when first handed a drink. Inside the glass, floating in the ginger ale, was a single cube of ice. Tom had expected a glass full. Europeans find odd the American preference for ice in beverages. Tom, a Yankee in every respect, considered it perfectly natural. Warm ginger ale was not to his liking, but, recalling the adage about visitors in Rome, Forester took a few sips and pretended satisfaction. As the ice cube inevitably melted, Tom contemplated pouring some of the beverage into a potted plant when no one was looking. However, his mother's voice reminded him that such a step would be inexcusable. He thus gamely sipped the warm ginger ale, concluding with amusement that iced drinks proved that life in the United States was better than in Europe where the phrase "on the rocks" referred either to a ship in distress or a broken marriage.

Forester was imagining a glass full of ice when Jane discreetly pointed to a man nearby who was conversing with an RAF officer. The man was in his mid fifties, slightly overweight, but with strong features that gave him a distinctive and not unattractive appearance. His hair was black, slicked down with hair cream. He wore formal attire, and had been circulating among the guests, all of whom greeted him with enthusiasm. Now he stood alone with the officer who listened intently. Given the noise in the room, neither Jane nor anyone else, save the airman, could hear what he was saying. The officer, a Group Captain, was fair in color and slight of build. His light blue uniform was well tailored, but bereft of decoration. He appeared upset.

"Colonel, have you met our host?" Jane turned Tom in the direction she had been pointing. "He's the man over there, talking to the officer in blue."

"No, I've not. Nor have I yet seen my hostess."

In response, Jane laughed. "I'm sure you'll see Helen soon. For now, come with me, and I'll introduce you to Sir Robert Trent."

to send a message to the other women in the room. He wondered whether that included Helen.

"I should introduce myself. I'm Tom Forester." He reached out and shook Lady Roberts's hand. As he did so, he felt compelled to explain his presence at the party. "I'm a friend of Helen Trent."

"I'm Lady Roberts. You should call me Edna."

For the next ten minutes, Edna proceeded to hold court with Tom. As she spoke to Forester, her mind was on Helen Trent. So this fellow was a friend of Bobby's wife. How delicious. It made the American an even more desirable catch. Helen was a complete bitch, a snob who, though not without a sense of style, was condescending to all but a select group of friends. Edna Jones knew she did not belong to the group despite her title. Seducing Helen's friend would register a victory over Helen and her types. It would demonstrate that the wife of Lord Roberts was not to be trifled with.

In conversation, Edna Jones thus played up to Tom. She asked him about P-47s and about America. She sought his opinions about the war on which he expressed strong views and about British politics on which he had none. Several times, she suggested he attend a party she was planning to give next week. More than once, she brushed up against him in a provocative fashion.

Forester enjoyed the attention. The woman was sexy and seemed attracted to him. Certainly, she was not playing hard to get. Tom began thinking about an assignation. What harm could come from a brief tumble in the hay.

"Too bad, this party will be over soon," said Edna. Intent upon seducing Forester, she could not imagine his not being receptive. "I'm really not ready yet to go home."

Tom recognized the remark for the invitation it was. For a moment, he contemplated suggesting they meet somewhere later in the evening. His brain had gone south. Forester was thinking that a night of easy sex might be a pleasant change of pace. Then in his head the alarm bells went off. Tom realized he was about do something truly stupid. *Wake up, you idiot, and don't screw up what you've got going with the lady who lives here.*

"I think you have more energy than I do. When this is over, I'm heading back to Bromley Park and my bunk."

"Why not stay over in London? Exciting things can happen in this city at night."

"It's tempting, but I'm going back to my airfield. It's where I belong, and in its own way, has plenty of excitement."

This time Edna got the message. She was not pleased. More often than not, Lady Roberts got her way. When she did not, the woman could be brusque.

"Well then, that's where you should go." Edna's tone suggested the anger she felt. Her next remark was sarcastic, as she deliberately emphasized the first word. "*Boys* do need their rest."

Tom welcomed her response, ignoring the insult Edna had just delivered. The woman would not pursue whatever plans she had for him. No doubt they would have been pleasurable. But Forester understood that he had come to see Helen, not pick up some woman he didn't know.

Tom now thought it best to remove himself from Edna's presence. "Excuse me, Lady Roberts, I need to check on my buddies."

"That would be wise," she snapped, "we wouldn't want you to be all by yourself." As Edna spoke, she turned and walked away. To herself, although not in a voice that could be heard by others, she said, "Bobby's quite right. These Americans are wretched little people."

With Lady Roberts's abrupt departure, Forester found himself alone. He now had little need to go find Collins, Williams, and Hawkins. They had only been an excuse to break off conversation with Edna. Besides, Tom knew the three officers were quite capable of taking care of themselves, especially given the abundance of liquor and the presence of females.

Forester enjoyed his momentary solitude. The party was in full swing. People were talking and drinking. Music from the Victrola was both loud and high spirited. Standing off to the side, Tom was conscious of the contrast. He was quiet and by himself. The room was crowded and full of noise.

Tom began to think about the people he had met so far. Most notable was Sir Robert Trent. Forester had imagined their meeting would be memorable, but awkward. It was neither. Helen's husband, Tom concluded, was polite, yet clearly disinterested in his wife's committee and its members. This led Forester to believe Sir Robert suspected nothing. Tom wondered if he would even care. He certainly didn't seem to show much interest in Helen. Not once had Forester seen Sir Robert with his wife. In fact, Tom observed, he frequently was in the company of Lady Roberts. The man seemed immensely popular. Throughout the evening, Tom noticed that guests at the party greeted him with fanfare and affection. They all were wishing him a safe and successful trip. Forester was glad Sir Robert would be out of the country. He hoped, and suspected, Helen would be as well.

If the conversation with Sir Robert was not memorable, Tom's encounter with the lady in the green gown certainly was. Forester found what had just occurred to be incredible. In Helen Trent's living room, he had been propositioned by a very good looking woman. Why, he was not sure. Most likely, Edna, who reminded him of Ann Sheridan, could have any man she wanted. Forester was puzzled why she had chosen him.

Tom had no idea that the woman's real target had been Britain's upper class represented so perfectly in Edna's mind by Helen and her friends. Edna Jones, born poor in Bristol, never felt welcomed in the circles she now frequented. Nor was she. England's elite, identified by their pattern of speech, education, and family lineage, were an exclusive group. Society in Britain was stratified, with little mobility between classes. So, despite having married into both money and a proper title, Edna, Lady Roberts would always be an outsider.

No American in England during World War II could help but notice the country's class structure. Tom had seen it during meetings of the Advisory Committee. Roger Baldwin had witnessed it on visits to Hadley in quest of RAF Mosquitoes. Ira Eaker had observed it in discussion with senior British officials. Class distinctions permeated England. Americans found them strange and distasteful. Raised in a land that promised opportunity for all and provided it to many, the Yanks had trouble accepting a social system that pigeonholed its citizens. The British cared not a whit for what the Americans thought. Nor did the English take kindly to occasional efforts to challenge this structure. They pointed out that the system was well established, having been in place for centuries. In their view, it enabled everyone to comfortably know their place, thus bringing to Britain an enviable stability. Moreover, they would note, the system had produced a great democracy and a proud people.

Tom thought the system was terrible. More than once he had told Harry Collins that it wasted human talent and seemed grossly unfair. Collins agreed. Harry said that in Britain, Abraham Lincoln would have remained a country lawyer. Both men liked the British. Both thought that in Britain, there was much to admire. Yet to them, and to numerous other Americans, England's class system was the country's most damning flaw.

"That and the food," added Collins, "It's truly awful."

"You're being unfair," replied Forester. "The war has brought shortages no chef could overcome."

"That's just a convenient excuse. Trust me, Colonel. I like the British. They're good people and plenty brave. But they can't cook. Even with all the food in the world, they wouldn't know what to do."

"Harry, I think you're generalizing."

"Perhaps, but answer me this. Back home, you've been to French restaurants and Chinese restaurants, and Italian restaurants. But have you ever been to an English restaurant?"

Off to one side of the living room and still by himself, Forester continued to think about the people he had met. As he did so, he moved toward a mahogany table on which several photographs stood. One of them, in a sterling silver frame, was of a young girl. Tom guessed the youngster was Helen's daughter.

"So here you are, Colonel Forester. I've been looking for you."

"Hello, Mrs. Ashcroft." Tom paused and smiled. "I'm supposed to call you Jane, aren't I?"

"Yes, you are, and I shall call you Tom, if that's all right?"

"Yes, I'd like that."

"Good. That's now settled. Well, I've not being doing my job."

"Ma'am?"

"My job, Tom, is to look after you this evening and to make sure you're having a pleasant time."

"Well I am. I've met some rather interesting folks."

"So I've noticed. One of them, a certain lady in green, seems quite upset with you."

Tom immediately became uncomfortable. He wondered if Edna and Jane were friends and how truthful he should be in relating his encounter with Lady Roberts.

Jane noticed Tom's discomfort and quickly put him at ease. "Don't say a word, dear boy. I suspect the worse of her, and by her reaction, the best of you."

In fact, Jane had watched across the room as Forester conversed with Lady Roberts. She assumed Edna had suggested something improper and, by the woman's response to Tom's reply, had been rebuffed. Jane considered Tom's action a good omen. So far, she had been pleased with what she had seen and heard about Tom Forester. Major Collins had been particularly complimentary.

As Jane spoke, both she and Tom noticed that Edna was deep in conversation with Jimmy Dixon.

"Our friend appears to have found an American after all," whispered Jane.

"Apparently so," replied Tom, "but don't be fooled by Jimmy's southern charm. Colonel Dixon can take care of himself. I suspect right now he's having a good time."

"I'm glad you're enjoying yourself as well."

"I am. My only complaint is that I've been here for more than an hour and still have not seen Helen." A touch of frustration was evident in Forester's response.

"Then you'll welcome what I have to tell you."

Tom peered into Jane's face, but remained silent.

"She's frightfully busy, playing hostess and making sure the party runs smoothly, but she's told me to tell you to be in the upstairs library exactly five minutes from now."

"I can do that." Forester looked at his watch. "Five minutes, you said?"

"Yes. She seemed to want you there on the dot."

"Jane, in my line of work, we pay close attention to timelines. So I will be there in precisely four minutes and forty-five seconds from," here Tom paused, "now."

"Good, but I want you to remember something, Tom Forester."

"And what is that?"

"Don't do anything foolish up there."

By this remark, Forester realized she was aware of his relationship with Helen. To his surprise, he found this reassuring. "I won't, I promise."

"I'm going to hold you to that. She's very dear to me and I don't want to see her hurt, now or later on." Jane then knowingly peered back at Forester. "Be careful. Just be very careful."

The upstairs library was small, about thirteen feet long and eleven feet wide. Two walls were lined with shelves filled with books. Another wall, the one facing Temple Court, contained a window that during the day admitted some, but not a lot of light. On the wall opposite the window were two very old maps, nicely framed. One, published in 1837, pictured the City of London. The other was a Royal Navy survey of the North American coast from the 1790s that had been a prized possession of Helen's grandfather. In one corner of the room near the window stood a small writing table and chair. In another corner sat a green well-worn upholstered chair. On the floor, a handsome Persian rug added warmth and color to an already cozy space.

Tom was examining the map of the coastline when he sensed someone's presence and heard Helen's voice.

"At last. I thought I'd never get to see you." As she spoke, Helen moved up next to Forester. She was wearing a tea length long-sleeved silver satin gown that fit tightly around her bodice and flared gradually from the waist down to the hemline. The sweetheart neckline accentuated her beautiful pale skin. Her thick hair was swept into a French twist, secured with a treasured mother of pearl comb that had belonged to her great aunt Martha. An impressive diamond and sapphire necklace sparkled, even under the dim light, as it laid against her bare skin. Tom thought she looked fabulous, but noticed that her hands were trembling.

"Are you okay?"

"I'm fine," said Helen. "Just nervous about this. But I needed to see you." She was not concerned about being caught alone with Forester. That could easily be explained. She was worried about giving in to her desire to be held by him. However, by sheer willpower, Helen took hold of herself, then instinctively reverted to the role of hostess. "Are you having a good time?"

"Yes. The party's very nice. The only problem is that I've not seen you."

"I feel the same way. But we can't, not here." Helen's hands again began to tremble as she touched his shoulders. "I must be crazy. Tell me that you care."

"Have no doubt of that, dear lady."

"I'm so glad."

Tom was about to take hold of her when Helen, wisely, moved away and switched her tone of voice. "Now, Tom Forester, I want you to stay right here for two minutes. There's someone special I want you to meet."

While Helen was gone, Tom browsed through the books. He noticed a section devoted to geography and a shelf filled with books about the Royal Navy. He was looking at a book about the Battle of Jutland published in German when Helen came back into the room. This time she was not alone.

"Tom, this is my daughter, Claire." Standing next to Helen was a beautiful young girl, age fourteen, whose face and body structure mirrored that of her mother. "Claire, this is Colonel Forester. He serves on the Advisory Committee with me."

With great poise, Claire stepped forward, extending her hand to Tom. "How do you do, Colonel Forester?"

Tom shook hands with the girl. "It's nice to meet you, Claire. Your mother has told me all about you."

For the next few minutes, Tom and Claire engaged in polite, but friendly conversation. Perhaps the presence of Helen, who remained silent, but was enjoying the moment tremendously, put each of them at ease. Tom asked Claire about school. Claire asked Tom about life in America.

Helen was about to bring the conversation to a close when the young girl posed a question to Forester.

"Is flying an airplane very difficult?

"Not really. It takes time to learn and plenty of practice."

"Just like the piano."

"That I couldn't say." Tom had never attempted to play a musical instrument.

"I would like to learn to fly someday."

"Claire, I've never heard you say that before." Helen was truly surprised.

"Yes Mummy, I should like to have an airplane of my own and fly to see all of my friends whenever I want to."

"I can't think of any reason why you couldn't," said Tom, "if you work hard and it's something you really want to do."

"Miss Evans says that once we've won the war, the world will change and women will be able to do just about anything."

Here Helen interjected, "Miss Evans is the headmistress at Claire's school."

"Well, Claire," Tom replied, "I don't know what the world will look like once the war is over." He now turned toward the girl's mother. "Let's hope it's a safer place where men and women, and their children, can enjoy many good things," here Tom paused and looked at Claire, "like flying an airplane."

The party for Sir Robert lasted well past midnight, and was a great success. Forester stayed until 11:30 P.M., remembering his mother's advice to leave while you're still having fun and before the party's over.

Once downstairs, after meeting Claire, Tom spent the rest of the evening in Jane Ashcroft's company. To ensure that he was entertained, she introduced Forester to several additional interesting people. Tom met Sir Robert's good friend, Donald Iverson, who held a senior position at the Foreign Office, although exactly what his job was, Forester never could determine. In fact, Iverson worked for British Intelligence. Tom also met Phillipe Dumas, one of General DeGaulle's aides. Monsieur Dumas, like the General, was aloof and proud. Yet at one time, he had served in the Armée de l'Air, thus giving him and Forester common ground on which to converse.

The most enjoyable people Tom met were Herbert Ashcroft, Jane's husband, and John and Harriet Pennington. Tom found them all to be extremely friendly, not at all stuffy. The two men were full of common sense. Harriet was outgoing and irreverent. Conversation centered on life in Britain compared to life in the United States. The talk was always friendly and often amusing. Later, Harriet told Jane that Forester seemed to be an extremely likeable fellow, and handsome to boot. Jane agreed, but said nothing to any of them about Helen's feelings towards the man.

As the evening wore on, Jane got to know Forester better. As she did, she liked him more and more. Forester, she found, was intelligent and good-natured. Being an American, he was informal and self-confident, but not brash and ill mannered. In fact, he was extremely polite, an attribute Jane admired. She also admired his modesty. Not once to anyone did Forester call attention to his achievements in the air. Only by talking with Harry Collins did Jane learn that Tom was an ace, with six kills to his credit.

"Why didn't you tell me you've shot down all those Germans?"

"It didn't seem relevant. Besides, many in the RAF have done better and, in any case, talking about one's own exploits is poor form."

"That's true, but six planes is quite an accomplishment."

"My crew chief, Sergeant McGowan, certainly thinks so." Tom then explained what crew chiefs do, adding a description of the sergeant.

"I suspect he's very proud of you."

"I guess so, but . . . "

"But what?"

"But there are lots of guys who risk their necks as I do. Some do well, some not so well. What counts is how we do together as a squadron or as a group."

"I suppose you're right. Yet six enemy planes is something to be proud of. It means you're good at what you do."

"I am proud of it, Jane. I just don't think I should talk about it. It would sound like bragging and that makes me feel uncomfortable."

"Major Collins and Major Williams don't seem to mind. They've been telling people all night that you are a real leader, on the ground and in the air. And that other fellow, Major . . . " Jane was searching for Fred Hawkins's name.

"Hawkins."

"Right, Hawkins. Well, Major Hawkins said, as only an American would, that you were the 'best in the business.'"

Tom was embarrassed and slightly annoyed. "Jane, I'd pay very little attention to what those three said. They've obviously had too much to drink and don't know what they're talking about." Tom made a mental note to himself to speak with all three men once back at Bromley Park. He then continued speaking to Jane. "All I do is my job and, while I try to do the very best I can, there are other group commanders out there who do the job just as well, if not better."

Jane put a hand on Forester's shoulder and spoke sweetly, but with conviction. "I doubt that very much, Colonel Forester."

By the time Tom was ready to leave, Jane could see why Helen was so attracted to him. Moreover, she had decided that Forester would be good for her. Not one thing about Tom had she found not to like. While Jane knew that no man was perfect and that Forester undoubtedly had flaws—Herbert certainly did—she believed the

American would bring comfort and companionship to her friend. She trusted he would bring love as well.

In effect, Tom had passed a test. He had gained Jane Ashcroft's approval. She now sanctioned a romance between the two. Of course, Forester had said very little to suggest any such relationship. Indeed, he had been most circumspect. Other than their brief exchange of words before meeting Helen upstairs, he had given no hint of his feelings towards Helen. Yet Jane sensed that he cared. That Tom treated Helen well mattered greatly because Jane, ever protective of her friend, did not want to see her hurt. Above all, she wanted Helen to be happy. *Tom Forester could probably do that though God knows where this will end.*

Only twice more that night did Tom again see Helen. She had said she would keep her distance and, except for the brief encounter in the library, had done so. The next time Forester saw Helen, they were in the company of three others. Helen was cordial, making introductions all round, but gave no hint of familiarity other than that expected of a hostess.

The following time was different. Just before leaving, Tom had gone upstairs to retrieve his service cap and coat. As he came out of the room, Helen was there. They were alone. Helen had made sure of that.

She took hold of his hand and squeezed it, speaking in a voice no louder than a whisper. "I'm glad you came."

"Are you okay? I've missed you."

"I've missed you, too. Jane thinks you're smashing."

"She's a nice lady, but I really only care what you think."

"I think I need you very much."

Hearing voices coming up the stairs, they moved away from one another. Tom spoke first.

"I will call you very soon."

"I shall be waiting." As the voices drew nearer Helen spoke in a more normal voice. "How kind of you to come, Colonel Forester. I do hope you had a pleasant time."

Tom said that he did and, passing four guests who had come to find their coats, walked down the stairs. At the bottom waiting for him were Collins, Williams, and Hawkins.

"You gentlemen ready to go?"

The three replied that they were. As Hoskins opened the door, Forester led them out onto Temple Court. The night was cold, yet comfortable. Rain had come and gone. Tom looked up into the black sky. A few stars were visible among the clouds. He decided he was one very lucky fellow.

FOURTEEN

Eight days passed before Tom was able to return to London. During this time, he flew seven missions. He also christened an ice cream plant and hosted the Sedgewick town leaders.

Harry Collins had purchased the plant the day before Helen's party. Colonel Tee had it up and running four days later. Churning out eighty gallons every other day, the ice cream it produced was extremely popular at Bromley Park. The ice cream also was a hit with the visitors from Sedgewick who, starting with lunch, spent an afternoon at the airfield. Numbering fourteen men and three women, they toured the hangers, mess halls, infirmary, and control tower. They received a briefing on fighter operations from Fred Hawkins and heard Harry Collins discuss the Luftwaffe, albeit in sanitized form. In addition, they inspected two P-47s Forester had ordered placed near the control tower. To prevent mishaps, Tom had insisted the aircraft be neither armed nor fueled.

The highlight of the visit was a dazzling display of aerobatics by a Thunderbolt with Lieutenant Leroy Richards at the controls. The Kid threw the plane all over the sky, concluding the performance with a perfect three-point landing. After Richards had taxied to a stop in a handstand adjacent to the two empty P-47s, Harry Collins remarked to Forester that the Kid had given the Sedgewick visitors quite a thrill. "No doubt they enjoyed it," Tom replied. "I'm just glad he was able to find Bromley Park when it was over."

None of Forester's seven missions involved escorting B-17s. The missions were all fighter sweeps. Mandated by General Harrison, they were intended to entice the Luftwaffe into combat. The Eighth Air Force called this type of mission a "Rodeo." They were aggressive in spirit and, in comparison with escort missions, simple to plan.

Unfortunately, they also were unproductive. Rodeos had not worked earlier in the year, and did not work now. Hence the Germans tended to ignore Rodeos. Only when the bombers were aloft did the Luftwaffe come up to fight. Thus, Forester's flights drew no opposition. Tom was frustrated with the tactic and disappointed with its results. In seven missions, the 19th Fighter Group registered no kills. The only benefit was the experience gained by new pilots. Forester acknowledged this. He knew that a pilot with a few missions under his belt was more likely to be useful when the enemy did appear.

Despite not traveling to London, Tom did talk with Helen soon after the party. He called her on Friday and they spoke for several minutes. She was delighted to hear his voice. He was thankful she was at home when he called. While their conversation was not awkward, it lacked intimacy. At times, the telephone can dissolve the distance between people. In this instance, it did not. Tom and Helen felt separated from one another. Neither liked the feeling. Thus, when Forester said he could get to London next Thursday, Helen was pleased. And when Helen said she would set aside the entire day, Tom was delighted.

Helen now looked forward to Thursday. More than once she wondered whether Tom would toss restraint aside and hold her in his arms. She hoped that he would. Forester, too, looked forward to their being together. But, unlike Helen, Tom spent little time thinking about next week's rendezvous. Until Thursday came, Forester focused primarily on affairs at Bromley Park. Only occasionally did his mind wander off to Helen Trent. These moments were sweet. A few were very sweet. Yet his attention almost always was directed to the business at hand. While he mused that the war was interfering with his love life, Tom knew he would give the Army top priority. He had come to England to fight, not make love. That he could do both without disservice to the other did not occur to Forester. In a short time, six days to be exact, it would. Tom would learn that work and play do mix, that he could have the pleasure of Helen's company while remaining true to Bromley Park and its P-47s.

They had agreed to meet at the Victoria and Albert museum. As the museum was not far from Temple Court, Helen decided to walk. She left the house early, giving herself ample time to meet Tom at 10:30 A.M., the time he said he would arrive.

She was wearing a green plaid skirt and a simple white silk blouse. Around her waist was a black leather belt with a pewter buckle. Her belt, blouse, and skirt were complemented by a green tweed sweater. The look was smart, yet subtle, certainly not dressy. Helen had chosen the outfit carefully. She wanted to be comfortable, yet suitably dressed for wherever they might go. She also wanted to please Forester. Thus, Helen's ensemble had to balance several competing interests. She thought she had found the appropriate mix.

The weather on Thursday was dreary. The sun was absent, replaced by dirty white misty clouds that dominated the sky. While rain had not yet appeared, the BBC weather service had forecast a light drizzle for most of the morning and afternoon. The temperature was 59 degrees Fahrenheit—almost chilly.

Despite the weather, Helen was in good spirits. With her pocketbook slung over her left shoulder and an umbrella in her right hand, she strode briskly down Cromwell Street, hoping to get some exercise, anxious to reach her destination.

As she walked, Helen saw evidence of German raiders. Destruction was noticeable, but here in the western part of London, most buildings were untouched. Most of the bombs fell on the East End near the Thames dockyards among working class homes and businesses. Despite receiving a disproportional share of Luftwaffe activity, the residents there harbored little class resentment at their more fortunate neighbors to the west. Loyalty to the Crown proved stronger than class-consciousness, especially after Buckingham Palace was bombed and the King, given the opportunity to leave, chose to remain in the city.

Along Cromwell Street, Helen saw many people, most of whom seemed to be in a hurry. She decided to play her game of imagining what purpose, contrary to their appearance, people had as they moved about. She saw a Royal Marine whom she decided was a drama teacher late for rehearsal. A studious looking fellow dressed in a striped suit and wearing a bowler was a sales clerk for a plumbing company. And, as Helen neared the museum, she saw an elegant, well-dressed woman whom she decided ran an orphanage.

When Helen arrived at the museum, Tom was getting out of a taxi. They practically bumped into each other.

"Hello there," said Tom, smiling at her

"What perfect timing." Helen's pleasure at seeing Tom was obvious. "How nice to see you. I've been looking forward to today."

"Me too." He took her hand and squeezed it. Forester would have preferred kissing Helen gently on the cheek, but restrained himself. He thought kissing a woman on the steps of the Victoria and Albert Museum so early in the morning might be considered inappropriate.

Helen, unaware of what Tom was thinking, asked an entirely reasonable question. "Do we have a plan?"

Before leaving for London this morning, Forester had realized that he would need to have at least suggestions as to what they might do, so he had obtained a tourist's guide to the city. Looking up the Victoria and Albert Museum, their point of rendezvous, he saw that the museum had much to offer. "I thought we might start here, at the museum. "I'm told it's rather interesting."

"It is that," replied Helen. With her eyes twinkling and her mouth about to break into a wide grin, she continued speaking, "and it does have one particular advantage."

"What's that?"

She took hold of Tom's arm and guided him up to the museum's front door. "Location, dear boy. It's but a few steps and we'll be inside."

They spent the next two hours in the museum. Although they saw much, Helen and Tom visited but a fraction of the museum's galleries, which stretch some seven miles over four floors. Opened in 1857, the Victoria and Albert concentrates on art and design, materials and technology. However, during the war, these galleries had been emptied of many prized possessions in order to keep them safe from damage and destruction by German bombs. Clothing and metal works were still on display, and it was these that Tom and Helen viewed.

By a little after noon, they had seen enough. They were now ready to focus upon one another. Tom suggested they have lunch. Hungry, Helen agreed, remarking that "lunch" was a term Americans used.

"I sometimes think," said Tom, "we speak a different language."

"Maybe our Advisory Committee should publish a dictionary," replied Helen.

"Not a bad idea, although upon arriving here in England, we were all given a booklet that listed a bunch of words translated into British."

"You mean English."

"I mean the language you speak here in Britain."

Amused, Helen decided to challenge Forester. "So you would know the American for," here she paused and thought a moment, "pram, bobby, and the underground."

Equally amused, Tom accepted the challenge. "Let's see, that would be a baby carriage, policeman, and the subway."

"Very good. Now it's your turn."

"All right." Now Forester thought for a minute. "Okay, I've got it. How about giving me the 'English' for a raincoat, a truck, and a string bean."

"The first two are easy. We call what you call a raincoat a mack-intosh. A truck is a lorry." Now Helen stopped. Tom could see she was thinking hard. When she spoke, Helen was throwing her hands up in surrender. "And I have absolutely no idea what a string bean is."

"A string bean, dear lady, is, according to my handy *Guide to Great Britain,* a vegetable you call a French bean. They're green and long like a string."

"And, one of my favorite vegetables."

"Mine too."

"Really?"

"Yes, honest. I do love them, along with carrots and cauliflower."

"I thought all Americans ate were steaks from Kansas City and potatoes from Idaho."

"We do, but we pile on the vegetables to stay healthy."

"You're making me hungry, Tom Forester."

"Well then, I will take you to lunch, or rather, I'll provide you with a noonday meal."

"A splendid idea. I know of a nearby place that will do nicely. There we can have," Helen paused and smiled at Tom, "something to eat."

A short distance from the Victoria and Albert Museum lies Walton Street where Helen led Tom to a small restaurant. There, they had a simple meal of cheese soup and corned beef hash. More important than the food was the conversation. They talked at great length, and, in doing so, came back together as a couple enthralled with one another. Any shyness that had been in evidence at the museum vanished. They occasionally held hands, and to a couple at the next table, appeared to be two people in love.

At the restaurant, they talked about their respective families and how all families seem to have an odd member or two. They also talked about careers, noting that the unexpected often derails the best of plans. Tom spoke of Dartmouth and the Air Corps, and how the war postponed admission to graduate school. Helen again men-tioned Peter and her decision to withdraw from the university to be with the man she loved. Boldly, Tom said that, despite a few girl-friends, he had not been truly in love, until now. Helen chose neither to ignore nor dismiss the remark. She responded almost sternly, hoping to hide the emotion she felt. She said that love was not a trifle, nor something to be confused with physical desire. Forester agreed, adding that a guy had to be honest with himself when confronting his feelings for a woman. Helen asked whether he had done so. Tom replied that he had. He then asked whether, in regard to him, she had done the same.

Before she could reply, to their mutual regret, the waitress came with the bill. This destroyed the intimacy of the moment. Tom had wanted to hear Helen's answer. She was about to say that she found in him someone to confide in, and hold close. Unfortunately, those words were not spoken. Her declaration of love was left unsaid. His question was left unanswered.

The meal cost two shillings and six pence. Forester paid with a half crown, a large silver coin worth exactly the amount required. In his currency, the coin, or "two and six," equaled fifty cents. As many Americans, Tom left a generous tip, a six pence coin. This was appreciated by the waitress who had no idea she had materialized at a most inopportune time.

Upon leaving the restaurant, Tom and Helen decided to go to Harrods, which was but three blocks away. Proving the BBC forecast correct, a light rain had spread across London. Helen opened up her umbrella, which Tom held as they, bunched together, walked to the famous department store.

In a conscious effort to recapture their intimate mood, Helen nestled up against Tom, and spoke with genuine feelings. "I feel much better when I'm in your company."

"I'm glad of that." Forester too wanted to rekindle their connection. He decided to speak frankly. Although he did not wish to pressure Helen, he was more conscious than she that their time together was limited. "Last week I told you that I think I'm in love with you."

"I remember every word. It makes me shiver."

"That's sweet of you, but I couldn't." Despite her words, Helen was pleased Tom had made the offer.

"But you must. I don't even like tea, and I know that you do."

"I do." As she spoke, Helen was trying to hand back the two tins.

"Please, no. You keep them, I'm a coffee drinker."

"Then, dear man, why did you buy them?"

"Because I wanted you to have them. I've come to learn how the English love their tea."

In Britain, tea was, and still is, a national institution. Not only a beverage, it was also a moment in time when the Brits, at home and abroad, stopped what they were doing in order to fix tea and enjoy a brief respite. Mid-morning and late afternoon, in company with their colleagues, comrades, friends, or family, the people of England had their spot of tea. Americans found the practice incredibly inefficient. The British thought it eminently civilized.

Thirty minutes later, having wandered about Harrods to their satisfaction, Helen and Tom walked out of the department store. Helen was holding the cans of tea. Tom was holding her umbrella, which he opened upon stepping outside. The rain had continued, but remained a drizzle.

People without umbrellas were scampering along the street. Those with them moved at a steadier pace. Helen had tucked her arm around Tom's and spoke first as they strolled towards Knightsbridge.

"I should like to walk a bit. You don't mind the rain, do you?" Helen asked.

"Not at all. I fly in it, so I certainly can walk in it. Besides, with you next to me, I won't notice the weather."

"Silly man."

"Where shall we go? When I fly, I usually know where I'm going," Tom responded jokingly.

"Let's just see where we end up. I just want to walk and have you beside me."

"That sounds good to me. I'm in no hurry to be anywhere."

Where they ended up was in Kensington Gardens. Beneath several trees, they found a spot where they could be alone. A park bench, which Forester wiped dry with his handkerchief, allowed them to sit. Before doing so, Tom turned to Helen and brought his right hand up to her cheek. Again he spoke boldly.

"I love you, Helen Trent. This may not be the best time to tell you, but it's true. And given this crazy world, it's probably not a convenient time to fall in love. But I have, with you."

Helen took his hand and kissed it. She was glad he had returned to the subject most on her mind. Setting down the cans of tea upon the bench, she replied in a trembling voice. "It frightens me to hear you say that, because I find myself wanting to be with you."

Forester leaned forward and kissed Helen. She responded willingly. They had kissed before, but not like this. Here in Kensington Gardens, the embrace was passionate. Each gave in to the urgency of their feelings. Tom dropped the umbrella and held Helen close. She offered no resistance and pressed her body into his. The kiss continued. Forester felt connected to the woman in his arms. She felt safe, eager to express her feelings.

Helen spoke first, but did not push Tom away. "I like that very much, but I need to catch my breath. I feel off center, as though my life is slowly spinning. I've not kissed like that in a long time."

Still holding Helen, with his face close to hers, Tom also was breathless. "I feel like nothing else matters but you and me. The war, your husband—they can all go to hell, and stay there. I do love you Helen. I'm not just saying some pretty words."

"I believe you. I want to believe you. But . . . "

"But what?"

"But what have we started? We could stop now and keep our lives intact, the way they were probably planned to be. I could go on playing wife to Robert Trent and you could fight your war and stay away from me. But we won't, I know we won't. And I don't want us to, anyway."

"Nor do I, nor would I let you. You and I belong together. We're good for each other. Trust me, Helen. Trust me and let me love you and take care of you."

"I will, Tom, but I'm scared. Not of you, but of the future. What will we do? What will happen to us?"

"We will love each other and take the future one day at a time. Remember, what we have is special, something to nurture and cherish.

"I will remember that, I promise."

"And please, don't be frightened."

"I am frightened, but it doesn't matter. What matters is this."

As she spoke the last four words, Helen put both arms around Forester's neck and kissed him. He in turn lifted her up off the bench and spun her around. When he stopped, they were still kissing. Neither wanted to stop. So they didn't. Both Helen and Tom were finding pleasure in the other's passion and in their own. Each understood they now possessed life's greatest gift—someone to love and be loved by.

Again, Helen spoke first. "I need to sit down."

"Are you okay?"

"Yes, thank you. I'm much better than okay. I just need to settle myself. I'm not used to this sort of thing."

"Me neither." As he continued speaking, Tom began to laugh. "But I think I could get used to it."

"You're going to have to," Helen was not laughing. She had spoken in grave tones, which remained as she continued speaking. "I don't think I'm going to be able to make do without you or your kisses."

Sensing Helen's mood, Tom ditched his lightheartedness. When he spoke again, his voice sounded almost stern. "Nor can I do without yours."

For a moment, neither of them moved or said a word. Then in unison, they came together and embraced. This time the kiss was brief, but still passionate.

Helen was breathing heavily. Gently, she pushed Tom away. "We'd better stop or this will get out of control."

"I suppose you're right." Forester kissed Helen gently on her forehead. "But God, I love being with you."

Consciously, Helen had decided to lower the temperature. She wanted the romance to remain, but here in a public park she concluded that the passion needed to be defused. With a bit of mischief in her eyes and a big smile, Helen responded to Tom's last remark with a question.

"More than flying?"

The tactic worked. Helen could tell Tom was surprised by the question, although she admired how quickly he recovered. At first, Forester thought he would respond positively, telling Helen what he believed she wished to hear, namely that her company was more enjoyable than flying. However, he knew that would be untrue. Nothing equaled the joy of sailing above the clouds, especially in a P-47. Yet Helen's company was extraordinarily special. Tom felt that Helen made his life complete. She heightened his senses, making everything more vivid. In her presence, he felt as though he never again needed to meet another female. In truth, he loved flying and this woman.

Tom decided upon a simple solution. He would tell the truth.

"I love you as much as I love flying. When I'm with you, I'm lost in the world we share. When I'm up in the sky, I'm aware of the power and beauty of flight and think of little else."

"You're an honest man, Tom Forester. It's one reason I care so much about you."

They sat down on the bench and spent the next several hours holding hands and conversing. The rain had stopped and, while the sun remained invisible, the weather allowed them to remain outside.

As always, they had no difficulty in finding topics to discuss. At one point, Helen was describing rationing when Tom pointed out that not only did the British government limit food and clothing, but it also rationed sunshine. "I knew it rained a lot in England, but not until I got here did I understand that the sun, like sugar, was in such short supply." Helen responded that too much sun was unhealthy and that all the rain accounted for England being so green. At another point, Tom was discussing the party for Sir Robert when Helen mentioned his encounter with Lady Roberts. Forester said she was an interesting lady, to which Helen replied that she lacked good taste and a sense of propriety. Tom was about to say that he found the woman attractive when he realized such a remark would be unwise. His silence led Helen to say that Jane Ashcroft had told her of Edna's proposition and that both she and Jane had greeted Forester's response with delight.

"Oh, she really wasn't all that attractive," said Tom rather lamely.

"You're a rotten liar, dear boy," Helen kissed Tom on his cheek, "but I appreciate the effort."

By late afternoon, they both were ready to leave Kensington Gardens. Helen suggested they have tea, which is what they did. At a small shop on Bayswater Road, they spent another hour together. Again, they enjoyed each other's company. After the waitress cleared their table, Tom was about to suggest they have dinner later in the evening when Helen, too abruptly, Forester thought, announced she soon would have to be leaving.

Tom reacted with surprise. "Oh, I thought we were going to have the entire day together."

"That's what I said, isn't it? I meant the afternoon and morning." Helen felt awful. She was disappointing Tom and introducing a sour note into what otherwise had been a splendid day. "I'm sorry. Truly I am. Robert and I have plans for the evening to which I'm committed. I'd rather be with you, but I can't."

Forester said nothing. He was trying to hide his disappointment, although not succeeding. However, the annoyance he felt he did hide.

Suddenly Helen's face brightened. She had thought of a solution, a plan that would please them both. "I am free tomorrow night, though."

"Tomorrow night? That's Friday. I just assumed you'd be busy."

"I'm not. Robert is having a dinner meeting at his club, so I'm not expected anywhere."

"So we could have dinner?"

"Yes, we could." Helen reached across the table and took hold of Tom's hand. "I'd like that."

Ten minutes later, harmony restored, they parted company. Outside the restaurant and still unhappy about the mix-up, Helen gave Tom a brief, but warm and loving kiss. "Til next time, dear boy." She then went home to get ready for the evening's engagement. She and Sir Robert were dining with Jock Appleby and his wife, Susan. A decent fellow, and old friend of Robert's, Jock was the family's solicitor.

Once home, Helen went upstairs, undressed, and took a lengthy bath. As she swished about in the porcelain tub, awash with suds, Helen became acutely consciously of her body. When she dribbled water over her breasts, her thoughts turned to Forester. *This whole thing is crazy, but I really do think I love him and need him.* She then wondered what tomorrow night would bring. She assumed the evening would be romantic. She hoped it would also involve pleasures of the flesh.

Unlike Helen, Tom had dinner alone on Thursday. By choice, he decided not to eat at one of the clubs frequented by Americans, deciding to spend a quiet evening with himself. Almost every night since coming to England, Forester had dined with others. This evening was different. He ate alone and over much of the meal, reviewed fighter tactics, hoping to improve the performance of the 19th Fighter Group. He also thought about the Advisory Committee whose subcommittee reports were circulating for comment. But over dessert, he put aside the business of the Army Air Force, turning his attention to the woman in his life.

At first, Forester wondered whether his attraction to Helen would affect his work at Bromley Park. The matter was not trivial. His job required total concentration and he had seen more than one pilot distracted by a woman. Tom decided Helen Trent would not interfere with his work either in the air or on the ground, because he would not allow it. Forester had always compartmentalized his life. Helen had become a new component, additive to the others. Tom did not integrate the pieces or permit mergers, and would not do so now. Helen would receive Forester's complete attention when they were together and when she was in his thoughts. But when other matters arose, such as those relating to P-47s, Helen would be put aside, tucked safely away in mental storage. This didn't mean she wasn't important. She was. It meant simply that Tom dealt separately with the different aspects of his life, as men tend to do.

Over dessert, Forester recalled how lovely Helen looked and how he treasured her company. Despite their differences, he thought they made a terrific couple. Forester found Helen fascinating and felt truly in love. He believed Helen was in love as well, despite her reluctance to use the word.

The next morning, Forester went back to Harrods before calling upon Jimmy Dixon in the townhouse at Grosvenor Square. The Colonel was at his desk when Sergeant Howard announced the visitor. Dixon put down his papers and warmly greeted Forester. The two men had come to like each other. They spent the next hour talking about Eighth Air Force tactics and the Advisory Committee. Regarding the former, they agreed that Rodeos were useless. As to the Committee, Dixon said he intended to have a completed report to General Eaker by December 1.

Before leaving, Forester obtained from Dixon the name of a restaurant where he might take Helen to dinner. Of course, Tom made no reference to Helen nor did Dixon, from which Tom deduced that the Deputy Air Attaché suspected nothing. Had Dixon even hinted at an involvement with Helen, Tom was prepared to bring up Lady Roberts whom Forester believed had enticed Jimmy to a private rendezvous following the party for Sir Robert.

After leaving Dixon's office, Forester went in search of a suitable hotel where he might take Helen after dinner. Tom had not far to look for he found a small one in Mayfair, just two blocks from Grosvenor Square. The hotel was three stories high and painted white. It had fourteen rooms, all expensive and all furnished nicely.

Forester took a room for two nights, paying in advance. At his request, the room had a double bed.

Tom was uncertain how Helen would react to the hotel room. He hoped she would be pleased. Twice now they had stopped kissing in public when the embrace became too passionate. A room in a hotel would provide much needed privacy. Yet Forester realized that a few such kisses did not automatically lead to a rendezvous in bed. Possibly, Helen might be offended by his action. More likely, she might be reluctant to take such a step. Tom thus intended to proceed cautiously. At the appropriate time, he would mention the hotel room to Helen. Hopefully she would agree to accompany him there. By now, Tom very much wanted to make love with her. To do so, he needed a place to which they could retreat. He was pleased he had found such a nice one.

They met at Trafalgar Square shortly after sunset.

Helen had dressed with the intent to dazzle Forester, and succeeded. She wore a prewar long silk dress that covered most of her body, yet in a subtle fashion accentuated her curves while still paying tribute to her slim figure. The dress was black, highlighted by an amethyst necklace and matching earrings. She had pulled her hair back and off to one side and, as always, used little makeup. In lieu of a coat, she wore a floor length, black woolen cape with a large hood, lined in red satin. Black evening gloves completed the ensemble.

Forester was speechless. The woman before him looked like a goddess. Never had he seen such a lovely creature. That she was to be his companion for the evening filled him with excitement.

When finally he spoke, it was from the heart. "Hello there. You look terrific."

Helen was pleased that Tom liked what he saw. While dressing, she suddenly had become conscious of her age and for a moment, feared that she would not be able to make this younger man take notice. This was the first time she had experienced such a thought. She found it most unsettling. Now, judging by Forester's reaction, Helen concluded her fear was unfounded. This too pleased her. So, when she replied she too spoke from the heart.

"Thank you. I'm glad you approve."

Helen then took hold of Forester and, to his surprise, kissed him. The kiss was tender. Tom held Helen close, delighted with the kiss, yet still in awe of her appearance.

Forester moved away and, to Helen's surprise, began to laugh. "I don't suppose we could just stay here and kiss?"

"I'm afraid not. One, you promised to take me to dinner and two, there are too many people around here."

"Well then, my lady, take my hand and we'll take care of number one." To himself, he said that number two would be dealt with later.

Dinner was a great success. Though its food was mediocre, the restaurant's ambiance was perfect. Colors were muted, lights were low, service was discreet, and a piano played by a man enveloped in cigarette smoke provided romantic sounds. On each table, candles cast a warm, reflective glow. Tom and Helen enjoyed themselves immensely.

At one point in the evening, just before dessert, Tom took out a cardboard box from beneath the table. He had given the box to the maître d' earlier in the day, shortly after making the hotel reservation. Helen had not seen the package, which was tied with a yellow ribbon.

Forester handed the box to Helen who was genuinely surprised. "Here, this is for you. I hope you like it."

"Aren't you sweet?" Helen untied the ribbon, which she rolled up and put in her purse. She then opened the box. "Why it's lovely. Aren't you a dear?"

She held up the cashmere scarf from Harrods. "It's beautiful and I love the color." As she spoke, Helen felt a tinge of guilt over her reaction to Tom not purchasing the scarf for her when she first saw it at Harrods.

"I'm glad. I saw you eyeing it, and decided then and there that you should have it."

"I shall wear it often, and when I do, I will think of you."

Dinner also was expensive. The bill came to three pounds six shillings, or $13.20. Having already paid for the hotel room, a bottle of sherry, the scarf, two days worth of meals, and several taxis, Forester was spending more money than usual. Of course, he could afford it. Tom's yearly pay as a Lieutenant Colonel was $3,500. This was supplemented by flight pay and an allowance for overseas service. Normally, Forester was frugal with money. Most of what he had earned since joining the Army had been deposited in two banks, one back in the States and one here in England. In October 1943, the accounts totaled a little over $3,000.

During World War II, American soldiers and sailors were well compensated. For example, Ira Eaker as a Lieutenant General drew a base pay of $8,000 annually. Generally speaking, Americans received higher salaries than did their British counterparts. At times, this led to friction particularly at the lower ranks. The Tommies often complained that the Yanks were "overpaid, oversexed, and over here."

Once dinner was over, neither Helen nor Tom wished the evening to end. Helen was hoping that Tom had planned something that would enable them to spend further time together. In fact, Tom had two possibilities in mind. The first was to go dancing. The second was to go to the hotel. Anxious to take Helen to bed, Tom chose the latter. Then Forester did something he had not done since his freshman year at Dartmouth. He lost his nerve.

"I had thought we might go dancing, although I should warn you I'm no Fred Astaire."

"That's a good idea." Helen had no inkling of what had just passed through Tom's mind. She simply was relieved he had not assumed their evening together consisted just of dinner. Helen liked to dance. She was about to ask where Forester would be taking her when Tom made the question unnecessary.

"I'm told the Imperial Hotel has a nice dance band and cocktail lounge. We could go there. It's not far from here. We could actually walk there."

"Sounds right on. And not to worry, Ginger and I have little in common."

This last remark was for Tom's benefit. In fact, Helen was a very good dancer. She had downplayed her ability in order to put Forester at ease.

She also cast aside restraint. Helen knew that dancing in public with Forester entailed the risk of being recognized. At this moment, she did not care. She wanted to spend time with Forester, on the dance floor and off it.

Helen and Tom left the restaurant, arm in arm, and began to walk to the Imperial Hotel, located a few blocks south of Grosvenor Square. The streets were dark and the two proceeded cautiously, anxious not to trip over a curb or bump into someone.

Halfway to the hotel, Tom saw a shape emerge from the dark in front of them. At the same time, he heard voices that he recognized. Within seconds, the shape came into focus. It was an American officer escorting a woman with a British accent. The man was Jimmy Dixon.

With the seasoned reflexes of a fighter pilot, Tom quickly took hold of Helen and steered her off to the side. He then pulled up her hood, making the woman invisible to anyone passing by. As Dixon and his companion approached, Tom kissed Helen with considerable fervor. At first surprised, she responded in kind. Forester prolonged the embrace. Finally, he let go of Helen, who spoke first.

"That was unexpected, though, mind you, I'm not complaining."

"I'm afraid, my love, while I liked it a lot, it was a bit of a diversion. That man who just walked by, well we know him. It was Jimmy Dixon."

"Oh dear." Helen seemed more saddened than alarmed.

"Not to worry, he didn't see either of us."

"That's good. But I suppose it means that dancing at the hotel might be unwise."

"Only if we're seen."

"Which we probably will be." Helen now became cautious and spoke more soberly. "I'm not quite ready for that, Tom." She nestled up against Forester. "So we'll need to do something else. I don't want our evening to end."

Now Forester, now. And stay calm. Remember, you're not the first guy to ever do this. "I don't either. Look Helen, I don't know quite how to say this, but I've taken a hotel room where you and I can have some privacy. It's not far from here and it's a very nice place. I can't promise you a band and a dance floor, but I can say no one will see us."

Helen's reaction was all that Tom hoped it would be. At first surprised, she then decided she was pleased, despite recognition that Forester has crossed an important boundary. Helen found Tom's awkwardness amusing, but was glad he had acted with the foresight and decisiveness she wanted her man to exhibit.

"Aren't you wicked?" asked Helen, taking hold of Tom's hand. "Well, lead the way, Colonel Forester. If I'm to sin, I'd prefer it be with you and you alone."

Tom's lodgings were on the second floor. Having kept the key to his room, he had no need to stop by the front desk. Thus, he and Helen, upon entering the hotel, proceeded directly up the stairs. Neither of them noticed that the hotel's owner, on duty at the reception area, gave them an approving smile. In 1917, he had been on leave in London and before returning to the trenches he had spent two nights with a woman he adored.

Once inside the room, Helen took off her cape, which Forester hung behind the door. Quickly glancing about, she commented to herself that the room was attractively furnished and in no way tawdry as she momentarily feared it might be. Off to the side of the bed was a small table on which stood a bottle of sherry and two glasses.

"Would you care for some sherry?" asked Tom. To Helen he appeared a bit nervous.

"Yes, I'd like that." Actually, Helen had little desire for sherry, but had responded in order to appear appreciative.

Tom poured the sherry and brought Helen her glass.

"To you, Helen Trent."

"No. To us."

They sipped their sherry and Forester appeared to relax. He soon went over to the nightstand. There he lit a candle he had purchased for this occasion at Harrods. Then he walked over to the wall and flipped the light switch so that only the flickering candle provided light to the room. His next step was to turn on the radio from which emerged soft music that blended well with candlelight.

"Better?"

"Very nice." Helen was pleased that Tom was creating a romantic mood, although she found amusing his deliberate, step-by-step approach. She made no attempt to block his next move.

"I should like to kiss you, for you are the nicest lady in all the world." With these words, Forester took hold of Helen and kissed her. Gently at first, then with increasing urgency, the kiss continued.

Helen very much enjoyed the embrace, but soon moved away. Tom's reaction was one of disappointment. Swiftly, she spoke to alleviate his concern.

"Not to worry. I only wanted to say that this time, at last, we're alone and don't have to stop."

She then pulled Forester close and kissed him. The kiss was passionate and lengthy. Their bodies came together and their arms held each other tightly. When they finally separated, Helen spoke first.

"Turn around and don't peek."

Tom did as he was told. He heard the rustling of clothes, and took off his service jacket. As he did so, he heard Helen's voice.

"Now you can turn around."

Helen had undressed and was wearing nothing but a satin slip and the amethyst necklace. Black, held in place by two thin shoulder straps, the garment billowed out at her breasts and then hung loosely, ending several inches above her knees. To Forester, she looked enchanting, both innocent and erotically tempting. He felt as though he had died and gone to heaven.

The soft light of the candle hid signs of Helen's age, which, to his credit, Tom would not have thought important.

Forester went over to Helen and put his hands upon her hips. Slowly and tenderly, as though caressing this woman with the palms of his hands, he brought his arms up to her shoulder, then past her neck up to her cheeks. He then kissed her as his hands gently moved about her body. Helen did not object. She enjoyed the sensation of having the man she cared for begin to take possession of her.

"I love you, Helen Trent."

"I'm so pleased that you do." Helen went over to the bed, drew down the bedspread, and lay down.

Tom took her seductive action to be the invitation that it was. He then removed his clothes and joined Helen on the bed.

He lay on his back next to her. Very soon, he pulled her on her side so that she faced him. Her softness, her smell, her smile all began to overwhelm him. When he began to speak, she quickly put her hand over his mouth and said now was not the time for words. Helen then slid on top of Forester and kissed him without restraint.

As they embraced, Helen and Tom came together. Their coupling was smooth and completely natural, totally consistent with their desires. As Tom entered her, Helen moaned. She felt filled up and remembered how much she loved making love. Helen wanted Forester to stay connected, to make their unity last her lifetime.

Tom felt enveloped by Helen. If he was penetrating her, she was surrounding him on all sides. Never had he felt such pleasure. He too wanted their connection to remain intact.

Slowly, in rhythm, they moved in unison. Each uttered sounds of intense joy. Tom looked up and saw Helen's face, beautiful, yet consumed in passion. She was smiling, yet concentrating fully on the man who had invaded her body, pleased that he had done so. Tom tried to stay in control in order to prolong their pleasure. For several minutes, he was able to do so, but as Helen moved back and forth, Tom began to feel surrounded by a swelling that gradually took control of his entire being. Nothing could hold back this feeling. As it rose within him, overtaking his entire body, he exploded in physical delight, crying out to Helen that she and she alone was the woman he needed and loved.

Helen held Tom close, offering soothing words and soft kisses. She had not realized the heights of passion Forester had, but her disappointment, though real, was much mitigated by the physical plea-sures she had experienced and by the knowledge that Tom had expressed in moments when men speak only the truth his total devotion to her.

For twenty minutes, they lay next to each other, exchanging kisses and vows of romance. Completely relaxed, Tom sealed in his memory the image of Helen's face looking up at him with her black hair scattered around the white pillow. Helen's mind was differently engaged. She was reflecting how odd it felt to first make love with a man, then comfort him in a motherly fashion. The only time in her life Helen had experienced a similar feeling was with Peter. She decided this was a good sign. She also decided the feeling repre-sented a unique attribute of women. Only a female could follow such stormy passion with gentle nurturing.

Helen's reflection was soon interrupted. Forester was kissing her. He had started with her feet and was methodically working his way up her body. By the time he reached her neck, Helen was focusing solely on the kisses, which felt marvelous. When, for a moment, Tom halted, she spoke up.

"Don't stop," she whispered.

With a slightly lustful look, Forester replied, "I don't intend to."

He then kissed her mouth, and as she began to respond, Tom pulled down the sheet, exposing her breasts. He then kissed one, twirling his tongue about the nipple. At first surprised, Helen responded approvingly, and encouraged him to continue. She felt enormously aroused. As Forester sucked her nipple, he instinctively dropped his left hand down to the soft mound between her legs. She took his hand and began to move it in a slow circular motion. As her passion grew, Helen pressed his hand down harder, still leading it round and round. Soon, she was succumbing to intense, compelling sensations. As the pleasure intensified, Helen no longer was aware of Tom, concentrating completely on what she was experiencing. She cried out saying simply, "Oh God, oh God." She then fell silent, let-ting a wave of warmth envelop her. Helen felt truly satisfied, immersed in a sea of serenity that matched in scope and enjoyment the pleasure that Forester, with her assistance, had just induced.

Sleep followed their lovemaking. Fortunately, Helen woke up an hour later. She shook Tom and asked him what time it was. Afraid that it was very late, Helen was much relieved to learn his watch read 11:30 P.M. Very soon thereafter, Forester got up and dressed, as did Helen. Only then did he notice she was not wearing a wedding ring.

Outside the hotel, Forester was insisting that he accompany Helen in the taxi to 28 Temple Court. She appreciated the gallantry, but was adamant that she ride alone. Seeing that her mind was made up, Tom relented. He remained on the sidewalk as she entered the taxi they luckily had found almost immediately upon stepping outside.

"I love you, Helen Trent. When will I see you next?" Tom was closing the door to the cab while simultaneously handing the cabbie three shillings, ample fare for Helen's ride home.

"Sooner than you think."

Forester had no idea what she meant.

As the taxi began to pull away, Helen continued speaking. "I don't think I can do without you now."

Tom was about to respond that he felt the same way when he realized Helen would not be able to hear him. Alone in front of the hotel, watching the taxi disappear, Forester became annoyed with himself for not firming up when and where they would next meet. Given their separate lives, arranging a rendezvous was not easy.

When Tom returned to his room, the tussled bed sheets in sight and smell reminded him of Helen. He missed her and went to sleep imagining her next to him. He also wondered when they again would be together.

That evening, Tom slept particularly well. No sounds of aircraft engines disturbed his rest, nor did fighter operations require him to rise at 5:30 A.M. Sprawled comfortably on his bed, he barely heard the knock on the door. At first he ignored it. When the knocking continued, he begrudgingly roused himself. A look at his watch told him the time was 8:45 A.M. Dressed only in undershorts he ambled to the door assuming the hotel owner, for some unknown reason, wished to speak with him.

Forester undid the lock and, still half asleep, opened the door. There, with a picnic basket in hand, bright and cheery, stood Helen Trent.

"Good morning, dear boy." Helen began to laugh at Tom's appearance and expression. "Are you going to invite me in?"

"Yes, of course. Please come in. I'm a bit speechless." Forester escorted Helen to a reading table where she placed the basket. "Have a seat and make yourself comfortable."

He grabbed some clothes and disappeared into the bathroom. "I'll be back in a flash."

Six minutes later, he emerged freshly shaven, bathed, hair combed, and wearing his last clean shirt.

Helen was impressed. "My, that was fast.

"Piece of cake, my dear, piece of cake. Now I need to say good morning to you properly." With that, Tom leaned over and gave Helen a lengthy kiss.

"Much better, much better. Now, I have two surprises for you. One is in this basket." Helen took out from the basket half a loaf of bread, some cheese, jam, two slices of ham, a small can of pineapple juice, utensils, and two cloth napkins. "I know you Yanks love your breakfast, so I've brought you some."

"Wonderful, I'm starving. I will go get us some tea."

"That's sweet of you, but in a few minutes that very pleasant man who owns this hotel and with whom I spoke on my way up will bring us a fresh pot and two cups."

"You're amazing."

"No, crazy perhaps, but not amazing." Helen was pointing to the bed. "You're the one who is amazing."

Breakfast was a great success. The tea arrived and the hotel owner, whose name was Albert Wade, greeted them both as old friends, winking to Forester as he left the room. After finishing his breakfast, Tom was about to ask Helen her plans for the day when a thought occurred to him.

"You mentioned two surprises. What's the second?"

"Ah good. I was hoping you'd remember. Here, have some more tea and sit over by the bed. I'll return in a minute. Helen got up and disappeared into the bathroom.

When she reappeared, she was wearing only a towel. Her hair was piled high upon her head, held together by the yellow ribbon. Walking over to the window Helen made sure the curtains were drawn. She then went to the door and locked it.

Approaching Forester, she said, "Your second surprise is me. Helen then leaned forward and kissed Tom with considerable fervor. "Now, pull the ribbon in my hair."

Forester did as he was told. There was no doubt that this morning he would do whatever Helen instructed. As he pulled the ribbon, her abundant black hair tumbled down.

Helen shook her head and ran her hand through her hair. "There, that's better. Now, Tom Forester," Helen put Tom's left hand on the towel between her breasts, "let's see if you can do an equally good job with the towel."

They spent the next three hours in bed and on the floor, exhausting themselves in lovemaking that was both torrid and tender. Around noon, they dressed and, after a brief meal, decided to see a movie. When they parted, Tom made certain they had agreed upon their next meeting.

Forester went back to Bromley Park. He flew six missions in the next eight days, yet found time for numerous administrative matters.

Helen returned home. On both Saturday and Sunday nights, and Mondays as well, she and her husband dined out with friends. With his departure set for Thursday, November 4, Sir Robert hoped to socialize as much as possible. He knew there would be limited opportunities to do so once out of the country.

On Tuesday, they remained at 28 Temple Court. Sir Robert spent much of the evening choosing clothes for his trip and then packing them into three large leather suitcases. Helen prepared a simple, but complete dinner, which he appreciated and enjoyed.

"Thank you, my dear, that was a lovely meal."

"I'm glad you enjoyed it," replied Helen in all sincerity. "Shall we be dining out tomorrow or should I be fixing dinner?"

"Ah, yes. Actually, my dear, this is our last dinner together before I leave. And a splendid one it was. We depart frightfully early Thursday morning, so I've made arrangements to stay at my club. I'm sorry, of course, but it's for the best."

To her surprise, Helen was disappointed by this news. Despite earlier suggestions to the contrary, she had expected Sir Robert would spend his last night in England with her, his wife. That she now loved another man did not matter. Robert was her husband and she thought he belonged, this one evening at least, with her in their home.

On Wednesday afternoon, Sir Robert came home from the Colonial Office to fetch his bags and to say good-bye to Helen.

"Good-bye, my dear, I'm off to do the King's business. And I will see you next in just about two months. This happens all over England these days, so we're not so different. Be a good girl and remember that I will be in touch with Hugh Williams by wireless so he'll know my whereabouts."

Sir Robert, who to Helen seemed to be acting a role, then said something Helen did not expect. "Now give me a kiss and I shall be on my way."

Helen obeyed, and kissed Sir Robert on the cheek. He did not return the affectionate gesture. She thought that odd especially with the role he seemed to be playing.

After Sir Robert was gone, Helen retired to the kitchen where she made a cup of tea. This is when the thought struck her, a thought that made her giddy with excitement, as well as slightly guilty. For the next two months, the only man in her life would be Tom Forester. She found this prospect pleasing in the extreme.

FIFTEEN

Forester returned to Bromley Park late Saturday afternoon. On Sunday, he attended church services in Sedgewick. Despite having doubts about church doctrine, Tom found both the sermon and the ceremony meaningful. Preached by the rector of St. Stephen's, the Reverend Jonathon Harper, the sermon emphasized the need for individual acts of mercy in time of war. The ceremony, standard Church of England fare, nicely balanced simplicity and ritual. Forester had gone to Sedgewick to cement Bromley Park's new relationship with the town leaders. He returned a morally strengthened individual.

That Sunday, the 19th Fighter Group did not fly. However, the next day the Group began a week of intensive operations. All the missions were successful. No aircraft aborted. Rendezvous were made on time. Losses were light, with only three Thunderbolts failing to return. Most importantly, the Luftwaffe was hit hard. The Group downed nine enemy aircraft, all Me-109s. Of these, Lieutenant Richards accounted for three, making the Kid an ace.

Forester did less well. Though he flew every mission save one, Tom merely damaged one Me-110. He missed altogether another Messerschmitt that flew right into his sights. Having permitted Sergeant McGowan to paint six small German crosses beneath his plane's canopy, Tom at first wondered whether vanity had jinxed his luck. He decided it had not. More important than luck, he concluded, was skill, especially the ability to shoot straight and hit the target. Forester concluded he had fired too soon, ignoring his own advice to get in close.

Miles away from Bromley Park, Mike McCready took notice of the 19th Fighter Group's successes. The Deputy Commander of Eighth Air Force fighters was looking for someone to become DFO, having decided he would convince General Eaker to remove Richard Harrison. Already, he had two candidates in mind. Now, with Forester's group doing so well, he had a third.

Tom would have been aghast had he known what General McCready was contemplating. Director of Fighter Operations meant a desk job at Wycombe Abbey. This would be ideal for someone looking to make a career in the military. Forester's goal was to become a college professor. He had little interest in becoming a Brigadier General, the rank accorded the DFO. For Forester, the war was an interruption, not a stepping stone. Tom was perfectly content at Bromley Park. He was leading P-47s into combat. He thought nothing could be more useful or as much fun.

Each day, paperwork awaited Forester upon his return from flying. Despite Wilbur William's best efforts to screen the flow of paper to the Group Commander, Tom faced a slew of administrative matters that required his personal attention. To properly deal with them, Forester grounded himself on Saturday, devoting the entire day to working at his desk.

Several of the matters concerned key people at Bromley Park. Tom dealt with these first. On Saturday morning, with fresh coffee and a donut by his side, he asked to see Harry Collins.

After participating in the briefing for that day's mission, the Intelligence Officer hurried over to Forester's office, having been told the Group Commander wanted to see him. Upon his arrival, he bumped into Wilbur Williams. Holding sheets of paper under both arms, the Adjutant told Harry to go straight in.

"What's up, Wilbur?"

Williams was smiling. "My lips are sealed. But relax, there's no problem."

Collins knocked at the door and entered. "You wanted to see me, Sir?

"Yes, Harry. Good morning. Have a donut. Some coffee? How'd the briefing go?"

"Well, I think." Collins accepted the proffered coffee, but declined the donut. "Hawkins did his usual good job. Weather's okay. And the pilots seem eager."

"That's good. Any news on the Intelligence front?

"Not much except we've learned Jerry has moved two groups of FW-190s up from the south. They're now based on Germany's border with Belgium."

The Fw-190 was a superb airplane. Fast and well-armed, versatile and rugged, over twenty thousand eventually would be built. In 1942, upon its entry into service, the 190 outclassed the Spitfire and was more than a match for anything the Army Air Force had. By 1943, in improved versions, the aircraft was key to the air defense of the Third Reich. Wisely, Collins had reminded the pilots at the briefing to be extra sharp when tangling with the Fw-190.

Tom now changed the subject. Like Wilbur Williams, he was smiling. "Harry, I've got some interesting news for you. The Army seems to think you're doing a good job, which I happen to agree with, so they've decided to promote you."

"Sir?"

Forester stood up, leaned over, and shook hands with Collins. "Congratulations, you are now a Lieutenant Colonel in the United States Army Air Force."

"Well, thank you, Sir." The Intelligence Officer was as surprised as he was pleased. "I had no idea this was in the works."

"It's well deserved, Harry. You do a great job."

"I appreciate your saying so, Colonel."

The two men then discussed Army life and how promotions are sometimes deserved and sometimes not. Forester told Collins he was working on a promotion for Wilbur Williams. Harry said the Adjutant deserved one, to which Tom agreed.

By voice and body language, Forester indicated he now had something important to say.

"Harry, there's something I want you to do for me."

The Intelligence Officer looked puzzled. Never before had Forester asked for a favor. "I'll be happy to do whatever you want."

From the top of his table desk, Tom took two sealed envelopes and handed them to Harry. "These are two letters I've written and I'd like you to mail them in the event I don't come back here one day."

Lieutenant Colonel Collins knew exactly what Forester meant. Tom's request was not unusual. In every airfield of the Eighth Air Force pilots were making similar requests. Harry looked at the two envelopes. One was addressed to Mr. and Mrs. John Forester in Port Washington, New York. The other was to Helen Trent at 28 Temple Court in London.

The second letter took Collins by surprise. He had no idea Forester was involved with the lady. More power to you Colonel, said Harry to himself. She seems very nice and you deserve the best. Harry put the letters in his pocket.

"I'll take care of these, Colonel. Don't you worry. Let's just hope they'll never have to be sent."

"I don't think they will, Harry." Here, Forester paused. "But just in case Jerry gets lucky . . . "

Now Collins decided to change the subject. The death of the Group Commander was not an eventuality on which he wished to dwell.

"I've heard an interesting rumor about Mike McCready. Seems he's out to dump our friend General Harrison."

"Really? Well I hope he succeeds."

"Rumor has it that he will. But that's not the interesting part. They're looking for a new DFO and guess who's apparently on the list."

"I haven't a clue."

"Well, Colonel, it's you. A buddy of mine is on McCready's staff and says McCready is impressed by how well the 19th Fighter Group is doing and attributes that to you. Which is right. Seems there are three names on the list, and one of them is yours."

"That's crazy." Tom was both surprised and dismissive. "That's a job for someone who's career army and likes to fly a desk. I'm in just for the duration, and have no desire to leave Bromley Park."

"That may be, but you're on the list. Seems McCready wants a pilot with combat experience, unlike Harrison."

"Well, I still think it's a terrible idea. Let's hope I stay right here."

"You may not have a choice."

"True enough, but I trust McCready will come to his senses and pick someone else. What else have you learned from your friend?"

"Something you'll be pleased to hear."

"And what's that?"

Well, General McCready really liked the ice cream we sent him. He's hoping we'll send him some more."

"We can certainly do that."

"I've already put in an order for some chocolate."

"Why chocolate?"

"My spies tell me that Mike McCready likes chocolate ice cream. Actually, my friend that works for McCready told me."

"Now that, Harry, is what I call good intelligence work. Seems the Army knew what it was doing in making you a Lieutenant Colonel."

The next words spoken came from Wilbur Williams. After first knocking, the Adjutant discreetly had entered the room, in time to catch Collin's remark about McCready's preference for chocolate ice cream. Curious about what had preceded the remark, he nonetheless stayed focused, speaking to what had brought him to Forester's office.

"Colonel, the chaplain's outside. He seems very upset, and wants to see you, if you've got a moment."

"Do you know what the problem is? Our padre is usually very calm. This seems out of character."

"It is. But the man is truly upset. It concerns Captain Granelli."

"Why am I not surprised," interjected Harry Collins.

"Harry," said Forester, "why don't you stay? You too, Wilbur."

"I will, Colonel," replied the Adjutant, "but there's one more thing you should know about Granelli. Last night, he got into a brawl in Sedgewick, took a swing at a member of the King's Royal Tank Corps, and busted the guy's jaw. Our M.P.s finally showed up and hauled him off. They put him in our jail where he now sits at this very moment."

"With Captain Granelli, when it rains it pours." Forester was half amused, half annoyed. He turned to his Intelligence Officer. "What do you think, Harry?"

"Colonel, let's hear what the chaplain has to say. Then deal with the Provost Marshal, our good friend, Hightower."

"Our own little Nazi," said Wilbur Williams.

"Now Major, let's be kind. Hightower does a good job."

"I'm just glad he's on our side," said Collins.

"Enough, gentlemen. We need to deal with Granelli, not Hightower."

As Provost Marshal, Robert Hightower served as police chief at Bromley Park. He commanded the detachment of Military Police assigned to the base. Hightower took his duties very seriously and performed them with German efficiency.

"Wilbur, let's do what Harry suggests. Ask the chaplain to come in."

Major Lowell Ackerman had been a Methodist minister in civilian life. He was one of five churchmen on duty at Bromley Park. There were two Roman Catholic priests, another Protestant minister, and a Jewish rabbi. All five provided comfort and religious services to their joint congregation. Of the chaplains, Ackerman was the oldest. He also was the gentlest, being a man of God who

"Wilbur's right, Colonel. The man has to pay a price. The question is how to fit the punishment to the crime. This guy is a bit of a bully and needs to receive a very clear message."

"So what do we do?" asked Forester. "Keep in mind, gentlemen, the man's a good pilot and we need guys up there like him."

"I vote to dock his pay," said Williams. "Even punks like Granelli worry about their bank accounts."

"I say we make Captain Granelli Lieutenant Granelli," responded Harry Collins. "We need to show our friends in Sedgewick and the British authorities that we've taken this thing seriously. A reduction in rank will convey that message."

Having listened, Tom made his decision. "Let's do both and confine him to base for ten weeks. Maybe he'll get the message."

"And if he doesn't?" asked the Adjutant.

"Then," replied Forester, "we'll court martial the s.o.b. and leave him in Major Hightower's care."

"Isn't it strange?" pondered Harry Collins. "We let Granelli go free after killing some guy in a parachute, but punish him for slugging some drunk in a bar who was asking for trouble."

As the Intelligence Officer spoke, an enlisted man entered Tom's office and whispered a few words to the Adjutant who, excusing himself, left the room. Very quickly, Major Williams returned and addressed Forester.

"Colonel, Colonel Jimmy Dixon is on the phone and wants to talk with you. Says it's urgent."

Exactly twenty-four hours before Dixon placed his call to Forester, Helen Trent was at home, about to start her morning's activity. This consisted of laundry and reviewing the section of the draft Advisory Committee report dealing with entertainment in London. She had decided to read the report first and was sitting in the living room curled up on the blue sofa accompanied by a cup of hot tea. To provide background music, Helen had turned on the radio, which she kept at a low volume. The sound was pleasing as the

BBC was broadcasting music from Verdi's *La Traviata*. Helen was about to begin her review when thoughts of Forester crept into her mind.

She smiled as she recalled their most recent rendezvous. Friendship and romance had brought about a truly wonderful time. The passion of Friday night and Saturday morning compounded their pleasure. Helen now felt more alive than she had in years. As of Thursday when they had visited the Victoria and Albert Museum, she was more sensitive to sights and sounds, more aware of her own feelings and desires. Not for years, indeed not since Peter, had she felt this way. All of a sudden, life had become full of excitement. Helen attributed this to Forester. She realized she was falling in love. That it had come unexpectedly added to the thrill.

Helen knew that Tom believed she could not say the word "love." Once he had been correct. No longer. She felt in love with Tom Forester and she looked forward to telling him.

There in the living room, Helen felt connected to Forester, as if they together had become something greater than what they were individually. This feeling she found enormously satisfying. It created in her a sense of completeness. She now longed for Tom, hoping they would see each other soon.

When Helen heard the knock on the front door, she was at first startled. Rising from the sofa, she had no idea who might be calling. Friday was not a usual time for guests, nor were any tradesmen expected. As she walked to the door, Helen imagined that Forester had come to surprise her. Before opening the door, she thus took a quick look in the mirror. All seemed well. Nevertheless, she straightened her skirt and ran her hand through her hair. Helen wanted to look her best should Tom be at the door.

He was not. Instead, Helen found herself looking at Hugh Williams, Sir Robert's assistant at the Colonial Office. He was accompanied by Group Captain Wilfred Grimes and a man she did not recognize. All three men looked tense and hesitant. Grimes appeared shaken.

Helen was surprised to see them. She had no idea why they were here.

"May we come in, Mrs. Trent?" asked Williams.

"Of course." Helen thought it odd they did not apologize for appearing at such an unusual time.

When the visitors were seated in the living room, Helen asked if they might like a cup of tea. Williams politely declined. Then looking directly at Helen, he spoke in a low, but reverent voice.

"Mrs. Trent, I have some dreadful news. There's been an accident—a terrible accident."

As Williams was speaking, Grimes looked to be in great pain. The other man, Reginald Fox, who served as one of two confidential secretaries to Sir Anthony Eden, remained silent, but appeared uncomfortable. He listened intently as Hugh Williams continued to speak.

"The plane Sir Robert was in, a Dakota, crashed as it approached Oran. There were no survivors. Dear lady, I'm afraid your husband has perished. I am so very sorry."

For a moment, Helen did not react. Her mind and body were frozen as she slowly repeated to herself the words that Williams had just said. When these words were linked into a discernable message Helen's first reaction was to deny what she had been told.

"Are you sure? Perhaps there's some mistake. I saw him two days ago. Maybe he survived the crash. People do."

"I'm afraid there were no survivors," replied Grimes. "That dear, dear man is gone."

Helen sat motionless. *Good God, not again.* She put her hands to her head as tears flowed down her cheeks. Rocking slowly back and forth, softly she spoke his name. "Robert, poor dear Bobby."

In an effort to comfort Helen, Reginald Fox reached over and put his hand on her shoulder. Like Williams, he too spoke in a low voice. "Mrs. Trent, Sir Anthony wanted me to be here to express his deepest sympathy and to pledge whatever assistance you might need."

Hugh Williams chimed in with a similar message. "At the Colonial Office, we of course will do whatever we can to help. And I personally am at your service. Please know that you can rely upon me."

Grimes remained silent.

"Thank you gentlemen. Now if you'll excuse me for a moment, I'll return shortly." Helen stood up and went into the kitchen. Feeling as though her knees might give way, she leaned against the pantry door. There, in private, Helen cried out loud. The tears were a trickle, not a torrent, but they were genuine. If she did not love Robert Trent, she at least cared for him. After all, he had always been cordial and generous, and they had lived under the same roof for several years. Soon, Helen forced the tears to subside and, by sheer willpower, she put aside thoughts of Robert. She concentrated on Claire. *I must protect my daughter.*

Within minutes, Helen, now composed, had returned to the living room. The three men rose as she entered and then sat down. They stayed with Helen for the next ninety minutes. The ensuing conversation was a mixture of recollections and planning for the immediate future. Helen decided a memorial service for Sir Robert should be held, choosing St. Andrew's, their parish church. Hugh Williams volunteered to make the arrangements. Reginald Fox said he would instigate the paperwork necessary to secure the pension benefits due the widow of a senior civil servant.

The pension would be modest, but reliable. Helen had little money of her own and required additional funds to live comfortably. She assumed these would come to her via Sir Robert's estate. The assumption was reasonable, although Helen had not seen Robert's will, nor had they discussed the matter in any detail.

Fox also said that Sir Anthony would be sending to *The Times* a letter expressing his high regard for his Oxford classmate. Group Captain Grimes said nothing. Of the four people in the room, he now appeared to be the most in distress.

When Hugh Williams and the others had departed, Helen remained in the living room. She sat quietly, thinking of Robert and recalling times, good and bad, they had shared. Reflecting upon their marriage, she acknowledged it had been a failure. Now, unexpectedly and unfairly, the marriage was over.

From her experience with Peter's death, Helen knew that much needed to be done. As people in mourning often do, as a way perhaps of absorbing the shock of a loved one's passage, Helen concentrated on identifying what she would need to do in the next few days. Her first task was obvious. She needed to inform friends of Sir Robert's death. So she began making a list of people to be told. The list soon became two. One listed her friends. The other was of people close to the deceased. Near the top of the latter were Donald Iverson and Jock Appleby. First on Helen's list were Jane Ashcroft and Harriet Pennington. Near the middle was Colonel James Dixon. She knew the American would wish to know and would inform other Advisory Committee members.

Excluded from her list was the name Tom Forester. Against her will, Helen realized that the news brought by Hugh Williams meant a different future with Tom was now possible. Though exhilarating, the thought made her uncomfortable. She considered it improper to be thinking of such things at this time. Helen felt she would be dishonoring Robert's memory by so soon contemplating another man. But she could not help herself. Forester kept intruding upon her consciousness.

Finally she decided to do what Tom said he did with fear—acknowledge its presence, but put it aside. Contain it. Concentrate on the task at hand. Forester concentrated on leading P-47s. Helen focused on her lists, and upon Claire.

Nothing, not even Tom Forester, was more important to Helen than her daughter. Helen understood she must be the one to give Claire the news. More importantly, she wanted to do so in person. She wanted to hold her child and reassure her that all would be well. Later that afternoon, having made a great many phone calls, Helen was on a train to Brighton to see her daughter.

—⁘—

When Tom took the phone call from Jimmy Dixon, he expected the Air Attaché to address matters pertaining to the Advisory Committee. What he heard instead stunned him.

"Colonel, I thought you'd want to know. Seems Helen Trent's husband has got himself killed. He was on some kind of mission to Africa when the C-47 he was in crashed into a mountain."

"Oh, God, that's awful." Tom was thinking not of Sir Robert, but of Helen. He knew she would be in great distress and no doubt fearful of the future.

"There were no survivors. Mrs. Trent rang me up a little while ago. I'm informing a few of our Committee members. Thought you'd want to know."

"I do, Jimmy. Many thanks."

"Well, I'm off to brief two visiting senators. Seems they want to know more about the Eighth Air Force, speaking of which, I've heard an interesting rumor about you."

"I assume it's the one about the DFO." At this moment, Tom had no interest in discussing any job, much less one at Wycombe Abbey. But he had no choice. Dixon had raised the topic and Forester felt compelled to respond, however briefly.

"It is indeed."

"Well Jimmy, it's a bad idea. I'd make a lousy Director of Fighter of Operations."

"That's not what I told General McCready when he asked me what I thought of you."

"Good Lord." The thought that he might actually be bounced upstairs now crowded out his focus upon Helen. "All I want to do is lead my Group and shoot down some Germans."

"That's what we all want to do, but some of us have to push paper rather than throttles. Listen, I gotta go. Take care of yourself."

"I will, and thanks for calling."

As Forester put down the telephone, his mind reacted to the news about Helen. The momentary focus upon the position of DFO had vanished. That had been nothing more than a distraction. Forester wanted to concentrate on the woman he loved, a lady now alone in the world. His mind raced in two directions. The first concerned how he might provide help to Helen who, unexpectedly, was in need of assistance. A number of possibilities came to mind. Most involved verbal reassurances and offers to do whatever she asked to be done. A few involved financial support. Tom had no idea if Helen would need money, but intended to provide some if she did. The second concerned implications for the future. Sir Robert's death meant Helen, in time, would be free and available. Forester realized that in order to merge their lives, he would need to proceed with patience and tact, and quite possibly persistence. Significantly, the prospect of not making Helen his bride never crossed his mind. To him, their differences posed only impediments that would be overcome. He believed they could live happily ever after.

Ideas on how best to do this were percolating in his mind when Harry Collins spoke, interrupting Tom's concentration.

"Sir, is everything okay? Did Colonel Dixon give us some bad news?"

"A bit of bad news, I'm afraid." Tom felt hypocritical. To him it was not exactly an unhappy state of affairs. "Helen Trent's husband just died in an airplane crash. The RAF plane he was in flew into a mountain."

"That's too bad," said Williams. The Adjutant meant what he said. But, in a time when Americans he knew were getting killed, the death of an Englishman he didn't know was not of great concern.

Harry Collins reacted differently. He had liked Helen Trent when they met at the party for Sir Robert. And he had appreciated her hospitality in inviting to her home four Americans from Bromley Park only one of whom she knew. Collins felt genuine sympathy for the woman. He wondered how deeply she and Forester were involved. Looking down at the envelopes in his hand, he concluded they were very much involved. *Now Helen will find out whether her relationship with the American officer we both admire was more than a wartime fling.*

Tom certainly believed it was. His involvement with Helen he considered honorable. With good reason, he believed it durable as well. Yet he realized that a situation he more than once had fanta-sized about now presented itself, thus occasioning choices of consequence. For the first time, Tom understood the advice he and Will received from their father while aboard *Reward*. "Be careful what you wish for, boys," John Forester said to his children, "for you might get it some day."

"It is too bad." Tom spoke sincerely. He had no wish for Sir Robert to die. He just wanted the man to go away. "And plain bad luck."

Harry Collins then added a thought, one with which Forester agreed. "His number must have been up. And when your number's up, you're gone. God knows not many people die flying C-47s."

Forester wanted to telephone Helen, to offer condolences and reassurances. He wanted her to know that he intended to remain faithful in both love and friendship and that, in the end, all would be well. He planned to tell Helen that he, Tom Forester, would make it so.

At first, Tom intended to call immediately, interrupting the busi-ness at hand. He even began to ask Collins and Williams to give him a moment alone. Then Forester changed his mind. Better to finish up with the work at hand, setting aside for later more private moments to converse with Helen. He could wrap up these administrative mat-ters in an hour. Then there would be ample time to give Helen his undivided attention. So, perhaps a bit callously, he put aside his con-cern for the woman he loved, and turned to Wilbur Williams.

"What's next, Major?"

"Colonel, we've received a nice letter of thanks from the folks in Sedgewick. They apparently had a great time on their visit."

"That's good."

"We've also received a letter from the lawyer for Sir Richard Wilson. He's the fellow who owns the house near Ipswich that Lieutenant Peterson buzzed."

"Knocking off a chimney, if I remember," said Harry Collins, smiling, "and a horse."

"Ah yes, Golden Arrow."

"Well, it seems Lieutenant Peterson has worked out a payment plan satisfactory to Sir Richard who now will not sue the U.S. Government. Peterson will be sending money each month for the next four years, if, of course, he lives that long. The lawyer, who's what the British call a solicitor, has sent us a copy of the agreement."

"Am I supposed to sign it?"

"No, Sir. I just wanted you to be aware of what's happened. But there's more to the story."

Forester looked puzzled. Before he could say anything, Collins spoke up.

"Wilbur's told me what it is, Colonel. You're not going to believe what's happened."

"I'm listening."

"Well," said the Adjutant, "it seems Sir Richard has a young attractive daughter and guess who she's fallen in love with, apparently with the old man's blessing."

"Not who I think it is."

"Exactly. None other than Lieutenant Oscar Peterson." Williams then explained what had happened. "He went over to the house, it's called Lincoln Manor and it's quite a place, to apologize and work out restitution and, presto, girl meets boy, boy meets girl, and they fall in love."

"So this crazy story has a happy ending?" asked Forester.

"Apparently so," responded the Adjutant.

"Except, of course, for Golden Arrow," quipped Harry Collins.

"Well, I always enjoy stories of romance in time of war," remarked Tom, thinking of one much closer to home. "What else do you have Wilbur?"

"Actually, Sir, you're not going to believe this one either. But our next order of business is another story of, as you put it, romance in time of war."

"And you'd never guess who's involved," said Collins, grinning widely.

Forester looked at Wilbur Williams. He too was grinning.

"Okay, I must obviously know the fellow. Let's hear it."

"None other than the 19th Fighter Group's Engineering Officer, Colonel Myron Tuttle," replied the Adjutant.

Harry Collins spoke next, "Our own Colonel Tee."

"Colonel Tee?" Forester was genuinely surprised.

"The very one," responded Williams.

"But he must be fifty years old," said Tom, ignoring the fact that love and marriage are not exclusively the purview of the young.

"Actually," said the Group Intelligence Officer, "Colonel Tee is fifty-three years old, meaning he was born, if my arithmetic is correct, in 1890."

"And he wants to get married?" asked Forester, still a bit incredulous.

"He does indeed," replied the Adjutant.

"To whom?"

"To a woman by the name of Dorothy Russell. She's an English lady. Must be about fifty herself. A widow, kind of pretty. She lives in a nice house outside of Sedgewick. Her husband collected antique airplanes, which were in need of repair. She found Colonel Tee to fix them and he, so to speak, found her."

"I suppose it's actually a sweet story," remarked Forester who was warming to the idea. "There isn't a better human being at Bromley Park than Myron Tuttle."

"That's for sure," said Wilbur Williams.

"What Wilbur hasn't told you, Colonel," Harry Collins was speaking, "is that Colonel Tee needs your permission to marry."

"That's true, Colonel. You also have to interview Mrs. Russell."

Both officers were correct. War Department regulations required soldiers overseas to obtain permission to marry from their commanding officers who also had to speak with and approve the bride to be. Paperwork for these marriages was extensive as the Army made such unions difficult to accomplish. The reason was simple. The Department believed single men were likely to be more devoted to their units and more supportive of the war effort. In addition, the Department shared the view that wartime marriages were less likely to succeed than ones originating in peacetime, although postwar evidence suggested otherwise.

Of course, marriage was not always the objective of the men of the Eighth Air Force. Many simply sought girlfriends. A common language, physical proximity, and the pull of hormones all combined to make romance among youthful Yanks and the girls of Great Britain an everyday occurrence. Most of the romances were sweet and innocent. Some were not. During the Second World War, over twenty thousand children fathered by Americans were born out of wedlock in England. Yet even this statistic does not spoil the success of the social relationships that occurred when the United States deposited well over a million men onto British soil. Most of the time, these men spent preparing to do battle with the Nazis. Much of their time off was devoted to the more pleasant task of pursuing females.

Forester, of course, agreed to the marriage. Feeling odd about having to approve the union of two people old enough to be his parents, Tom was particularly uneasy about interviewing Mrs. Russell. He need not have been. The interview went smoothly. Dorothy Russell put Forester completely at ease. Afterward, she told Colonel Tee that Tom was an extremely pleasant, likeable young man. The man she was to marry agreed.

Myron Tuttle admired Forester and the feeling was mutual. Thus, Tom was honored when Colonel Tee asked him to be his best man. The wedding itself took place nine days later in Sedgewick at St. Stephen's. After a three-day honeymoon in London, Colonel Tee moved out of the Cottage to live with Dorothy at her home. But his devotion to his job did not suffer. The P-47s at Bromley Park remained well serviced and fit to fly.

Fifty minutes later, Forester completed his discussions with Wilbur Williams and Harry Collins. The three men had accomplished much. Matters of personnel, supply, and morale had been reviewed and effectively dealt with. So too had matters related to training and transportation. Unlike other Group Commanders, Forester found these issues interesting. Keeping Bromley Park administratively up to date was like running a small city. Tom considered the task challenging and rewarding. Yet he was aware that the Adjutant was the primary reason the base functioned smoothly. Forester devoted most of his energy to the P-47s. Wilbur Williams made sure everything else functioned well. And he did so in a manner that kept the Army Air Force happy, and off Forester's back. As the Adjutant departed along with the newly minted Lieutenant Colonel Collins, Tom renewed his commitment to secure a promotion for Wilbur Williams.

Back in his quarters, Forester found the slip of pink paper on which was written Helen's telephone number. Oddly, for he and Helen had not yet spoken, Tom felt intimately connected to her. She was his woman, now in need of comfort and support.

As he crossed the room to the telephone, he marveled at how a single unexpected event can recast the content of one's life.

Thinking about what he would say to Helen, Forester decided he first would express his sorrow at Sir Robert's death and then reassure her of his love. He would tell her that she was not alone in the world and that they together had a future of great promise.

In fact, Tom said none of this to Helen. When he called, the telephone at 28 Temple Court went unanswered. Forester tried a second time, in the event an incorrect number had been dialed. But again, no one picked up. The house was empty. Helen had left for Victoria Station to catch a train to Brighton in order to see Claire.

Forester decided he would call again that night and, if necessary, the next day. If by then he had not reached her, he would go down to London and find her.

Thus, after flying an early mission along the Dutch coast, he appeared at Helen's home late Sunday afternoon. Tom knocked on the door and was relieved when, moments later, the door was opened. He did not recognize the woman standing before him. She was elderly, and wore an old fashioned black dress. Petite in size, the woman spoke in a clear gentle voice.

"Do come in, young man. My name is Clara Harris, a friend and neighbor of Mrs. Trent. She'll be back shortly. I'm sure she'll be pleased you've come by."

Helen was pleased. Very pleased. Upon arriving home, she brightened noticeably upon seeing Tom. Despite efforts to put aside thoughts of Forester, thoughts she considered inappropriate given the situation, she had thought about him often.

Before Helen came home, Tom and Clara chatted pleasantly. Mrs. Harris enjoyed their conversation, as did Forester. Both began by commenting how tragic Sir Robert's death was. Then, each from a different perspective, they spoke of Helen, agreeing that she was a remarkable woman.

"She is a loyal and dear friend," said Clara Harris.

"A woman," noted Tom, "of great charm and intelligence."

When Clara left, Helen and Tom were alone. Both were aware that the moment was delicate. Yet neither felt awkward. Nor did they feel uncomfortable with Forester being where Sir Robert had once lived. Tom was relieved he had met up with Helen. She was glad he had done so.

Tom spoke first. "I'm terribly sorry about what's happened."

"Yes, it's awful. Thank you."

"He didn't deserve this."

"No, he didn't. We were not getting on, as you know better than anyone, but he was not an evil man. And I feel terribly, terribly sad over what's happened." Helen added a comment she had told no one else, "And a little frightened."

"Please don't be scared. I will make sure you're okay. Is there anything I can do for you now?"

"No, not really. Hugh Williams is handling the arrangements, the few that there are, along with Jane Ashcroft's husband. They've both been just super. There's going to be a memorial service on Wednesday. I'd like you to come, if you could."

Wondering who Hugh Williams might be, Forester nonetheless responded promptly, and sincerely, "I'll try to be there."

"There is one thing you could do now, though."

"Just tell me what it is."

Helen moved closer to Tom and reached for both his hands. "Just hold me and tell me again that what we have is real."

Not with passion, but with warmth, they embraced. For several minutes, Tom held Helen in his arms and, by his presence and soothing words, provided comfort, as well as reassurance that in the end all would be well. Then he spoke more directly to her.

"Helen, this world of ours is full of surprises, some good and some, like this one, just plain lousy. I don't know why such things happen, but they do. I do know that despite all the pain and suffering around us, there is still much to be thankful for. And what I'm most thankful for is you."

Helen said nothing. She just nestled her head upon Forester's shoulder. Then Tom noticed she was crying.

"I am truly sorry."

"I'm crying, my love, not for what I've lost but for what I have— Claire, you, my friends. They have all come to my side with loyalty and love."

"Helen, all those pretty words I've said to you, when things were easy, well, they're all true. I loved you before all this. I love you now." And then, in words Helen would never forget, indeed, she would recall them on the day she died, Forester continued, "And I will love you until the end of time."

Helen responded with a kiss, a warm and lengthy kiss that almost led to unplanned passion. Unexpectedly, each of them now wanted to make love. However, thinking better of it, they drew apart, albeit slowly and reluctantly.

"I love you, Helen."

"Yes, I know that you do. And I love you. You once said that I was afraid of the word. Well, I'm not. Not now anyway. I love you, Tom Forester. God help me, but I do."

Tom remained silent, but felt wonderful upon hearing what Helen said. But the feeling would not last as Helen continued.

"What a crazy time to tell you, but I do care so very much for you that it can only be true love. And because I do love you, I'm going to ask you to do something. And I want you to do it."

"Anything, Helen."

What Helen was about to say had been percolating in her head ever since she had learned of Sir Robert's death. Only on the train back from Brighton had she concluded she would make this request of Forester.

"I want you to go away. Not forever, but for a while. A few weeks, maybe a month or two. I need time to get my life in order. I need time to act like a proper lady in mourning. And I can't do this when you're around. I can't think straight when I'm with you. Everything gets out of focus. So I want you to go back to Bromley Park and let us live separate lives, at least for a while."

At first stunned by what Helen said, Forester recovered quickly.

"Helen, what you're saying is crazy. I can't do that."

"You must, for my sake."

"People in love don't walk away from one another."

"Sometimes they do. And you must now. I don't have the strength, but you do. Please."

"Helen . . ."

"I'm begging you, Tom. I need time alone, to regroup, to get my life in order. This love of ours is special and I believe it will survive. I love you Tom, totally, without reservation, and that's really why you must go."

Forester said nothing. He looked at the woman he loved. As always, she was beautiful. Yet, for the first time, Tom thought she looked fragile. Helen was pleading with him, as though seeking a life jacket aboard a sinking ship. Against his better judgment, and simply to do what she seemed so desperately to want, Forester agreed to her request.

The next ten minutes were spent in quiet conversation, none of it trivial, yet none of it focused upon what truly was occupying their minds: Tom's departure and their ensuing separation. During this conversation, the dramatic intensity occasioned by Helen's request receded only to reignite when Forester stood up to leave.

"Must you go now?" Helen's voice was trembling. Confronting the reality of Tom's absence, she now was uncertain of what she really wanted. Torn, she nonetheless said nothing, thus encouraging Forester to speak.

"I'm afraid I must." Upset over what Helen had requested, and angry with himself for acceding to her wishes, Tom had decided to face the inevitable sooner rather than later.

At the doorway, Forester said nothing to Helen. He simply smiled and, as he might a child, kissed her on the forehead.

Helen was surprised and hurt by his silence. She wanted to hear again the expressions of love Tom so often had spoken. As he walked through the doorway, tears flowed down her cheeks. She wondered whether she would ever see Forester again.

SIXTEEN

The memorial service for Sir Robert was well attended. Sir Anthony Eden delivered the principal eulogy while Lord Roberts, Edna's husband, spoke for several minutes, as did Donald Iverson. Eulogies contain only positive references to the deceased, and these were no exception. All three praised Sir Robert. They made particular mention of his erudition and of his devotion to King and Country. Occasionally, eulogies, at least the better ones, contain elements of humor, which, in addition to signaling affection for the departed, help to relieve stress. In this case, the remarks fell short. This was due to Sir Robert himself whose life seemed devoid of characteristics others without malice might have found amusing.

Forester did not attend the memorial service. He had been called to a meeting with Mike McCready. Even Tom was aware that Lieutenant Colonels respond promptly when summoned by Lieutenant Generals. So when Sir Anthony was speaking at St. Andrew's, Tom was sitting in the office of the Deputy Commander of all U.S. fighter aircraft in England. McCready was interviewing Forester. The General was about to convince Ira Eaker to remove

General Harrison and figured he'd better have a replacement in mind.

Not wanting the job, Forester was relaxed in the interview. The result was that he did extremely well. Tom spoke frankly, told a joke McCready enjoyed, and sensibly discussed fighter tactics. When the interview was over, the General was impressed. He wished Forester well, which Tom appreciated. He also said that Wycombe Abbey was a splendid place, a remark Forester considered ominous.

Despite the presence of Britain's Foreign Secretary, Helen was the dominant individual at the memorial service. Dressed entirely in black, including a stylish, yet restrained wide-brimmed hat, she looked striking. Everyone present commented on her regal appearance. Noteworthy too was her composure. Holding back tears, Helen remained calm, conveying to all the deep sadness she felt. She was also gracious, fully appreciating the many expressions of sympathy she received. Only a few friends, Jane Ashcroft in particular, were aware of the fear that lay behind Helen's stoic exterior.

Sir Robert's death had been untimely and unwarranted. To those in attendance at St. Andrew's, his loss seemed totally unfair. Of course, death often is unfair. People who have lived exemplary lives die young while villains at times enjoy the pleasures of old age. Sitting in the front pew, with Claire tucked safely next to her, Helen reflected upon death's vagaries. She had seen first hand the accident that took Peter away. Now she sat in a church mourning Sir Robert. While doing so, Helen could not but wonder whether death would claim prematurely the man she now loved. Deliberately, she then pushed thoughts of Forester out of her mind. The present moment belonged to Sir Robert.

Sitting three pews behind Helen was a man whose world, like Helen's, had been reconfigured by Sir Robert's death. While she carried herself with dignity, he did not. Tears ran down his cheeks throughout most of the service. More than one person at St. Andrew's that day thought his behavior odd, especially for an officer of the Royal Air Force.

Helen noticed the man's behavior, but paid little attention. So many people spoke to her before and after the service that the entire event, with its parade of individuals, seemed like a continuous blur, with men and women all saying much the same thing. Only later, in the office of Jock Appleby, did the behavior of Group Captain Wilfred Grimes come to make sense.

The next Monday, Helen was walking along High Holborn Street in company with Jane Ashcroft. They were on their way to meet with Appleby so that Helen could learn how Sir Robert intended to have his assets disbursed.

The day was cold and damp, and windy, with nondescript clouds blanketing the city. The unpleasant weather mirrored the task at hand.

"Are you sure you want me to be here?" asked Jane.

"Absolutely," replied Helen in a manner that suggested complete certainty.

"Some would say it's not my place."

"They would be wrong. You're my best friend and I have no secrets from you. And I need your support, especially now."

"That you'll have, and my love as well."

"How strange all this is. I mean, here we are, about to learn what Robert put in his will. I have trouble believing he's gone. It's as though he's away on holiday and will somehow return soon, except he won't."

"No, my friend," said Jane, "he won't."

"Poor Bobby. I feel so very bad. For him, not for me. People have been so kind, offering condolences. Yet I'm alive. He's the one who's gone."

"People do and say what they think is best."

"I know that, and I appreciate it. It's just that I feel their sympathy is misplaced. It should be directed to Robert and to his memory, not to me."

"I understand what you're saying, but only you are here, so people naturally focus their attention on you. His death is your loss."

"Of course you're right. It's just that his suffering was so much greater than my own."

At this time, Helen noticed a brass sign affixed to the entrance of a five story rather plain office building. The sign read simply *J. B. Appleby*. Helen was pleased to see the sign, for she wished to change the subject. "Ah, here we are. I recall Bobby saying Jock's office is on the second floor."

To Helen's surprise, and to Jane's, the first person they saw once inside the solicitor's office was Wilfred Grimes. Cigarette in hand, he appeared uncomfortable in their presence, although he greeted both women politely.

Alerted by the secretary, Jock Appleby entered the room, just as Grimes, with the greetings over, had begun to make conversation.

"Good morning, Helen. How nice to see you." Appleby, who had not been looking forward to this meeting, spoke with sincerity as he continued speaking. "You're well, I trust?"

"Yes, thank you." Helen then turned to Jane, but spoke to the solicitor. "This is my good friend Jane Ashcroft. I've asked her to accompany me today."

"My pleasure, Mrs. Ashcroft," said Appleby, further acknowledging Jane with a smile and a handshake. At first, Jock Appleby was displeased that Helen had brought along a companion. Then he decided it was fortunate she had.

"Let's go into my conference room," Appleby said to everyone. "And excuse all the papers. A solicitor thrives on the written word, even in wartime."

The room they entered was small, and surrounded by shelves filled with books and folders tied neatly with red string. Dominating the space was a rectangular table and six chairs. At one end of the table was an open folder containing numerous papers carefully subdivided. Appleby sat closest to the folder. To his left was a secretary. To her left was Wilfred Grimes, across from Helen and Jane who were to Appleby's right. Before proceeding with business, the solicitor offered everyone tea, which they accepted. Without a word from Appleby, the secretary, a Miss Gaines, stood up and fetched the tea, which she served in an ornate silver teapot that once belonged to the solicitor's mother.

"I'm afraid there's little sugar," said Appleby apologetically, "but I do have some cream and some biscuits."

Once tea was served and Miss Gaines seated back in her chair, Appleby picked up the folder, withdrew some papers, and began the meeting. He first reviewed the legal procedures typically followed in cases of death. He then asked Helen to sign three documents, which she did. Clearing his throat, Jock Appleby came to the issue of Sir Robert's assets and their disposition.

The assets were considerable. Sir Robert's estate was not huge, but most Londoners would have considered him a wealthy man. In addition to the house, he had a modest investment portfolio, two savings accounts at Barclay's Bank, his civil service pension, and a small piece of commercial real estate outside London near Croyden.

How these assets were to be disbursed would now be disclosed. Speaking in a calm voice, as though saying nothing out of the ordinary, Jock Appleby began reading from the will. As he did, he looked directly at Group Captain Grimes and then at Helen. Sir Robert, announced his solicitor, left one-third of his estate to Helen, one-third to Claire, and one-third to Wilfred Grimes.

Helen's surprise was total. She was completely dumfounded, barely stifling a gasp when Appleby revealed Grimes as a co-equal beneficiary. Helen Trent was not a greedy individual. She had no desire to possess all of what Sir Robert owned. Indeed, she expected him to leave a portion of his estate to others, most probably a charitable organization. But that he left so much to someone she considered simply an office colleague astonished her.

Quickly, astonishment gave way to a realization that Grimes was something else. *Good God, Wilfred Grimes and Robert Trent were lovers. Robert was a homosexual.* Now suddenly, like an avalanche, everything about Robert's behavior made sense. His lack of interest in her sexually, his overnight stays at the Collingwood, his long hours at the Colonial office.

Immediately, Helen's surprise gave way to anger. Anger at herself for not knowing her husband's most intimate preference and anger at Sir Robert for the deceit implicit in this discovery. She felt betrayed and humiliated. He had kept from her a vital piece of knowledge about himself. She had thought she had known him well. Now she realized she had not.

As Helen looked across at Grimes, her anger intensified. Finding the idea of two men sharing sexual pleasures inconceivable, she was more upset by the deception they had perpetrated upon friends and family.

All these reactions took place in her mind, and in her heart. They were all internal, invisible to those at the table, even to Jane, who, having reached the same conclusion as Helen, was horrified. On the outside, Helen appeared calm and under control.

"Well then, if that's what Bobby wanted, that's what we shall do. Perhaps Jock, we could meet tomorrow or the day after to discuss how best to carry out Robert's wishes. By that, I mean, how we might sensibly divide things into three equal shares, if," and here Helen paused, "that would be agreeable with Group Captain Grimes."

"Certainly, Madame, however you would like to proceed." Grimes was not an evil individual. He felt sorry for Helen and wished her no harm. Indeed, he too had been surprised by Sir Robert's largess. Turning to the solicitor he said, "Mr. Appleby, please schedule a meeting at a time convenient for Mrs. Trent and I will be there."

One hour later, Helen and Jane were at Fogarty's having a scotch and soda before partaking of a midday meal. The latter was now particularly glad she had accompanied Helen who, still shocked by the revelation, remained angry at both Sir Robert and herself.

"He deceived me, and I was such a fool not to have noticed."

"Don't be so hard on yourself. I suspect a number of men we know favor boys over girls."

"Perhaps, but I feel like such an idiot. At one time I even thought there might be another woman. How ironic."

"True. But outside the five of us, Appleby, his secretary, Grimes, and I, no one knows or needs to know. Besides, it's in the past. What counts now is the future."

Helen was not willing to let go. "And Robert was so terribly clever. He knew I'd be horrified by Grimes, so he leaves a full third of what he has to Claire. That will keep me content and quiet, which is exactly what he wanted."

"Clever man, Sir Robert," Jane agreed.

"Yes, he was. In one sense I suppose he was also being generous. He knew that she is what I care about most in this world, so in his last act he does something very kind."

"Generous, I'm not sure I'd use that word. While he was alive, you did all and more of what he wanted from a wife."

"I did what I thought was expected of me."

"That and more."

"And so in gratitude, he makes this grand gesture."

"I think he was giving you your due as well as making amends for living such a lie." Jane was less forgiving than Helen.

"That too, I suppose. And now he's gone. Despite everything, I find it so terribly sad."

"Sad?"

"Yes. He must have been a terribly lonely man, living with me, yet not finding from his wife the kind of love and companionship we all need and want. I of all people can understand that."

"You're much too kind. Robert had his career. He valued that above all else."

"Perhaps. But the fact he carried on this clandestine affair suggests his life was not the success he wanted us all to believe it was."

"You sound sympathetic."

"I don't approve of what he did. How could I? I think it's wrong. But part of me feels sorry for anyone who feels compelled to live a secret life. Bobby must had had a hard time of it, and now his life, both the good and the bad, is over."

"Yes, it is. But Herbert always says that life belongs to the living so now, slowly at first, but most definitely, we must begin to focus on you and the future." Jane no longer wanted the conversation to focus on Sir Robert.

"I shall do fine. I always have."

"You know of course that Herbert and I are here for you, if you need us."

"I do, and I'm very grateful."

"There is one question I have for you. And it has nothing to do with pounds sterling or Claire."

"I think I know what it is."

"I suspect you do, especially now that I see you smiling, a welcome sight, I might add. Whatever are you going to do about the American, young Tom Forester. I must say I rather like the boy."

"I do too. I've told myself and him that I love him, so I might as well tell you. I know it's crazy, but the truth Jane, is that I'm quite sure I love him, and I know I miss him."

"That's perfectly reasonable, and rather sweet."

"God it is sweet. Only once before have I ever felt this way."

"So what are you going to do?"

Helen then related to Jane what had transpired when she last saw Tom.

"So, basically, you sent him away?"

"Yes, but just for a time. I needed to be alone. I needed to mourn, and truth be told, I wanted to keep up appearances. But I think about him all the time."

"What in your heart do you want to do?"

"In my heart? In my heart I want to be with him, I want to hold him and be held by him, and I want to tell him that I love him."

"Then that's what you should do."

"But I'm afraid, Jane. Afraid of what people might think and afraid now that I'm no longer off limits so to speak, he might find me less compelling."

"You need to have more faith in yourself, and in Tom Forester. From what I've seen, he's a terribly decent fellow. And for what people think, let them think whatever they wish. It's your life, not theirs."

"I need to hear this, and listen to you."

"Yes, you do." Jane now took hold of her friend's hands and spoke earnestly. "Helen, life is short and good men are in short supply. If you love this man, then go to him and tell him so. And do it soon; these are dangerous times in which we live."

Before Helen acted upon Jane's advice, Forester telephoned her. Ever since he had agreed to Helen's request for time alone, Tom had been annoyed with himself. He now believed that acceding to her wishes had been a mistake. According to Forester, people in love need time together, not apart, especially when their time together is so limited. Except when involved in a mission, Tom had been unable to put Helen out of his mind. He thought about her constantly. These thoughts were pleasant, but distracting, particularly to someone who liked to keep his life on an even keel. Both Harry Collins and Wilbur Williams noticed the change in their Commanding Officer, but said nothing to him.

"The symptoms are obvious. It's woman trouble, pure and simple," remarked the Intelligence Officer. "Who but a female could drive a guy like Forester up the wall."

"Imagine," responded the Adjutant, "Herman Goering and his entire Luftwaffe can't rattle him, but one dame can. I wonder who it is."

"I think I know, but discretion requires that the lady's identity remain a mystery."

Having accepted on Monday Jane's advice to seek Forester out, she intended to telephone Tom on Friday. Tuesday and Wednesday were earmarked to matters pertaining to Sir Robert. Helen expected them to be difficult, and they were. Thursday she planned to rest in the afternoon after revisiting St. Andrew's in the morning to offer a prayer in private for her late husband. This would mark her farewell to the man she had married in 1935. Friday, she intended to start her life anew. And what better way to do so than to reconnect with the man who'd won her heart. Any guilt she may have felt at shedding so soon the image of a widow in mourning was erased by the still painful discovery of Sir Robert's hidden life.

Tuesday found Helen back in Jock Appleby's office. Grimes was there as well. Together, they and the solicitor, reached agreement on how sensibly to split Sir Robert's assets. The meeting was entirely cordial. Everyone was on their best behavior. For Helen, the only painful part was the realization that the house at 28 Temple Court would have to be sold. Graciously, Group Captain Grimes invited Helen to remain in the house until she was able to find suitable lodgings for herself and Claire. He said he was in no rush and wanted Mrs. Trent to feel no pressure to move quickly.

Wednesday was particularly difficult. With the assistance of Clara Harris, Helen packed up Sir Robert's personal belongings. Clothes she gave to the local air raid warden for distribution to those in need. Of the other items several she kept, for memory's sake, placing them in a small storage box. The others she decided to give to Grimes, in appreciation for his relaxed attitude regarding the sale of the house. In giving these items to Wilfred Grimes, Helen thought she was acting rather magnanimously, given the revelation regarding him and Sir Robert.

Thursday was less difficult. Helen attended a morning service at St. Andrew's. She listened intently to a particularly timely sermon entitled "As We Forgive Those Who Trespass Against Us." While she agreed conceptually with the sermon's obvious message, Helen was unable to forgive Sir Robert totally for his liaison with Grimes. But she made progress in doing so and, with genuine faith in the Almighty, prayed for his soul. She also recalled with affection the good times she and Robert had shared. When the service was over, Helen left St. Andrew's spiritually refreshed. As importantly, she felt a chapter in her life was over. Though anxious, she nonetheless was looking forward to the next one.

Back home, Helen planned to spend a relaxing few hours. The strain of the past two weeks was considerable. Each day had imposed emotionally demanding tasks. Thus, Helen was looking forward to an afternoon free of stress. She intended to read and enjoy some music before taking a leisurely bath, all prior to joining Jane and Herbert Ashcroft for dinner.

Helen had disrobed and was standing naked about to step into the bathtub when the telephone rang. She contemplated not answering it, but decided the call might be important, so she walked quietly to her bedroom, and, still naked, picked up the receiver. The voice she heard made her insides tremble and her hands grow cold.

"Helen, it's me, Tom. Are you okay?"

"Yes, I'm fine. I'm so glad you called. I've missed you."

"Listen, we've got to see each other. I understand why you wanted to be alone, but I'm going nuts without you. I love you, Helen Trent."

"And I you, Tom Forester. You're safe and well?"

"Yes, I'm okay except I can't seem to get you out of my mind."

Helen giggled. "That sounds like the title of a song."

"It's true, song or no song."

"What would you say if I told you that I was somehow going to ring you up tomorrow and tell you that I need you and wanted to see you as soon as possible?"

"I'd say hooray and give thanks to Venus, the goddess of love."

"Not a bad idea, for both of us. So you're not angry with me?"

"Why would I be angry with you?"

"For sending you away."

"No dear lady, you did what you thought was right."

"But it wasn't, or at least it isn't now. What I need now is not time by myself, but time with you."

"And what I need and desire above all else is to hold you and be with you."

"So you'll come to London?"

"You bet. Let's see, today is Thursday. I can come down on Saturday."

"Splendid. Just splendid. I'll be waiting."

"Where?"

"At the Abbey, of course."

"I'll be there, around ten o'clock."

"I'll be waiting. Jane Ashcroft said to me that I should tell you that I love you. So I am, because I do."

Forester then said to Helen something no man had ever said before. The words she found provocative, but pleasantly so. "You're my woman, Helen Trent, and that's all you need to know."

"Yes, I am," she responded, accepting the designation. "And pleased that I am."

—⁂—

On Saturday, Helen was standing outside Westminster Abbey, awaiting Forester. The day was sunny, yet cold. Helen wore a heavy coat, charcoal in color, and, to send a message to Tom, had wrapped around her neck the burgundy cashmere scarf purchased at Harrods. On her head was a light grey wool beret. This she had pulled down around her ears to keep warm. But, deciding the look was unattractive, Helen repositioned the beret so that her ears and much of her hair were left uncovered. Though satisfied that she looked better, she wondered how long her ears could withstand the cold.

Helen also wondered whether she and Tom would hit it off as they had in the past. Their differences were great and now, with her situation altered, Helen was concerned that Forester, despite all the devotion he had expressed, might pull back. True, she was now available. However, that alone might frighten him. Moreover, she was an older woman, and one with a child to rear. As Helen expressed these concerns to herself, she became conscious of her age. She realized she was not twenty-six, Tom's age, nor did she feel twenty-six. Outside Westminster Abbey, the thought occurred to Helen, not for the first time, that Forester might prefer someone younger.

When Tom stepped out of a taxi and sprinted over to Helen, her concerns vanished. One look at his face reassured her. As did her own reactions upon seeing Forester. She was excited by his presence and thrilled that they would spend Saturday together.

Tom spoke first. "God is it ever good to have you in my sight. I've missed you, and I'm worried about you."

"Don't be. I expect to be fine." Then, more assertively, she added, "I am fine."

"I do hope so."

"Except for one thing."

"What's that?"

"I've told you I wanted to be apart from you. And when I was, I felt empty and incomplete. And now here you are. You must think I'm an idiot."

Forester did not consider Helen an idiot. Quite to the contrary. "I think you're the best woman in the whole wide world. And I am absolutely crazy about you."

"So you forgive me?"

"There's nothing to forgive."

Helen wanted to be kissed. So she moved closer to Tom. Uncertain as to the propriety of embracing a woman on the steps of Westminster Abbey, Forester nonetheless took the hint and complied with her wish. He was glad he did. Her lips were warm, her mouth moist. The kiss was lengthy. They held each other tightly as if to make certain the other knew that now nothing, save Tom's responsibilities at Bromley Park, would keep them apart.

When Forester drew back Helen protested. "Don't stop."

"I don't want to, but we seem to be drawing a crowd." Tom had noticed that several people outside the Abbey had stopped and were staring at them. Most seemed amused at the sight of a young American officer embracing his English girlfriend.

"Oh dear, I hadn't realized." Helen now noticed the people around them. "Well then, I guess we'll have to stop."

I guess so." Forester then spoke with reluctance in his voice. "I'd really like to do it again."

Looking straight into Tom's eyes Helen smiled mischievously. The words she then spoke echoed the expression on her face. "Not to worry, my boy, the day is still young."

Because of the cold they decided to again tour Westminster Abbey. But once inside, they found the church dark and chilly, and not conducive to intimate conversation. So they reversed course and went outside where the weather, though winter-like, permitted a brisk walk along the Thames. This they did for the next twenty-five minutes. Arm in arm, they strolled along Victoria Embankment finding pleasure in both the sunshine and each other's company.

Tom told Helen about Colonel Tee and Dorothy Russell. He also related the tale of Sir Richard Wilson's daughter and her American boyfriend. Enjoying both stories, Helen remarked that the lesson to be learned from these accounts is that people sometimes encounter romance in the most unlikely places. Kissing Helen gently on the cheek and, mentioning the Advisory Committee, Forester replied that he had already discovered that.

On a more somber note, Helen told Tom about Sir Robert's memorial service. She then recounted her meeting with Jock Appleby. Hiding no details, Helen revealed to Forester the nature of her late husband's liaison with Wilfred Grimes. Tom was surprised. Forester could not imagine how one man could be sexually attracted to another. Indeed, he found the subject uncomfortable even to discuss.

Helen also revealed that the house at 28 Temple Court would have to be sold. This news distressed Forester.

"Where will you live?" Concern was evident in Tom's voice and expression.

"Not to worry. I will find something suitable here in London. Much smaller of course, but room enough for me and Claire."

"Now I am worried."

"Don't be. I can manage."

"I don't want you just to manage. I want you to be comfortable and secure."

"That's sweet of you to say."

"I mean it. Listen Helen, I don't know how best to say this, but money is not something to treat lightly. This may not be any of my business, but if you're short of funds now or later on, well I've man-

"In the middle of the afternoon?" Grinning broadly, Helen spoke in mock horror. "I'm not sure proper English ladies do that."

Gently pulling her towards him, Forester replied in a knowing voice. "They do, but only if they're in love, or," here Tom paused, "they wish to express gratitude to those Americans who have come so far to help protect this sceptred isle."

"Well then," said Helen, still grinning, "I pass muster on both counts."

Ten minutes later, they were in a spacious room on the third floor. Decorated in quiet shades of creamy yellow and ivory, the room featured a double bed and a small sitting area. Through two large windows, the sun cast rays of linear light. Yet, despite the sunshine, the room felt chilly. The absence of a fireplace and the presence of several blankets upon the bed suggested the chill would remain throughout the night.

Upon entering the room, Helen looked about and pronounced herself satisfied. The room was certainly attractive, and larger than she had expected. Having dined at the Savoy several times in the past, she never had stayed in its rooms and had been curious as to their size and decor. Nor had she ever spent an afternoon with a man in a hotel room. With great amusement she realized she thus was about to have two virgin experiences. Continuing the thought and her amusement, she concluded that at her age such experiences were rare.

As she focused her eyes upon Forester, Helen felt desired, wanted as a woman. This she found extremely satisfying. The feeling, moreover, had no artificial dimension. It was natural and as sensual as it was pleasing. Helen attributed this feeling to Tom. He understood what all wise men know. Namely, that not only can a man make a woman feel attractive. By word and deed, he can cause her to feel sexual, confident, desirable.

As Tom made sure the door was locked, Helen pulled the drapes closed, thereby darkening the room. She wanted their private space blacked out for reasons having nothing to do with German bombers. When the drapes were drawn, Forester walked over to

Helen, kissed her on the cheek, and guided her down to a chair near the bed.

"Do you realize how odd this is?" said Tom, who smiled as he spoke.

Helen had no idea what Forester was talking about. She looked puzzled, so he continued.

"I mean, here we are having just sat downstairs in front of a fireplace wearing heavy clothes only to go upstairs to a cold bedroom to take them off."

"It makes perfectly good sense to me." With an index finger, Helen indicated she wanted Forester to sit next to her. "Clothes are like formal dinners, they have their time and place."

Helen then kissed Tom. He put his hand through her hair then down around her cheek as the embrace continued. Her lips were inviting and Forester sensed the urgency that lay behind them. Briefly, they stopped kissing only to start again.

"I love kissing you," whispered Tom.

"Kisses also have their time and place."

Their kisses grew in intensity. Tom drew back to catch his breath. As he did so, Helen stood up. Forester started to do the same, but Helen gently but firmly pushed him back onto the chair.

After kissing him once more, she slid out of her clothes gracefully and without embarrassment. The look on Forester's face told her she could do anything she wanted with or to him. First, she took off his service jacket. Then she unbuttoned his shirt. With one motion, she pulled off the shirt along with the T-shirt underneath. Kneeling in front of him, she moved her hands lightly over his bare chest, staring into his eyes, not saying a word. It was clear who was in charge.

Forester had never been with a woman who moved with such sensual assurance. Nor had he ever been so completely aroused, until she slowly, expertly, began to remove his trousers. As her hands reached under the trousers and touched his skin, he took in a breath and held it.

Still kneeling in front of him, Helen encircled his body with her arms, resting her head against his chest and then slid downward. Her breasts rubbed against his erection as she took it in her hands and began to move rhythmically, still looking into his eyes. Forester moaned.

"I love you, Thomas Forester. Never doubt it."

With that, she took him in her mouth. After a few moments, overcome with pleasure and excitement, he took her head into his hands and gently tried to move her up to kiss him.

"Not yet."

He surrendered to her, feeling physically and emotionally unlike he had never felt before. Time collapsed.

At last, Helen threw her head back and stood up, only to sit down again, this time facing Tom on the chair, taking him inside of her. For the first time, she gasped. The look on Helen's face told Tom that control of the moment had shifted.

He carried her to the bed and laid her on her back. His eyes and his hands gently caressed her entire body. He kissed her closed eyelids, then each cheek, and then, repeatedly, and with great care, her mouth. Her small hands were enfolded into his as he climbed on top and came into her. Again, she gasped as her eyes opened and her body began to move with his.

As he exploded inside of her, stripped down to the essence of his soul, the words came spilling out in a torrent. "Helen, I love you. I love only you. I need you. Promise me you'll never leave me."

In that sweet special moment that only lovers know, Helen held him in her arms, stroking his hair as a mother would a child, gently kissing his face, his hands, his shoulders. As she stroked his chest, his eyes closed, his breathing slowed, and he fell asleep. She pulled up the covers, lay her head on his chest, and soon, she too was asleep. Body heat and blankets kept them warm. Of the cold that had remained in the room, they were unaware.

Later that evening, Helen and Tom had dinner in the Savoy's dinner room, which they visited again early Sunday morning prior to Tom's departure for Bromley Park.

At breakfast, after spreading orange marmalade on a piece of toast, Helen addressed Tom on a subject now dear to her heart. "When will I see you next?"

The question was not unexpected. Having given the matter some thought, Forester was ready with an answer. "On Thursday, I'm hoping you'll be free late in the afternoon."

Pleasantly surprised that Tom would return to London in just a few days, Helen's face brightened.

"Yes, I'm free." These were the words Helen spoke to Forester. To herself, she used a different set of words. *I'll be free whenever you want me to be.*

"That's great. Thursday, of course, is special."

"It is?"

"Yes, my dear English lady. Thursday is Thanksgiving, a national holiday back in the States and, I guess, wherever there's an American. It's my favorite holiday."

"Mine is Christmas. But I know about your Thanksgiving. It's about pilgrims and festive dining."

"Very good. Those pilgrims were actually your pilgrims who became our pilgrims." Now Forester spoke more seriously. "Helen, Thanksgiving is very special. It's a day we set aside to give thanks for all that we have, which is plenty."

"What a sensible idea, and how American."

"It is an American holiday and one I'm very proud of. Sometimes we get too concerned about the food, but I think the spirit of it survives nonetheless. It's a day when families gather and give thanks. I think it's wonderful."

Helen agreed, but she was more interested in Forester than in an American holiday.

"So we'll be together in the afternoon, on Thursday?"

"Yes, the late afternoon. Traditionally, Americans eat turkey on Thanksgiving and Uncle Sam goes to great lengths to feed the troops a special turkey dinner on Thanksgiving Day. We're doing it at Bromley Park and I need to be there. Then I'll hop a train and meet you in London."

"And have two Thanksgiving meals?"

"Yes indeed." Tom took hold of Helen's hand. "I have much to be thankful for."

"As do I, my love, as do I." Helen then asked Forester another question, this one not expected.

"Then you'll be here the next day as well, yes?" Helen could tell that her point did not register with Tom. "Friday we have a meeting of the Advisory Committee."

"I've forgotten all about that." Indeed he had. Among Tom's priorities, the Committee had not been at the top. To be sure, Forester had carried out General Harrison's order. Tom had attended all meetings and participated in discussions. He was very much a member in good standing. But the Advisory Committee did not occupy his thoughts. P-47s did. And when he was not concentrating on Thunderbolts, Forester spent much of his time thinking about his lady in London. "But, you're exactly right. The Committee meets the day after Thanksgiving, so I'll be here."

"Splendid. I shall look forward to that."

"Me too."

—⁂—

As planned, Tom and Helen met late in the afternoon on Thanksgiving Day. However, Forester had only one turkey dinner, at Bromley Park. Dining with Helen that night at Fogarty's, Tom ate steak and potato pie in which, due to rationing, the potatoes vastly outnumbered the steak. But the meal was tasty, especially when dessert turned out to be an old fashioned chocolate cake baked by Mrs. Fogarty. Of course, the food was secondary to the company. Helen and Tom reveled in being together. Their pleasure was enhanced by knowing that at night they would share the same bed, this time at the hotel near the American Embassy.

At 9:50 A.M. on Friday, they stepped out of a taxi at Hamilton Place in front of the Royal Aeronautical Society where Taffy Edwards greeted them in his booming voice. This last meeting of the

Advisory Committee, set to start at 10:00 A.M., was to take place where the first one had occurred.

The meeting started on time and was a complete success. Committee findings and recommendations were discussed. A few last minute suggestions were adopted. Colonel Jimmy Dixon who chaired the gathering was delighted. He had worked hard and, with great skill and tact, had gotten the group to produce a solid report. At the meeting's conclusion, he thanked the Committee members for their effort, praised their product, and expressed gratitude on behalf of the entire Eighth Air Force. He then said he would draft the final report over the weekend and have it typed at the Embassy on Monday. He told the assembled body that he personally would deliver the report to General Eaker on Wednesday, December 1. Dixon was an experienced staff officer. Deliberately, he had built a one-day cushion, Tuesday, into his schedule. This would allow for production slippage or the unexpected.

On Wednesday morning, Jimmy Dixon drove to Wycombe Abbey to see Ira Eaker. Ushered into the Commanding General's office by Major Hull, Dixon immediately noticed two Army Air Force officers in the room. They were colonels. One, standing next to the fireplace, was Roger Baldwin. The other was Keith Davenport.

"Hello, Jimmy," said Eaker, greeting the Deputy Air Attaché informally. "Keith's been telling me about your committee. Apparently it went well."

Dixon acknowledged General Eaker with a salute, and said, "Yes, Sir, it did." He then greeted Davenport and Baldwin.

For the next thirty minutes, the four officers discussed the report after which the General said he would read the entire document that evening, which he did. The next day, Harris Hull was directed to prepare a set of orders implementing the Advisory Committee's recommendations.

After Dixon left Ira Eaker's office, the General asked both Baldwin and Davenport to remain.

"Colonel Baldwin," said the Commanding Officer of the Eighth Air Force, "earlier this morning I spoke with the RAF and they told me something I think you'll be pleased to hear."

"Sir?" Roger Baldwin had no idea what Eaker was about to say.

"The British are going to let us have twenty deHavilland Mosquitoes. We should receive them in February. Several will be used for weather reconnaissance."

"That's great news, General." Baldwin was delighted, and a bit surprised. He had not known that the Eighth had worked hard to obtain the British aircraft. "We'll be able to scout the targets and send back accurate weather forecasts to the strike force. It will be a big step forward."

"Well, Colonel, it was your idea and a very good one. Well done, Roger."

What Eaker did not say was that he had written a special letter of commendation for Baldwin. This was placed in the Colonel's personnel file.

As promised, the Mosquitoes were delivered to the Americans. Later, additional numbers of the deHavilland aircraft were supplied, a total of 145 in all. These planes and their crews performed admirably, providing necessary meteorological information to the Eighth Air Force. At war's end, the surviving Mosquitoes were all returned to the RAF.

Eaker now took a pipe from the rack on a nearby table and began the process of lighting it, starting with a pouch of tobacco he took from his pocket. The tobacco was a special Virginia blend supplied to him monthly by his sister back in the States.

"Now, Colonel," Eaker was still addressing Baldwin. "What kind of long-range forecast can you give me for December? November's been terrible."

Weather conditions in November 1943 had been dreadful. Frequent cloud coverage over Northeast Europe precluded accurate bombing. Even with newly developed radar targeting devices, results were unsatisfactory. For example, on November 7 in a raid against Duren, the Eighth Air Force scattered bombs for 100 miles along the border of Holland and Belgium. On a November 26 mission to Paris the B-17's returned to England with bomb loads intact, having been unable to identify the target.

"Well, Sir, I wish I could give you good news, but I can't. Our long-range forecasting is not as good as we'd like it to be. My best estimate is that clouds will be covering our target areas at least more than half the time. December doesn't look all that good."

"Hmm," Eaker sucked on his pipe, "that's what I was afraid you'd say."

Throughout the strategic air campaign against Germany, the weather proved to be a formidable obstacle. During the Eighth Air Force's operational lifetime, from August 17, 1942 to May 8, 1945, bad weather kept the bombers on the ground one fourth of the time. In addition, clouds caused missions underway to turn back and bombardiers to miss their target. To Ira Eaker, the weather seemed to have taken sides and favored the Germans.

"Well, General, the weather may be lousy," Keith Davenport was now speaking, "but there's good news regarding the buildup of the bombers. The Eighth is starting to look like the air force you planned back in 1942."

"True enough, Colonel," answered Eaker. "The days of our dispatching a few hundred bombers are over."

Nothing better illustrated the General's point than the mission of November 26, 1943. On that day, 633 heavy bombers were dispatched. Clearly, Eaker's force was growing. Losses continued, and remained high. But bombers and crews that failed to return were replaced. And new squadrons were arriving in England. America's industrial might was flexing its muscles. All of East Anglia was becoming crammed with B-17s and B-24s.

Eaker was determined to use these planes to destroy Nazi Germany. He still believed in the supremacy of air power. The last several months had been difficult. But now, as the number of aircraft swelled, the General believed his air force would render irreparable harm upon the enemy's war machine.

Eventually, the Eighth Air Force would inflict such harm. But only when the P-51 Mustang was available to escort the bomber formations to every corner of Germany and back. In a three-month period, February through April 1944, the Mustangs and Thunderbolts too out flew and out fought the Luftwaffe, turning the tide of battle in the air. However, in early December 1943, victory was still in the future. Much blood remained to be spilled. The Eighth was to be called upon to give more than its fair share.

As Ira Eaker and Keith Davenport discussed the buildup of the bomber force, Roger Baldwin excused himself. Davenport continued talking with General Eaker for the next twenty-five minutes. He too then excused himself.

As Colonel Davenport was leaving, Eaker asked him to stay for one last piece of business.

"Sir?"

"Keith, do you still want to go back and command a bomb group?"

Surprised, Davenport responded, attempting unsuccessfully to hide his enthusiasm. "Yes, General, I sure do."

"Have you learned anything from your experience with the 918th?"

"I have, Sir. I'll still care about the men, but I'll be tougher and harder on them."

"Like Frank Savage?"

"Yes, Sir, like Frank Savage." Brigadier General Frank Savage had replaced Keith Davenport as commander of the 918th Bomb Group. Savage was known to be a hard ass.

"Good, well I'm giving you the 311th. It's a new group, just in from the States. Their C.O. was just killed in an automobile accident. The group is yours, Keith. Go knock the hell out of some Germans."

"I will, General. I'll do just that."

SEVENTEEN

Forester was aware that the Eighth Air Force was expanding. As a fighter group commander, he could see for himself. Since returning to Bromley Park, Tom had flown several missions. He noticed that bombers were attacking in much greater numbers than in August when he first had led the 19th into combat.

The Group was now a veteran outfit. Constant training was paying off. Each time the Bromley Park P-47s took to the sky, Forester was confident they would safeguard the bombers. And, in doing so, they would directly challenge enemy fighters. November 29 was a particularly successful day. The 19th Fighter Group knocked down nine enemy aircraft, all Me-109s. Forester got one of these. His score now stood at seven. Sergeant McGowan was ecstatic.

For the commander for the 19th Fighter Group, December 13 started off like any other day at Bromley Park. He rose at 5:30 A.M., washed and dressed in the same sequence as always, and enjoyed hot coffee and two donuts before driving over to the Group Operations building. There he received a summary of the Field Order that had arrived shortly after midnight. He then approved the plan for the resulting mission. B-17 Flying Fortresses were attacking the port city of Bremen. Start Engines was at 10:19 A.M. Take-off at 10:25 A.M. Rendezvous with the bombers was scheduled to take place exactly one hour and forty minutes later, at 28,000 feet.

Harry Collins drove Forester out to his plane. As the Intelligence Officer did so, Tom retained his customary silence. He was using these few moments to get himself ready. Once again, he was about to risk his life. By habit and willpower, Forester contained his fear, setting it aside for later. Right now, he was too busy. He had to fly to Germany, leading forty-seven Thunderbolts.

Climbing into the cockpit, Tom noticed the new black and white German cross adorning his aircraft. McGowan had painted the victory symbol the same day Forester had achieved the kill.

Settling in, Tom did something he had never done before. He thought of Helen. He pictured her smiling, holding onto his arm. He recalled the sweetness of her kisses. Forester considered himself a lucky guy. She was a terrific woman. They had agreed to spend Christmas together. He would secure a three-day pass and, together with Claire, they would put the war aside and enjoy the holiday. Briefly, Tom wondered how he and Claire would get along. *Later Forester, later. It's time to get going.* With that, Tom banished all thoughts of Helen and her daughter. As the huge four-blade propeller of the P-47's Pratt and Whitney engine began to spin, Forester was focused. He was ready to fly.

The P-47s reached the rendezvous point on time. So did the Fortresses. Together they made an awesome sight. Three squadrons of Thunderbolts escorting the vanguard of the strike force. Over two hundred aircraft in formation, armed and seemingly unstoppable, were heading to Bremen. December 13 was a Tuesday. More than one American in the air that day thanked God it wasn't Friday.

Along the route, German defenses were attempting to jam the P-47s' radio transmissions. The clue was the whine Forester heard in his earphones. The sound was annoying, but hardly disruptive.

More threatening were the Fw-190s some ten miles ahead of the B-17s. Guided to their position by Luftwaffe ground controllers, they soon would slam directly into the path of the oncoming bombers, unless Forester and his Thunderbolts could stop them.

In less than two minutes, Tom caught sight of the enemy.

"This is Trumpet. Bandits in sight, eleven o'clock." Forester was flying with the 340th Fighter Squadron. They were providing top cover. "Okay, Snowflakes, follow me. The rest of you stay put, your turn will come."

Sixteen P-47s, in four flights of four aircraft, peeled off to their left. Tom took the Thunderbolts directly into the middle of the enemy. He was attacking thirty-two Fw-190s. A tumultuous air battle had begun.

At first, Forester flew through the enemy formation unscathed. He then rolled his aircraft, dove, and came back to engage the 190s. One of them he got in his sights. *Stay calm. Get in close. Closer Still. Now!* Eight machine guns erupted, sending streams of .50 caliber shells into the fuselage of the German. Forester kept the trigger down and brought the stream forward. The Fw-190 exploded. Forester flew safely through the wreckage. Immediately, Tom felt a sense of exhilaration. The deadly game had been played. Once again, he was victorious. Now he would go find more Germans.

Instead, they found him. Two Fw-190s had Forester's P-47 in their sights. As their guns erupted, Tom instinctively banked his plane to the left, turning into his attackers. This caused the Germans to miss. Simultaneously, Forester pointed the Thunderbolt downward and advanced the throttle. Gathering speed, he expected to outdistance the Focke-Wulfs. However, the geometry favored the Germans. They retargeted the P-47 and, as the American plane began to pull away, fired again.

Piloted by men who knew their trade, the aircraft pursuing Forester were Fw-190A-6s. These were heavily armed machines. They carried two machine guns that fired through the propeller and four 20 mm cannons, two in each wing. When the Germans again opened fire, the results were explosive. Tom's plane was struck in several places. Pieces small and large flew off the P-47. Holes appeared in the tail, fuselage, and right wing. The engine was also hit. By the feel of the controls, Forester could tell all was not well. A glance at his instruments confirmed the bad news. The aircraft was badly damaged.

Confidently, the Fw-190s lined up for another shot. With trigger fingers itching, the pilots were eager to score. Both figured just a two-second burst would finish off the Thunderbolt.

The Germans never fired. Their attention was diverted by three P-47s boring in on them. Quickly, the two pilots maneuvered to face the onrushing Americans. Guns at the ready, the Focke-Wulfs prepared to fire. So did the Thunderbolts. In the few seconds before flight paths crossed, five planes let loose. Instantly, the space between them was ablaze with gunfire.

One Fw-190 escaped unscathed. The other did not. Hit in the engine, the aircraft caught fire and began to roll whereupon its pilot took to the silk. He fell free for ten seconds. Then he pulled the ripcord and, after two minutes floating free, landed safely. By the next morning, he was back in the cockpit.

Two of the P-47s flew past the Germans without damage. The third was less fortunate. Some 20 mm cannon fire converged at its propeller hub, then crashed into the Pratt and Whitney engine. The results were devastating. The aircraft was ripped apart. When its fuel ignited, a bright orange fireball enveloped the entire plane. The pilot of the P-47 was killed instantly. Mercifully, he died without pain, without even knowing his life was over. The pilot's name was Robert Ennis.

As the three surviving aircraft turned to do battle again, Forester had leveled off at 16,000 feet. His plane was still flyable, though barely. In no condition to engage the enemy and with no other aircraft in sight, Tom pointed the plane towards England. As the P-47's compass registered a westerly direction, Forester assessed his situation. He was alone in hostile airspace, miles from home, in an aircraft that was about to fall apart. Tom the instructor told Tom the pilot that prudence required him to bail out.

Forester told the instructor to go to hell. Tom preferred to think of his parachute as a seat cushion rather than as a safety device.

Parachuting was measure of last resort, to be taken only when everything else had failed. *Besides, the situation is not all bad.* He was alive, the plane was still in the air, and he had sufficient fuel to reach home. With luck, he could make the coast of England, maybe even touch down at Bromley Park.

Then, unexpectedly, something occurred that had never happened before. Forester panicked and became truly afraid. Afraid of dying, afraid of being alone, afraid of disappearing forever. Fear gripped his entire body, permeating flesh and bone. Tom attempted to contain it, but was unable to do so. He began to shake and felt sick. He wanted to throw up. The reality of his situation, of the likelihood that the good times were about to end, overwhelmed him. He realized he would never see Helen again. Forester was about to concede defeat when two thoughts interjected themselves.

The first concerned Lieutenant Samuel Ordway. Framed as a question, the thought was whether the lieutenant felt like this when he climbed into his P-47 on the day he jumped. Tom visualized Ordway stepping out of the Thunderbolt and wondered where the young man was. He hoped Ordway was resting safely in a POW camp, free of airplanes and the terror they brought him. The second thought was more personal. Tom realized he was doing what Ordway had done. He was giving in, throwing in the towel. The realization made Tom angry. He told himself that in doing so he was betraying the Army Air Force and, more importantly, himself. Forester began to regain his confidence. He put aside thoughts of death and defeat. *Not yet, God damn it, not yet. Stay calm, get a grip, and you just might get yourself out of this mess.* Tom took charge of the situation, a process that itself instilled confidence. He soon began to feel much better and started to calculate what he must do to survive.

There was much to do. Nursing home a crippled Thunderbolt would require considerable skill and total concentration. When the engine coughed and the aircraft shook, he knew luck would be needed as well.

For the next twenty minutes, Tom's P-47, its airspeed just 140 mph, flew toward England, slowly losing altitude. As the plane neared the Dutch coast, Tom was on the lookout for enemy fighters. Though his guns still worked, he realized his chances of survival were slim should the Luftwaffe appear.

At 7,000 feet, he was over the North Sea. No ships were in sight. Forester felt very much alone. Below, the water, although calm, appeared dark and uninviting. It stretched as far as he could see. Finding a downed pilot, assuming he survived the cold temperatures, was unlikely. In 1943, rescue operations were hit and miss affairs, even when another pilot saw you ditch. There was simply too much water in which to spot a single figure bobbing among the waves. Moreover, water landings were dicey. Most P-47 pilots who tried did not succeed.

As Forester coaxed his plane westward, his spirits brightened. He began to think he would survive. At 5,000 feet, his heartbeat accelerated. Off to the right, above him, were two shapes moving quickly. As they drew closer, their form as aircraft became more recognizable. They were single engine fighters, with large radial engines. Were they P-47s, he was safe. Were they Fw-190s, he was a dead man.

They were Thunderbolts. The two P-47s pulled up from their dive and formed up on Forester's aircraft. Tom then heard a voice he recognized.

"Hello Trumpet, this is Cowboy Red 1. Glad to find you. We've all been worried."

Cowboy Red 1 was Ken Browne. He had been leading ten aircraft of the 87th Fighter Squadron back to Bromley Park when he sighted Tom's P-47. "Your plane looks like Swiss cheese. Can you keep her flying?"

"Red 1, Trumpet here. I think so. So far so good."

"How's your oil pressure, Colonel? You've started to smoke." Thick black smoke had begun to billow from beneath Forester's aircraft. "I'm going to take a closer look."

Browne took his P-47 down beneath Tom's plane, coming up on the other side. What he saw he didn't like.

"Colonel, your aircraft looks pretty bad. There's a piece of rudder missing, tail wheel is all shot up and up front, down near the oil cooler doors, it's all a mess. It doesn't look good, Colonel."

Forester had to agree. The situation did not look good. Then it got worse. Tom noticed that his aircraft's oil pressure, up to now okay, was starting to drop.

"Just a few minutes more, Major, and I'll set this crate down on some soft English real estate."

"Colonel, maybe you ought to jump. The coast is coming up and we'll circle about until they come pick you up."

"No thanks, Ken." As the situation worsened, Forester dispensed with call signs. So did Browne, though the Major was still employing Tom's military rank, one grade higher than his own.

"Your choice, Colonel. I'm sending my wingman home. I'll stick with you till you're on the ground." To himself, Ken Browne completed the sentence, "or in the drink."

Forester watched as the other P-47 banked sharply to the right, heading north to Bromley Park. As the aircraft departed, Tom heard a sharp grinding noise followed by a loud bang. His Thunderbolt shook and began to falter. *Come on, come on. Not now. Just a little longer.*

"Time to set her down, Colonel. You're about two miles from the coast."

Gently, Forester pushed the stick forward. The P-47 responded. It began a shallow dive. Tom also advanced the throttle. He needed airspeed to keep the plane from falling in. The speed would allow him to maintain some semblance of control, assuming the engine, already overstressed, did not break apart.

Now a mile from shore, Tom was at 900 feet, with a rate of descent that alarmed Ken Browne. Forester was too busy to be worried. He was trying to keep the plane aloft and aligned with a field just in from the beach that seemed suitable for a wheels-up crash landing. No buildings were in the glide path, nor were there trees in the way. The only obstacle, as far as Forester could tell, was an old stone wall that marked the field's eastern boundary. He would have to fly over the wall and then quickly bring the Thunderbolt down onto the field. Forester knew the landing, if it could be called that, would be a close call.

Tom's plane fell short. It struck neither the wall nor the field. The engine tore itself apart and the Thunderbolt hit the water at 160 mph, 100 feet from the shore. The P-47 plowed into the sea. Water cascaded as if an artillery shell had exploded. The plane did not bounce. It cleaved through the water, coming to an abrupt stop in seven seconds. Whereupon, after a few seconds pretending to be a boat, it began to sink, nose first.

Forester had taken the precautions of tightening his harness. He also had pulled the canopy back and braced himself for the oncoming shock. In those few seconds, Tom undid the straps and pulled himself out of the cockpit. When the plane began to nose over, he was on the wing about to dive in when he became aware of something odd. He sensed it first before his brain recognized what had caused him to pause. The Thunderbolt was not moving. It was remaining stationary, its front end submerged with its tail pointing skyward at a 50-degree angle.

Still wearing his Mae West life preserver, Tom sat down on the wing, and feet first, gingerly pushed himself into the water. Immediately, he received a surprise. He was standing in three feet of water.

The water was very cold. Tom told himself all he had to do was wade some sixty yards to the shore. He thought that would be easy. It wasn't. Forester used every ounce of energy he possessed to reach the beach. Fortunately, the surf was low. For the last fifteen feet, Tom crawled on all fours, water washing about him. Once ashore, he stayed on hands and knees, forcing himself to get a few feet above the high tide mark. Then, stretching out on the sand face down, he breathed deeply over and over again. Exhausted, he had come close to drowning after nearly being killed in the air. Now on land, Tom was thankful to be alive.

As he lay on the sand, a noise forced him to sit up. The sound was loud and utterly familiar. It was deep and thunderous, extremely powerful, yet sweet and reassuring to those who recognized it. Tom smiled as he sat up and, out to sea, past his now useless Thunderbolt, saw the source of the sound.

Ken Browne was taking his P-47 low across the water at full power. He came straight towards Forester, zoomed overhead, then circled and flew parallel to the shore. Wagging his wings as he passed Tom, Browne headed north, climbing for altitude, on course for Bromley Park.

Tom knew he should get off the beach. He was cold and wet and might come down with pneumonia were he not quickly to find shelter and dry clothes. He also needed to find out where he was, and get a message through to Bromley Park to confirm Major Browne's report. Wilbur Williams could then arrange a ride back to the base.

Instead, worn out and still shaken by all that had transpired, Forester decided to stay right where he was. At least for a while, Tom wanted to rest and enjoy the unexpected tranquility of the moment. No people were nearby or even in sight. No aircraft were present, nor were any automobiles disturbing the peace. Only a few sea gulls off in the distance broke the silence. Tom thought it strange, but wonderful that after all the commotion he'd just experienced he found himself alone on the seashore surrounded by such beauty. Up and down the beach the view was lovely, truly picturesque. The water was still a slate grey, foreboding as before. Streams of clouds covered the sky, permitting light to pass through unevenly. The coastline, itself meandering for miles, appeared endless. Off to the north, a small fishing village displayed houses of brown stone and reddish slate roofs that North Sea weather had bombarded for years. Forester had a fleeting desire to paint the image before him, to capture it forever. Until he reminded himself that he had little talent as an artist.

Despite the cold and wind that now was stirring, Tom remained on the beach for ten minutes. They were minutes he would always treasure. In 1943, moments of solitude to appreciate nature's beauty were uncommon along England's eastern shoreline.

—ɱ—

Three days after the respite on the beach, Forester was sitting outside the office of General Harrison, having been summoned to Wycombe Abbey by the DFO. Tom had no idea why the Brigadier wished to see him.

Forester assumed Richard Harrison was up to no good. Harry Collins agreed and, a day before the meeting, offered to accompany Tom. Politely, Forester declined the officer, saying two lieutenant colonels were unlikely to persuade Harrison from doing whatever he intended to do.

"True enough," replied the Intelligence Officer who knew of a certain lieutenant general who might. The difficulty would be in getting to this senior officer in a timely fashion. The goal would be either to preempt Harrison from issuing orders regarding Forester or to have them countermanded before they were implemented. Collins was determined to block General Harrison from damaging Forester and his career, objectives he was certain the DFO had in mind.

By that afternoon, the 19th Fighter Group's Intelligence Officer had a plan. Step number one was to place a call to the American Embassy in London and speak with the colonel he had met at Helen Trent's party. Step number two was to telephone his buddy on the staff of the general he needed to see. After completing the first call, Harry soon was on the phone again.

"Okay Benjamin, my friend, you owe me one and I'm calling it in. I need to talk to the Big Guy and I need to do it real soon, sometime tomorrow."

"Jesus, that's going to be hard, Harry. He's real busy. I've got generals wanting to see him," answered Lieutenant Colonel Benjamin Stillwell, an intelligence officer serving as chief aide to Lieutenant General Michael McCready.

"So what? You work his calendar. He trusts you. You can get me in."

"This better be good. It would help if you could bring someone with you, someone, how shall I say this, a little more imposing than a Group Intelligence Officer. No offense."

"None taken. How about Jimmy Dixon?"

"The Air Attaché?"

"The same. He's actually the Deputy Air Attaché and destined for bigger things. I just spoke with him five minutes ago. He's on board, and will show up with me. And relax, there won't be any egg on your face from this."

"He'll do. Okay, Harry, I'll see what I can do."

"Not good enough, Ben. I need to see him. And it's not about me."

"Are you going to tell me what it's about?"

"Do you really want to know?"

"No, but I need to, in case McCready asks."

"Okay. This concerns Brigadier General Richard Harrison and a certain Lieutenant Colonel in a certain fighter group who happens to have eight kills to his credit."

"I think I know what's going on. Okay, come down first thing in the morning. I'll get you in. I may get some heat on this, but for you, I'll do it."

"Thanks, Benny. I knew I could count on you. Besides, what are old friends for?"

—⁓—

As Forester waited outside his office, Richard Harrison was lost in thought. He was thinking about aerial dogfights, imagining what it must be like to engage the enemy in deadly combat among the clouds. He pictured himself victorious, a pilot on the winning side gaining laurels by virtue of courage and skill. General Harrison longed to succeed. He wanted to be in a position to boast of accomplishment and then not do so thereby winning further kudos as a modest All-American hero.

Harrison knew that at forty-one, though youthful in appearance, a tour of duty in fighters was unlikely. A tour in bombers might be possible, but here again age worked against him. So Harrison switched images, envisioning a different scenario. He was in charge of an air force combat command. He led an armada of airplanes that overcame obstacles and crushed the enemy. He was a warrior whose tactical and strategic talents resulted in a triumph of American arms. The victory would earn him respect and fame. His name would be known here in England, as well as back home. Advancement in the Army Air Force would follow. A second star would trumpet his arrival as an officer to be reckoned with. Once the war was over, the Air Corps was bound to become a separate service. Richard Harrison saw himself as a leader of the new United States Air Force. A third star was then likely. He would wear it well. Then, perhaps, certainly not out of the question, he would cap his career with appointment as Air Force Chief of Staff.

Jody would like that. She wanted what he wanted. Jody found pleasure in his success and enjoyed the deference accorded the wife of a senior officer. Harrison loved Jody. She nurtured his ambition and was a loyal, accommodating woman who placed his needs above her own. He thought she was quite good looking, in a June Allyson sort of way. She was, he believed, an ideal spouse. The daughter of a general, Jody was comfortable with army life, wise in the ways of the military. Stern with wives of junior officers, accommodating to those married to more senior men, Jody added to the pleasure Harrison had in wearing the uniform. She made him feel important. In good times and bad, she helped to advance his career.

Now was a good time. Director of Fighter Operations was a position ideal for advancement in rank. DFOs were officers considered to have bright futures. The job itself was not all that difficult, or so Harrison thought. Pay attention to the wishes of your superior officer and the powers that be. That meant pleasing General Eaker and the Bomber Boys. Let your staff do the planning and let them attend to details. On both counts, Colonel Arnie and his people were doing a fine job. Stay in touch with Washington and attuned to Army politics. That was being done by private communications with friends at Hap Arnold's headquarters and by Jody, who constantly socialized with the wives of senior officers. General Harrison believed these efforts constituted a formula for success. They had worked well in the past. The DFO was confident they would continue to do so.

Images of senior command and of Jody merged as Richard Harrison dreamed of the future. By the end of next year, he hoped to be a Major General. He and Jody might then take some leave and look for property in Texas. He had always wanted to own a ranch. Jody wanted a place to call home. Someday they would need to retire. They both wanted to live comfortably.

Again, the images shifted. Now Harrison saw himself in the cockpit of a P-39 leading a squadron of aircraft that was blasting enemy tanks. Then he was the pilot of a B-24 leading a mission to Berlin. This recalled to mind the time he had brought down safely a twin-engine Beechcraft whose motors had conked out. He had glided down, using stick and rudder, landing the plane at high speed on a highway in the California desert. The feat was noteworthy. Not every pilot could have done as well. The episode brought Richard Harrison his first taste of recognition. He and Jody discovered they liked it.

Thoughts of the Beechcraft dissolved with a knock on the door. Colonel Arnie entered, and saluted the Director of Fighter Operations.

"How's it going?" said Harrison, to whom the words were a standard greeting devoid of meaning.

"Fine, Sir. Thank you," said Arnie who, despite responding, recognized the lack of sincerity implicit in the remark. The Colonel had heard Harrison say these words may times. He knew they were not an expression of interest. "Lieutenant Colonel Forester is outside, General, as you ordered."

"Let him wait. I'll get to him in a moment."

Arnie did not say anything. Instead, he reflected upon the individual before him. Harrison certainly was bright and had been a fine pilot. He also was ambitious, itself no sin, but in Richard Harrison, ambition appeared paramount despite conscious efforts to disguise it with informal behavior and charm. As a commander, Arnie considered the DFO a disappointment. This surprised him. At first blush, Harrison seemed perfect for the job. Yet over time, Colonel Arnie had found his boss wanting. General Harrison was cocky, and extremely critical of others—traits Arnie found unattractive. More importantly, the General appeared incapable of grasping the true nature of his responsibilities. The Director of Fighter Operations needed to understand fighter tactics so as to make the Bomber Boys understand why these tactics made sense. His job was to represent Fighter Command at Wycombe Abbey, to ensure that fighter operations could and would mesh with those of the B-17s and B-24s. Harrison did not do this, nor did he realize that his failure to do so jeopardized the entire Eighth Air Force.

For the next several minutes, Arnie and Harrison conducted business, mostly of an administrative nature. When the business was completed, Arnie moved toward the door. As he did so, he asked whether he should send Forester in.

"No, not yet, Colonel. I want Forester to twiddle his thumbs for awhile."

Harrison now pictured Tom in the outer office. No doubt the man had no idea of what was about to happen to him. All the better. Ever since the court martial fiasco, the General had mulled over how he might seek revenge, despite telling himself that both Forester and the incident with Eaker were unimportant. General Harrison did not like being thwarted. He did not appreciate being told not to do something he wished to do. He did not enjoy looking bad in front of his superior officer. Forester had made all three of these take place. The 19th Fighter Group Commander had led a charmed life. He thought himself a crackerjack pilot with a big reputation. Well, that was all about to change.

Harrison realized that the key to punishing Forester lay in making the action appear to be a promotion. Eaker, and McCready as well, would not countenance any downgrading of Forester's responsibilities, nor anything obviously punitive. So the task was to sack Forester without appearing so do so. That meant transferring him to a job that went nowhere, but to an outsider seemed both reasonable and impressive. Richard Harrison had given the matter much thought. When at last he had located such a job, he was pleased with himself.

General Harrison intended to ship Forester back to the States as Commander of Flight Training, First Air Force. Based at Mitchell Field in New York, the First was primarily a training organization fielding replacements for the European Theater of Operations. For Forester, as for any pilot interested in combat or hoping to make a contribution to the war effort, it was a dead-end job, despite the fancy title. At last, Harrison concluded, Forester would be put in his place No longer would he win fame in the air or hold a combat command. This so-called hotshot would get what he deserved.

To make the assignment seem what it was not and to deflect possible criticism of himself, Harrison was going to recommend that Forester be promoted to full colonel. With that, even Eaker could not object.

"Perfect, just perfect." said the DFO to no one. "I get Forester out of England, sidetrack his career, and deprive him of opportunities to win anymore DFCs." Harrison was rankled that Tom had received the RAF medal. "Let's see how many medals you can win flying over Long Island."

An hour later, Forester still was sitting outside General Harrison's office. When Colonel Arnie discovered this, he went into the office and tactfully announced, "Forester is ready to meet with you, Sir, whenever the general is ready."

Slightly annoyed, the DFO responded that in five minutes, Arnie should tell Forester to come in.

When Tom did so, General Harrison ignored him. Standing at attention, Forester had said simply, "Lieutenant Colonel Forester, Sir, reporting as ordered."

Harrison continued to take no notice. Aware of the slight, Tom decided to inwardly relax. Harrison obviously was going to give him some bad news. As he could do nothing about it, Forester decided to calmly await his fate. Finally, in a brusque voice, Harrison broke the silence.

"Forester, I'm reassigning you to a job where your talents can better serve the Army Air Force."

Tom was about to respond that his talents were best utilized at Bromley Park when, realizing the futility of any response, he chose to remain silent. Forester began wondering where Harrison was going to send him. Tom prayed he would remain in England. That way he could still see Helen.

"And this time, the RAF won't come to your rescue."

Tom did not understand what Harrison meant, but he did recognize the General's less than pleasant tone.

The General was about to continue speaking when, with a knock on the door, Colonel Arnie appeared, accompanied by a lieutenant colonel neither Harrison nor Forester recognized.

General Harrison did not like interruptions. He spoke to Arnie with ice in his voice. "I trust this is important."

"It is, General. I apologize for coming in like this, but this officer is under strict orders to see you at once, and in person."

Taking note of the situation Forester spoke next. "Excuse me, General, I will wait outside."

"Yes, fine." Still annoyed, Harrison turned his attention to the newcomer who, surprisingly, addressed Tom.

"But don't go far, Colonel Forester, I have a message for you as well."

As Tom withdrew, both General Harrison and Colonel Arnie thought it odd that the colonel, on a mission to see the DFO, had something to say to Forester. The messenger who did not wear wings on his uniform was pleasantly surprised that the two men he needed to find were both at Wycombe Abbey, in the same office no less.

Now for the second time, the visiting officer spoke.

"General Harrison, I am Lieutenant Colonel Benjamin Stillwell. I carry an urgent message for you from Headquarters, Eighth Air Force Fighter Command. My orders are to deliver this message to you personally."

Harrison took the envelope proffered by Stillwell. He then opened it. What Harrison read came as a great shock. Later, alone in his quarters, there would be anguish and regret.

16 December, 1943
To: Brigadier General Richard Harrison
 Effective immediately, you are hereby relieved as Director of Flight Operations. Report to me, 17 December 1943 for reassignment as commanding officer Air Depot #2, Liverpool.
Lt. Gen. Michael J. McCready
Deputy Commander, Eighth Air Force Fighter Command

Dumfounded, Harrison looked up at Stillwell and Arnie. Saying nothing, he laid the message down upon his desk. Then he stood up and walked out of the room.

Despite surmising what had just transpired, Arnie asked a question of Stillwell. "What was that all about?"

"Can't say. You'll have to ask General Harrison. The message was for him and him alone, although God knows it won't be a secret for very long."

Colonel Armstrong Dwight Arnie had been in the Army for twenty-seven years. During this time, he had seen general officers come and go. This time, he suspected one was going. Arnie had sensed that all was not well during Harrison's tenure as DFO. On more than one occasion, the Colonel had tried to steer General Harrison on a corrective path. But to no avail. Harrison had kept to himself, indicating clearly that unsolicited advice and counsel were not welcome. So Arnie did what he always did, which was the best possible job under the circumstances.

"I'll probably be having a new boss soon. Got any suggestions?"

"Not really. Although I might want to have a staff car with a full tank of gas ready in the morning."

Stillwell then remembered he had a second communication.

"If you'll excuse me, Colonel, I need to go find Colonel Forester." As Stillwell was leaving, he turned towards Arnie. "Thanks for your help."

"My pleasure. Forester should be right outside the door."

Tom was where Arnie had said he would be. Stillwell handed him a sealed envelope.

"Colonel Forester, here is a message I've been instructed to deliver to you after seeing General Harrison."

Tom took the envelope and opened it.

16 December 1943

To: Lieutenant Colonel Thomas Forester

Effective 1 January 1944, you will report to Headquarters, Eighth Air Force Bomber Command, and assume the position of Director of Fighter Operations (DFO).

Request you provide recommendation regarding new Commanding Officer, 19th Fighter Group.

Lt. General Michael J. McCready

Deputy Commander, Eighth Air Force Fighter Command

Also inside the envelope was a handwritten note on a single sheet of formal stationery. The note had dropped to the floor when Forester had opened the envelope. Stillwell retrieved it and handed the note to Tom.

"Thanks," said Forester as he read the note.

Colonel Forester,

Congratulations. I'm sure you'll do a splendid job as DFO. Keep our friends at Wycombe Abbey happy and honest, and in six months you can have another group.

Regards,

Mike McCready

"Congratulations, Colonel," said Stillwell.

"You know what it says?"

"I do. General McCready read it to me as I left his office."

"Not to sound ungrateful, but I'd rather stay where I am."

"McCready knows that. That's why he's letting you finish the year out with the 19th. Then it's up to Wycombe Abbey for you."

"I don't suppose I get a chance to appeal?"

"Are you kidding? This is the army we're in."

"Well, I guess I'll go back to Bromley Park and fly while I still can. I left my Jeep in the circle by the front door. I hope it's still there."

"It is. I saw it when I came down. Right now, there's a friend of yours in it waiting to drive you back. And be nice to the guy. He came to your rescue, in the nick of time."

Tom had no idea what Stillwell meant.

McCready's aide then shook Forester's hand as he made to leave. "I'm off too. Best of luck to you. And don't let the Big Guy down. Generals come no finer."

Left standing alone, Tom went in search of his coat and service cap. Finding them, he went outside to the Jeep. There, behind the wheel, was Harry Collins.

"Hello Colonel," said the Intelligence Officer, "fancy meeting you here."

"Harry, what in heaven's name are you doing here? Or do I want to know? I have the feeling that somehow you're involved in all that's happened."

"Let's just say, Colonel, that Jimmy Dixon and I paid a visit to a general."

"Dixon's involved in this?"

"Up to his eyeballs."

"Okay, Harry, start this thing up, and tell me what's been going on."

"You want the long version, or just a short summary?"

"The former. We've got a long drive ahead of us and, with you at the wheel, we've got plenty of time." Now a broad smile formed on Forester's face. "Mostly though, I want the truth, and nothing but."

"Well, Colonel," replied Collins, "in that case, our story begins fifteen months ago back at Army Intelligence School where sitting next to me was a fellow lieutenant in need of my help by the name of Benjamin Stillwell."

—〰—

On December 17, the day after Richard Harrison was relieved of command and Tom Forester was appointed DFO, Roger Baldwin was standing in Ira Eaker's office, next to the fireplace.

"I wish I could predict good weather, General," said Baldwin, "but I can't. All the indicators suggest more of the same."

"I'm sure you're right, Colonel," replied Eaker. "I just wish you weren't."

"This is among the worst weather Europe's seen in years."

"I wouldn't know about that. I do know it makes our job harder."

"General Anderson tells me that despite the weather, we'll be going back into Germany."

"That's true, Colonel. Our force is growing and come next year, in the next few months, I promise you we're going to hit the Nazis where it hurts, deep inside Germany, in a place called Berlin."

"I'll try to conjure up some good weather for that, General." Baldwin was smiling. He knew Eaker would appreciate the remark.

"Do that, Colonel, and I'll be the most grateful person in Europe."

A knock at the door caused both men to stop talking. Turning, they saw Harris Hull enter the room.

"Excuse me, General, but I have a message for you from General Giles. I also have some bad news for all of us."

In response to this last remark, Eaker queried Hull. "What is it? Barney Giles can wait."

"I can tell, Harris, I'm not going to like what I'm about to hear," interjected Roger Baldwin.

"No, Colonel, you're not." Hull then faced Eaker. "General, I've just learned that Keith Davenport's been killed. His plane took a direct hit over Bremen. Apparently, it was a rocket from an Me-110. Reports are that the plane just blew up. No survivors."

The Eighth Air Force Commander shook his head in sadness. As a military leader, he knew losses were inevitable, and he accepted them. But as a man, he found them painful. "Keith Davenport was a fine officer. He'll be missed."

"Yes, Sir, he will be," said Harris Hull. Eaker's aide found Davenport's loss particularly hard to take. The two officers had become close friends after Davenport has been assigned to Wycombe Abbey.

"Well, the sooner we end this war the better chance that men like Keith Davenport will get home safely." As he spoke, Eaker's tone changed. He was trying to focus on the future, on the battles ahead. "Harris, ask General Anderson to come in. I want to review targets in Germany. We need to get on with this damn war."

Ira Eaker would help win "the damn war," but not in the manner he would hope. The next day, December 18, was the worse day in his life. Once again, Harris Hull entered his office with a message from Washington. However, this message did not originate with Barney Giles. It came from Eaker's friend and superior officer, Hap Arnold.

The message stated that Lieutenant General Ira C. Eaker shortly would take command of Allied Air Forces in the Mediterranean. Jimmy Doolittle, also a three star general, would take over the Eighth. Eaker was being fired. Having brought the Eighth Air Force into being, guided its growth and shaped its character, Ira Eaker was to be denied its finest hour.

Eaker was dismissed because Hap Arnold was dissatisfied and because Dwight Eisenhower, appointed Allied Supreme Commander, wanted to select his own senior commanders. To lead the bomber force in England, Ike chose Doolittle whom he knew from North Africa where Doolittle had commanded the Twelfth Air Force.

The departing general left England on January 1, 1944. Fittingly, he departed in a B-17. The day before, the RAF held a farewell dinner in his honor. Eaker was widely admired in Britain's air service and the dinner was well attended. Several RAF officers spoke, among them Air Vice Marshal Philip Sidney.

At the podium, the Air Vice Marshal first acknowledged the senior officers present. He then addressed Eaker.

"General, I want to say publicly how much we in the Royal Air Force admire the courage and determination of the air force you created.

"As we in the RAF flew at night, your brave men took to the sky in daylight. Together, we did what you told our Prime Minister could and must be done, and that was to 'bomb Germany 'round the clock. Give the devils no rest.' That's what we're doing and will continue to do until this great conflict comes to an end when, at last, the flags of freedom will fly above Europe.

"Now it will surprise no one in this room if I say that on occasion, we in the Royal Air Force have had differing views on tactics with you Colonials."

This remark was greeted with amusement by both British and American officers. Sidney continued.

"As you leave us, I have a small, but highly sophisticated device to assist you should the American air force choose to follow our example and fly when the sun goes down."

At this point, Air Vice Marshal Sidney reached down by his feet and picked up a small box he earlier had placed by the podium. Handing the package to General Eaker, he encouraged the American to open it. Eaker did so, and laughed out loud as he held a flashlight up for all to see. As Eaker displayed the gift, the audience broke into broad smiles and applause.

As the laughter died down, Philip Sidney turned serious.

"Here in Britain we consider General Eaker to be one of the architects of air power. No one has spoken about the role of aviation in wartime with greater clarity or commitment. More importantly, no one has turned these words into action better than the gentleman we honor tonight.

"With great persistence, force of logic, and endless energy, you, Sir," here Sidney turned toward Eaker, "have represented your great country and led its magnificent Eighth Air Force with professional skill and personal integrity.

"As you leave our shores, know that you shall always be welcome in England, both as a friend and comrade in arms.

"Now, gentlemen, please rise and join me in toasting one of America's great warriors, Lieutenant General Ira C. Eaker."

All eyes in the room focused on Eaker. He was genuinely touched by the good will evident in the room, but appeared to some as slightly embarrassed. In fact, he was caught in a moment of reflection. The General was picturing in his mind the day he and six officers arrived in England. Their orders were simple: establish and operate a strategic air force. To Eaker, that day in February 1942 seemed a lifetime ago.

As the party continued, Air Vice Marshal Sidney had further words for the American general. This time, the RAF officer spoke in a whisper, not wishing others to hear.

"General, when first in Africa, do indeed go visit Colonel Holt."

Eaker wondered who this Colonel Holt was. Earlier, the RAF's most senior officer, Air Chief Marshal Sir Charles Portal, had suggested he pay a call upon the colonel. Impressed that Portal had made the suggestion, Eaker did not need convincing by Philip Sidney.

"Yes, I shall do so." Eaker's voice did not betray the curiosity he felt.

—m—

Landing in Casablanca, General Eaker went to a waiting hotel where he bathed and put on a fresh uniform. He then sought out the officer he had been urged to see. To his surprise, Eaker found him at the same villa at which he had made the case for daylight strategic bombing the year before.

A British army brigadier general greeted Eaker at the door of the villa and escorted him inside.

"Please make yourself comfortable, General, Colonel Holt will be down in a moment or two," said the officer whose name, much to his chagrin, was Richard Lionhart.

Lionhart disappeared and Eaker waited alone. Looking about the room, he could not help but notice its large windows and numerous pieces of rattan furniture. The decor was decidedly informal. The room was full of sunshine and, with ceiling fans to push the air about, completely comfortable. Eaker realized he was far away from the cold and wet of Wycombe Abbey.

"Ah, young man, good of you to come."

The man speaking, coming down the stairs, was Winston Churchill. "Colonel Holt" was the pseudonym he used when traveling. The Prime Minister was in Africa recovering from an illness. Few people knew he was not in England.

At first surprised, Eaker recovered and stood up as Churchill moved slowly to a chair. Wearing a unique one piece, grey cotton coveralls, Churchill looked either like a gardener or an auto mechanic. Eaker couldn't tell which. More conventional was the cigar, which the Prime Minister, despite suffering from pneumonia, smoked with undisguised relish.

"Please sit down, General, and tell me what you propose to do while in command here in this ancient land where Rome once ruled."

Eaker explained his plans, careful to speak briefly and to the point. Churchill disliked long speeches, unless he was giving them.

"That sounds fine, eminently sensible. Give the Hun the bashing he deserves."

"I will, Prime Minister."

"Good. Now let me speak my mind and tell you why I summoned you here."

"I know of your disappointment in coming to this theater of war. But I beg you to remember, young man, that here in the Mediterranean, you will have British forces under your command. They are among the finest we have. If we did not have faith in your leadership, we would not have given them to you."

"Yes, Sir." At this point, Eaker felt like a schoolboy standing in front of the principal. That would soon change.

"A year ago, we met in this villa with the great generals and admirals of this war. But I remember you and what you said. You said to me that we should bomb the Germans 'round the clock. Give the Hun no rest. Well, that is what we're now doing and I believe it will lead to victory in Europe. On the wings of your aircraft and those of the Royal Air Force, we shall witness the triumph of democracy.

"In this war, on lands from Norway to North Africa, from Egypt to Iceland, from Russia to the South Atlantic, we have seen great courage and accomplishment among the men who have fought and fight still today. But none shine brighter than the men of the air force you established and led during most difficult times.

"History, General, will treat you well," here Churchill puffed his cigar and appeared much amused, "because I shall write it. And I will record that the American Eighth Air Force has earned its place at the table reserved for freedom's great warriors."

With this last remark, Churchill began to cough and, waving his hand, indicated that the audience, for it could not be called a meeting, was over. Lionhart appeared, and, much to the Prime Minister's annoyance, helped Churchill up the stairs. Eaker was left alone in the room.

Taking a last glance at the room, the General quickly left the villa. As he stepped into the sunshine, he was thinking of the Eighth, hoping that Doolittle would lead the men with the courage and conviction they deserved.

EIGHTEEN

On the day Forester was appointed Director of Fighter Operations, Helen was lunching with Jane Ashcroft. The two women were to meet at Fogarty's and spend the afternoon together. Jane wanted to enlist Helen for volunteer work at the hospital. Now that the Advisory Committee had completed its task, Helen was agreeable, although she wondered whether a paying job might be preferable given her changed circumstances.

Helen arrived at the restaurant first. She quickly found a small table off to the side, and awaited her friend.

Helen's eyes took in the restaurant, but her mind was elsewhere. She was thinking about Sir Robert, despite a resolution made at St. Andrew's to focus only on the future. Her husband's death had caused her to reflect upon their marriage and about the man himself. Not for the first time she asked herself why she had married him. Each time she came up with the same answer. She had agreed to his proposal because she was alone in the world with a child to care for. At the time, the rationale appeared compelling, if a bit calculating. Claire needed a safe and secure world and, to Helen, that seemed primary. She also knew that she herself faced an uncertain future. In 1935, economic conditions were difficult, especially for an unmarried female.

In the building where once she worked in a dress shop, Helen wondered whether she would have married Robert Trent had no child been involved.

Robert always had been charming. He was witty, well dressed, and attentive. He enjoyed many of the things she enjoyed. Theater, literature, and travel were interests they had in common. Moreover, Robert, "Bobby" as she called him in moments of endearment, had been persistent. He had courted her with determination. Helen felt she understood this engaging, ambitious individual. He wanted a wife, a companion to share life's ups and downs. And he promised to be good to Claire.

So marriage seemed entirely sensible. If their union then and later lacked passion, Helen reasoned that affection, respect, and comfort were satisfactory substitutes. As the years passed, Helen had found no cause to change her mind.

Passion had been Peter's purview. While married to Sir Robert, Helen had put aside the memories of the romance and lovemaking that characterized her first marriage. With Peter, there had been moments of indescribable pleasure. But, in Helen's mind, those sweet memories had happened to a younger, different woman.

At first she and Robert had been intimate. Yet, Helen felt his lovemaking perfunctory. He seemed far more comfortable in the library than in bed. She had tried to seduce him, but succeeded only on occasion. Helen thought she was an attractive woman. Over time, she concluded he did not. Their sexual intimacy dwindled. This troubled her. At times, she would blame herself. Other times, she chose to ignore this facet of life. Only recently, on that day in Jock Appleby's office, did she realize the true obstacle.

Now in 1943, eight years after marrying Robert, Tom had rekindled feelings Helen believed were part of her past. He had caused her to rediscover her body. This pleased her immensely. However, she wondered whether by involving herself with the American she was acting impulsively. Sometimes she told herself that she hardly knew Forester. They had met only in September and saw each other but occasionally.

In the restaurant while Helen was thinking of Forester, she became conscious of her age. This had happened before, though most often in the past three months, a coincidence that had not gone unnoticed. Helen realized that her youth was gone. Certainly, she did not feel old. She just did not feel like a person whose life lay largely ahead of her. The evidence was in her hands. Where once her skin had been smooth as silk, it now was etched with wrinkles. Both her hands and neck showed signs of aging. Peter had never seen her skin this way. Robert had, but presumably paid no attention. Helen wondered what Tom thought. Had he noticed? Did he care?

If her skin was that of a middle-aged woman, her feelings were a different matter. Helen felt truly alive, emotionally involved, as a teenager might with a first love. There was a man in her life who with words and deeds had awakened feelings she thought no longer relevant. He had come along unexpectedly and, much to her delight, had brought passion with him. That he was a twenty-six-year-old American, she told herself, did not matter. Indeed, it added to the excitement.

But would the excitement last? Was there a future to this relationship? Were not their differences, so intriguing at present, the seed to problems later on? Was this romance simply a product of the times? Or was it an affair of the heart, so true and so compelling that nothing could separate them as lovers and friends?

These questions and others like them Helen asked herself as she waited for Jane Ashcroft. Helen did not have the answers nor did she pretend to. Her mind wavered. At times, she felt optimistic regarding the future. Somehow she and Tom would last as a couple and do well together. Other times, she considered such optimism to be naive. How could two people so different remain together once life in England and America returned to normal?

Helen remembered that Tom had said the future would have to take care of itself. They had been outside Harrods when the subject had come up. Tom said he didn't know what would happen, but that they should be thankful they had each other to share the present. Helen accepted this. She was thankful, but she still pondered the future. She wondered if Tom did as well.

"Hello, Helen. You look lost in thought." Jane Ashcroft had arrived.

"Hello, Jane. Yes I am. It's good to see you." Helen rose and the two friends exchanged kisses on the check.

"Have you been here long?"

"No. I was a few minutes early."

Jane laughed, and replied, "You almost always are. I wish I could. I never seem to get anywhere early."

"That's because you don't do what's absolutely necessary."

"And that is?"

"Leave a few minutes early."

"I knew you were going to say that."

At this point, a waiter arrived and announced the special of the day. Fogarty's was serving a steamed fish roll, made with cod, carrots, and cabbage. This sounded unappetizing to both women, so they elected to have instead a hearty scotch broth supplemented by fresh bread that, like the soup, was flavorful and filling. Tea, and later on, a cup of apple pudding completed the component of lunch devoted to food. More important was the conversation, which began when Jane described opportunities for Helen to serve at St. George's Hospital. Mrs. Ashcroft said help was needed everywhere, but particularly in physical therapy, pediatrics, and treatment of burns. Helen thought she might be useful in, and comfortable with, physical therapy. But she remained silent, not committing to any aspect of hospital service. Helen first wanted to meet the people involved and get a better sense of what service at Herbert Ashcroft's hospital entailed.

More importantly, Helen felt uncertain as to whether she should accept a volunteer position. With finances unsettled, she told her friend it might be wise to put off a decision for a week or two, in order to see more precisely what her situation would be regarding income and expenses. Jane's response was immediate. She said that Helen indeed should delay a decision regarding volunteer work. Then Jane spoke words that Helen, though touched by her friend's generosity, had hoped not to hear.

"Remember Helen, Herbert and I are here if you need us."

"That's generous and so very dear of you both."

"I know it's an awkward subject. Just know that we will help however we can."

"I do appreciate your offer, Jane, I truly do. I think I shall be fine. I just need a few weeks to settle into my new life."

"Which raises the question of how exactly is your new life."

Jane intended her remark to change both the topic and mood of the conversation. Talk about the hospital had been pleasant, but serious. Talk about money, if brief, had been more serious and was not something upon which either woman wished to dwell. Jane wanted Helen to know that she and her husband would help out if necessary. Helen wanted Jane to know she was grateful for the offer. Once these wishes were expressed, both women desired something else to talk about. Jane spoke first.

"You do have a new life, my friend. I do hope you will take advantage of it, despite the sadness that brought it about."

"Yes it was sad, awful really."

"Of course, it was dreadful."

"I find myself in this new life of mine, thinking about my old life."

"That's very natural."

"True enough, I suppose. Sometimes I find it difficult to believe that Robert is gone."

Jane remained silent. She sensed Helen wished to continue.

"You knew, of course, that our marriage was not entirely successful. And now we both know why. I still can't believe I was so blind. I feel like such a fool."

"Don't. You did your best and made every effort. The fault, my friend, lies with him, not you."

"I'm not so sure of that. After all, I agreed to marry him. I stayed with him when he became distant. I enjoyed the comfort and society he brought into our lives. Maybe it was I who took advantage of him."

"That's rubbish. You did what was expected of you, and more."

"Yes, I certainly gave it a go and thought at first I was succeeding."

"Helen, you have nothing to be ashamed of. If I may speak frankly, Robert betrayed you. He mocked the sanctity of marriage."

"Perhaps."

"Not perhaps. Definitely so."

"But I married him. I said yes to his proposal."

"And with good reason. You had a young child and a life of your own to lead. He came along with not inconsiderable charm and promised to care for you both."

"That's true, and in many ways he did."

"But I will say this to you directly, as your friend."

"My best friend."

"Yes, your best friend. What Robert Trent did was wrong. It was deceitful to marry you and he was wrong to take up with that man Grimes."

"Yes, I suppose he was. In truth, though, my anger seems not to last. I just feel sorry for Robert. God knows he had his faults, but deep down he was just another human being trying to make his way through life. Mostly, I feel sorry for him."

"I don't. I think he betrayed you."

"He did and I know that. It's just that I can't seem to hate him. Maybe I failed him."

"Absolutely not. Helen, you're speaking nonsense. You're being much too kind and taking blame where none is deserved. He failed you. His life was one of deception and perversion."

"Yes, but if I had tried harder or done things differently, perhaps he would not have . . . "

"Stop!" Jane was visibly annoyed. She saw where her friend was heading and was not going to allow Helen to proceed. "Robert was what he was. Nothing you could have done would have changed that. He deceived you and led a secret life, one that decent people everywhere condemn."

Helen did not respond. By remaining silent, Helen acknowledged agreement with what Jane had just said. Helen Trent could not fathom how one man might be sexually attracted to another. Moreover, she considered Sir Robert's relationship with Wilfred Grimes to be contrary to what the Church of England taught and what English law sanctioned. In her view, it was simply improper. Yet she would always wonder whether had she behaved differently, he would have changed his ways.

Jane was aware that she was becoming agitated, so she decided to again shift the topic of conversation. She took hold of Helen's hand and spoke to a subject she believed more important than Sir Robert's innocence or guilt.

"Helen, all that is in the past. Now you must look to the future. You now have a new life and a chance to find some happiness."

"That's a good way to look at it."

"Sometimes happiness comes when and where it's least expected."

"Yes, I'm finding that out."

"Good. I just want you to have someone who takes care of you and makes you happy."

"I seem to have found that someone."

"Young Tom Forester?" Jane asked.

"I'm in love with him, silly as that sounds."

"It doesn't sound silly to me."

"I'm forty-three years old. I'm not supposed to fall in love with someone his age. He's twenty-six. What will people think?"

"Do you care?

"Part of me does. The other part says everyone else should mind their own business."

"That's good advice."

"Yes it is, and I need to remember it."

"If you love this man, how old he is doesn't matter. Differences matter only if you let them. My advice to you is to follow your heart."

"I want to, so very much. I'm just afraid it may not work out."

"It may not. But if you don't try, you'll never know. Let me ask you a simple question. Do you love this man?"

Helen did not hesitate. "Yes, I do."

"Well then, you have your answer."

"But isn't it too soon? I've just met Tom and here I am carrying on like a schoolgirl when I'm supposed to be a grieving widow."

Jane replied with assurance. "Whatever you owed Robert, you've paid in full. Your life now belongs to you, not him. As to Tom Forester, all I can say is that life is short and not everyone gets a second chance or, in your case, a third. I'm going to say to you what I once told you before. If you love this man, go find him and tell him so. Hold on to him and make him a part of your life."

The two women remained in the restaurant for another hour. As they continued their conversation, Helen, as she had done many times before, reflected on her friendship with Jane Ashcroft. Jane, she concluded, was loyal, generous, sensible, and completely trustworthy. Helen felt comfortable with Jane. Between them, tension never occurred. They could discuss any subject imaginable, and since Roedean, had spent more than one night talking until sunrise when one or the other was in need of a sympathetic listener. Helen considered herself fortunate. Not everyone, she realized, was blessed with such a wonderful best friend.

When the waiter brought the bill, Jane insisted on paying.

"I'll let you pay this time, only if you remember next time that it's my turn." said Helen.

Then they both laughed. Helen Trent and Jane Ashcroft had been paying for each other's noonday meals for over twenty years and never could remember who had paid last. Both knew that soon they would forget who had paid this day at Fogarty's. Neither of them thought it mattered.

newcomers' chances of survival as well as to enhance their value to the 19th Fighter Group. The other two flights were operational missions. On December 20, the Eighth returned to Bremen, losing twenty-seven aircraft. Two days later, the bombers visited Osnabrouk. On both missions, the 19th did well. The pilots of Bromley Park made their rendezvous on time and broke up numerous Luftwaffe attacks, downing a total of thirteen Germans. Forester's score was less impressive. He damaged two Me-109s.

—〟〞—

On December 23, Tom caught an afternoon train to London. He had hoped to leave earlier, but a stack of paperwork needed his review, and he was determined to dispose of it properly before departing. Wilbur Williams worked hard to keep administrative matters up to date. Tom believed he owed it to the Adjutant to do the same.

At Bromley Park station, Forester did something he never had done before. He purchased a first class ticket. He did so just to see what first class accommodations were like. Not surprisingly, he found them plush and comfortable, though pricey. He decided that, as he easily could become spoiled, he would henceforth ride second class.

Soon after Tom found a seat in the first class coach, a member of the clergy entered the compartment accompanied by his wife. The man looked to be his father's age and projected an aura of authority and distinction. His wife was equally imposing. Forester guessed that unlike him, they were used to traveling first class.

The churchman's name was William Temple. He introduced himself and his wife, whose name was Frances. They were friendly and eager to engage Forester in conversation. The Temples lived in Lambeth, which Tom learned was across the Thames from Westminster. Francis Temple was about to say something about their residence when William threw her a stern look. She then said simply that their home had been bombed and they were "making do."

The Reverend Temple asked Tom what he did. In response, Forester explained the role of Bromley Park and its P-47s.

"And who commands these men and their airplanes."

"Actually, Sir, I do."

"Oh, I see." Temple was surprised. "You seem rather young for such responsibility."

"Well, perhaps I am, but many group commanders are my age. Some are a little younger. I think it's the same in the RAF. Combat flying is a lot like athletics. You need to have quick reflexes and be in top physical shape. It tends to be a young man's game."

"I suppose that's true. That's one of the terrible things about war. Young men have to fight and die because old men cannot agree."

"I've never thought of it that way."

"You will, my boy, when you're older."

As the train moved along, the conversation continued. Often, Frances Temple participated. Forester noticed how the clergyman listened intently to what his wife had to say. Clearly, he respected her views. Tom could see why. Frances spoke sensibly and with compassion.

At one point in the conversation when Frances mentioned recent public statements by several outspoken Anglican bishops, William Temple shook his head and sighed in frustration. Tom then recalled that since coming to England he had wondered about the relevance of Christian teachings in time of war. To Forester, the Reverend Temple seemed an appropriate person to query.

"It must be a difficult position for you, Sir, given your line of work. War is about death and destruction, about killing the other fellow, which your air force and mine do everyday over Germany. Yet the Church preaches just the opposite. It emphasizes love and compassion, peace and good will. How does one reconcile that?"

William Temple pondered Forester's question. The American had raised an issue of supreme significance, one that the bishops had debated and been unable to reach unanimity. As the state religion of Great Britain, the Anglican Church had to be supportive of the war. Chief Defender of the Faith was George VI, King of England.

Temple himself had struggled with the issue, discussing it often with Frances. His answer reflected what they both thought.

"All human life is precious. We are all children of God. And to all true Christians taking a life is morally repugnant. Yet we live in a time when a monstrous evil exists and threatens all that is good and decent. Evil, my boy, is not some old fashioned concept relevant only to Milton and the Bible. Evil is something real and tangible. In our time, it is a political Black Plague that has infected Germany and wishes to spread about the globe.

"Crushing such evil has become an absolute necessity. Of that, I have no doubt. Nor does the Church of which I'm part. We in this kingdom are not just at war. We are engaged in a crusade, to rid the world of something truly terrible. We confront and must defeat an Antichrist whose powers, like that of Lucifer, challenges the very existence of Christian civilization.

"I do not like many of the actions we must take to stop Herr Hitler. I'm not sure I myself could do them. But I accept them as necessary and condemn them not.

"On Sundays and everyday, I pray for the safety and success of men such as yourself upon whose shoulders rests the burden of victory. You are all Christian soldiers, marching on to war."

The words had been spoken with heartfelt feelings. Tom felt he had heard a great man speak. For a moment, Forester said nothing, absorbing the message. He felt reassured. What he did was not wrong in the eyes of the Church. That made Tom feel comfortable, although he recognized the inconsistency in that he did not believe much of church doctrine.

Frances Temple was gently patting her husband's hand. The Reverend had spoken with emotion and now, with his wife's assistance, was calming down. The subject was one William Temple felt strongly about. His wife decided a less serious subject was in order.

"Tell me, Colonel, have you met many people in London?"

Forester replied that he had met a few, mentioning both members of the Advisory Committee and guests at the party given for Sir

Robert. He did not speak of Helen, but as the train approached the city, she was much on his mind.

Minutes before the train pulled into the station, Tom and his two traveling companions had said their farewells. William Temple and his wife were extremely cordial and remarked that when convenient, Tom should call upon them. The clergy handed Forester his card on which printed below his name and above a telephone number were the words "Lambeth Palace." Tom took note of the unusual address, but said nothing. He quickly forgot about it when stepping off the train. Instead, he was picturing in his mind the woman with whom he had come to spend Christmas.

Helen was excited that Tom and she would be together. On her favorite holiday, Helen would have as company the two individuals she loved above all others. She was determined this Christmas would be a joyous one. Not the war, not even Sir Robert's death would be allowed to mar the holiday spirit.

Claire had come up from Roedean on Tuesday, two days before Forester arrived. In that time, she and her mother had been insepa-rable. Helen had taken Claire Christmas shopping though, mindful of money, they had limited their purchases. Mostly they talked. Claire told her mother about her friends at school, about her stud-ies, about the latest gossip regarding Miss Evans, and about several boys she had met while at a supervised party earlier in the month. This last subject made Helen realize her daughter was now of the age when interest in the opposite sex accelerates. This both pleased Helen and made her worry. It was another sign that Claire was maturing. Her daughter was more and more a young woman, less and less a little girl. At the same time, Helen believed that Claire's newfound interest signaled the beginning of heartache, which the mother considered an inevitable consequence of romance. For proof, Helen looked at her own life. It was her own past experiences she was contemplating when Claire, sitting on the blue sofa in the living room, was asking a question, or rather trying to.

ment. Knocking over a lamp, they simply laughed. Reaching the stairs, they experimented, finding old pleasures in new positions. Several times Tom exploded in ecstasy. More than once Helen was enveloped in orgasm.

Later in the evening, after passion had subsided, they were sitting on the sofa, resting and holding each other's hand. Forester was wearing only his dress shirt. The rest of his clothes were strewn about the room. Helen had put on a robe after taking her clothes upstairs. She was in a mood to talk.

"I love you, Tom. I can hardly believe what's happened to me, to us. But I'm happier now than I've been in a very long time."

"I'm glad of that, Helen. You deserve to be happy."

"Do you love me?"

"God yes. Can't you tell?"

"I can tell that you love to make love to me."

"I do that. But my dear, dear lady have no doubt that I love you truly and always will."

"That's so sweet to hear."

"Especially since it's true. You're my woman, Helen, and I'm your guy."

Thinking of the last two hours, Helen sighed. How wonderful to be passionate again, to feel a man's touch, to make love without restraint or shame. Better still to be in love and have that man be in love with you. Helen felt her life had come full circle. She believed a new chapter was underway.

Turning reflective, Helen spoke to Forester.

"I wonder how all this will end."

"What my love?"

"Us. What will become of us? In the months ahead and when the war is over."

"We'll do just fine."

"Do you really think so. Tell me the truth. Aren't we a bit of a long shot?"

"Not at all. What matters is who we are and how we feel. I love you, Helen. I truly do. And I believe that you love me. And if we remain true to one another and true to ourselves, then things will work out."

"I want to believe that. I'm just not sure."

"Helen, we can't predict exactly how the future will unfold . . . "

"So we . . . "

"No, let me finish. But if this love of ours is special, if it's more than two lonely people in the middle of a war, as I believe it is, then the future will take care of itself. We have each other and together we can handle whatever lies ahead."

Forester's optimism registered with Helen. She wondered if he felt this way because he was young, or in love, or because he was an American. Then she realized Tom was all three.

They talked for another twenty minutes. During that time, she explained what she had planned for the next two days. He asked if she were free on New Year's Eve. When Helen replied positively, Tom suggested they spend the last night of 1943 together.

"That would be super." Helen's enthusiasm was genuine.

"I report for duty at Wycombe Abbey at ten o'clock the morning. And since I plan to leave Bromley Park that afternoon, the evening is free."

"Splendid. We shall celebrate your new position and the beginning of 1944."

"Yes indeed," replied Forester. *And something else as well,* he thought happily.

As they walked upstairs to the bedroom, Tom stopped Helen on the stairwell. He turned her around to face him and, to her pleasant surprise, kissed her. Softly at first. Then harder.

"I love you, Helen. All of this has happened quickly, and I'm sure you wonder if these crazy times have made us do crazy things."

Helen started to speak, but Tom gently covered her mouth with his hand.

"Just know that whatever happens, I'm your guy and that if this war has done anything good, it's brought me to you and you to me, and for that we should be truly grateful."

—⁓—

Forester returned to Bromley Park on Sunday, December 26. He had had a wonderful three days. The Christmas Eve service at Westminster Abbey had been particularly moving. Clara Harris, Claire, he, and Helen had arrived at the Abbey early in order to obtain good seating. Hundreds of candles provided light while the organ and choir combined to create majestic sounds of Christmas that enriched all who were present. When *Silent Night* was sung, Tom felt suspended in a moment of stillness and peace, as though the war had gone away and everyone in the Abbey shared a common bond, united in their humanity, bound together by good will.

Forester could not sing well, but with conviction he joined the others:

> *Silent night, holy night*
> *All is calm, all is bright*
> *'Round yon Virgin, mother and child*
> *Holy infant, so tender and mild*
> *Sleep in heavenly peace*
> *Sleep in heavenly peace*

Dinner at the Ashcrofts also was a success. Jane made a special effort to have Forester feel welcome, which he appreciated. Herbert Ashcroft kept Tom engaged in conversation, which Helen appreciated. Together with Jane's two sisters, they all dined as one extended family. This eased Tom's sadness at being far from home on Christmas Day.

Helen thought Jane's menu was outstanding and its execution excellent. Mrs. Ashcroft served perfectly grilled lamb chops with mustard sauce, fried potatoes, and a medley of green beans, mushrooms, and carrots. Dessert was simple, yet superbly prepared. It was a chocolate raisin cake. Tom enjoyed the meal and thought the cake the best he had ever eaten. He did not realize that the Ashcrofts used a week's worth of ration coupons to obtain the food. Gestures such as this happened often in Britain when gracious English families invited Americans to dine. The families would sacrifice in order to provide for their guests, many of whom had healthy appetites, with plentiful food.

Helen was aware of what the Ashcrofts had done. What she did not know, until the meal was over, was how Jane had pulled off such a splendid feast. Her friend was a wonderful person, but not a terrific cook. Throughout the visit, she had kept Helen out of the kitchen, saying forcefully, "I want you in the sitting room with Tom and not to worry, I can cope." The mystery was solved at the conclusion of the meal when Jane brought François Sabotier out to the dining room to accept a round of well-deserved applause.

Prior to his departure from Bromley Park, Tom spent most of his time on administrative matters. His priority was to obtain a promotion for Wilbur Williams, which occurred after he left. He flew only three times. One flight was a training mission. The other two were escort missions in which the 19th Fighter Group was assigned to cover the strike force on its way to the target. On December 30, the Fortresses visited Ludwigshaven. The next day, Eighth Air Force bombers hit airfields in France. On both operations, enemy opposition was intense.

On the last mission of 1943, Forester led the Bromley Park P-47s to Nantes where the Germans based maritime patrol aircraft. The Thunderbolts made their rendezvous with the B-17s on time and were well beyond the French coast when the Luftwaffe came up to fight.

Tom was flying with the 340th Fighter Squadron.

"Snowflake Red flight, this is Trumpet. Bandits nine o'clock."

Two seconds after alerting the flight, Tom rolled his aircraft to the left and attacked. Eleven P-47s followed.

The Germans were not surprised. They met the attack with one of their own. Fourteen Me-109s roared towards the Thunderbolts.

Forester fired at the lead Messerschmitt, but missed. Circling around, he renewed the attack. This time his aim was true. The

P-47's machine guns spit forth a stream of fire that struck the left wing of the Me-109.

Then, unexpectedly, Tom heard an explosion, a loud crushing sound of metal accompanied by the crackling of flame. As if in slow motion he saw his cockpit erupt in smoke and fire. Tom looked at his left arm and both legs. They were drenched in blood, which spattered the canopy and instruments. At his feet, he could feel the heat of approaching fire. Instinctively, he knew what was about to happen.

War is an ugly business. Good men die in war, on land, at sea, and in the air. Tom Forester was a good man, and on this final day of 1943, he died.

In the seven seconds of life remaining to him, Forester at first got angry. Not at the intrusion of death, but at himself for not flying the way he should have, for letting the Germans destroy his P-47 and its pilot.

Quickly, the anger subsided. Tom expected to see his life flash in front of him. It did not. Instead, he saw the future. He caught a glimpse of the life he would have led had he lived. The image was serene and pleasant. He was, as he had hoped to be, a university professor. Life had been good to him. There were children, even grandchildren. However, the edges of the image were frayed and unclear, although at its center he could see with clarity. Next to him, in front of a grand Victorian home, was a woman, his wife. She was lovely, and they were holding hands. Then inexplicably, she walked away. He could not tell who she was. He had not seen her face.

The woman continued to move away. As she did so, her image blurred. Yet Forester recognized her. She was the Lady in White, elegant as before. Her dress sparkled, reflecting bright sunshine that hurt his eyes. Her hat was different, yet still lavender and white. This time she held a parasol, also white. Together they created a picture of Edwardian perfection. The woman moved gracefully and seemed full of gaiety. Tom could see that she was smiling, and reaching out to him as though, this time, she wanted him to join her. Tom was anxious to do so. He found this woman irresistible. Compelled to act, he approached, eager to place his hand in hers. When they came together, he felt at peace, totally content. She kissed his forehead and told him that love was all that matters.

Then the Lady in White and her surrounding image dissolved in flames. Forester gasped for air, but found none. He slumped forward. Life had vacated his body.

When the P-47s returned to Bromley Park, the news that Forester had been killed spread rapidly. Everyone was stunned. Intellectually, they had known he might someday be lost. But no one believed it would ever happen. Like Forester himself, they thought the man was destined to survive. When he did not, gloom settled over the airfield.

Sergeant McGowan was inconsolable. Long after the fuel supply of Tom's Thunderbolt would have run out, the crew chief remained at the hardstand, hoping first to hear and then see the Group Commander's P-47.

Lieutenant Leroy Richards finally went out to the flight line and ordered McGowan to leave. He told the Sergeant that Forester was not going to return. The Kid had seen Tom's plane get hit and confirmed its destruction. Richards scored another victory that day. However, more noteworthy was his navigation. On December 30, the Kid flew directly back to Bromley Park. Never again did he land at another airfield.

Wilbur Williams and Harry Collins attempted to put on a brave front. The two men tried to pass off Forester's death as just another loss in a business where losses were to be expected. They convinced neither themselves nor anyone else. That night, along with Norman and Colonel Tee, they got hopelessly drunk, which helped to temporarily ease their pain.

—ɯ—

On Wednesday morning, the Intelligence Officer went to London. His sole purpose was to visit Helen Trent. Harry Collins had a letter to deliver.

Upon hearing that Tom had been killed, Helen went into a state of shock. She felt paralyzed, unable to feel, unwilling to speak. Collins became alarmed. He was about to go find a doctor when Helen, in a calm and normal voice, told him she would be fine. Then she went into the kitchen. When she returned, carrying a tray of biscuits and tea, tears were streaming down her cheeks.

Harry Collins did his best to console her. He told her about life at Bromley Park and of Forester's indelible impression upon the place. He recounted Tom's routine of coffee and donuts in the morning, of his weekly solitary drives around the airfield, and of his preference for Coca-Cola at the post flight interrogation. Collins also told Helen about the ritual of their silent ride out to Tom's P-47, of Forester's delight in leading Thunderbolts into action, and of the faith the pilots of the 19th Fighter Group had in their Group Commander.

Helen listened intently, aware that Collins represented the best and most likely the last opportunity to hear about the man she loved. Each time Harry spoke, Helen would learn more about Forester. She absorbed everything she heard. Consciously, Helen Trent was building a storehouse in her mind whose contents were memories of Tom to be recalled when their time together had entered the distant past.

When Harry Collins left Helen felt disconnected, adrift. A profound sense of loss and loneliness pervaded 28 Temple Court.

That afternoon and evening Helen remained at home alone. Claire was visiting Regina. Helen neither answered the telephone nor made any attempt to communicate with others. For the moment, she shared her grief with no one. Mostly she cried, often uncontrollably. Unhappily, Helen had been reminded, once again, that fate can be unkind and that life is a random mixture of good times and bad.

That evening, Helen took from the drawer to her dressing table a small wooden box. She then went downstairs to fix some tea. With her cup of tea in hand she went back upstairs and climbed into bed. The house was dark save for the small table lamp next to her bed.

She opened the box and took hold of its now treasured contents, a set of U.S. Army Air Force wings. She kissed the wings, put them back in the box, and opened the letter Harry Collins had given her.

My dearest Helen, I am writing this at Bromley Park. Hopefully, you will never have to read it. If you do, you will know that I am gone. Of course, I am but one of the many who have died in this war. Yet despite my death, I am glad to have fought, to have played a part in this great conflict. This war is a crusade, a fight of good against evil. I have no doubt that we will win. You will see the triumph of democracy and the defeat of tyranny. As for me, I have heard the battle cry of freedom and flown the wings of victory. That's more than enough. Yet I have been doubly blessed. For when you entered my life, so did love. The truth is that I love you and have since the moment I saw you that first day at the Royal Aeronautical Society. Never had I known what love encompassed. Never had I lost my composure at the mere sight of a woman. Never had I prayed for a woman to be safe and happy. Never had I been dazzled by someone so utterly compelling until you came along. When you came, my world changed. I became more sensitive to sight and sound, more aware of how truly precious life can be, and so very grateful for our time together.

These last months have been wonderful, truly the best of times. You taught me what it means, and feels like, to be in love. How marvelous it's been. How wonderful to simply walk with you beside me, your arm tucked around mine. How much fun it was to have dinner together or visit a museum or walk around Westminster Abbey. And how fantastic to touch you, to caress your body, and hold you.

Helen, I have been the luckiest guy in the world, for I have shared life with the best woman that ever lived.
Forever yours,
Tom

Helen read the letter twice, then once more. Then with great care, she folded the letter, placing it inside the envelope. This she placed on her night table beneath the wooden box. Helen let thoughts of her sleeping daughter soften her grief. Soon she found herself extremely tired and turned off the light. Sleep came quickly. Her last conscious thought centered on Forester, as well as her daughter. She prayed that in time Claire would come to understand, as she had with Tom, that to experience the richness of life, one must find someone to love.